COMPANIONS

Christina Hesselholdt, born in 1962, studied at the Danish Academy of Creative Writing in Copenhagen. Her first novel, *Køkkenet, Gravkammeret & Landskabet* [The Kitchen, the Tomb & the Landscape], was published in 1991. She has written fifteen books of prose, and received critical acclaim and awards for her books, including the Beatrice Prize in 2007 and the Critics' Prize in 2010. She was included in Dalkey Archive's *Best European Fiction 2013*. *Companions* is her first book to appear in English. Her latest work, *Vivian*, a novel about the photographer Vivian Maier, was published by Rosinante in 2016. It won the Danish Radio Best Novel Award 2017 and was shortlisted for the Nordic Council Literature Prize in 2017.

Paul Russell Garrett translates from Danish and Norwegian. He serves on the management committee of the Translators Association and is Programme Director for a new theatre translation initiative, [Foreign Affairs] Translates!

Fitzcarraldo Editions

COMPANIONS

CHRISTINA HESSELHOLDT

Translated by
PAUL RUSSELL GARRETT

CONTENTS

I. CAMILLA AND THE HORSE

THE RAMBLE 15

ANIMALS 49

DEATH HOUSE 55

CAMILLA AND THE HORSE 68

CAMILLA AND CHARLES 80

II. CAMILLA AND THE REST
OF THE PARTY

CAMILLA AND THE REST
OF THE PARTY 88

CAMILLA'S GPS 100

IF ASHES HAD EYES 144

NATURE AS A SERIES OF BACKDROPS 157

THE FACE OF RUBBISH 161

THE HOUSES AND THEIR BRILLIANT
SUICIDE VICTIMS 164

CHARLES REVISITED 187

A THEATRE OF SOULS, OR
THE ENTIRE PARTY 198

RELOCATIONS 203

III. THE PARTY BREAKS UP

THE PATIENTS OR CAMILLA
AND ALMA'S EARLY YEARS 216

CAN I APPROPRIATE HER MUM? 269

WEDDING 279

THE WORLD'S GO-GO POLE 282

THE HAIR IN THE DRAWER 285

NOT DIVIDING, SUBDIVIDING 290

A TEA PARTY
(AROUND CHARLES'S BED) 303

FROM THE HORSE'S MOUTH 308

THE MARCH HARE 328

IV. MAROONED

ALONE IN PARADISE, WITH
THE GARDENERS AND THE
HEDGEHOG'S HEART 334

BERNHARD'S SHOES, A NOTE 362

THE BOSS 364

THE VETERINARIAN'S BROTHER 368

COLUMBIA, THREE LITTLE CHINAMEN
(AND A WILD HAPPINESS) 370

FRAGMENTS OF THE COMPANIONS'
CONVERSATION IN THE GARDEN 380

QUEEN OF THE JAMS WITH
THE STICKY LEGS 386

THE LIST OF ITEMS AND MATTERS
ALREADY WRITTEN 388

EEYORE WITH A STICK OF DYNAMITE
IN HIS MOUTH 390

ONCE THEY START TO LOOK 393

MY TWO MAIN CHARACTERS 396

BY THE BANKS OF THE BOOKCASE 400

I. CAMILLA AND THE HORSE

'... and the blood of love welled up in my heart with
a slow pain.'
—— Sylvia Plath

THE RAMBLE

[Alma]

Last summer I rambled through Wordsworth's rolling landscape, where the shadows on the hills are so dark and so pronounced that the hilltops look like they are drenched in water, and the lakes are so deep that... when suddenly a fighter jet appeared and without thinking I threw myself to the ground, terror-stricken. I had neither seen nor heard the jet until it was directly above me. It wagged its wings, turned on its side and disappeared between two hills. It was so elegant, so fast and so sudden, and from that moment on I lived and breathed to see another one, preferably many more. I was lucky, because that summer RAF fighter pilots were performing training exercises there, weaving in and out of the hills of the Lake District, and perhaps they continued all the way to the Scottish Highlands before departing on a mission to Afghanistan; like predatory shadows above the endless opium fields and endless mountain ranges, 'bearing their cargo of death', something I repeated to myself in order to curb my enthusiasm – in any case I managed to see one or two every day. I made a few notes, this is what I came up with: 'Typhoons, the sublime, flashing, wagging, a terrifying noise – then gone. In the very landscape where WW had one vision after the other, where in sudden flashes of insight, he looked and looked.'

As I walked around in Wordsworth's landscape, dragging myself up his steep hills, I thought of the fighter planes as an embodiment of his inspiration, the sudden insight, a divine flash of realization, a thought like a bolt from the blue and full of load-bearing force – enough to carry a poem through. These are not words I would ordinarily use, but I do not think William Wordsworth would have shied away from them.

Though what consumed me more was that I could get so excited, so fulfilled by the sight of these fighter jets. I was not shameless. I was ashamed to sense delight at observing a phenomenon that was brought into the world to cause death and destruction. I was ashamed and I couldn't wait till the next one arrived. The fact that the plane only appeared for a brief moment certainly played a part. I never tired of looking. I pursued my own ocular pleasure.

Perhaps I also pursued the inundation of the senses it entailed – the noise, the shock at its sudden appearance. I reminded myself that the suddenness which fascinated me... the purpose of which was so that the plane could appear out of nowhere, drop its bombs and be gone before anyone could even think of shooting it down; but it was no use. I simply waited for the next one. And they flew so low! It provided a sense of connection. The pilots might have seen me, and the one who saw me throw myself to the ground probably smiled.

The *we* that once existed, it no longer exists. How I loved that we. How it fulfilled me.

My husband was with me. He is tired of me never saying *we* any more, only *I*. But I forget to be mindful of that, and the next time I talk about a trip we went on, an experience we shared, I hear myself saying *I* again.

He was with me on my ramble through the Lake District, and Dorothy Wordsworth had rambled through these hills just as much as her brother William had; on several occasions WW wrote poems based on her notes. But regardless of whether the event was witnessed in the company of Dorothy or was Dorothy's own unique experience, he always used the personal pronoun 'I' in his poems. For example, she was the first to see the daffodils, (hundreds of daffodils along a lake) and her description formed the basis for what must be his most famous poem of all, 'I Wandered Lonely as a Cloud'.

Dorothy writes: '... as we went along there were more and yet more and at last under the boughs of the trees, we saw that there was a long belt of them along the shore, about the breadth of a country turnpike road. I never saw daffodils so beautiful they grew among the mossy stones about and about them, some rested their heads upon these stones as on a pillow for weariness and the rest tossed and reeled and danced and seemed as if they verily laughed with the wind that blew upon them over the lake, they looked so gay ever glancing ever changing.'

I don't know whether it is a matter of fairness; a simple acknowledgement that my husband was also present; that Dorothy was present. Why would I say 'I' about an experience that we shared... because I felt alone during it? Or because my entire focus is on the currents streaming through my own consciousness; how I experience things – the fighter jets, for example – though he had also thrown himself to the ground.

As for William Wordsworth, not only did he write 'I' in the daffodil poem, he later denied that Dorothy had had any influence whatsoever on his poetry. He wrote her out of it.

When he got married, he cut her out of his heart, at least her-being-his-muse. He had to. Just like he had to get married. People talked. Bear in mind that Byron had a child with his sister. WW was known to embrace Dorothy and kiss her on the mouth when they met up in the landscape; maybe she had gone to meet him and stood there waiting. And there he was, finally he arrived – she rushed into his arms. They had been seen. They had been spied on in the hills.

He wanted to see his literature as the sovereign product of a sovereign I. He distanced himself from, practically renounced the note-method in his old age (which he had used for the daffodil poem, in this case Dorothy's notes), and writing poems from notes altogether, including his own; he wanted to view his poetry as a more original practice, as something that came directly from his consciousness: he went into the landscape, he saw, he thought, he wrote.

But allow me not to diminish Dorothy. She had a practice that bore traces of William's. She did not borrow words or ideas from other people. (Which during our century is taken as a matter of course as being entirely unavoidable, and had WW not denied this practice, I would have no objection.) But she did borrow people's clothes. When she was to go on a trip where she would be away for a few days, or maybe a good while, she did not bother to pack. She relied on the wardrobe of the hostess. Even the most intimate articles of clothing, by all accounts, without any thought to the hostess, that she might have wanted to keep her underwear to herself.

While I walked at his heels or scampered off in front of my husband, (never beside, as William presumably did on his walks with Dorothy) I recited the daffodil poem to myself:

> I wandered lonely as a cloud
> That floats on high o'er vales and hills,
> When all at once I saw a crowd,

18

A host, of golden daffodils;
Beside the lake, beneath the trees,
Fluttering and dancing in the breeze.

Continuous as the stars that shine
And twinkle on the milky way,
They stretched in never-ending line
Along the margin of a bay:
Ten thousand saw I at a glance,
Tossing their heads in sprightly dance.

The waves beside them danced; but they
Out-did the sparkling waves in glee:
A poet could not but be gay,
In such a jocund company:
I gazed – and gazed – but little thought
What wealth the show to me had brought:

For oft, when on my couch I lie
In vacant or in pensive mood,
They flash upon that inward eye
Which is the bliss of solitude;
And then my heart with pleasure fills,
And dances with the daffodils.

Incidentally, the verse 'They flash upon that inward eye/Which is the bliss of solitude' was written by his wife, Mary Hutchinson. Three pairs of hands have played at that piano; the daffodil poem.

I heard the poem for the first time when I was seventeen or eighteen; there was a TV broadcast about Wordsworth and Coleridge, some kind of dramatized documentary, at any rate someone was romping deliriously about in a landscape reciting this poem; it was windy, the grass was like a raging sea, the clouds were sailing past. Nature sang on its own, while the actor playing WW sang about the abundance of flowers.

My husband does not believe I have a flair for words. Nor does he think I know how to move. One night when I couldn't sleep, I went into the kitchen to fetch some water, and when I came back to bed he said: 'Your shuffling is keeping me awake.'

I shuffle. I stomp. I shuffle & stomp & trudge about. Shuffle-shuffle-stomp-stomp-trudge-trudge.

I can't sing, hence my husband thinks I am unable to hear music. By *hear* he means understand, relate to.

For years, I didn't sing. I refused to sing. I trudged around the Christmas tree like a silent vessel.

I sing off key. And I am so unfortunate as to be able to hear it myself. I remember the few times in my life when I was able to hit a note, great and unforgettable experiences – fusion, the feeling of not being on the sidelines, but on the contrary, of belonging. Then something happens. At the time I was working as a supply teacher. To earn some extra money while I studied. I was in a nursery class that day. Working as a classroom assistant. A little girl had to go to the dentist. Her parents couldn't go with her. I was asked to accompany her. We could take a taxi, there and back. I was happy to and the girl agreed. She sat very quietly in the back of the taxi.

The dental clinic was inside a school. We entered the building. It smelled both of school (an unfamiliar school) and of dentist. That's almost too much for one building. The girl took my hand, or did I take her hand?

The dentist chair. The girl refuses to open her mouth. The dentist discusses the concept of free will. She says she never holds anyone down, never forces anyone's mouth open. I say that sounds like a very good policy. The girl squeezes my hand. I encourage her to open her mouth. The dentist changes tack. She now appeals to the girl's collective consciousness. She mentions how the girl's classmates have already been in her chair and they managed alright. Surely she will be alright if all the others were? Apparently not. Her mouth remains shut. The dentist gets sentimental, she tells the girl how much people like her, how she couldn't hurt a fly, how much her own children love her, would they love her if she wasn't nice? The girl opens her mouth and says: 'Of course they love you – you're their mum.' Her mouth remains open, the dentist pokes her hands inside, calls her sweetie and promises to sing throughout the long winter, and says the teacher has to join in, and the dental assistant too. They break into song. 'I Can Sing a Rainbow'. I remain silent, they look at me sternly. The dentist somehow nudges me in the side. The girl has a big cavity and needs laughing gas. A contraption is placed over her nose. She clings to both of my hands, I am practically lying on top of her. She is close to going into a panic, despite the song. And then it happens. I do it. I open my mouth and sing. The others die down. I sing 'I Can Sing a Rainbow'. My voice sounds wild and strange, a perfect accompaniment to all the steel instruments.

'She who conquers herself is greater than she who captures a fortress,' I tell the girl when we are back in the taxi, her with a filling, me with a solo under my belt.

He is full of contempt. He is plagued by loathing. He lacks kindness. He has no sense of humour. (And his flaws go beyond these.)

The thought of growing old with him is chilling. How

is he going to look at me when I'm fifty-five or eighty-five and I am dragging my feet around, not out of fatigue or because I'm in a bad mood like now, but quite simply because I am no longer capable of lifting them.

Perhaps age will temper him.

'Last summer when I was rambling through the Lake District ...' I say.

But he was there too.

'Is there room for that ego of yours?' he asks – and smiles for the sake of the listeners.

Nonetheless sometimes when he gets into his stride I get the sense that we were not on the same holiday; or living the same existence; enduring the same punishment. We, the anaemic shadows who drain each other's lives of happiness. I long for a different life; for kindness and a generous body. I get the feeling that I am drying up at the age of thirty-five. And I find myself in a kind of slumber. I cannot act. When I have to cross the street, I almost hope that I will get run over – a crash and an awakening. Maybe I should dream of being shaken instead.

Every night I have to look away when he chews his dinner to death. It's his tense jaw, I cannot stand how he turns his beautiful mouth into a waste disposal unit. He listens to classical music the same way he eats: clenched, tense, his pointy elbows on the table, his fingers gripping his skull like an iron ring: concentration, slavish discipline. I am not allowed to utter a sound during this séance. Music is sacred. 'Can't you *try* to hear the music?' he says. I am in doubt. I have never connected it with effort. (When Dorothy pointed out nature to William – which she did by all accounts – it doubtless took place in a more friendly manner.) Why don't I leave...? And so I will.

I wonder what my dry husband thinks? First and

foremost he is preoccupied with safeguarding his own eccentricities and therefore incapable of stepping into character as a man: socially, I mean, and so he waits, shrouded in his peculiarity, downright proud of it, but in actual fact it is merely so that I will get fed up and leave him.

There is a man I can't get out of my head. Occasionally I call him forth in my mind. He was on a ramble through the Lake District, or he was there at least. He sat beneath the clouds, on a roof. I saw him from below. He seemed like a lovely man. It was with a sense of a life wasted that I continued walking with my own man.

Well, isn't it mad... We did not so much as exchange a single word, yet still I latch onto the thought of him. I would like to be able to fall in love, just one more time in my life; to be consumed by life and sense the abyss.

[Edward]
There is something about art that annoys me, I realized that last summer. Then suddenly it dawned on me what the essence of art is.

I was tired that day and had set out on a short hike. I walked along the old Coffin Trail from Grasmere to Rydal, the path the bereaved once took when they had to bring the deceased to the churchyard in Grasmere. There were several large, flat stones along the way that were used to rest the coffin on. I thought about all that effort, all the trouble they had taken, in a place I now strolled along so easily, carrying only a small rucksack.

At the Ramblers Tea Shop in Rydal I was told about a small grotto by a waterfall that I definitely should not miss out on. The grotto was a so-called 'viewing station', the waitress told me, the first of its kind in England.

Towards the end of the 1600s, that is at a time when people were only just developing a taste for landscapes and appreciating the beauty of nature, Sir Daniel Fleming, with his interest in nature and art, had built the station just a stone's throw from his manor house, Rydal Hall.

This little grotto, let us call it a house, a shack, a shed, a vantage point, had one window (without glass) through which the waterfall could be observed. There was a painter inside with her back to the door, facing the window; I felt it would be cheating to look at her painting. I tiptoed behind her and was sure to only look outside.

The window framed the waterfall.

The frame turned the waterfall into a picture.

The frame established a point of view to the waterfall.

The frame carved a rectangle out of the scenic view, the romantic motif, the waterfall.

Sir Daniel Fleming's viewing post enticed (and continues to entice) many tourists and artists. One of the most famous paintings of the waterfall is by Joseph Wright of Derby in 1795 (I bought a postcard of it in the tea room). In this picture, where the falling water resembles streaks of white paint (or perhaps a well-combed head of hair with traces of the comb still visible), nature's true wildness is found in the tree trunks around and behind the waterfall, living their own twisted, pathless lives. The water is neat and still. Both the falling water, and the pool of water formed by the rocks – the water in the rock pool is by and large unaffected by the water falling into it.

Behind the waterfall is a small bridge, a perfect wooden arch, which the demented trees will soon get the better of.

Perhaps the water is so tame because the moment it was selected as a motif it was cultivated.

I got so annoyed that Sir DF had determined how I should view the waterfall, the part I was actually able to view, that after a single glance from his perspective, I exited the small house and climbed up on the roof so that I could view the waterfall as it suited me. Straddling the roof (which cut me on the crotch, I later discovered I was covered in splinters) like some kind of Hamlet, with my legs dangling on either side of the ridge, I realized that the essence of art is to force a particular way of viewing upon others.

Yes, I know – without an angle, a choice of subject, narrowing, zooming in, focusing, there is no work. I am perfectly aware of that.

The fact that Sir DF had carved out this segment of the view using the window as a frame... how should I put it... I suddenly realized that it was an act of power; he had made himself master of the angle, he had cut into the view, and like sheep the tourists and painters had flocked (and continue to flock) *into* the house in order to stare *out*.

Fortunately for my mood, a young woman with a shapely figure in a purple bathing suit and with visible goose pimples suddenly entered my unobstructed view. She balanced delicately above the rocks in front of the waterfall and then settled into the pool of water with a gasp. A couple of strokes carried her behind the curtain of water. When she reached the rock wall, she turned and looked at me.

I was just about to wave to her – whatever that might have led to – when I spotted a man standing on the bank, clawing at the dirt with one foot like a raging bull. I felt a tad ridiculous, me, Prince Roof Ridge. I don't know what they thought. Maybe they thought I was one of those so-called cloudspotters.

I sat on the roof and below me, inside the house, the painter made a noise. A thought entered my mind, that in a sense I was riding her. The house was a Trojan horse: place a man astride the ridge of a roof and immediately the building becomes a horse, in this case it contained a painter, and a horse filled with people – that sounds very Trojan.

Maybe they thought I was inspecting the house, looking for damage, that I was a builder; or even worse: that I was one of these sensual creatures who feels the need to touch everything – down on his knees to touch the withered leaves, up on the roof to feel it between his thighs.

[Kristian]
There are so many deodorizers in our room that we both develop a migraine while staying there; I am worried about getting brain damage so we keep the window open, living in a constant draft, to Alma's great irritation, and she has developed quite the cold; I keep thinking of the long-haul lorry driver I saw on the news who was forced to retire early because he had kept deodorizers in the cab where he spent most of his life, in that case it would have been far healthier to have a small plastic skeleton, as long as you don't suck on it or touch it too often.

Naturally there is a deodorizer hanging over the rim of the toilet, no surprise there, and it has two functions, it colours the water purple and eliminates odour; but we are also met by a synthetic pong in the shower cubicle, meaning you can't smell yourself until you turn the shower on and the problem goes down the drain. And in the wardrobe, and on the shoe rack – and in every single drawer there is one of these small poisonous thingamajigs. And today I spotted one above the bed!

That reminds me of something! Once at my organic hair salon, a male stylist sprayed a fragrance into the air for a male customer to sample... When asked by the customer when the fragrance might be of use, I heard the hairdresser reply: 'Well, when the gentleman is shagging in the morning, for example.'

The salon went completely quiet. I am certain that each and every customer, hairdresser and sweep-up-the-hair-boy thought they had been the victim of a misunderstanding. And I pictured an amorous couple, regularly refreshing the air above them, particularly the southern region, as they say, with a few puffs. My hairdresser froze for a moment, her scissors hovering in the air, then abruptly launched into some nonsense about wigs: 'During the Renaissance,' she said, 'people used white lead, both on their face and in their hair, it caused large open facial wounds that would not heal, and their hair fell out, so by the time the baroque era was reached, there were very few people who still had hair, and that is how the wig was invented. Poor people had wigs made of felt, they probably looked more like hats than hair.'

And I was forced to imagine these wretched people, hairless, lingering on, era after era with large lesions, hundreds of years old, until they entered the age of wigs and found salvation.

The landlady is very fond of lime and strawberry scents. She has a rather synthetic appearance herself, and a very intense smell, also from these smelly things that she most likely has hidden in various places under her clothes. She has a slight lisp, because she has one tucked inside her mouth like a wad of chewing tobacco, she would prefer cancer to bad breath any day. Faced with all this unnaturalness... it really surprised me when the landlady told me that she held a kind of badger show in her drive every night, for her guests; there was an entire family of badgers living under her rhododendron (a very lush and extensive specimen) and every night around eleven she fed them leftovers from breakfast, bacon, eggs and fried sausages, 'they are probably the only badgers in England with high cholesterol,' she said, and I could tell that was a line she got a lot of mileage out of. And no sooner had she said it when, like an echo, (slightly nauseating; tell me: what became of the joy?) I hear myself repeating the line when I describe the incident upon returning home, and I pictured Alma looking away – it does not require much imagination, she often does that.

That same evening we took our seats on folding chairs as a couple of bright floodlights suddenly bathed the drive in a light worthy of a prison yard or a prison camp, and the landlady arrived wearing a pink dressing gown and offered these final instructions: 'They are practically blind,' she said, 'so if you just sit completely still, they will come right up to you. But the slightest movement...' and she made a sudden movement with her hands. Lost, disappearance, whoosh-away-they-go. Then she generously scattered leftovers across the drive and retreated into her castle of scents.

Only a moment passed before the animal poked its head out of the rhododendron bush. And a little later a plump, short-limbed creature with snake-like movements appeared, sniffing loudly, and approached us with its nose to the ground, entirely at the mercy of its sense of smell, ready to die for the titbits (I felt a stab of envy; I longed to have something to die for). It munched on the bones, and of course I was reminded of how in the past, when the woods were teeming with badgers, people filled their boots with charcoal when they were hunting because badgers bite until they hear a crunch.

Its nose guided it to the next bite, it came right up to the leg of my chair where there was a fried potato, and I glanced nervously at my sandalled foot. It munched and moaned. Then it heard something! And bolted! The air was full of galloping and pattering body parts. It sounded like a fat naked woman running. When your wife starts to take her clothes with her into the bathroom in the morning, and her nightgown in the evening, in order to avoid your gaze while she gets changed, there is something wrong. Alma is not fat, on the contrary. The bath in our room doubles up as a jacuzzi, if only she could be tempted into the waves. Hardly.

She sits watching the cat – the pink lady has one just like it. And the cat looks at Alma. She makes little sounds in a distinctive feline tone – a combination of hissing and deep, cuddly noises – the kind you learn to use on cats from an early age. And it starts to purr and rub up against the rubbish bin, the sound alone is enough, she does not need to touch it. It submits. It positions itself in her vicinity, in front of the door.

Our landlord arrives home, parks and is about to go inside – to join the pink angel of the house who has run rampant with a feather duster all day long. He greets us; he has a very masculine appearance, tweed and pipe. A pie probably awaits him in the oven. While he eats, she will kick off her slippers and place her anointed feet on his lap. He will put down the knife, eat and squeeze her sweet little toes a little. I am dying for a similar idyll. Like marzipan.

The cat is disturbed. It needs to move or the master of the house cannot get inside. It looks at him, wronged and defiant. It does not think of itself as his cat. He has long since disappeared inside the house. There is nothing to be done. Nobody to complain to.

[Alma]

If you did not want to be the angel of the house in the time of the lake poets, you had to climb into bed. There were plenty of illnesses to choose from and nothing to cure them other than opium and brandy. You could lie there and lose yourself in reading, in translation, in opium visions; you could write. While other people looked after the children, relatives, master of the house, housework, callers, dinner parties and churchgoing. May I introduce a breathless Sarah Coleridge:

At the hour of nine we all assembled at the breakfast table – S. his wife & two eldest daughters, myself and Sara, all well, except the good Lady of the house [Edith] who is in a very complaining way at present, (Mrs Lovell always breakfasts *alone* in the schoolroom & Hartley *alone* in his study.) A note is brought in – Sir G. & Ly B[eaumont]'s compliments hope to see the whole party to dinner including the young ladies. We promise to go – Away fly the two cousins to Shake the Pear Tree before dressing for Church – in a minute Edith arrives, breathless – "Aunt Coleridge, Sara has shaken something out of the tree, into her eye, & she is distracted with the pain." After bathing the eye & lamenting over it, & and deprecating the *folly* of the poor sufferer for nearly an hour, S. raps at the door with all the children ready for church, except for one. Where is Kate? "She has such a bad headache she can't go to church, her mother is going to stay with her to give her James's-Powder, so I hope Sara is better & you are both ready for church." Sara was too blind to go, but I huddled on my things and got to church as the last Psalm was reading, found our pew full, obliged to go into another, & when the communion plate was brought round, had left my purse at home, & sitting among strangers looked very foolish... On our return, Kate was in a high fever; Mama [Edith] very unhappy, poor Aunt Lovell on the couch in *her very worst way*, & on entering the bedroom, I found it quite darkened, and Sara in tears... We sent off for the Dr who tried with a camel's-hair pencil to clear the lid of the eye, but made it worse; prescribed for Kate who was put to bed, and Sara lay down again in despair, & I sat by her bedside reading... I had hardly prepared myself to be with her for the night... The maid comes up – Ma'am, here are two gentlemen who *must* see you, they are friends of Mr Coleridge – "pray call Hartley to them, I am nearly undressed" "Mr Hartley is just gone to the inn"... Well, after sitting a full hour with these gents, I suffered them to depart without asking them to stay for supper, for which I got a trimming from S. who did not venture to ask them himself not being *sure* whether there was anything in the house to give them...

With a talent on a par with that of her famous father, longing for immersion and peace and with a similar opium dependency, Sara Coleridge (without an h; daughter of Sarah and Samuel) often lay down on the sofa, or once she simply disembarked the stagecoach on a journey, and pleading poor health (she truly was in a bad state), she lodged at a guest house for weeks where she wrote, until her husband, after sending numerous letters in an effort to tempt her home, appeared in person and brought her home. Maybe it was on that occasion that she wrote the poppy poem, which later, strangely enough, and despite the protests of her family, was published in an educational rhyming book for children, written by her:

The Poppies Blooming all around
My Herbert loves to see,
Some pearly white, some dark as night,

Some red as cramasie;

He loves their colours fresh and fine
As fair as fair may be,
But little does my darling know
How good they are to me.

He views their clustering petals gay
And shakes their nut-brown seeds.
But they to him are nothing more
Than other brilliant weeds;

O how should'st thou with beaming brow
With eye and cheek so bright
Know aught of that blossom's pow'r,
Or sorrows of the night!

When poor Mama long restless lies
She drinks the poppy's juice;
That liquor soon can close her eyes
And slumber soft produce.

O' then my sweet my happy boy
Will thank the poppy flow'r
Which brings the sleep to dear Mama
At midnight's darksome hour.

We left the Lake District, all the beauty, the hills and
the glittering lakes, the sinewy ramblers with their sil-
ver-tipped walking staffs and long strides, and drove
through Discount England; at each stop the bus grew
heavier; 150-kilo teenage mothers boarded the bus with
overweight children with close-cropped haircuts stiff
with hair gel.

Kristian has got tar on the back of his white shorts. He tried to wipe off the worst of it with kitchen roll. Naturally the paper stuck to the tar. So now he is walking around with a large blotch on his backside with kitchen roll stuck to it. It goes without saying that it looks rather unfortunate. But he perseveres. I feel like a pubescent teenager who is embarrassed of her parents. I maintain a vain hope that people won't think we are together, as long as I stay a couple of metres ahead of or behind him. I'm happy when he sits down; I leant my head against the window of the bus, and it felt like the landscape rolled through my left eye and out the back of my head at a ferocious speed.

Hands have seized them from below and shaken them: the gravestones are tilting, pointing in every direction. They are meant to be in straight rows, they are wild and tooth-like, it would take a strong set of braces to straighten them. The churchyard lies in the village of Haworth, we (I'm learning!) have to walk through it to reach the path to the heath. We cross the churchyard in the morning, we cross it again in the afternoon.

'Also' is written before the names of family members, also her, also him, also her, and one stone reads: 'also or enough!' yet another child lost, perhaps the exclamation mark is addressed to God; enough already! To have buried an entire family, where you have to wander aimlessly in wait, perhaps with a lock of your loved one's hair in a locket around your neck, wound around a lock of your own hair. People were obsessed with keeping locks of hair in the 1800s. Displayed in a glass case at the Brontë museum, the hair of Father Brontë and one of the daughters is married together in a small open container. Did someone occasionally open the locket and put their nose up to the interwoven plait in the small grave? A lock from each of the deceased, that could add up over time, so much love, and so, so dry! in such a small space. The last surviving member of the family roaming around with a miniature churchyard around the neck.

I remember an entire wall teeming with hair, it was in Turkey, in a cluster of caves where the first Christians had lived in hiding, one of the caves was furnished as a bar, and the wall of the cave was covered with locks of women's hair, thick layers of hair that you had an urge to stroke, and dangling from each lock was a note with the name of the owner. An eager Turk with a pair of scissors ran after Alwilda and me, but I do not think we yielded. Or else in the end we really did bow our heads for the short man; and two amputated Scandinavian giants boarded the waiting bus in annoyance.

At the church where Father Brontë preached, summoning all of his strength after losing his wife and over the course of the years his six children – Emily died on a sofa, I stood behind the rope barrier of the Brontë Museum and looked at the sofa and attempted to conjure up the, by all accounts, short and chunky image of Emily, possibly made ethereal by tuberculosis, a body worn down by all the coughing, but the sofa remained empty – in the church we meet a man who is in a bad way. He violates my personal space, which like most people is just under a metre, and he sticks his face right up to mine and asks about my relationship with the Lord Jesus Christ. I say that I was baptized, so I should belong to his kingdom, but that was about as far as it went.

'What's your opinion.'

'I suffer from violent fits of rage, yes, I suppose I shouldn't be saying that in here.'

'You needn't worry,' I said.

'I could tear this church apart in ten minutes.'

I looked for the exit, I don't know how we had made it so far inside, I slowly retreated.

'That's why I'm trying to have faith,' he bellowed, 'faith, faith, faith,' the room echoed, 'and that's really helped me,' he whispered.

His face glued to mine – during operation exit. Goodbye fury, goodbye sound; it is always a relief to escape such difficult people, but at the same time a tragedy, so many people, using myself as an example, whom I have left behind, standing or sitting, homeless, hungry children with lightning-quick movements in the Third World, you name it, and you always carry a little of that tragedy with you: sorrow and regret. The unfortunate person you leave behind.

Oh, all the people I should have taken by the arm and walked away with, but where would I have kept them all, all the life-sized people.

[Kristian]

Haworth is a dark city, built from dark stone, or stone that time has darkened, the streets are narrow. Many of the houses are decorated with flowers at the front, orgies of flowers, the blue and red in particular can be gathered under the term spinster-flowers: leaves like earlobes that time has made large and loose, and in garish colours that even weak eyes can capture; dangling from the façade in pots, pots on the ground lining the wall of the house, each house an entire flower shop. The landlord at our guest house is English and the landlady is French; when we arrived, she came to greet us with open arms, I put the suitcase down, and she bonjoured and directed her lips at my cheek; somehow or other my mouth was too open, or she turned her head too much: instead of planting a kiss in the air by her cheek, I got a mouthful of her ear. It tasted of pepper. And before she managed to withdraw, I pictured (in a flash of lightning) the duchess from *Alice in Wonderland* stirring a huge pot.

We are staying at a guest house right by the churchyard. By cutting across the churchyard, opening a gate, following a narrow dark path for a hundred metres, opening another heavily sloping gate: you reach the heath. Haworth Moor. The fairy tale spreads out before us. We are still miserable, and again we are rambling in the realm of a powerful love: Catherine and Heathcliff. Their love was equally impossible as Dorothy and William's, which we had just experienced, so to speak. And our own is also utterly impossible. Though for other reasons. Reasons I don't understand. If I run my hand across Alma's body, she shudders and says it tickles. She does not move my hand, but stops it by placing her hand over it. It feels more like a funeral than a sign of affection.

Today we visited Top Withens, a building that is said to have inspired Emily Brontë to write about the storm-battered house, Wuthering Heights, now a ruin.

The heath. Sparrowhawks circled above us. The heath was white with cotton grass. In moist areas grew bracken. It causes cancer. And I was walking bare-legged. The weather changes incessantly. The sun is shining. Then it starts to rain. The rain lashes the face, and the wind is severe. We put on our woolly jumpers. A little later we take them off again. Yesterday Alma bought a pair of long woollen knee-length stockings. From a specialist shop (regional wool) in the town. We got to chatting with the owner. He wanted to leave England. Because of the way foreigners are treated. He wanted to move to France.

36

Alma made a few comments about how the conditions for new arrivals (wasn't that the word the Danish queen had used in her latest New Year's speech? A carefully selected neutral word, a proper queen word; but maybe so neutral that it lacks precision) had also become rather harsh in Denmark. He looked at us blankly. 'No, no.' He wanted to go home to Le Pen. Le Pen knew what needed to be done. Only a couple of days earlier I had read an article in *The Independent* about the prison-like conditions English asylum seekers face; about an African woman who had been forced to give birth in handcuffs so she didn't use the hospital visit as an opportunity to make a run for it and join the mass of undocumented immigrants. By that point Alma had already paid for the stockings. Otherwise we would have left without them. Now we are using Alma's long racist stocking as scarves. One for each of us, with the foot of the stocking smacking the middle of the chest; Alma ventures a smile; the ridiculousness unites us. That's how cold it is.

On the way up to Top Withens, we passed through a valley that was nothing less than delightful, in a place that the Brontë sisters were fond of sitting. Steep rock faces. A waterfall. A brook with stepping stones: an invitation to joy. I removed my shoes and hopped from stone to stone. In the meantime Alma walked back and forth across the Brontë bridge and sat down for a while on the Brontë chair (also a stone).

'I would like to return here,' Alma said, and then we continued walking.

When we arrived at the ruin, sweaty and out of breath, we were immediately surrounded by moorland sheep, they were greyish-brown and freshly sheared. They flocked around us. One had a large growth dangling from its chin. Maybe it was from the ferns.

The ruin consisted of only a few rooms, two or three. The inside walls were so low that I could look over them. In the novel, Wuthering Heights, the building that gave the novel its title, seems to be a property of considerable size, full of corridors and dark rooms, where dogs leap out from hidden corners. The Wuthering Heights of the novel is like a fortified prison where an incredibly poor atmosphere incessantly reigns. A place that is difficult to escape from. First the adult Heathcliff keeps his son imprisoned in the house and later his daughter-in-law, the daughter of his beloved Catherine, whom you would think he would treat well out of love for Catherine; but no, on the contrary.

The violence takes place within the confined rooms.

The ruin is open. The heath, as well as the weather, has forced its way in. The building cannot hold anyone in, as the house in the novel does in abundance. Nowadays Heathcliff would have to chain his prisoners there. The only thing resembling the description in the novel is the isolation of the building; located on a hilltop, surrounded by a desolate heath. Windswept. The wind takes hold of the stocking foot and swings it over my shoulder, 'it is very wuthering'.

Heathcliff is a savage, avaricious (he usurps two entire properties), vindictive brute, and Catherine is a hysterical, manipulative and rather violent monster. Why is their love so famous? How can two such monstrous people love? And how is their famous love represented? Is it a noble phenomenon set against a backdrop of violence (the house and a number of violent minor characters) between two equally violent people? For them love is to know no difference between each other's souls, to believe they are one:

> My love for Heathcliff resembles the eternal rocks beneath:
> a source of little visible delight, but necessary. Nelly, I *am*
> Heathcliff! He's always, always in my mind: not as a plea-
> sure, any more than I am always a pleasure to myself, but
> as my own being. So don't talk of our separation again: it is
> impracticable,

Catherine says and shortly after marries Heathcliff's opposite, a cool man.

Only in death do they become one. Heathcliff digs up Catherine's coffin and releases the boards on one side so that it remains open; he ensures that the same will be done to his own coffin after his death – threatening the powerful anger of his ghost if he is not obeyed; thus at long last the two become one flesh.

In contrast to the true love of these two, where the truth is that one is (like) the other, the love between Heathcliff's son and Catherine's daughter is a love artificially creat-ed by Heathcliff, again with material gain – and revenge – in mind. It is obvious that the two lovers have different wishes, the proof that their love is false:

> One time, however, we were near quarrelling. He said
> the pleasantest manner of spending a hot July day was
> lying from morning till evening on a bank of heath in
> the middle of the moors, with the bees humming dream-
> ily about among the bloom, and the larks singing high
> up overhead, and the blue sky and bright sun shining
> steadily and cloudlessly. That was his most perfect idea of
> heaven's happiness: mine was rocking in a rustling green
> tree, with a west wind blowing, and bright white clouds

flitting rapidly above; and not only larks, but thrush-
es, and blackbirds, and linnets, and cuckoos pouring out
music on every side, and the moors seen at a distance,
broken into cool dusky dells; but close by great swells of
long grass undulating in waves to the breeze; and woods
and sounding water, and the whole world awake and
wild with joy. He wanted all to lie in an ecstasy of peace;
I wanted all to sparkle and dance in a glorious jubilee. I
said his heaven would be only half alive; and he said mine
would be drunk: I said I should fall asleep in his; and he
said he could not breathe in mine and began to grow very
snappish,

Cathy tells the housekeeper, Nelly.

I read the piece out loud to Alma, and she said: 'Such
an amazing piece about the heath. You could only write
like that about a place you know inside out. And such an
amazing piece about the joy of moving.'

She put her arms around me and said: 'Such poetry!'
and I was just as happy as if I had written it myself and
had not merely possessed it for a moment with my voice.
I said: 'Heathcliff's son had tuberculosis, that is why he
did not have the energy for all of her running and dancing, but preferred to lie about and sleep. It felt like he
had burning milk running through his veins. He experienced it as though lying between heaven and earth, as
though breathing through the eye of a needle.'

She looked at me suspiciously and said that sounded
like something from a book, not that she had anything
against it, but where was *I*? The last part was in fact a
quote, from-god-knows-where, in any event not from
Brontë. Maybe she grew tired of all the talk of illness.
In any case I got a sense of having missed an important

40

moment – it had been a long time since we had been so close, both physically, with her arms around me, and mentally – until she got up and walked over to the window. We were back at the guest house. She looked like someone who was trapped, and I felt inferior. Like the skinny cucumber on the label of the vinegar bottle.

[Alma]
Kristian has come down with something. Ill in Wales. Snowdonia. He has a fever and sleeps most of the day. We have taken lodgings at the Heights Hotel in the village of Llanberis. It is a relaxed location, a bit hippyish, but not outright psychedelic, you can come and go twenty-four hours a day, there are rooms and dormitories, the music is a little loud, but it is clean and tidy, and there is no danger of having your things stolen. It is a young area, in contrast to the Lake District which is mostly for the prosperous middle class. There are a lot of mountain climbers. The area, with its grey, naked mountains and Snowdon itself, the highest mountain in Wales, is a Mecca for climbers. Today I saw one being rescued from a mountaintop by a yellow helicopter, I don't know if it was due to a broken bone, or if the person in question simply could not or would not climb back down, like the cat that has to be helped down from the roof by the fire service.

Kristian has told me to just go out as much as I like. There is no reason for me to sit on the edge of the bed watching him sleep. No, probably not. Still I felt a bit bad when I went down to the hotel bar at night. I don't like going out alone. I don't know what to do with my hands or where to look. When I am out at a restaurant alone, I normally read. In short: I'm afraid of someone getting the wrong idea. I tell myself how unreasonable it is that men can go out alone and feel free and at ease, own the world... in other words: I think I should do it. And so I do. But of course I can't force myself to feel at ease.

I set foot in a room packed with people and smoke; there were evidently a lot of locals, a number who looked a little inbred; that is what the mountains do to people. I bought a beer and looked for a table. I found an empty seat at a table for three. Sitting at the table was a small, sharply-dressed, quick man, whom I estimated to be in his early forties. He could be a jockey. Weighed next to nothing. And looked wily as hell. Next to him was a very different man, far younger and heavier, with dark curls, well-built under a striped (purple and burgundy) North African hooded cloak. He had probably been to Morocco. I've been there. Maybe it is one of those jella-bahs, or else it is some other, long, cloak-like outfit. His eyelashes were so thick and long that his eyes were veiled when he blinked. His name was Michael, and his friend was called Tony. They were both from Leeds. They were here to climb. They came as often as they could. Tony was a car salesman, and Michael a carer for the disabled. They lived and breathed mountain climbing. I was told all of this at once. Because no sooner had I sat down than they leant across the table and started to talk to me. Tony talked the most. And leant forward the most. The other one had his elbows on the table, a little stooped; but he looked at me alertly enough. My only contribution to the conversation was to tell them that I had a fear of heights. And how it came about.

Up until fifteen years ago, the time I climbed the Leaning Tower of Pisa, I had never had problems with heights. I could choose to walk up to an edge or not. I was neither attracted to nor afraid of heights. Not one

42

of those people who always says, oh dear, afraid of accidentally throwing themselves over the edge. Not at all. Just indifferent. But on the uppermost colonnade of the Leaning Tower I suddenly got scared that I would fall onto the sloping foundation. I got nauseous and dizzy and had to lie down. I lay close to the centre of the tower and clung to the side. You know how an old wall like that smells – almost like a well. (Tony tapped his fingers on the table, he did not have the patience for descriptions.) I was blocking the way and brought traffic to a standstill, there was not much room beforehand. I lay on my side and pressed my face against the body of the tower and felt the precipice tugging at my back – as though it was trying to tear my hands loose. Finally I agreed to be helped down. The trip down the narrow staircase was a nightmare, let me tell you. I promised myself I would never ever climb to any great height again. I sat on the ground and looked at the Leaning Tower, it looked like a chess piece from there, but I knew better, and everything was swimming before my eyes.

When I had finished, Tony said that there was only one way to cure me.

'Don't say another word,' I said, 'I can guess. Desperate diseases call for desperate remedies, right?'

'Exactly,' he said, 'we'll take you up with us tomorrow. We can lend you some gear.'

I looked at Michael and nodded. I felt exhilarated. I felt anxious. I felt intoxicated. I wanted to be brave. I wanted to be admired. By then, I think that we had already made up our mind. But I couldn't know one hundred per cent. I felt like I was being torn apart from the inside. I had another beer and pushed the image of Kristian out of my mind and asked if we were going to climb Snowdon (1085m). No. They were going to take me to a place called Suicide Wall. The name caused me to emit some strange sounds, I had wanted to say 'hah, hah.'

Tony reminded me of a restless bird. A tough bird, with short, sharp movements, back and forth across the table. A bright knife. With no further presence, only really present in flashes. Where did he go. Everywhere. Scanning the bar. Quick glances at every woman that stepped inside. Restless, restless, restless. Michael, on the contrary. I don't care for the expression 'grounded'. But that was what he was. He was anchored in himself. Present. And if there is one thing that stimulates me, that is it. To have somebody at home. And here I had found a mountain climber so firmly rooted to the ground.

There was a commotion on the dance floor, more and more people got up and stood in a circle until there was an entire throng of observers. Curiosity brought us to our feet; oh, a stripper had arrived. With bad skin and breasts like pears. She probably worked at the supermarket during the day. She stripped naked and tried to get a man to join her on the dance floor. She held out her arms and grabbed several people's hands, but nobody dared, they held their hands behind their backs and retreated a little. Then a couple of men pushed their friend into the centre. He tried to hide in the flock, but kept getting pushed into the middle – he was now sacrificed by the entire throng, all of the people who had personally declined to dance made sure he stayed on the dance floor. As long as they kept him there, they were safe. The stripper danced up to him and tugged his shirt out of his trousers. He tried to tuck it in again. Then she started to unbutton it. He raised his hands in surrender and pulled off the shirt by himself. Then he put his hands in the air and started to dance a dance that was all about shaking his belly. Cheers from the throng. He reached for the stripper's breasts, but she evaded his grasp and made a snake-like attack on his belt. Soon his trousers were hanging around his ankles. He was wearing red underwear. There was no end to the excitement, the shouts grew coarser, a few people threw beer on the couple. And the man on the dance floor was handed beer after beer, which he drank and poured over himself and over her. Loads of foam that disappeared down their bodies and onto the floor. It was starting to seem Prussian. He pulled off his shoes and threw them into the crowd. One shoe just missed my ear. Of course he couldn't resist swirling his trousers in the air like a lasso before letting them fly.

Tony had pushed all the way to the front; I could see that only a small part of him was shouting, the rest of him was busy keeping his bearings. If he had only belonged to the upper class, he could have worked at an embassy. The stripper must have signalled someone at the bar, because suddenly the bartender threw a love doll onto the floor. I looked at M and he shook his head in embarrassment. The stripper held the blow-up plastic doll in front of her and got the man to touch it. He threw himself at her gaping fish-mouth and glaring eyes, and the stripper left him there, with this creation that belonged to a hot summer day at the beach in his arms. She pulled away relatively unnoticed, the man threw the doll on the floor and pulled his underwear down to his ankles and made a show to penetrate her, but something went wrong, because she burst like a balloon, and only a sea of coloured plastic remained beneath his fat hips.

Kristian was feeling no better the next morning; I forced

a little yoghurt and juice between his dry lips. He managed a smile before he drifted away again. I decided that if he was not better later that day, I would fetch a doctor. And then I went down to meet Tony and M. I thought his initial encompassed him better than his full name. Maybe initials are always sexy. They hint at something more. Something that might come. Might not.

I was afraid, but I pretended I was fine and climbed into the back seat of Tony's car with a smile. M sat in the front seat. I sat right behind his curly head. And then we drove off. Faster than I have ever driven in my life. Into the mountains. With the music at full blast, with the tyres screeching. I was in love. I didn't care. We could die in this car as far as I was concerned. I don't know why such powerful feelings of being alive make people indifferent to losing their life. Because you're on top of the world? And you would prefer to go out on a high? Once in a while M turned and said something to me. I was shy and had a hard time coming up with an answer.

Half an hour later when I was hanging halfway between heaven and earth there was only one thing I could think of: survival. And of reaching our goal quickly, so I could get my feet back on the ground as soon as possible. I was hooked up to a rope, so that if I fell, I would just dangle from it. But I was still terrified. They had supplied me with a pair of soft-tipped shoes that were created to dig in and find footholds in the tiniest cracks. And it was incredible how many cracks and crevices there were in the cliff, which had looked perfectly smooth from the ground. So I burrowed my fingers and toes into the holes and cracks and pulled myself up. The first couple of metres were relatively painless. But about five metres up the terror and fear struck me. I pressed my body against the cliff while I searched for cracks. And suddenly it was like I had never seen a rock before in my life. The wall felt like the most implacable and brutal thing I had ever faced. I clung to it for a moment, breathing heavily. Tony had advised me not to look up or down. Now I looked up at the plateau, my terminus, took a deep breath and practically darted upwards. Afterwards they told me that they had never before seen anyone climb that quickly. I did not tell them that it was to get it over and done with.

My recollection has furnished the plateau, where I sat soon after, with yellow flowers; like they signified life and happiness itself; but how could they have grown there?

I climbed the wall once more. And again, and in the end I enjoyed it and started to think – maybe the rock face had not outright invited me – but... 'I want to fall. Just to try it,' I shouted down to the two men on the ground. Hanging and dangling from the rope, I meant. I looked up. I looked down. The sky did not make me dizzy. The ground did not make me afraid to fall. Not in that moment.

'She wants to fall. Just to try it,' M said to Tony in admiration.

And it occurred to me that it was just like in school – when we used to play catch and kiss . I thought for a long time it was a matter of running fast. Not about getting caught. Twenty-five years later, I was hanging from a rope and again it was my speed I wanted to be admired for. It was foolish and narcissistic. Maybe not when you were ten, eleven or twelve years old. But at the age of thirty-five? And then it was time to return to the hotel and try to force a teaspoon between Kristian's lips again. M craned his neck back and looked me in the eyes, and

something sprung forth inside me, my heart twisted and
nearly stopped, it was the blood of love.

ANIMALS

[Edward]

I have started to spend a lot of time at the pet shop, even though it smells wild and foul, and the birds make an infernal racket, whistling and chatter, 'hello' and 'good day-good day,' the parrots say with resounding voices that sound like speakers from the early days of radio, a long since antiquated technique. Apart from that, it only takes a moment to get used to the smell.

I do not stand there thinking that to a certain extent we are all in cages, animals as well as people, I do not stand there looking at the animals because I feel like a prisoner in my own existence, I know all the modernistic pitfalls & platitudes ad nauseam. There is by no means any sense of identification. I don't feel bad for the animals, I don't even feel sympathy for them. Nor do I think that these feathered and scaly creatures are the building blocks my species was founded on, so to speak. But as the thought emerges, I realize that I *could* think that.

I stand in contemplation in front of the cages and aquariums. I seek out the eyes of the animals and like to imagine that they seek out mine. They can't remember me later, they can't remember me even a second later. They don't recognize me when I return five minutes later. Likewise it is impossible for me to distinguish between one goldfish and the next. Our eyes meet, and zilch. Am I the kind of person who says 'zilch'... Our eyes meet across the battlefield of evolution, across millions of years.

I have learnt to grow accustomed to mice, I would not have thought that possible, what with their scurrying, their tails, etc. The birds' eyes shine with intelligence, do not stick your fingers into the fish tanks to pet them, they can get fungal infections. One day there was a rabbit that (possibly) sensed me watching it, in any case it turned its head and looked me in the eyes, lingering and lazy. Would it have done the same with any old object, dead or alive? Is there life on Mars? It was grey and probably soft as silk, as they say.

There are sharks there, and now I am getting to the point. I come for the sharks in particular. My frequent returns are down to the sharks. I had not noticed them at first, and I thought I had misheard when the trainee asked: 'Are there any sick fish to feed to the sharks today?' And the owner must have nodded, because he continued: 'I want to feed them, I want to feed them.'

At first I thought it was a metaphor, that shark meant something else. And I looked around suspiciously. I was afraid of being ridiculed. I was afraid to ask: 'Do you have *sharks*?' Slowly I scanned all the aquariums. I dress sharply, I'm not the type who wears clogs and has a snake around my neck while I walk down Strøget, (or worse still, and here is a story I was told once: a man who was in the habit, when there was a knock at the door, of opening the door, shouting 'catch' and throwing his snake into the arms of his visitor!) not the overweight kind that keeps stick insects or millipedes – oh, millipedes! Once on a dusty road in Africa I saw three monstrous millipedes come sweeping along, their legs made the most cheerful turn, black as old-fashioned locomotives they far outnumbered sightings of cheetahs and lions, and every time a couple wearing pith helmets stopped their four-wheel drive and asked us: 'Have you seen any game today?' I said yes and told them about the millipedes, 'There, over there, that way, be careful you don't run them over.'

Not the poor, lonely, sad type. Not perverted, not even introverted. I don't keep pets. My love life is rather ordinary, like that of a country bumpkin (strictly speaking I did not need to share that with you). I have a degree, I'm slim and light on my feet, the rambling type. Does that sound like a personal ad? It is.

The aquariums are stacked three high at a length of ten metres, it's a large pet shop, and the sharks are placed at the very top, almost at the end of the row, that is, deep inside the dark heart of the shop, where the room curves and opens into a warm side wing with glass doors where the birds and rodents are kept.

There are five small, eager devils side by side, they stay close to the glass and bump into it aggressively, like a team of horses stuck in a rut.

'Nothing but mouths,' the pet shop owner says; menacing mouths. The sharks can grow up to one metre in length, and I don't know what people do with them then. Maybe they butcher them. In Iceland I was served shark with gravy and fried onions. It was disgusting. But Björk was sitting only a few tables away, wearing something that resembled rompers. I had just landed, went into the first restaurant I came across, and who should be sitting there but Björk! That would be like... no, there is no comparing. Not because they are cuter when they are small (the sharks), because they are not the least bit cute, but at least they can be kept in a normal-sized aquarium.

'Maybe,' the pet shop owner says, 'people keep them (when they are fully grown), but I guess they would not have much room to move.'

They are grey and look like ferocious anchors. I have an urge to buy them and leave them on the windowsill at my office. Every time I would look up, I would meet their gaze, they would keep close to the glass and stare at me, consumed by a single thought: to escape and take me. In the end I might relent to all of the excited, concentrated will and stick my arm in. When somebody wants something from me, I am not very good at saying no, that was how my ex-girlfriend Alwilda got me, that is how my students take up all my time. I picture the sharks, one hanging from each finger; as long as the fingers remain. Now I picture myself pulling my hand out of the aquarium with a shark (about ten centimetres long) hanging from each finger, and masterfully continue typing on my computer, striking the sharks against the keys, typing with them until they expire on a keyboard ruined by blood and water.

I only have one animal at my office at the moment. A teddy bear that I bought at the Russian Museum in Saint Petersburg; one of these museums where you have to walk through the gift shop in order to reach the exhibitions. And in a display case in the shop, there were three bears, one large, one medium and one small, designed by Malevich. Bing-bang-boom. Father-mother-child. Oh, how I wanted to buy all three. But it was too much. I could only justify buying the smallest one, the baby. Buying all three – it made me imagine an old spinster, her bed covered in porcelain dolls, her liver-spotted hands pressing their yellowed backs and yellowed dresses against the wall every morning, dumb as rabbits. I knew someone like that as a child. Her name was Gerda. At night, when the bed was Gerda's, what did she do with all those dolls? The task of removing them and putting them back is what concerned me. I do not want to go there.

In the beginning, my heart would race every time I was going to show the bear to someone. Now the object has been normalized, displayed on my desk, on most days I pay no attention to it. But originally, in the very beginning, I felt a need to display my conquest.

It is neither soft nor adorable. It is like the Russian peasantry that Malevich stole it from and returned it to, now Malevich-coloured, clear red, clear blue, white, black, yellow. It is tough and proud, it works until it drops. It goes to bed with the chickens, rises with the sun, and once in a while, it gets to eat a little millet.

I kept it in my bag, god knows why. I was waiting for the right moment to pull it out, waiting for a lull in the conversation. When it arrived, I struck.

One time when I was in a restaurant with two of my best friends... it was seething in my bag throughout the main course and dessert, the bag was behind my chair. Under the pretext of having to grab my cigarettes, I loosened the flap a little and looked at it, it was sizzling. We were having a conversation about our likes and dislikes – they are both painters – and we jogged through the history of art, through a series of exhibitions. Should an explanation to my exaggerated state of excitability be sought in the past: I had a toy dog as a child, it was just as firmly stuffed as the Malevich bear, you sang about it while it danced: 'Look, here comes the chequered dog, it has a rattle in its nose, it wants to sing you a song, it is a curious creature.'

And now I really wanted to display my curious new creature. I finally managed to do it after we had paid and were putting our coats on: 'I'm not usually the type to collect dolls and stuffed animals, you know that,' I said, 'but look!'

'Ooo,' one friend said and stepped forward.

But my other friend made a small noise and stumbled back, as if he had seen a ghost or an aesthetic phenomenon in the flesh.

Which track would you prefer to follow, the beautiful one that leads you into the arms of a piece of handicraft that makes your heart race, or the one that leads back to 'Once upon a time', hearing the legs of a stuffed dog as your hands make it waltz on the edge of a cot?

DEATH HOUSE

[Edward]

People with the need for order and perhaps also a belief in progress have invented the concept of stages of grief; here I imagine a system of locks. As though the person in mourning was a boat on a river, the river of sorrow, you might say, full of locks that ease the person ahead, and further ahead, towards the open sea, the reconciliation with death and loss where a new future is possible.

I am the kind of man who lives in a death house. Literally. I moved into my parents' home when they passed away. Joint suicide. They loved to demonstrate their rock-hard realism whenever possible. Their realist and Socratic position, I would say. Life as an illness. Goodbye and thank you, we're slipping away now. While we can still do it ourselves. Very considerate. Nonetheless a shock. For a long time. Death by hanging. Whoever had to kick out the chair from the other then had to kick out their own chair. It was probably my mum. I was a child of older parents. I am now the same age as my mum was when she gave birth to me. Forty-five. I was ashamed of their sagging faces when they turned up at school among the crowd of athletic activist parents, primarily young parents. There were a few with potbellies. I did not change the house much. Once in a while I go down to the rec room, a monument to the seventies; if you put your ear to the wall, you can hear the faint echo of Abba; I take a seat by the dark, wooden bar and grab a glass (I suppose I am lonely), or I continue my losing battle with the billiard table, just a couple of shots. Thirty years ago, we used to kiss down here. With the old folks pacing nervously back and forth in the room above. And once in a while they would poke their heads down to make sure nobody got pregnant. I remember seeing my dad standing in the doorway once when I was crawling on the floor drinking Bacardi from the bottle; he pretended not to see me and shut the door behind him. Then everyone drove off on their mopeds and it was over. Someone had thrown up in the hedge. It is a terraced house, meaning the neighbour woke up to find white garlands hanging from their side of the hedge.

The house is filled with unusually large, low-flying flies. Filled might be going too far. There are four or five in each room. I get them with the hoover. It's easier than swatting them. A little later there are just as many again. I don't know if they are the same flies from before; did they really crawl out of the pipe? Or have new ones already hatched? They should be tagged so I can follow their routes.

The tube of the hoover is like a pistol (only something will soon shoot in, not out of it), the black opening approaches the black fly where it sits calmly, until the moment of perdition arrives and flight is no longer an option, the air it had previously travelled through so comfortably has become evil, a whirlwind that can lift a man on a donkey high in the air and a fly off a wall, tipping it into a noisy black tunnel – which it might be able to crawl out of when the machine is switched off.

Things have been rather gloomy since Alwilda left me. Almost a year ago. Maybe I should just sell the house. Put the past behind me.

There is only one kind of man worse than me. The kind who never leaves home, but spends his entire adult life sleeping on a sofa in the sitting room or in his former childhood room with old posters on the walls and a collection of crumbling crab shells on the windowsill. I moved out though, at the normal age of nineteen. But as soon as I spotted my chance, I moved back in.

I want to abandon the castle of my old folks, my childhood palace, their arena of death. I want to move forward in time instead of constantly being whirled back through the black tube of the past.

I moved into my parents' bedroom without considering whether it was healthy or not. I could say that I was sleepwalking, and that would fit in nicely with what comes next. In the same bed where they tossed and turned, sweaty and sleepless, decade after decade, I lay down to sleep each night. Insomnia was their great common theme, and their addiction to sleeping pills, they even gave me sleeping pills when I was a child; I struggled through my childhood dizzy and drowsy, until one night at the age of ten I gave a definitive no to the white pill held between the two fingers of my father's outstretched hand, the little almond he was about to pop into my mouth. It equated to violence: 'Are you turning against your own father?' he asked. He might just as well have said: 'Are you laying a hand on your own father?' It sounded biblical.

In the bed where I had been conceived and where they had lain sleepless, I voluntarily settled down to sleep after they died. In the very room they had chosen as the setting for their death. The place where I arrived one day to find two chairs tipped over, two old people dangling from hooks in the ceiling. And when Alwilda used to visit, she would lie down next to me. I never told her that it happened in there. I don't think she would have wanted to sleep there. On the rare occasion when she couldn't sleep because she had drunk too much tea, pleasantly and without complaint, she would count the flowers on the brown, floral wallpaper until the pattern blurred before her eyes. We had some crazy times; I hope she looks back on them with rapture, or rather: with moisture.

It happened on the same trip I saw millipedes come cheerfully sweeping down a dusty African road. We found ourselves in a reserve for large wild cats in the Kalahari Desert. For security reasons it was forbidden to get out of the car. But Alwilda considered it an invitation. She stopped the car in the middle of the plain, pulled her knickers down to her knobbly knees, climbed out of the car and pressed her face against the hot chassis of the car; she bared her arse and urged me to sink my teeth into her neck, 'just like the cats,' she said. And standing there, rocking and swaying, it was an enormous turn-on for her that at any moment we could be attacked from behind by a leopard, a cheetah, a panther or a lion. I had a harder time giving in to it. I listened attentively for soft paws, rustling in the grass. I thought more about the distance to the car door than her body. During one of these hot, rocking, anxious bouts of intercourse, the millipede, long and black like an endless set of carriages (it turned out there were three in a row) came sweeping around the turn on the dusty road; it made me think that a situation similar to the Tom Kristensen poem with the beetle and the condemned man – where in the lengthy moment before the executioner's sword falls, the condemned man spots a beetle and focuses all of his attention on it – might be about to develop; with one of the great cats serving as executioner.

Alwilda was driving and she stopped a lot. She called it 'hitting death squarely on the noggin'. I wished she had held onto me. First she wanted me. She was the one who pursued me. Then she got me. And slowly but surely I began to want her too. Just as I began to feel that it was love, despite her large knobbly knees and single-mindedness, she came to the realisation that it was not after all and left me.

At night we were in a campsite, separated from the animals by a tall wire fence. We lay in our tent and heard the cats on the prowl. Their screams and those of their victims rose and fell and cracked and rumbled, close by and far away. I have never witnessed so much sound, such a lively night.

When I work myself up to do something about it all, I quickly begin to feel faint and devoid of energy. So I sit down in an armchair and swing my legs up over the armrest. The hoover is never far away. My rear end sinks into the seat. I can sit like that for a long time. I call it staring.

They had only been dead for a few hours when I found them. They had invited me over to dinner that day. When nobody answered the door, I went around to the garden first, as though it held an answer, while I half-heartedly called for them. They had been hard of hearing for many years. Then – feeling like I had crossed a line – I inserted the key in the lock. I had not let myself into that house for fifteen years, not since the time they went to Poland and I had to water their flowers; it is the same key and key ring that they handed to me as a child with the message that I was now a latchkey child – they both worked late. When I moved away from home, I attached my own keys to that ring; unmistakably a child's key ring.

They no longer went out because they were so unsteady on their feet, so I knew something was wrong. But it was difficult to imagine them both dying at once. Still I was jubilant on the inside – it's over now, they are at peace, they're no longer in pain, they can sleep now.

What they have long awaited has finally happened. A wave of triumph passed through me on their behalf.

For years, whenever I asked my dad if there was anything I could do for him, he would reply: 'You can shoot me,' still he faithfully took his vitamins every day and got the flu jab. He retired at the age of sixty, and then lingered on for thirty years with an idleness that made him unwell. He could not grab hold of anything. He mentioned again and again his longing for a 'project', but never found one. My mother was a little younger and continued to work after he retired.

Then I grew fearful of the sight that would greet me, and I started to call out 'Mum,' the gentlest of all words, and I called out 'Dad'.

It was as though I only dared to enter another room if I called out to them first, as if the words dragged me along, or meant I did not think too much about walking forward, and what might meet my eyes; I stifled my own momentum, so to speak. Finally there was only the bedroom left – and this was it. And then I opened the door.

I saw them again the following day at the funeral parlour. They looked like the product of an African wood carver. I don't know if all dead people resemble one another, but they did. Death had turned them into twins.

They had passed into another state. They no longer belonged to me.

Their mouths were slightly agape, giving their faces a slightly scheming look that they had never had when they were alive. I squatted down on the floor to find an angle where I could avoid their scheming, shrewd, calculating mouths. They had died in the same way, and they looked the same. Their skin was so frightfully cold but their hair looked normal. So I stroked their hair. I later asked the undertaker to cut off a lock of their hair but he cut off far too much; it was like a disfigurement; for that reason I never again looked inside the envelopes he handed me before the funeral service. There was too much; too alive; like scalps.

I realized that I moved between a series of positions – in my mind. They were all there from the beginning. There was my fear of forgetting. I recalled and repeated the conversations we had had during our latest meetings, with the same energy as someone who is about to sit an exam; I remembered their expressions. I could picture them sitting directly across from me. They were inside me.

There were times when I could not conjure them up in my mind, where they moved back in time like a rocket, away from me, so that I lost them entirely. Other times it was not the speed with which they disappeared, but instead they were behind a frosted window, they were blurred, impossible to get hold of. It hurt me when they diminished in clarity. But they always became clear again. Then unclear. Then clear.

I was overjoyed on their behalf that their troubles were over; the autumn approached and with that, the darkness that they feared; I was glad that they did not have to stay inside the house lighting candles, oppressed by the darkness with all their sufferings. I never realized how much it helped them that they had had each other. The more disabilities that turned up, the less so – I think. Their pains isolated them from one another. I think so. I have no idea how they managed to get up on the chairs, she with her osteoporosis and a compression fracture in the spine, he with his Scheuerman's, the failed operation on his herniated disc, the numb leg that he had to drag around; how did they even get up there; one final, caring, joint endeavour, or did he snap at her, even in that situation?

And then there was my longing for them, to see them again, just one more time. Sometimes my happiness at their release could completely rid me of my longing. Other times not.

I was never angry that they had arranged for me to find them – by inviting me that day. You might imagine that I would feel deceived. I was the closest. Who, if not me? It was an expression of trust. The house quickly filled with people that day; the police, doctors and the emergency services, into whose hands they passed. I liked all of them.

I liked the mortician too. Even when he said: 'I worked so hard for you that my fingers are bleeding,' I thought it was a rather tactless bodily reference, and he must have realized it and backtracked; but even after that he said: 'I've got your parents in a cardboard box.'

(Only much later did I begin to wonder if he had an occupational injury, or if he was just trying to see what he could get away with; whether it was out of spite, or from having the upper hand – I was clearly down; was that the reason he had cut off too much hair? Stop it, I told myself; and so I did.)

And the florist. And the priest. And the staff at the funeral parlour. I liked them so much that I wanted to see them again. Not only did I want to see them again, I had a hard time letting go of them.

On the other hand, people who had known them, neighbours, a few old friends, I did not want to hear what they had to say about them. I wasn't worried they would say anything bad but I did not feel like having their lives interpreted by other people. It was down to two things; I had a sense that they belonged to me; and I did not feel like having more added to my image of them; I did not feel like having to grapple with new 'material'. I thought I had enough. So much so that on occasion I had a hard time getting my bearings.

One morning one of their old friends called me; he had arranged a memorial for my parents on the fortieth day of their death; he was a member of the Russian Orthodox Church; he invited me to participate; he told me that they believed – well no, he served it up as fact – that for the first forty days their souls were bound to the earth, and that this ceremony would help them let go; people would pray for their sins to be forgiven and ask God to receive them; my first reaction was that I did not want them to leave the earthly realm, (I wanted to keep them close, if possible; where they were had not crossed my mind until now, previously I had thought that everything ended with death) and my next reaction was that I did not think they had done anything wrong.

They were both critical-rationalists; I am too, none of us believers. Still, the new material that had been dumped on me, I could not simply dismiss it out of hand.

I was afraid of joining the memorial because I felt unstable – if I could feel a connection to the florist who handed me a bunch of flowers from behind the counter, who knows what would happen to me in a gathering of chanting believers? I decided not to go. Even though it felt wrong to let people who had not known my parents – only one of them had – pray for their souls without me even being present.

I realized that I had a constant sense that my parents were floating above the house that I had immediately settled into, and that they could see what I was doing.

However I had not, as I previously thought, imagined that everything ended with death; that was only my common sense (speaking). I realized that after the phone call. Now, whether I wanted to or not, I had to start thinking about how they were doing, whether they liked what they saw me doing. From the very first day (after their death) I kissed a photograph of them several times a day; it was a comfort to press my lips against the glossy surface; I decided not to frame the photos, because glass would mean greater distance. The surface of the photograph was all I could get, not living skin, or even cold, dead skin (they had long since been cremated), there should be nothing separating us, no glass.

Now when I did it, kissed them, I thought about whether I did it out of fear – of what they would think of me. I suddenly understood that you can be afraid of the dead; all of this came pouring down on me after hearing the word soul on the phone.

I went to the churchyard and read their names on the gravestone; their urns (containing half their ashes, the rest were to be scattered at sea) were buried in the earth, this little patch of garden; but were they truly there? I did not think so. I did not think that this place had anything to do with them.

I knew very well that they were not floating above the house, yet still I believed it; they were not in the churchyard; sometimes they were inside of me; other times they were not. Everything ended with death; maybe their souls were tormented. One day I heard a sentence inside my head, spoken in my mum's voice: 'Maybe you'll discover that you don't love us nearly as much as you thought you did;' she had actually said those words to me once, once when we talked about death; that I might feel that way. The sentence had entered my mind and now

I had to decide if that was the case. How was I to know that? I am sure I protested when she said those words. Now she was no longer there to protest to. New material streamed in from all sides, I was like a person writing a thesis that could not be delimited.

There was a lot of light and a strong wind on the November day I drove to the island where my parents were born to scatter their ashes; after the cremation I had their ashes divided up into four urns. They had wanted their ashes scattered at sea. I wanted a grave. And a grave without a little of them seemed senseless. Hence all the urns. Two for the earth, already buried, and two for the sea.

I stopped the car and grabbed the white cardboard boxes and a bunch of yellow roses from the boot. I had to walk past a field of sugar beets to reach the water's edge. I had chosen a place where they used to enjoy swimming, where the three of us used to swim when I was a child. Along the edge of the field, even though it was well into November, there were still a few poppies and daisies in bloom, though somewhat brown at the edges. The wind tossed the light around and took hold of everything. The wind added some wildness to the day. I had chosen that day because of the light. I had waited weeks for it to stop raining, racked with guilt at leaving their urns in the boot. But I would have been unable to face black trees and bushes, a dark sea and a grey, wet sky – a landscape that was practically dead.

I had not been there for years; there I walked on one of my childhood haunts; even returning is something special; it makes you notice more; with one look you see the changes, with one look you recognize the place; with one look you recollect. And of course all of this was intensified by the fact that I was walking with my parents' urns in my arms.

As a child I identified this place with the Stone Age; it seemed so old to me, the coast and its bays, black underbrush, all the seaweed and rows of large stones jutting out from the coast, an hour ago someone dressed in fur could have slurped down some mussels here.

I remembered how my mum used to swim; she always swam on her side with one arm stretched out behind her, she loved the water; it was a source of enjoyment that she was robbed of when she was no longer steady enough on her feet to be able to get into the water; now she was returning to this place in the form of ashes.

I pulled the urns out of the cardboard boxes and put a couple of rocks in each box so they would not fly away. I removed the name tags from the urns and cut open the steel wire that sealed them with a pair of pliers. Then I balanced on the stones in the water. I reckoned the breeze was at my back. Halfway out I stopped and removed the lids. Then I leant forward, with one urn in each arm and poured from each one at the same time. Immediately the ashes blew back in my face. I got them in my mouth, my nose, in my eyes. My coat and my suede shoes were grey with ashes. I leant forward even more and managed to empty the urns. The ashes were clearly visible on the sandy yellow bottom. I threw both urns against a stone and kicked the shards onto the seabed. I was a little worried that some bathers might step on the shards next summer. But by then the current would probably have carried them away. I threw the yellow roses into the water above their ashes. Then I rubbed my eyes, spat out some ashes and brushed off my coat and my shoes – their final loving embrace.

The yellow roses – I could see them when I was back on the beach. I had a peculiar taste in my mouth and wiped it away with my handkerchief; I had ashes in all of my facial cavities.

Note to my *Mourning Diary*: When I saw them dead, I thought they no longer belonged to me: they had passed on to another state. I struggled for a long time with whether I could miss something that was no longer accessible. I missed them as they were when they were alive. But they were no longer alive. The image of them being dead had placed a dividing wall between us.

It was like being forced to undergo a particular exercise in logic. It seemed like I was running the gauntlet between my lines of reasoning.

CAMILLA AND THE HORSE

[Camilla]

We go to an expensive Italian restaurant across from the strip club and drink a bottle of wine to kill some time, and it soon becomes apparent that the waiter is attracted to my husband, who may be getting on in years, but is hot-blooded. The waiter is getting on in years too, he has had his photograph taken with Sophia Loren and Helmut Kohl in this very restaurant, which gets my husband out of his seat. Would you look at that, it's nine o'clock, and we head across the street. We pay admission. I start by asking at the bar if it is okay for me to be here even though I am a woman. I do that to initiate contact and get on their good side. No problem, we are the only guests here. The girl behind the bar is from Romania, sturdy with short hair. My husband thinks I am good at making contact with people and at relaxing. People have to be careful not to praise me too much, I get terribly stimulated and can easily overstep the mark, then there is no stopping me. There are so many prostitutes here I don't know what to do; we are the only guests and we have no intention of buying sex, I tell that to the girl at the bar several times. That's quite alright, we can just have a drink, you get three free drinks with admission, so I choose the strongest one and knock it back in a hurry. On stage, the show begins, with a mixed-race girl doing all the expected stuff and manoeuvring up and down and around a go-go pole until she is naked. It reminds me of the circus and of extreme fatigue, routines, because I hate to say it: of a tired circus animal. The moment she walks off the stage, she goes all shy, bowing her head and clutching her clothes against her stomach.

In the meantime at the bar: a woman has sat down

next to me, she is also Romanian (from this point I refer to her as my darling), I ask her if she knows Herta
Müller, she asks me to name titles, I mention *Even Back
Then the Fox Was the Hunter*, which is quite a mouthful
in German, especially with my German; her German is
not great either, she is taking lessons and claims to speak
eighty-five per cent grammatical German. I am not sure
how to respond, 'modal verbs, you know,' she says.
Those I know. But it dawns on me that I have completely forgotten that articles and nouns conjugate, meaning
nothing I have said has made any sense. Apparently I
have been speaking zero per cent grammatical German
so I switch to English. I am sitting with my back to my
husband, he is very interested in our conversation, and
once in a while I turn around to fill him in. He nods and
poses supplementary questions. I ask my darling if she
sends money home to her parents, because you always
read about that, but no, they have never helped her, so
she does not help them. 'Does that sound a little harsh?'
my darling asks. I think so. My darling thinks so too.
Whenever my husband gets drawn into the conversation, she treats him with the utmost respect, giving him
all the time he wants. It makes me jealous, I want her full
attention.

'Do you want to buy him?' I ask. 'Three hundred
euros.'

She looks at him to see if he finds it amusing, he does.

'Oh, that's expensive, very expensive,' she says.

'He may be a bit old, but he's good,' I say. 'He fucks
like a stallion.'

'Oh, a superboy,' she says.

'There are boys and then there are boys,' I say.

'Prince Charles,' she calls him, and he likes that.

My husband leans back in his barstool and laughs, my

69

darling laughs, I laugh. I realize I am taking up her time, so I ask her if she wants some money for speaking to me.

'Oh, Camilla,' she says. 'Money, money, money.'

I hold out a note in front of her and see that she does not think much of fifty euros, but the note disappears down her top. She is dark-skinned and could be a Roma. My husband is getting bored now, he gets up and strolls over to a group of girls sitting round a table, including the Romanian barmaid who is studying mathematics, he fancies a little chat with her. He wants to know about Romanian living standards, differences and similarities in the time before and after Ceaușescu. It makes me a little insecure seeing my husband speak to other women, 'oh mein Schatz,' my darling says, 'just let him be, that's just the way it is sometimes, everyone needs that.' 'Mmm.' I ask her if she has a boyfriend. She does, but she does not seem particularly enthusiastic. I ask her if it is difficult being in a relationship when you work as a prostitute. She takes a deep breath and says something about Orgasmus, she is about to make a speech about various types of Orgasmus, or the lack of Orgasmus, when some customers arrive, three little Chinamen, and now she has to run. I feel lost. She weaves around them. I get up and join my husband and the women at the round table.

'This is going to be expensive,' I tell him, 'you are conducting an expensive conversation.'

'No,' he says, 'this is the staff table. And I'm speaking to the girl who works behind the bar.'

'Trust me,' I say, 'it's going to be expensive. It's like sitting in four taxis at once.'

'Rubbish,' he says, 'we're talking about Romania.'

'Rubbish,' say the girls.

'All right then,' I say. 'Just call me paranoid.'

I join the small group that consists of:
1. The mixed-race girl, twenty-four, a sceptic.
2. A pale woman who introduces herself as an alcoholic.
3. A woman with black hair and a small face, she has just had a facelift.
4. The barmaid.

'Mein Schatz,' my darling says when she sees me (the Chinese men are getting ready to leave) and plants herself on the chair behind me and wraps her arms around me, 'Camilla and the horse,' she says to the others, pointing at my husband and me. Then she wags a finger in front of her nose and corrects herself: 'Prince Charles,' she says and points at my husband.

I duly compliment the mixed-race girl's performance and ask her: 'Do you want to buy him? He may be a bit old, but he's good.'

Before she gets a chance to answer, the alcoholic leans across the table and introduces herself as an alcoholic again. I tell her that she is very clever and incredibly good looking and I encourage her to stop drinking and be happy with herself. I show her how I give myself a pat on the back every day, unfortunately I can't remember what that technique is called, but it works (because for every day that passes, I am more and more content with myself), I got it from an article in *Reader's Digest*. I force a promise out of her, that she will not have a drink first thing the following morning, I start to see myself as a kind of barefoot doctor, moving from bar to bar, I order champagne for the table to celebrate the alcoholic's decision, and my darling kisses me, her tongue is very pointy, mine is very dry, this is going to be expensive, and I tell her that married life with my husband is like one looong German porn film, he is a superboy, he is falling apart, I have also completely fallen apart, my darling's one breast slips out, and her skirt is twisted halfway around, she is about to fall apart, but she strokes me and caresses me, she wants to go home now, so I give her a slap, not very hard.

'She hit me,' my darling says in shock.

'Blame it on love,' the woman with the small face says, 'I prefer gentlemen, but once in a while I like a woman.'

'Sorry, sorry, sorry,' I say, it's morning, and I ask her how much it will cost to get her to stay for just one more hour, please-please-please, but she lives wayyy out in the suburbs. I picture my darling, alone on the U-bahn, alone on the S-bahn. I want to buy more champagne for her, for everyone.

We have to go now, the bar is closing, it's seven o'clock, I have a husband who fucks like a stallion, I cry, 'oooooh,' they jeer at the sight of my tears: 'It's true love,' I give the alcoholic one final admonition, she has to manage without her trainer now, because Camilla and the horse are leaving, 'no no no: Prince Charles,' my horse is my cane this blistering morning; suddenly it is the last summer ever.

I wish I was Žižek. Žižek can get everything to make sense, if I had been Žižek now, right now, I would be lying in a Punic bordello having a fucking match with Houellebecq, the whores would not be trafficked, just glo-ba-lized – can you hear it being sung by Gregorian monks, or maybe a eunuch: glo-ba-lized pro-sti-tutes.

Ohhh, the human, the oh-so Žižekian need to make sense of things where none exists. What is it that I cannot make sense of? My memory? My love life? We will have to take a closer look at that.

I miss my Romanian darling. I never discovered her name. My husband says: if you want to see her again, you'll have to hurry back, they are flighty people. By which he means she might be working at another bar already, in another city: or that so many people have slipped through her fingers that she will have forgotten me, or soon will.

'Flighty people' – the expression surprised me. Like he was in possession of an experience I was unaware of – and was only now revealing a small piece of it.

At first I could not remember her either. I mean: I could not picture her. And I could not really remember what had happened.

The very first thing, when I woke up later that morning after only a couple of hours of sleep (we left the bar at seven and stepped outside to face a morning light as sharp as needles, with me crying over my lost love, over parting as such, over the brevity of life) with a horrific hangover, maybe even drunk, the very first thing I found in my handbag was the address and telephone number I had extorted from her. She had handed it to me with a shrug (maybe it was fake), and I quickly tore the note into tiny pieces and flushed it down the toilet so I would not be tempted to contact her. A memory arrives on the platform of the cerebral cortex, bleak as a freight train. One loss carries another with it. Loss opens up loss opens up tear ducts. Even as a child I feared the worst. I was secretly in love with a boy in my class and wrote him love letters that he was never meant to see, never ever, my love was hopeless, I wrote the letters (well, they were not exactly Shakespeare, were they?) because I felt closer to him when I wrote, when I communicated, when I placed his name in a heart next to mine. Fearing these letters might somehow fall into his hands, or anybody else's for that matter, I tore them into a thousand pieces as soon as I had written them and flushed them down the toilet. Almost as soon as I had done that, my nightmare began. I imagined him walking into his bathroom many kilometres away, and lying in the toilet water was – my torn up letter, which he would immediately fish out, dry, piece together. Then he would throw his head back and laugh, and I would change schools. A fatal flaw in the sewer system was to blame for this frightful event, his pipe and my pipe were connected! The next time I burnt my love letter. The wind caught a couple of singed flakes and carried them out the window. I began to daydream instead and was thus let off having to destroy evidence. The memory is now departing from platform cerebral cortex, do not cross the tracks. And hold onto your portmanteau.

We are staying on the twenty-fifth floor of a hotel on Alexanderplatz, with a view of the restaurant in the TV tower. I could draw the curtains and make the small hotel room even darker, even closer, or I could offer an unobstructed view of my wretchedness. Not that I think anyone could see into our hotel room from the restaurant in the TV tower, they would need binoculars to do that. Not that I thought anyone would even consider doing that. No, the TV tower itself was so observant, a massive observer with red flashing eyes, right outside the window.

The WC and shower were in a green, marbled glass space *within* the hotel room, a shower cubicle with a toilet. For a long time, I threw up in fits and starts within this tiny cage, where there was barely room to kneel down and which did nothing to block the noise from the surrounding room (I hoped Charles was fast asleep). Who could vomit noiselessly? It was practically pouring down. Like the expression: Life flows out of you. As though life was a small brook. I coughed up in convulsive jerks, kneeling in the most humiliating position with my arms flung around the white bowl, clasping it (oh, how I would have preferred to be kneeling amongst sheep by a brook and drinking amongst sheep).

In that respect, I have always imagined dying in a bathroom, a clean death, practically antiseptic, slumped against white enamel, a sampler of the coffin's white calm, but I hope that the bathroom I die in will be bigger than this cubicle in the hotel room on Alexanderplatz, a little more spacious, a little more *Todesraum, bitte*. When I was finished vomiting, I went to bed, closed my eyes and tried to remember. Next to me, Prince Charles was snoring.

The first thing Charles did when he woke up was squeeze my hand. A gentle squeeze that meant: we belong together, the two of us; even though our eyes may have been turned by other people last night. Or it could also mean: I didn't hear you vomiting. Very reassuring, very affectionate. I squeezed back. Then he leapt to his feet and started to rummage through his pockets, pulling out all the receipts from last night's festivities. The Visa had been swiped many, many times. The bar did not accept Visa, they wanted cool hard cash, but the barmaid had offered to have Charles driven to the nearest cash machine in the bar's six-door white Cadillac with tinted windows, one of those ones that looks like an oversized hearse, (if I could choose my death, I would be run over by a hearse, death is my best *friend* // my raddled follower to the bitter *end*, tra-la-la, it sounds like one of my friend Alma's halting, drawling rhymes, the mortician would gather me up from the street and place my bruised body on top of the coffin, skip the hospital and the chapel, get right to the point, straight to the grave) but more precisely, at least in this instance, it serves as a bordello on wheels. Charles had declined. He was more than happy to walk. And so he had – more than a few times – back and forth between the cash machine and the bar, the evidence of all his walking was presented, a pile of crumpled-up receipts.

'Ouch,' he said, 'that was one expensive night.'

'Let's check how much cash we have in our pockets,' I said optimistically.

There wasn't much.

'We spent nine grand last night.'

'Nine thousand euros?'

'Kroner.'

'What's that in euros?'

'Why euros?'

'What's that in yen?'

He looked at me. And I knew we were thinking the same thing. He had insisted it would be free, free and easy, to have a conversation with the girls at the staff table about Romanian living standards et cetera, et cetera, and I had known it was going to be expensive, that it would mean we ended up paying for all their drinks over the course of our conversation. I said nothing. Thereby doubling my enjoyment: not only was I right but now I could act magnanimously by saying nothing. I smiled. And pocketed my point. Then we started to discuss the possibility of deducting the amount. Charles is a food critic. But even though we had sat in the bar dipping nachos in guacamole (from a jar) it could hardly be deemed a restaurant. I started to feel nauseous again and said: 'Dear sweet Charles, would you mind stepping outside for a while?'

'In the corridor?'

76

I nodded: 'Yes, quickly though.'

He quickly put on some trousers and a shirt and opened the door to the corridor. As I squeezed into the cubicle, he said: 'You do realize that the fruition of a party is suicide.'

The Balcony. Jean Genet.

'Yes,' I replied, 'we should have chosen the monotony of the lily fields.'

'Genet,' he said and closed the door.

We have just read *The Balcony*. We read to each other before going to sleep. I read novels, poems and plays to Charles. And Charles reads recipes to me. In the foreword of one of his cookbooks it states that there is nothing to prevent people living to the age of 140. We eat according to that book. By the time he is finished reading, we are starving. We head straight to the kitchen, and that's why we've got a little, only a little mind, rotund. But as long as we walk along the bulging highway of life together, where your love handles are mine, and my love handles are yours.

The only thing I have left of her is her lighter. Charles found it in his jacket pocket and gave it to me. It's black. With palm trees. And a couple dancing in evening wear. A bungalow can be made out in the background. Slender and elegant, they dance through the boundless tropical night. He wearing a tuxedo, she wearing a white cocktail dress. He with a hand on her enticingly curved back, his hand placed right there, in the curvature. She with a hand on the broad shoulder of his tailored jacket. A waiter crosses the terrace of the bungalow carrying a tray. Bungalow, from Banglā, a single-storey house for Europeans in India. It is another era. All, I presume, very colonial, (apparently the only thing missing is some pillars, it ought to have been a house with colonial era pillars) scorching hot, the sea in the near distance, and snakes in the grass. Occasionally a snake enters the bungalow. The servants scream, and the woman in the white dress screams loudest of all. Small, underdeveloped men in white coats, slender as crickets, come running in from the garden with sharp instruments and make short work of it. The driver leans against the large car, bored, he has lit one of his master's cigars and has to smoke it discreetly, concealed in his hand, if that's even possible with a cigar. The couple are in the honeymoon stage of their marriage. They can still contrive to dance on the terrace at night.

I keep the lighter. A keepsake. At one point I dragged her out onto the dance floor – I went first, in the depths of intoxication, throwing my arms in the air like a skating queen and shouting: 'I'm an architect.' Even though I most definitely am not.

Charles and his companions at the staff table: the alcoholic, the mixed-race girl, the barmaid and the black-haired woman who had recently undergone a face lift and whose small face resembled a tight raisin: they observed us, hooted. I was wearing an improbable amount of clothes. A half-length skirt, flat boots and a thick black sweater. She was more appropriately, more lightly dressed. I probably looked like an ageing, slightly chubby panther. Though not without a certain suppleness. But. By that point she was already yearning to go home. When we sat down the barmaid said, pointing at Charles: 'He has children.'

'He got them in Hamburg,' the alcoholic said.

'Uh, do not go to Hamburg.'

'No, do not go to Hamburg.'

'I've never been to Hamburg,' Charles said and put

his wallet back in his pocket. He had obviously shown them a picture of his two grown-up sons. Two enterprising men in their twenties. Business, this slightly woolly word. By the age of sixteen his youngest son had already made his first million. A happy story. He's not my son. But I also have expectations of him.

Charles leaned back in the chair and exploded with laughter as he looked at me and shook his head, we had ended up surrounded by surrealists. (I happened to think of Gulliver, what he had been subjected to, of how surprised he was. As a child I could not get enough of the illustration of giant Gulliver waking up surrounded by Liliputians, finding himself tethered to the ground by countless thin strings, with an army of miniature people teeming all around and all over him, industrious as ants, all holding something useful, on their way to complete some useful errand.)

'He's a stallion.'

'Uh, a superboy,' my darling said, then pulled up a chair behind mine and embraced me.

'Little devil,' she said.

Shortly after that was when she grabbed me by the head and kissed me. And I began to think that she was taken with me. Our acquaintance lasted from about nine o'clock, when we arrived at the bar and she sat down in a chair next to me, until seven o'clock, when we reluctantly (at least I was reluctant) vacated the premises.

Over the course of those roughly ten hours, every time she left me, for example in favour of the short Chinese men, I felt I was missing something. As if to exist was to pull something out of thin air (which it possibly is). It was exactly like that when I met Charles. Empty, lonesome, hollow, wrong whenever he was not in my direct vicinity.

CAMILLA AND CHARLES

[Camilla]

Charles and I count among the small minority of people who found out about the events of September 11 after a delay of about twenty-four hours. Owing to a combination of factors, including language barrier, love and general distraction. We were in Lisbon, at the shabbiest hotel you can imagine. The corridors, furnished with damp-stained runners that were apparently only there to conceal missing floorboards, were filled with junk that had never made it any further; worn-out suites were piled up, beds that had been slept to death, chairs that had been sat to death, tables covered with thumbprints left by melancholics who probably thought in circles, round and round the table. Outside our room there was an old typewriter. When you struck a key, the slender metal typewriter leg got stuck halfway between the ribbon and the other letters (a flowery meadow of ancient letters) as though trying to say: No, I won't do it alone.

Who can deny having a weak spot for typewriters? Every time I returned, every time I left the room, I struck a key. I simply could not resist. Like seeing a piano that just *has* to be played. Recollection arrives, everyone knows the platform: I must have been nineteen, I had not written a single word, much less a poem, when I hauled my 7.5-kilo typewriter along on a train journey with stops in Rome, Florence, Venice, without ever managing to write a single word, but it was completely worth it when a young American girl told me that she understood why I was dragging that heavy beast around because 'what is an author without her typewriter,' she said. And I was sold. Recollection cancelled. It leaves a pleasant tingling, but also an insipid taste in the mouth because nothing much ever came of it. I feel like the typewriter key, dangling between heaven and earth. No, I won't do it alone. But I still like typewriters. And I like to read Charles's food reviews and suggest a change here and there. The reviewer's reviewer, that's me.

It was not only the recollection of the American girl's assertion that made me tingle inside. Florence, New Year's Eve, a quarter of a century ago, she had long black hair and was wearing a red duffle coat, just like Paddington, and perhaps that was why I thought of her as a small bear, I've never been able to resist that kind of button, wooden and oblong, buttoned crosswise.

Back to Lisbon. Our hotel room was stained with damp, just like the rest of the hotel. When I plugged my blow-dryer in to the outlet, I could use it to switch the lights in my room on and off, but I could not make it blow. And there was a mirror in which you could faintly discern yourself, and each other – naked and locked in an embrace we appeared, Charles and Camilla, duly flattered, only contours, somewhere deep inside the rusty night of the mirror while (we were doing it all the time, we were probably doing it all the while) the aeroplanes flew into the towers. Afterwards, hungry from all of that love, we left the room and I struck a key as always, perhaps 'd' for disaster that day, and we walked with our arms around each other, hungry and happy along the dangerous corridor and down the dangerous staircase, the lift was simply too dangerous, even for soldiers of fortune like ourselves. Downstairs in reception, one of the Indian owners emerged from his room under the staircase, said something to Charles and tugged at his sleeve. He was tugged into the room. And I followed. He was visibly agitated about something on TV. I saw a mass of smoke and assumed it was a forest fire.

'No, we are not interested in seeing a film right now,' Charles said in a friendly tone, because he is always friendly, and tugged his sleeve back.

'It's not a film,' I said, 'I think the forests in his native country are on fire.'

'Argh,' Charles said, leaning forward and stroking the Indian on the cheek, 'I'm sure everything will turn out all right.'

The Indian was at a complete loss. In the end he let us go with a shrug. And without realizing it, we stepped out into a world transformed. But of course people do that all the time. I would hate to overestimate the significance of the event: so much evil has happened prior to and since then, and perhaps society would have isolated itself anyway. And perhaps we would have isolated ourselves out of anxiety anyway. Perhaps the collapse of the Twin Towers was just an opportunity. That's what Charles thinks, for example. Unfortunately I am unable to produce an independent, an original political analysis; I'm not trained for that so I rely on and repeat what I have heard and read. Good thing I have my newspaper. Good thing I have Žižek. And not least, good thing I have Charles. And good thing I have Alwilda, too. She is tough.

I was riding my bike one day when I got stopped by a journalist, asking if I could explain why I wore a helmet. How many answers could there be? But in an attempt to surprise him, I told him I was afraid of something falling on my head. 'From above?' he asked. 'From above,' I repeated. 'I belong to a nation of nervous Nellies, we're scared of everything these days.'

'Would you mind confining your reasons to you,' he said.

'No,' I replied, 'I would prefer that. Long before 9/11,

I began to fear the worst. Always. The only thing I'm not afraid of is salmonella. I eat raw eggs with complete disregard for death.'

'I'm hearing and writing disregard for death,' he said, 'but we're not talking about eggs. Although, an egg landing on the kitchen floor and a head landing on the asphalt, of course they can be compared.'

And then he rushed off, with the idea of opening his short feature on cycle helmets with a slow motion shot of an egg being smashed against a hard surface. How he ran. So nobody would steal his idea.

Let's talk about flowers then, I say (the journalist is gone). I am sitting directly in front of a bunch of almost black-red gladioli at home in our living room and I wonder what it would be like to walk inside such a velvet funnel. Now don't go thinking this is about female genitalia, caution, this is about death again. Walk inside such a funnel of velvet, turn around and watch it close behind you. Be surrounded, enclosed, suffocated in a delightful scent, with soft walls, and be allowed to die a flowery death.

But where does it come from, I ask myself, and sometimes Alwilda asks me that too, and Charles, this circling around death. For a long time I could not come up with an answer. I shrugged, turned away and decided to keep death to myself in the future. As though it was my problem alone, mine and only mine. For that reason I was happy when I found a possible answer in V. S. Naipaul's *The Enigma of Arrival* one day.

I learnt the piece by heart, and the next time Alwilda asked me, I replied: 'To see the possibility, the certainty of ruin, even at the moment of creation: it was my temperament. Those nerves had been given me as a child in Trinidad, partly by our family circumstances: the half-ruined or broken-down houses we lived in, our many moves, our general uncertainty...'

'Trinidad,' Alwilda said in disbelief, 'but we lived in Jægersborg the entire time, and your home was so nice, it was certainly no ruin.'

'The uncertainty,' I said sombrely,' the uncertainty, the furniture was shifted round a lot, for long periods at a time I was put out to graze with relatives, there was much illness, my life was abruptly turned upside down, people arrived and departed.'

'Yes, childhood is a quagmire,' Alwilda said, 'you get stuck. Every single day I blindly repeat what others have told me. Who is speaking through me now? I ask myself, is it my dear mum or my dear sweet granddad, who was it now that got ill from having cobwebs on the broom, who was it now that shouted at me when I swept the webs off the ceilings and forgot to clean the broom, with something resembling mouldy porridge stuck to the bristles. And now it is my turn. I don't care what the broom looks like. But when Daniel forgets to clean the broom after sweeping up, a shout escapes me (nonetheless)...'

'Isn't it a little simplistic to fall back on the idea that someone is speaking through you? Shouldn't we take responsibility for what we say?'

'But now that someone is being spoken through. First I have left – yes, what have I left – the figure of my granddad shouting at me. And then, when I am shouted through, am I also meant to take responsibility for that?'

'At least you have the pleasure of shouting at Daniel.'

'Who will then shout at another person who will shout at ...'

II. CAMILLA AND THE REST OF THE PARTY

'He had a bestial relation to literature as though it were the sole source of animal warmth. He warmed himself by the side of literature, he rubbed up against its coat with his bristly red hair and unshaven cheeks. He was a Romulus who hated the she-wolf which gave him suck, and hating, he taught others to love her...'
— Osip Mandelstam describing his teacher V. V. Gippius

CAMILLA AND THE REST OF THE PARTY

[Camilla]

Charles is ill. He is the one that pain rides. This is the second year. He takes morphine. I sit on a chair by his bed every night – not even on the edge of the bed, because he cannot cope with the mattress sloping – and gets terribly impatient. Or restless. I have a hard time staying seated for long periods at a time. And depressed. And very upset to see his pain-ridden face. I am not good at being the next of kin. I feel sorry for myself, at the turn life has taken. And for him, most of all, the one ridden with pain.

On the odd occasion that Charles gets up, I sometimes throw myself onto the bed where he lay, in an attempt to try to mull over the situation, and as I do, I view the room from his position – see what he is surrounded with every day. Still on the table are the gifts this week's visitors have brought, a jar with a brown label dangling from a fiery-red bow: 'Alwilda's Strawberry Jam with Cumin,' there's some tea, and a silk pillow towering there, all gifts from young women with sunny dispositions; a little to the right are the dark gentlemanly things – rum and bitter chocolate.

The windowsill is lined with flowers and rocks, and there are a number of red items, a red plaid blanket over the back of a chair, a red glass on the table. The yellow orchids do not have the dead waxen characteristic that orchids often have, there is a swarm of small light flowers, and the height of the plants (nearly a metre) and the colour of the flowers (warm yellow) with the grey sky as a backdrop, makes you think of the yoga routine, Sun Salutation, where a person sits and salutes by stretching their arms high in the air. My maths tutor (at secondary school) tried to teach it to me, he struggled to cross my stiff calves over my thighs, into the lotus position, it felt like sitting on a see-saw. In the corner of the room is the rocking chair that he seduced Alma in, its seat and back are made of wicker, it was given a new seat, there were holes in the old one. The upstairs neighbour has a golden Buddha in the windowsill facing the street, in our windowsill Ganesha is standing with a rat, also visible from the street. Approaching the property, you would think you were approaching a couple of sanctuaries: Hindus on the ground floor, Buddhists on the first floor. Charles loves flowers. Charles loves rocks. I have an equally difficult time with rocks as with the sky – I stare and wait for something to happen, but nothing happens, and after a moment I give up. Or I just send short, dutiful looks at rocks, at stars. I have a strong desire and an expectation for something to happen inside me during my encounters with the world.

We, Charles and I, used to characterise our love with the words 'speed, motion and momentum'. We never thought we would get stuck. Now we are. 'Locked,' visibly, just like something in his back, him to the bed, me to the chair by the bed.

The morphine has taken away Charles's appetite, he lives on oranges. First his stomach became as flat as that of a young man, and I stroked it with desire. Now he is practically hollow. I lean over him gingerly – I need to be an angel or some other winged presence so that I can float above him weightlessly, touch him without making the pain worse – and kiss him and I am terrified that he will disappear from me entirely, 'ow, ow, ow,' he says. Back to the chair. I have become a sister. I recall: Torremolinos, God knows what year exactly, but there was an air of hippyness to it, and we were all reading *The Drifters* (it was passed round between us) by James A. Michener, that was why we were in Torremolinos, one of the chapters was set there, and that was why we later travelled to Marrakech (and then returned to Torremolinos just like in the book) where we arrived in moonlight, and I provoked my boyfriend, Tim was his name, by saying that the walls and the ground were yellow, not red, the red walls of Marrakech, as Michener had described so enticingly, and which at long last we now stood by. Alas, all of this because I sit looking at Charles's brown pill bottles remembering a man with brown hair (who constantly had to toss his head back to get the long fringe out of his eyes, was missing a couple of teeth and must have had a name like Jimmy) with a guitar on one of the beaches, very quietly singing 'Tell me, sister morphine, when are you coming round again,' and I thought: yes, that's how it is, ('it' likely meaning life – but actually things are only like that now, just under twenty years later (now: morphine & immense pain that I am a neighbour to here on the chair) while at the same time feeling left out and, quite rightly, like a complete idiot. My self-consciousness made me quiet as a clam; but within my muteness I kicked against the pricks – against the idea that there was something wrong with me, even though I was unable to fit in with the crowd.

I was envious of those who were happy and easygoing. In particular a Norwegian girl whose laughter rose and fell as she played ball, wearing only knickers and with a couple of long hairs (though blonde) poking out from one nipple; she had been an intravenous drug user and saw it as her new mission in life to smuggle hash into Norway – to somewhere far north where she came from, to give young people there an alternative to heroin, which was much easier to smuggle, and for that reason it was far cheaper and more accessible (she explained to us in a rare moment of gravity) – swaddled in packages around her tall Norwegian waist, maybe around her legs too. I remember that her legs were not even that long. It occurs to me that the one time we were alone together (which was easier for me than being in a crowd, I kept seeing myself from the outside, and it cast an enormous damper on me: it meant that there were two of me and I found myself walking in a never-ending circle, treading on my own toes) and in an attempt at intimacy (which maybe I was able to reciprocate, maybe not) she told me about a house she had lived in, along with several other junkies, where they had slept in one big pile and every night they would simply reach out for whoever was closest, from somewhere deep inside 'the blind night of intoxication,' and I envisaged a Hieronymus Bosch scenario, it was also the first time I heard the Norwegian words for cock and cunt. And I should not have begrudged her for all the happiness available to her. But I did.

She was with a German named Uwe who spent his life in a VW Breadloaf, he was such a warm and beautiful person, with long, thick curls and a laugh that went on so long that I seized up, that is, moved a notch below my base condition – like a clam. And I had an unpleasant feeling that my mere presence, my essence, was placing a damper on the group; once in a while they looked at me with concern. Of course, it was frisbee she was playing, or they were playing frisbee, the happy Norwegian and the happy German, the beautiful couple, one fair, the other dark, that is whenever they were not simply bent over the hooka (which for my part definitively and conclusively severed my connection with the group, as

I sailed off in a darkness of grief and regret. A little later when they slipped down to the beach to get high on LSD, they were clever enough to leave me in the VW, which (by the way) Uwe had placed at his girlfriend's disposal for her project. They collected the hash in Morocoo, hid it behind the hubcaps and in a couple of hollowed-out surfboards that were secured to the roof, and I don't know whether I came down one day and saw her preparing to leave with all the packages fastened to her body with thick tape, or whether that was something I saw in a film) and he shouted 'Go for it, Cathy,' with glittering teeth; and maybe later he would lean his magnificent German bite over her breast and snip off the hair. Or not. Because what was there was natural. Just as she burped when she had to – in a straightforward and graceful way, like a small and lovely sound had been released inside a seashell and now rolled between its mother-of-pearl walls.

After a couple of months I managed to tear myself away – it felt like I was glued to the spot, and in all that time by the sea, in the southern sun, I had not bathed, neither in the sea nor the sun, I was liable to fits of monological rage (with my family as the focal point), which the hash had clearly unlocked, and which kept going, for years – without additional fuel, a kind of perpetual motion machine of the mind.

'Here comes the spring,' I said to Charles as I walked past his bed with a yellow glass vase (I had just bought) and placed it on the table where he could see it. At Østre Anlæg, the slopes are yellow with buttercups. The vase is more of an old-fashioned yellow colour, however that is supposed to be understood. I also bought one for Alma. Now, as I sit by Charles's bed, I keep turning to look at it. The colour is outright soothing.

Later the forsythia arrive, but perhaps yellow is not comforting, but a sheer maddening energy; because Charles just lies there. Charles just cries or turns away. And now the mirabelle is powdery white, in long white strokes with all that brownness still around it. Charles turns over and says, so that was how life turned out.

'Who knows what constitutes a life,' I say, it sounds matter-of-fact, you would not think it was the title of a book by Ashbery.

Outside the miracle continues, the colours rise from the brownness; the miracle continues to be miraculous, year after year, and the older you get, the more you seem to love the spring, it is the coldness of the grave in the bones that this love comes from. There stands the tree, Charles, with lead weights dangling from his arms, a pendulum round his neck, no, he has become a grandfather clock, a staggering and bandy one. He stands as though on a sloping floor. And the mirabelle loses all its leaves in a single night.

We have two pairs of boxing gloves, mostly for decoration now, but once, in another lifetime, Charles used to box with his two sons. Listen, we haul Charles out of bed, make the bed and to begin with, we position him on top of the bedspread.

We say: 'That can't be right, two people who together had so much speed. Let's have a little party.'

(We, it is always Charles and I.)

Who's that coming? It's jolly well Edward, and he has brought his dog with him, it's white with black freckles, and it jumps up on the bed and grabs a corner of the bedspread in its mouth and spins round twelve times while it whimpers as though it was painful work, 'to make sure there are no snakes in the grass,' Edward says, 'the primitive mind, you know, when dogs were wolves,' before eventually lying down. But then there is another knock at the door, and it has to get up and say hello, the entire ritual was in vain, my beloved Alma arrives, and she has Kristian with her, the dog spins round again, the bedspread is getting properly wrinkled, 'easy now, lie down, there are no snakes.' Alma and Edward have never met before, but they seem very familiar to one another, and poor Kristian gets jealous – until suddenly Edward is positive that he has seen him before too. Charles places the morphine on the table, who wants to try, Edward does. Edward is always in need of relief, first there were his parents, then Alwilda, his life is far too empty, he has to fill the great void that the dog alone has been unable to. I lug in an entire case of champagne from the kitchen, 'the majority of eye injuries in the sixties were caused by champagne corks,' Kristian claims and covers his face with his hands, he has never been much of a hero, in actual fact he would prefer to crawl under the table, and I tell them how during my time as a waiter I hit a man in the forehead. The corks fly, and the anticipation of the intoxication is like standing at a great height and looking across a kingdom, I seldom drink, but when I do, I drink far too quickly.

'Slower, Camilla, slower,' Charles says, but it is probably too late, my mind is already galloping – ahead, across the kingdom. Edward is talking dog-talk, and I place my watch on the table and say 'okay, Edward, you have ten minutes, and then I don't want to hear another word about dogs.'

'You're so cynical, Camilla,' Edward says.

I crank up *Sexy Back* in order to avoid hearing him

94

tell how dogs are such sensible creatures yet again, then Edward asks Alma what kind of music she prefers, and she says: 'Gloria Gaynor and Shostakovich,' Edward can appreciate that, and they both get up and browse the shelves of music, I notice that Kristian is in the mood for a fight, and I go and fetch the boxing gloves, 'I've thrown down the gauntlet,' I shout and drop them on the table in front of my companions, one pair brown and the other lacquer red, a promise that blood is going to be spilt – when good manners crack. Charles is talking about the dog's long legs, it has jumped down from the bed, its lofty legs, and I am on the verge of being jealous, but isn't it a he, I check under the belly, yes, no.

'Charles, give Edward some more morphine,' I shout, because he has brought the lovely dog with the lofty legs into the living room.

'I had decided not to speak to it,' Edward says to Alma, and I can see that she is already bored, 'at least not outdoors, but I was unable to follow through on that, as it is well known that language cannot be blocked, it trickles or crashes out of you. A gaze that meets your gaze, and a will that can be guided in the right direction, or can't – that is sufficient. Language takes hold. It enquires, it persuades, it threatens and reasons. But I try to curb it and do not use the conjunctive, subordinate clauses or irony. Not like the lady with the black labrador. When it finally comes to her, she forces its head up, it looks at her sluggishly and she hits it: "What's wrong with you? Didn't you hear me? There's no way you didn't hear me. I'm not falling for that, my friend. You know that when Mummy calls, you have to come to Mummy." I tried to tell her that the dog does not want to come to her when it associates that with being hit. "It understands," she answered. Towards me, she is rather curt.'

'Your ten minutes is up, Edward,' I shout, because now I can only express myself by shouting and only move by running, and he nods and falls silent, maybe he has nothing else to talk about today. In any case Alma can probably hear how bright he is. Edward was the last friend to arrive. It feels like someone is missing, 'where has Kristian got to?'

'He has probably got his head in the fridge,' Alma says, and he probably has, because he always fancies something other than what is being served, and he is always hungry, even though the table is groaning with sausages and cheese, but he is most at ease when he can slink around on his own in the kitchen and open cupboards and drawers and nibble a little here and there. 'Should we take a look?' I ask, because then I can have Alma to myself for a moment, (I am a possessive and jealous person) and she takes me by the arm, and we slip through the rooms and down the long corridor, and then Alma jumps into the kitchen with a howl, and just as we suspected: the fridge door is open, and Kristian has one hand on his chest, 'jeez,' he says.

'Can I help?' I ask, 'or can you find what you're looking for on your own?'

Kristian nods, a sandwich in the other hand, a scrap here and a scrap there, his nose is running. Kristian is a doctor. 'Hoping that he won't become a patient,' Alma says. He is terrified of illness. The patients' eyes meet the shifty gaze of the doctor, shake his sweaty hand, receive their diagnosis from a cracking voice. I know nothing about all of that. But he looks nice in his white coat, I have seen him, stern and slender. 'Since our time here is so brief...,' is how he often starts his sentences. It sounds beautiful and it is sad and true. Just as, according to Alma, in the final moment of abandonment, near the

96

conclusion of the seething, pounding finish, he shows the whites of his eyes – so she is forced to close her eyes and to think: Here it is, the death you fear so much. And now it arrives, now, now, now.

I sit down at the kitchen table, 'Doctor, doctor, I think I'm ill,' I say. Alma sits down next to me and swings her legs, 'Doctor, doctor, I've broken a bone,' she says.

Without resembling each other one iota, Alma and I are often mistaken for sisters, because after having known each other for so long, we are like two sides of the same coin, Alma is the queen and I am the ship or the throne or the tower or the statesman.

'Doctor, doctor, I have appendicitis,' I say.

'I'm leaving the scene of the scandal,' he says and exits the kitchen, his face contorted as though he has smelt something awful; the scene of the scandal is the intoxication, we realize, he is right and never gets intoxicated.

Nobody says no within me. Everything within me agrees.

'Doctor, doctor, I have flat feet,' I shout after him.

It might be appropriate to reveal a little about my friends here, just a little:

1. Alma is my number one. When I was fourteen and had known Alma for seven of my fourteen years, it struck me like a bolt of lightning when I was standing in the shower: 'Oh no, I've fallen in love with Alma.'

I caught my gaze in the mirror and soothingly repeated my mum's words (said in an entirely different context) in my mum's deep voice: 'It's easy to mix up one kind of love with another.' Why did I think of her round breasts back then? But it passed. Maybe even by the time I climbed out of the shower a moment later.

2. Charles has large features, a seductive mouth,

Kristian is sophisticated, and Edward is handsome, in good shape and has well-developed calves. He spends the majority of his life walking. Such men, such times.

3. Alwilda. But she couldn't come.

Back to my companions. The living room has become a boxing ring; Charles, who can hardly walk, but is the only one who can box, is bouncing around on the floor, along with Edward; the combination of champagne & morphine gives them wings. Until he receives a sudden blow that makes him collapse. He deprecatingly raises both arms in the air, the gloves quickly resemble bandaging. A moment later he is lying on the bed again, now with the dog at his side, and Alma is extricating him from the gloves, 'Doctor, doctor,' I say, because now the pain is shooting up through the champagne and through the morphine, 'where's the brown pill bottle?' Finally I can be still.

And now Edward leans towards Alma and tells her about the ducks dozing in the sun by the lakeshore, about how the dog races after them, sends them splashing across the water; if one of the ducks is too slow, it swipes at the air with its paw, because not for a moment does it consider killing them, it merely enjoys the pleasure of forcing them into the water – this takes place off the island with the rhododendron, in Østre Anlæg, where at the moment a long pink reflection drags the flower down into the lake, and there are also white, crimson and purple rhododendrons. The flower bushes are close together, practically a thicket, white stretches up and peers over the shoulder of red, but they jostle all the same. There is a denseness resembling a tropical forest.

When Edward begins to talk about the reflection,

Alma wakes up. He has nudged her with his eloquence. Now they look at each other. Edward imagines a life with Alma and Alma imagines secret meetings with Edward, on Rhododendron Island, for example, where she will lie with her head in his lap while he raises her limp hand and speaks about her simultaneously pointy and round fingers.

'Oh,' Alma says, 'I'm in love with the spring. I can't sit still. I can't stay indoors.'

'But most of all, I love the lilacs,' Edward says.

'That's not even an island,' Kristian says.

'Kristian,' I say and reach for the gloves, 'now it's our turn.'

CAMILLA'S GPS

[Camilla]

I had to go to Belgrade to give a couple of lectures, and Charles was unable to travel with me. I am a literary figure, but might have preferred to be an architect. I have a strong sense of space, I am touching my heart at this very moment. My hotel was red on the inside, *Twin Peaks* red; the receptionist was a legal practitioner. His life had not turned out as he had imagined. Unlike mine, he commented, referring to my visit to the institute as evidence. Though his current position, working as a receptionist for his younger brother – this was his brother's hotel – did give him the opportunity to put his law degree to use on occasion. For instance when he had to communicate with and show around the supervisory health authorities, 'because it demands an understanding of the law'. I wondered what it might be comparable to. Perhaps, for example, if a qualified house painter only used his qualification to buy paint for his own house, no, consider the opposite instead, how when her daughter lay dying in hospital, the author Joan Didion purchased surgical clothing and walked around the hospital ward wearing it, all the while offering sound advice to the doctors, until finally they told her that if she did not stop interfering with their treatment, they would have nothing more to do with her case, she would have to take over herself. That would be equivalent to a person, while a painter is working on their home, wearing white paint-stained clothes and standing on a ladder next to him. Welcome to my labyrinth.

I had no desire to commit my usual blunder of isolating myself in the hotel room. At one time I enjoyed staying in hotels; staying in a room that was not mine and which I had no responsibility for, where I could quickly make my peace with any possible aesthetic qualms, and where unseen hands swept away the dust. Now I regard them as waiting rooms where it is impossible to sleep, all night long the unfamiliar objects change shape every time I blink; everything solid becomes fluid. During the day I am lightheaded and dizzy, it's like I'm breathing thin air. My feet are heavy. I drag myself along. The minibar. No, no alcohol. Chocolate. Salted nuts. Lonely, a veritable waste of my life, munching in bed, albeit in safety. And exempt from having to find my way home-out-and-home-again. I mean: find my way around the city and attempt to find my hotel again. My sense of direction is terrible. Non-existent. Better to stay home. (Of course I did not neglect my lectures, that was the entire reason I had come, but I allowed myself to be picked up and dropped off so as not to disappear somewhere in between the two destinations, I'm talking about the rest of the time, my spare time.) But as Eliot has taught us:

We shall not cease from exploration
and the end of all our exploring
will be to arrive where we started
and know the place for the first time.

(Which does sound reassuring: as though you can be confident of returning home, automatically, so to speak.)

As a compromise, I spent quite a lot of time in the reception (not out, not entirely in) hovering on a barstool, I drank one espresso after the other. It was a small hotel, with only six rooms. And at one point I was the only guest. The staff, on the other hand – if anything they were overrepresented. I have no idea how many thin,

101

dark chambermaids in red dresses walked aimlessly around, blending in with the walls. They weren't prostitutes, were they? If that were the case, they might just as well have been leaning against the sunset in a deserted landscape. Nevertheless when breakfast was served in the basement, all six tables were laid. To keep up the illusion. It was called Hotel City Code, a name I was not quite sure how to interpret. Was this hotel the code to the city? When I said the name, code quickly became coat.

Before leaving, I had decided to spend every waking hour exploring the city. I wanted to be a tourist. I wanted to get to know Belgrade. And then I lost my courage. The reception, as mentioned, was my compromise.

But the receptionist talked incessantly. In a rather mumbling and unintelligible English that meant I had to strain every nerve to understand him. He had plenty of time for his only guest. As soon as I stepped out of my room, he moved towards me as though carried by a gust of wind. He was dark, slender, nimble, indefatigable, with surprisingly kind eyes hidden behind his glasses, but he kept going on and on until my mouth went dry, the room blurred and I nearly fainted. I knew the names of his siblings, I knew his cholesterol level and I knew his doctor's instructions: 'fifty grams of almonds, four squares of dark chocolate and a glass of red wine every day,' he said, his small friendly face beaming, 'and obviously eat plenty of fruit and vegetables and walk at least three kilometres.' He bent forward and drew a curve in the air to indicate the progress of his blood pressure. I also knew that his grandfather had written an account of his experiences in World War Two, but unfortunately the manuscript had gone missing. I knew more or less what it contained. And I was starting to get the idea that it was hidden in a barn somewhere in Croatia. I was also starting to suspect that he was encouraging me to go in search of it. He considered me to be an unusually kind person – with a lot of spare time. Ear, vagina, a mirror that makes you look twice as big; you little devil, I suddenly thought, not a chance in hell. And with that I grabbed my coat and left the reception with barely a nod. I had chosen a good time to leave. He had just stated that no matter how much money society poured into the Roma community, all they did was spend it on beer and cigarettes, and on chocolate for their many children. That was what drove me out into the world. Though I was afraid of encountering a Roma who behaved like the one I met in St Petersburg. I had given her what corresponds to a hundred kroner, and in gratitude she lay down in the middle of the street and started to kiss my shoe. 'No, no,' I said, 'please get up.' 'Not until you give me another hundred,' she said, and only then did she release my shoe, allowing me to continue walking towards the Spilled Blood Church, the one with the candy-coloured cupolas, which even up close did not look real.

As soon as I walked out the door, a sense of loss swept over me. With absolutely no desire to do so, I took my first steps in Belgrade. Like I was learning to walk. I knew nobody, nobody knew me. I was nobody. I did not understand the language. I understood nothing. I might as well have stopped looking where I was going, because when it came down to finding my way back, maybe I would have a vague recollection of what met my gaze, but I would not be able to remember where on my journey it had occurred. The order of the elements is not arbitrary when it comes to finding your way. Instead of trying to find my way back to the hotel later,

I should have checked out and taken my luggage with me. Then, exhausted from exploring and lugging everything about, when I could manage no more, I could have dragged myself to some new, unknown hotel – and then when I absolutely *had* to, I could set off again. I am not that helpless. I had the address of the hotel in my pocket, and when I grew tired of walking, I hailed a taxi and rode back. An unfortunate experience in my youth had taught me to always carry the address of the hotel or guest house on my person. Greece, half a lifetime ago. Me, young, wearing a gauze Iphigenia dress, light as a feather, so white that I had had to cover my nipples with toothpaste. It was before the time of strapless bras. In any case, I had been out dancing, night-time, the flowers falling from the flowering trees. Alma, my faithless friend, continued to dance with her Greek. I could not find our *pension*. The longer I searched, the smaller I became. A man had been observing me for some time. In the end he cut across the street and kindly asked me what I was looking for. He had a hard time believing that I could not so much as remember the name of the *pension*. That which you do not understand, you simply have to accept. So at the first hotel we came across he rented a room for me and promised to return the next morning to help me. He left. He had a moustache, but he was not without some charm. Had he been less chivalrous, it might have led to a slightly lengthier encounter. The next morning he returned, paid the bill, swung onto the saddle of his moped, and with me behind him, headed for the local office of the Tourist Police. There they had a copy of my passport, which the owner of the *pension* had dutifully submitted upon check-in – with the name and address of my temporary residence attached! Such efficiency, and in Greece, at that. Back at the

104

pension, I found my beloved friend Alma wringing her hands, half-dead from dread, certain that I (my head) was lying somewhere, detached from my body, under a sprinkling of browning flowers, even though we were used to ditching each other whenever some handsome mutt crossed our path. Ah, adolescence, one long mating season, a parade of brilliant memories, an entire repository of bright young passion for tougher times – did I really have a piece of red glass (grenade-like) attached to my navel and did I really display it to my temporary chosen one in a tunnel by simply lifting my dress? Yes, you bet I did! It was me, to give one final little toot. Now I use the word 'toot', which is Beckett's expression for drawing out the text as much as possible, not to tie bows, but to make curls, and earlier today, duly escorted by a lecturer from the institute, on my way back from a lecture, I came across some graffiti. Sprayed on the wall were the words:

Books, brothers, books
Not bells

The lecturer translated for me and said something about bells and Santa Claus – when he arrived in his sleigh.

'Santa Claus, you know, on a creaking carpet of cotton wool, jingle bells jingle bells, until we all hygge our arses off. Even his beard is creaking.'

Bells probably referred to church bells. So neither church nor kitsch, no thank you. Moral graffiti. Lovely to see graffiti that encourages reading, the lecturer said.

'Exactly,' I answered and hoped he would offer to carry my bag. Because it was heavy. With books.

Now, halfway through my fourth decade, grown-up, to

put it mildly, I stood near the ruin of a Turkish fort, high above the Sava (I had thought it was the Danube but that was on the other side of Belgrade). A long, black barge was floating past. Oh, the endlessly glittering river and now this long barge. Who doesn't like river barges, who isn't reminded of *Huckleberry Finn* or Venice at the sight and the sound of their gentle gliding. I ought to have been happy. Once upon a time people did not think they owed it to nature to enjoy it; it was simply an infernal nuisance; something that stung you when you stormed through like a savage; when you did not think of nature as a deficiency within yourself if it did not reveal itself to you – and trickled into your soul like sweet, white wheat.

Has my soul grown too fat?

Has it hibernated?

Or the exact opposite – suddenly nature is a music where everything flashes before our eyes before we drown, and faced with this denseness we have to close the shutters?

My friend Edward said to me one sultry summer: 'At last I sat down on a chair in the garden. But the garden did not speak to me, it was as though my surroundings were dead – and then suddenly it came to nonetheless, and within ten minutes I was enjoying the birds and the wind in the trees.'

The mind as your own worst enemy. Furious monologues, scenarios where everything ends in disaster; catastrophes; attacks against imagined enemies; not to mention demonic fits of doubt, forsaking all that is good – as if you are truly possessed by a demon, and maybe in the midst of everything you think: If God were to look into my soul right now, the punishment would be horrific; but it is not a demon, nor a God, merely a carousel that you cannot get off; the giraffe, the fat pink pig with the blue trousers and the straight back and the team of horses in front of the revolving coach, it mists before the eyes. And you think: Now I am going to die of dizziness. I'll never get off.

And yet suddenly, mercifully – it slows down, the mechanism groans faintly (something is stuck) but then it goes quiet, and the outside (nature, for example, an irresistible person, for example) is allowed to enter and fill the space.

I ought to have been happy, or at least not quite so lost, standing before the Sava; considering my age. (I find myself in a situation where I constantly have the chance to gauge the temperature of my soul; I have to get out and dig ditches.)

Why does the journey reinforce this existential loneliness – never am I closer to death and the abyss than when I am alone on a journey. I know the answer already. An unknown among unknown faces. And unknown, unmemorized stretches. Kingdom of the dead, glittering, indistinct features, averted eyes, withdrawal, fleeting shadows, bloodlessness. I was all but longing to return to the receptionist. Horrified I think that is how it will be for me one day back home – if I survive everyone I hold dear. You ought to be able to pop your clogs in time, let me keep time.

This city is incredibly ugly; it consists primarily of concrete buildings that are leaning forward or backward, some of the walls have stomachs, sagging in the middle and studded with criss-crossed supporting beams. And the windows are like eyes under too much pressure, bulging. But there are trees too, this rustling green complex, planted for the enlivenment of the citizens and the dogs of the city, and the rivers are likewise enlivening, old Sava, old Danube. Some buildings in the city have survived the many bombardments, first by the Germans, then by Nato, the first floor is wider than the ground floor, perhaps to save on precious land, that was something the lecturer also drew my attention to. The older houses are the ones with stomachs.

Every time I stood by the Sava, I considered taking the bridge across to Novi Beograd. Not to enjoy a glass of the local water, which contains uranium, leaching uranium from the bombing in the nineties, likely featuring on a list of the most polluted water supplies on the globe, but to visit the art museum there. In the end I did just that. I stepped out onto the bridge. There were no other pedestrians on that stretch, but plenty of traffic, so heavy it made the bridge groan. Belgrade has no ring roads. Every car has to drive through the centre. And below me was the blackish-green water. I would probably get hit by a lorry and be sent flying over the railing. Get run over first, then drown. I hurried along. In an attempt to get the trip over and done with.

No sooner was I across than I longed to return to the other side, which had apparently become a kind of home to me.

'You're hopeless,' I told myself, 'you finally make it across, only to long for a return.'

Even though I was not hungry, I felt like the starving protagonist in *Hunger* that day. I wonder whether my temperament can be compared to his; in a sense, he is more or less constantly in the dumps; there is something artificial and terrifying about his sudden euphoria. Luckily it seldom lasts long. The head quickly sinks between the shoulders again.

I clambered down a staircase, also concrete, and stood

on a seemingly deserted quay. Below the bridge were traces of an abandoned Roma camp. You are always at risk of being robbed. My easily awoken uneasiness was awake. Then another pedestrian appeared. I asked for directions to the museum. The pedestrian pointed towards a public park with trees and said that she would dissuade me from walking through it. It was not safe. I should keep to the water instead. I stared at the desolate park and nodded. The river ran in front of this deserted park. And there were houseboats, and restaurants, also on boats.

Nothing happened. And the museum was under renovation. So I had to go back across the bridge. I sat for a while on a bench and stared at the opposite shore of the river. I am the offspring of Homesickness and Departure sickness, the descendent of Melancholia and the Great joy. Easy now, you're not Bruno Schulz in the posthumous publication of *Sanatorium Under the Sign of the Hourglass*, which consists entirely of poetic extracts and for that reason is largely unreadable, every living creature needs to breathe, don't go over the top, you have to move. I got up, in an attempt to walk off my thoughts. I left the hysterical poetry on the bench, bent over (fallen into a reverie, staring at a small great object down in the gravel), wearing purple, the messianic colour of the soul, with a soft, effeminate lower body, strong arms and a small but finely-formed head. A head like a thoroughbred with quivering nostrils.

I made it across the bridge in one piece, turned my back on the Sava and strolled towards the town centre. Suddenly something I recognized, I felt a pang in my heart. The art film cinema, Art Bioskop Museum, where the lecturer in 2005 or 2006 had seen a French film where the only other person in the cinema was the academic Mihailo Marković, the SPS ideologue, the party of Slobodan Milošević; there they sat in the darkness, and before the film began, Marković, who was in his eighties, asked the lecturer why, young as he was, he was not with a girl. In those years very few people visited the cinema in Belgrade, and sometimes the cinema staff crossed themselves when the lecturer arrived because he had strayed into the darkness. This expression, 'strayed into the darkness', as he described it, made me think of him as a werewolf. (Incidentally his eyebrows had also grown together, the sign of the werewolf par excellence.)

Shortly afterwards, I arrived at a street where the air was as fresh as an early morning. The street had just been hosed down. Trees grew on either side of it, their crowns full and leaning towards one another, so that the street was covered by a green, rustling roof, with the light drizzling down through it; I walked upon a living pavement, light and shadow fluttering about; it was dim beneath the trees. Outside of this oasis, the world was an oven. I turned around and walked back down the street and felt a gleam of pure adventurousness, which must be the opposite of loss. In my mind, there is a connection between adventure and early mornings. Or in any case there was in my childhood, and for that reason I made sure to get up early, and then wandered about, across the golf course, along the beach and through the woods. The sense of adventure was most present at dawn, it gradually wore off as it grew light and people appeared. In all likelihood, the sense of adventure was connected with being alone; alone in a world devoid of people. Because I don't recall anything special ever happening. Or perhaps what was exceptional about it was that I began to notice myself; the absence of gazes gave me an incipient view of myself. Nobody to look at me with a gaze shaded by some preconceived notion of who I was. And for that reason I could arrive there on my own. In order to discover yourself, you have to be alone. In all probability the opposite also holds true: You do need the gazes of others (in order to discover yourself).

Back then I was never afraid of getting lost outside. And nobody worried about me. I could leave the house at four o'clock in the morning without any form of protest, without getting told off later. On the other hand I did get told off when I refused to go to school later in the morning; and I did that often. The time when I had the best conditions for wandering about as the merry daughter of Mother Nature, when I jostled with nature as soon as I opened the door, was in Year Three. We had moved to Helsingør for a year. We had a rather plain, very basic house in the midst of the great outdoors. The house had brown and ugly doors, like at a school. I had had to change schools, this time the school was yellow. My classmates and I did not have our own form room; we were a so-called wandering class. I never knew where to go when I arrived in the morning. Somewhere in the vast building there was a noticeboard displaying a message about where we were supposed to proceed to. The noticeboard did not change location. A number and possibly a letter indicated a room. But I did not want to (circle around for ages looking for an abstraction such as B29, I did not want to be contracted in that way).

'If you don't start attending school soon, I won't like you any more,' my mum said.

('I could have bit off my tongue,' she said years later.)

But by and large I stayed home. And spent the day mixing fruit juice powder with a tiny amount of water and eating it with a spoon: pineapple powder, raspberry powder, pineapple powder again. Once in a while a young girl was hired to keep me entertained, she brought me buns and cocoa from another world. The kitchen was so small that we had to edge past each other.

Apparently, hidden in a corner somewhere inside of me is the child who, in the strange school and in the kitchen with the strange young girl, did not really feel like flesh and blood, but like bricks and mortar. A stubborn wall of silence, of enormous inconvenience. I now believe I have studied loss under a magnifying glass. Things (like this) take time, one might object. But I have long thought about this, because who wants to be a helpless idiot; this is obviously a condensed version of a longer, more zig-zagging thought process. I am back to where I started, with the dissolution of pineapple powder and young girls in a cramped kitchen. Facing the walls of Hotel City Code and the minibar with its sweet & salty temptations – like a bullet that has hit its target. More by accident than by design. That should wrap things up with Eliot.

And who was standing around waiting for his dear guest?

Alma has arrived. She could tell from my voice how I was doing. It has always been like that. Friendship is golden.

The last few days I have not really left the hotel, only to cut across the square to a small shop where I buy toasted bagels with tofu or salmon. I then devour them in bed, and afterwards do the same with large pieces of fruit pies while on my computer I watch Serbian films with English subtitles, bought on the cheap from street vendors. When watching Emir Kusturica's *Underground* and *Black Cat, White Cat* (I watch them several times, I brought them with me), I turn down the Balkan music, which normally makes me feel like dancing and drinking, so that the receptionist does not come in and join my party (my opulent meal would send him directly to his grave) or attempt to drag the fox out of the den, for espresso & monologue in the reception. A couple of times I hear him stop outside my door. I recognize his small pointed footsteps. Incidentally, he wears a pedometer on his belt, at the behest of his doctor. Oh yes, and then the lecturer and I went for a melancholy afternoon stroll along the Danube where I reflected my frame of mind on the barges and was at a loss to keep death at bay, while the lecturer observed the mafia ladies.

'I'm Camilla's GPS,' that was how Alma introduced herself at dinner last night, and everyone understood what she meant, as they have all taken turns shepherding me around, picking me up at the hotel reception and dropping me off again like I was a large package – with the string coming loose. Now Alma has taken charge of me for my final days in the city. She did not come exclusively for my sake, but also because she was a little confused with what was going on back home and with herself; but first and foremost she was here because her book has been translated into Serbian and she is taking part in the Belgrade book fair. The dinner took place at the embassy where Alma was the guest of honour, and the lecturer had forgotten to inform them that I do not eat meat. As soon as the individual portions of sliced fillet were brought in for starters, the receptionist's voice echoed in my head: 'Almonds, dark chocolate, red wine – every day. And no meat: But who can survive without meat? Nobody! Nobody can survive without meat,' he yelled.

As he yelled, he had cocked his head like an affectionate woman – an attempt to obtain agreement without a struggle. 'I can,' I objected, and reached for my room key, but he quickly placed his hand over it and continued talking. I politely swallowed the delicate fillet. The main course consisted of rare roast beef, also individually portioned, which I cut into pieces that were small enough to swallow, barely touching my teeth. All the while I thought of a film about the survivors of a plane that crashed in the Andes in 1972, where the dead 'lent' the living their muscles; in the film, the survivors file off infinitely thin slices from the frozen bodies. I had not eaten meat for twenty years, but the rigid ambassador was not the type to cock her head (otherwise she would never have made it that far, unlike the stranded receptionist with his cocked head working at his little brother's hotel), I preferred not to be an inconvenience, and at long last I managed to clear enough of the red mountain away that the bottom of the plate was visible. Besides the ambassador, the cultural attaché, the lecturer, Alma's translator, Alma and I, there was a dramatic Serbian poet present. She had brought a selection of her works with her, in English translations, as a gift to the host. I expressed an interest in her books, and the ambassador said that I could keep them, the poet could bring her some more on another occasion. The two were old friends – she could permit herself to speak on her behalf. 'No, no,' the Serbian poet and I exclaimed in chorus: they were for the host. When the Serbian poet said no, I hurried to repeat it a number of times, and I got up and put the books down in the middle of the table, demonstratively, out of my reach. Meat-free dessert. Thank you for a lovely dinner, leave the table, the others went into the adjoining room, I reached for the books and looked at them a little more – then I hurried to join the small gathering. I am a little careless in my conduct with my bag. I never zip it shut, meaning someone can just slip their hand in and pull out my wallet. Later, the next morning, I suddenly recalled how both the host and the poet had looked at my bag strangely. Well, instinct or the experience of moving in more exalted circles must have told Alma that since she was the guest of honour, she had to bring the evening to a conclusion. 'Thank you so much for this evening,' she said and put down her coffee cup, and as if by command, everyone got up and said their goodbyes. Two minutes later we stood outside. In the hotel room I put my bag down and gave it no more thought until the following morning when I went to find my lipstick. In the bag, oh horror, were the Serbian poet's books. In a fit of absentmindedness, perhaps confused by all that meat in my stomach, I must have stuffed them into my bag instead of putting them back on the table.

'Now they're going to think I'm a kleptomaniac,' I whimpered to Alma, 'how did that happen?'

'The lecturer will sort it out,' Alma said, 'he'd be only too happy to help – seeing as you had to eat all that meat.'

And so the lecturer did sort it out. He returned the books personally.

A lot had gone awry in connection with this trip. I had not felt like travelling there in the first place. (Not least, as I mentioned, because I hate travelling alone.) I had convinced myself that my plane would crash, and for that reason I tidied up all my drawers and threw loads of things out before I left – so that Charles would not be left to deal with everything. I had also just about finished spring cleaning the entire place, in an attempt to force myself to calm down.

I had promised Edward to walk his dog the afternoon

of my departure. He had told me I could easily take it off the lead, but I almost never got it back on again. I had chased it through all of Fælledparken and had ended up on the square in front of the post office. It was pouring down, the dog and I were the only living creatures outside that Sunday afternoon, and the dog had sought shelter under the roof of the post office. I perched on the statue in the middle of the square, staring at it impotently, drenched and furious. I tried to recall some of the condescending and funny things PH had said about the bombastic post office and its bulging pillars, or where I had read about it, but I could not remember. The dog looked small and lost next to the pillars, but make no mistake – as soon as I moved closer, it leapt down the steps with a crooked grin, nimbly striking them like it was practising the scales on the piano. When I returned to my position in the rain, it went back under cover and looked at me again. 'Do you want to swap places, you filthy mutt,' I shouted and considered letting it find its own way home, when a lady holding a massive umbrella fortuitously made contact with it, and it practically leapt into her arms. I sneaked up behind it and grabbed hold of its tail. At home I said my goodbyes to Charles, as though it were for ever, and with a heavy heart I went to Kastrup and with heavy steps I walked to my gate – apparently a group of Chinese tourists and I were the only ones flying to Belgrade that day, and nobody was in a hurry to get us on board. When, according to my ticket, it was time to depart, I asked a short Chinese man if he had heard about any delays to Belgrade. 'Beijing, Beijing,' he said. And I realized my mistake. I ran like a madman, and even though my gate (the right one) was already closed, I forced my way through and boarded the aeroplane. 'Why didn't you call me – over the

116

loudspeaker?' I piped up to a stewardess, she gave me the 'Stick a pipe in it and sit down' look, 'but they always call passengers who don't come to the gate,' I said, 'I've heard them do it before,' and with a sense of being completely unwanted, I sat down in my seat.

Alma has another man, and for that reason she buys two of everything when it comes to gifts. Two identical sweaters. And in addition, two identical bottles of aftershave. That way she does not carry different coloured wool from one set of arms to another, or different male scents. It reduces the risk of being found out. What about hair, I ask, you always hear stories about that; but she has a lint roller in her bag that she just runs up and down herself, and close-cropped men do not shed much hair. She flirts with every man we come across; in the department store she approaches three different men to hear their opinions on aftershave before she settles on one for her two men back home.

In reality there is a third person she is thinking of and longing for, but she can't have him, and not even having two men can make up for that one. When she describes his kiss, I can almost feel it myself: 'He placed his hands around my mouth – he shielded my lips so that they were the only thing in the world, and then he kissed between his hands; his tongue was slow and light; he used only the tip, and after a moment it was as though I was made of a weightless, floating material.'

But she could not have him; he was a mountain climber and would not leave his Welsh mountains behind. They spent a single night together, in an empty dormitory at the youth hostel. Kristian was lying ill at the other end of the corridor. The door could not be locked, so they dragged a table in front of it and then positioned

117

it so the handle was forced upward and the door could not be opened from outside. They were sitting in their underwear in the barricaded room, drinking wine and smoking cigarettes and listening to music, when suddenly Alma saw herself from the outside and said: 'You would think we were sitting on a beach.'

Outside there were mountains, it was not even a little bit warm. He replied that physically speaking, she was certainly very beautiful. And it reminded her of how black as coal, how deceitful her insides were.

When she awoke in the morning, lying with him in the upper bunk, the only thing on her mind was that she had to have him one more time. She woke him up so there would be enough time. And she had him once more, and it was so bittersweet because they were to be parted, and because one day we are all going to depart, everything heeled over and capsized and broke and turned into I want and I want, and then I think she said something about pomegranates, or no, he had said that she reminded him of one of those fruits that are soft on the outside and hard on the inside. But then they had to part. She caught a final glimpse of him as she passed through reception where he was huddled over a map with a couple of friends. When she opened the door to Kristian, or rather threw it open, she stood bolt upright like an Olympic rider and had never felt more alive in her entire life. The following day she wrote a letter to him that sounded like it came from *For Whom the Bell Tolls* or *A Farewell to Arms*, where she was overrun with love, and later when she had arrived home from the trip, she wrote another letter, before finally receiving a reply. She put his letter down and grew sober and cold. His letter contained a description of a minor incident about him climbing a cliff in darkness, the only good part of the letter; the rest was a plea to abandon any thought of them because of the distance and the different lifestyles, (she had even aired the thought of studying mountain climbing at a school on Bornholm in order to approach *his* way of life) and then a pale request to write back. She decided to liberate the short passage from his letter and wrote:

We were climbing a cliff that is around one hundred and fifty metres high, when it began to get dark (my watch had stopped, and we had left much later than we had thought). We were around fifty metres from the top when it went completely dark, and we could not go back down because the water had risen and there was no longer a beach beneath us, but a sea.

We climbed the last fifty metres in darkness – but the beam from a lighthouse flashed against the cliff around every seventeen seconds. When the light fell upon the cliff, we searched for the next crevice to place our hands or feet and pulled ourselves up, blinded by the light that washed across us. It went dark again, and over the course of the following few seconds our eyes would grow used to the darkness. Then the light returned. It went on like that until around midnight, when at long last we reached the summit.

She later binned the letter and lay down on a floor that smelled of wood and soap, because then she could not get any lower, and she remained lying there for what must have felt like six months. And later she sent the story about the cliff to a journal, together with a couple of other pieces she had written herself, and had them published in her name. The theft was not revenge for her unrequited love, it was just an excellent, if not unassuming bit of prose that deserved to see the light of day – to be read, Alma thought. And the mountain climber would have had no objections. He had no literary ambitions.

Once in a while she reached out for *Ulysses*, because as she now felt so terrible, she might as well attempt to finally make it all the way through the book. And now she was here, with me, and was able to say that it would never have worked out.

'But during those six months on the floor, you still managed to meet someone to buy aftershave for?'

'Yes.'

'And you kept Kristian.'

'For the time being. Yes. I do not have the energy to rid myself of him.'

'Do you also want to rid yourself of the other one?'

We lay on the bed. It could have been anywhere in the world. Because Alma was there, I felt at home.

'I wanted a daring life for myself,' she said, 'like on the cliff, a life lit up by flashes from a lighthouse.'

'A life with lighthouses, cliffs, flashes and a sudden and total darkness,' she sighed.

'Remember to turn off the heating pad before we leave,' I said.

'And hold on tight until your nails turn white,' I said wearily, because she could not seem to let go of the cliff in her mind.

'Only the nails, which have been completely abandoned by the blood, illuminate the darkness,' I continued, 'but now I need something to eat.'

'Oh,' Alma said, 'then we had better get going' – and then she reminded me for the God-knows-how-many-times of the night in Venice, half a lifetime ago, when I was so hungry and she couldn't decide on a restaurant, that in the end I slapped her across the face, but as soon as I had done it, I said: 'Hurry up and slap me, otherwise I'll hear about it for the rest of my life.'

And so she did, but she looked as though she had been forced to cross a line, whereas my slap, I am sorry to say, had practically grown out of my hand naturally. Half in shock and with one hand against her cheek she stepped forward and slapped me on the cheek I had turned to her.

Before we set off, Alma looks at the map. A single glance is enough, then she is familiar with it. We are going to the Nikola Tesla Museum. Just who is Nikola Tesla? Nikola Tesla is ostensibly one of the greatest geniuses, physicists, electrical engineers and inventors of the nineteenth century; Serbian, born in Croatia in 1856, emigrated to the USA where he was initially employed by Thomas Edison (proponent of direct current, obstinate opponent of alternating current), later financed by J. P. Morgan, and died, unnoticed and alone, in a small room in the New Yorker Hotel in 1943, considered an eccentric (because he spoke at length about the possibility of transmitting images, among other things), after having presented humanity with the gift of alternating current (think of Tesla when you switch on the lights), the radio (even though Marconi received the credit, Tesla was awarded the patent two years after his own death), the remote control, the robot and more still (he held hundreds of patents) and after, it should be added, many years living the high life, keeping company with the greatest minds of the time, Mark Twain among others. He would go to work like he was attending a banquet, wearing white tie and tails and gloves. He was lean and elegant. He loved pigeons and was often seen pictured with them up and down his arms, like a statue.

And that's all from the bag of myths. Except of course that there was a terrible thunderstorm the day he was born – electricity welcomed its master with the greatest of orchestras.

'We're here,' Alma says and plants a finger on the street the hotel lies on, Dobračina, 'first we have to cross Aleksandra Nevskog,' ('that's the square with the equestrian statue where a crowd of Serbian nationalists protest every day, and which I have to cross when I buy bagels,' I say, 'they want Kosovo back') 'down Francuska, continue along Bulevar Despota Stefana, let's take that one for the name alone, though it might not be the fastest route, down Dečanska and Bulevar Kralja Aleksandra – and yes, then Krunska, where the museum is situated.'

She checks the map again.

'Should we take it with us just in case?'

Alma shakes her head three times like a circus horse. And then we leave.

This museum is also under renovation. But half of it, the ground floor, is still accessible. I stare at Tesla's machines but they are beyond my understanding. But this much I can say: there is something resembling a golden egg, standing on the pointy end of something resembling a truncated drum (or a small arena) and it is the same green as an examination desk.

Tesla's urn stands on a pedestal, round as a globe but with small feet. I doubt it really contains any ashes. And if there are... then is the dust able to rest amongst shrieking Serbian schoolchildren on a tour and surrounded by inventions of 'the porter of dust': a button is continually pressed, and a noise follows as the mechanism activates, the machine clicks into gear / but perhaps for the dust it is music to the ear. I could gain access to this world, but it would take time. On the other hand I immediately recognize the description of the mind that created the inventions:

> In my boyhood I suffered from a peculiar affliction due to the appearance of images, often accompanied by strong flashes of light, which marred the sight of real objects and interfered with my thought and action. They were pictures of things and scenes which I had really seen, never of those I imagined. When a word was spoken to me, the picture of the object it designated would present itself vividly to my vision and sometimes I was quite unable to distinguish whether what I saw was tangible or not. This caused me great discomfort and anxiety.

This, the tangibility of intangibility that Tesla describes in his autobiography, *My Inventions*, later made him capable of envisaging his discoveries (they also presented themselves in flashes of lightning) as ready-made, as though they were already on the table in front of him. Then all he would have to do is construct them according to 'his vision', so to speak.

In 1926, another genius of the twentieth century, Virginia Woolf, wrote in her diary:

> *Returning Health*
> This is shown by the power to make images: the suggestive power of every sight and word is enormously increased. Shakespeare must have had this to an extent which makes my normal state the state of a person blind, deaf, dumb, stone-stockish & fish-blooded. And I have it compared with poor Mrs Bartholomew almost to the extent that Shakespeare has it compared with me.

... Is it not conspicuous that two minds, one of a physicist and one of an artist, can be endowed with the same kind of power? That the same power can offer such diverse yields, alternating current and *The Waves*.

But now to the book fair – to the book fair in Belgrade. We meet the lecturer outside a new, grand exhibition centre, a kind of oversized glass cage. To some extent the lecturer has acted as a middleman between Alma and her publishers, speaking Serbian as he does, and a resident of Belgrade and friendliness incarnate. But the lecturer looks mortified.

'Why the mortified look, lecturer?'

There are two reasons.

The publisher has not arranged for our passes to the fair. ('Do I have to pay to attend my own reading?' Alma asks incredulously. The lecturer can only nod.)

But there is no reading. The publisher did not expect anyone to show up to Alma's reading (with the lecturer serving as interpreter) or to hear her speak about the book, since she is completely unknown in Serbia. (But that's the very reason I've been flown here, Alma says.) However, a number of interviews have been arranged. 'Oh,' Alma says, brightening up.

We buy our tickets and as we go inside we are warned that if we exit, we cannot get back in – without purchasing new tickets. There is a poor indoor climate at the temple of books. Lots and lots of stands. The lecturer leads us through the labyrinth. We reach the stand for Alma's publisher. Alma's publishing house was founded by a blind man. Alma's publisher looks like an intellectual from decades past. Wearing a corduroy jacket et cetera. Charming. Sitting round a table is a group of older men wearing overcoats and dark glasses. 'Those are the blind people,' the lecturer says. They are drawn to this place like bees to sugar water, now they sit and drink in the background. I myself am extremely short-sighted. I don't wear glasses, only sunglasses with lenses, I use them when I watch TV. Charles thinks it is a little sombre when I sit on the sofa on a winter afternoon hiding behind my sunglasses. Alma offers her hand. There is one person who is not blind. She has read Alma's book. She does not care for it, we can tell. Maybe it has been translated nonchalantly. Suggests the lecturer. In any case Alma has found a name in the translation that she does not recognize. 'Who is that?' she asks the translator and points at the name. The translator shrugs.

'You've simply introduced an extra character,' the lecturer says.

'It's post-modernism,' the translator says.

I feel like I should contradict him, or ask him to expand on it, but the exhibition hall has a sleep-inducing effect on me.

Alma gives six interviews over the course of the next hour. None of the people in attendance have read her book. But the more Alma speaks, the less important that is. 'And now the author is going to say something funny,' one of the journalists says, and Alma recites some muddled nonsense about Hamlet, something along the lines that if Hamlet had been Finnish, then... no, it's impossible to remember. She goes on and on. The publisher hands her a shot, and then she talks even more. Now Serbian TV arrives. She insists on being shown with her publisher, 'my Serbian publisher,' and places an arm around him. His shoulders stiffen. A sighted friend of one of the blind people makes a video of her for personal use, 'she's quite the character,' he says, almost to himself, and Alma beams. 'It's difficult to stop talking,' she says during a break. The publisher suggests she get a little fresh air. He wants to lend us some employee passes so we don't have to pay to re-enter. All we have to do is ring his mobile when we return. So we do that – after a long and liquid lunch – and he comes out of the exhibition centre and drags us around to the car park and gets us to duck down behind some cars so the guards at the entrance (who look like proper skinheads) can't see us, and then he clips the book fair cards to our clothes. He very nearly breaks out in an innocent whistling when we pass the guards.

[Alma]
So it is done. I have left. (The day after I returned from Belgrade with the journey still lingering inside me.) It was like pulling up an enormous root from of the earth – I fell back with a thud and found myself on the pavement, with a suitcase in each hand. Goodbye windows, and goodbye brick. And goodbye Kristian, I can see you behind the curtains, goodbye dry, dusty life, goodbye rules, goodbye worries, goodbye terrible and devastating quarrels, and goodbye sweetness (by now, you only fell in drops) and goodbye beautiful, practically translucent eyes, but I have to be careful now, otherwise I'll just walk back up the stairs, goodbye goodbye, because I mean it. This morning I informed him of my decision. It is already afternoon. At first he began to pace around the living room with long, vigorous steps, round the dining room table, over to the sofa. His body was moving so powerfully that it frightened me; like there was a cliff lurking somewhere in the living room where he could drag us both into the abyss. I wrapped my arms

around his chest and tried to keep him calm, but he took no notice of my embrace, he tore himself away and stormed round the table again and into the kitchen and back into the living room. But suddenly he went quiet. He lay down on the bed and did not say a word while I packed my clothes. He just followed my movements. When I was finished, he got up, almost mechanically, and strode after me to the door. He closed it immediately after me. For a moment it was like I was pasted to the door.

It is Sunday, there are families out on walks. Frederiksberg is very red and very heavy. The road is as wide as a racing track. I feel a twitching inside me to move fast, I sense it as something equine. Good thing we never managed to have a child and become one of these families behind a heavy red brick wall. Kristian asked me about it once, and as ill luck would have it I replied: 'You're like a child yourself. I'm not having another one.'

Seven years and not a moment longer. My man-child. Child because he clung to me. (When we would lie face to face and I turned my head away, towards the room, he grabbed it and turned it back so that I could see him again. He could not get enough contact. He could never get enough. The more he made his demands on me, the more I preferred to write. The more insistently he turned my head towards his, the more defiantly I looked away.) And then he was so afraid of dying if he got a bone caught in his throat or scalded himself on a teaspoon of hot porridge or got stung by a mosquito (Lake Victoria, safely entrenched behind malaria pills). You should be able to surrender your life with a grand gesture. I believe that. At this moment.

I have torn myself free. My heart is pounding

something fierce. I am alone. I am heading into the unknown. I am going to live with Alwilda for a few days,
on Sankt Peders Stræde, that will be my first stop. But
when will I know that I have truly left? That I will not
fall back; like when you have thrown something in the
rubbish bin and an hour later you regret it and take it
out and clean it off. Or a longer period of time will pass,
and it will be like opening a house that has been empty
all winter long, and the first thing you do is sweep out
the cobwebs.

Nobody's back is straighter than Alwilda's. She never
uses a backrest but still manages to sit ramrod straight.
Then I am aware that I am sprawled out, my back is
an arch, and I straighten up a little in the chair out of
embarrassment. Alwilda has ironclad discipline. Me –
I need a broom to sweep myself together. I sleep until
noon. I have become dependent on my heating pad. I
make a cave out of my duvet. I wrap myself up and disappear inside it; I want to sleep within my duvet like in
a snowdrift, burning hot. Then I think that it is lovely
to be a person, with breasts, wearing a white nightgown.
Alwilda hangs the strangest objects to dry in her bathroom, requisites for exotic sports, are these for the knees,
Alwilda, or the elbows? The other way around, it's the
other way around. Such a nice red kayak. What would
it feel like if I headed out in one, alone among seals and
icebergs or merely a silhouette against Rungsted Havn.
Alwilda chose a short, sensible education and lives for
her free time. She became an elementary school teacher
because of the long holidays. She has no problems with
noise in her classroom. She is firm but fair, and her heart
is in the right place. My work has no beginning and no
end. When Alwilda grew tired of Edward, she made

short work of it. I don't know how many years it took me to leave Kristian. Now I am about to fall asleep again. On Alwilda's hard chair. I close my eyes and dream about a man I saw in the park. I am alone and searching for someone so I can send my thoughts in their direction. What am I going to do with my longing? Where am I going to send my notions? What am I going to do with myself? I take up too much space, I am overflowing. But now the door opens. Alwilda is back.

'If you don't have a boyfriend, you need to get yourself a vibrator,' she says firmly.

I am caught off guard and let out a laugh. Is that what she has been out shopping for? No, she just happened to think about it on the way up the stairs, which she took in long strides.

'I'm more the dreamy type,' I say, 'thanks all the same.'

What more could I say? I could say: I am romantic, but precise. The ringing of a bell out in the blue yonder. I ring incessantly. Plant me firmly on the table.

And I think about how as soon as Obama was elected, all kinds of objects were produced with his face plastered all over them.

'Why are you shaking your head?' Alwilda asks, 'Why are you sighing? It sounds so melancholic.'

In return, maybe I could ask her where she gets all her energy from, this staunchness and lack of doubt? Tearing along in a canoe, is that life? Are there not all kinds of reasons to sigh? Is life not fundamentally sad, we enter through one door with a scream and soon after we slip away through another (oh, now I sound like Kristian) and someone has taken my tail; I want to lose myself in my work, I am at my best when I do not feel like I am here (maybe only when I have sat in the same

position for too long and have to stretch my neck a little).
Why do I get so terrified when I see women with infants,
the exhaustion spreads through my limbs, I don't like
all the chalky white delicate skin (the children's) with all
the throbbing blue veins that suggest the frailty of life
(over, over) and the mothers' skin when they bend down
to pick up yet another fallen object, and their tops slip
above the waistband to reveal a patch of skin that is almost blue-white, but then there are also two children in
the pram, and maybe one holding her hand, no time for a
moment in the sun for the blind handmaidens of broods
& breeding. Alwilda is different than the rest of us. She
goes to protests and does not shy away from clashes with
the police. Myself, protests make me cry, I cannot manage large (or even small) crowds in motion, something
works loose within my chest, and the sight of the long
lines of police, shield to shield, makes my legs tremble.
I am afraid of these black beetles. I hide my face in my
hands and sob silently when the megaphones crackle,
and the crowd sings and hollers and feels like one great
body. I cannot join the crowd; nor do I long to. I long
to be free of myself – with just one other person. And
now it is June, and the graduating students drive past in
open lorries and shout and wave, and people wave back
and honk, and my face contorts idiotically so I have
to hurry down a side street. The other night Alwilda
was nearly run over. She chased the car at breakneck
speed, and at the first red light, she dropped her bike
and jumped into the front seat and put the driver in a
chokehold. That's Alwilda. Not much talk. Someone
who acts. And she does not care much for the idea of
part of Nørrebrogade being made car-free, if you don't
want cars side by side with us, move to the country, now
I recall a protest to have cars banned from the city, the

parents shouting in time: 'Our young / shouldn't have black lungs'; a capital city should look like a capital city. She will do everything in her power to ensure that the same does not happen with Vesterbrogade. There are groups for everything; the first Saturday in the month dog owners meet on a hilltop in Østre Anlæg to fight for the right to walk their dogs without leads, Edward told me about that, there was shouting, clenching and shaking of fists, the dogs bay at the red sky, a lot of people wearing Hunter boots and looking like landowners, but apparently landless and reduced to parks; there is one group for the Metro and one against, and so on and so on, every time an issue arises, two groups arise. So much activity, so many leaflets. As for Edward, she says that he needs to sell his house; that he is presiding over a death house, running a death cult, 'the house is a ghost ship,' she says and I picture him standing on the bridge of a long black ship with worm-eaten sails.

'Poor, lonely Edward,' she says, 'he feels so sorry for himself.'

'He does have the dog,' I interject.

'Yes, he's married to that dog,' Alwilda says, which is also wrong.

She does not believe that he will relinquish the sorrow that is his last link to his parents, if he relinquishes that sorrow, he loses them entirely. It sounds like night school wisdom, but I say nothing. I think she is brutal. I once confused this brutality with honesty. I found her honesty laudable. I imagine her orgasms are like a smack with a fly swatter, swift, hard, and practical. Afterwards she leaps up and tightens her belt. Not much of the sea about it, oceanic movements, I mean, drawn-out Atlantic breakers and then a sweet sleep, no. But she is the only one of us who does not want anything other than what she already has. As far as I know.

Kristian wants a child. Charles wants a new back. I want a life without heating pads, where I write like I played the piano, flip page after page until suddenly I have pumped out an entire book. Camilla wishes her mind did not resemble greasy dishwater, or how does she describe it: like a bag filled with slips of paper, you stick your hand in and pull one out: Guilt, it reads. Defensiveness. Bitterness. The need to blame.

But all of this I am unable to recognize – in Camilla.

I think (with regret) about what has been left at Kristian's. All the things I could not take with me when I left; things that could not be taken back. And things I would prefer he not preside over. My life story, for example. Intimate confessions. Embarrassing incidents. My idiosyncrasies. My pettiness. All the things he knows ad nauseam; but things which, when we were together, could be smoothed over and placed alongside my more excellent & redeeming qualities.

Is it how he will remember me that concerns me?

I would like to be gone completely, to be able to remove all traces. I am not prepared for him to be wheeling and dealing with 'me' when I am not there, where he can add and subtract.

Oh, and then there are my letters; once glorious, now cringeworthy scraps I would like them back, please. And if he refuses? Then I will be forced to break in and collect what is rightfully mine.

Kristian was (is, unless he is suddenly over it) a nudist, not an avowed nudist, but one who is happy to strut about naked, which can be viewed as a protest against the puritanical upbringing he was subjected to, despite being born in the late twentieth century – but isn't that a tedious way of thinking, third-class thinking, originally stemming from 'the Viennese quack', as Nabokov calls him, and then diluted and diluted again into pop psychology, like a sandwich we are all thrashing about inside, enough already – in support of this (his upbringing) his sister Cecilie recalled the time when she was watching a movie with her mother, when two lovers abandoned themselves to a long kiss, the mother clucked and raised and lowered her hands and attempted to distract her and in the end, she suggested they turn it off, because the kiss just went on and on, but 'no, I would like to watch this,' and I wonder whether the mother then got up and disappeared into the kitchen, or did she simply cover Cecilie's eyes? My suggestion is that Kristian regarded nudity as a form of communication, wordless; when we are naked we have something in common, we have nudity, so we do not need to make an effort to reach one another through all these layers of clothing, these inhibitions and reservations. The one who remained clothed was, translated into Kristian's system, the silent guy of the group. Jack of spades. And wasn't that also why he became a doctor, to be among the undressed, or partially undressed. Then he was forced to take illness as part and parcel. In any case, every time he threw off his clothes, he became equally sheepish and content at being able to parade his body around freely. No, he did not 'throw off' his clothes, because as happy as he was to be naked, he was equally meticulous with his clothes. He had a lot of clothes, expensive clothes, good clothes, and he always hung his clothes neatly over the back of a chair. He got angry if a dog, big or small, in its eagerness to reach his face, placed its paws on his legs, then he brushed off the fabric angrily even though there was nothing to be seen. He had always been good at getting his girlfriends to walk around the house & garden naked, though not me, I am very modest, (maybe as a result of my liberal upbringing) but not as much as Camilla's well-swathed Indian friend who says: 'I have never understood why people would want to expose their body when the world is full of so many beautiful materials,' but I remember seeing Susanne, an old friend of his, trotting briskly around a corner, bare-arsed, wearing a sunhat and red clogs, carrying a trowel, one hot summer's day when I stepped into the garden unannounced.

Personality cannot be encircled, Camilla says, and then I imagine a sheepdog barking in ever smaller circles as it herds its flock. Or a prisoner tethered to a pole.

[Alwilda]
'Tonight I want to present you with an example of fear and an example of greed. When I was in Africa with Edward, we spent a week at a mission in Mozambique. We were given room and board in return for helping out. Edward worked in the fields, and I looked after children. There was a house with orphaned children, and there was a schoolroom. The children immediately grew attached to me, they called me "Sister Alwilda"; they were locked inside an enclosure (when they were not sleeping or receiving tuition) like little goats, but they received clean clothes every morning. It was a dirt pen they walked round in, and a moment after they had been shut inside their clothes were dirty, and their hands and feet embroidered with filth. I don't think there were any toys. They had their hands and their bare feet.'

(And the dust, Alma thought. And God, flapping above like a big, crumpled-up coat.)

134

'During the day, the laundered clothes were laid out to dry on bushes, we, Edward and I, were told to iron our clothes (when they had hung to dry outdoors) in order to kill off the eggs that certain insects lay in moisture, and whose larvae can burrow under the skin (but the children's clothes were not ironed) and when the children caught a glimpse of me – outside of the enclosure, they crowded together by the fence and called me and enticed me, "Sister Alwilda, Sister Alwilda." I was enraptured by each and every one, there were probably twelve or fifteen of them, but I was particularly enraptured by two beautiful children, a small boy by the name of John and a little girl named Mary (and now that I think of it she might have learned to adopt the right facial expression a little too early on, I now think of John and Mary as the youngest in a musical) and as I mentioned they were all enraptured by me, their Sister Alwilda. There was one child who was not terribly charming, and she was also listless, her name was Mildred. She was probably five. Mildred reminded me of how happy I had once been to vaccinate my big filthy Dorthe Doll with a potato peeler.

One day in the schoolroom – I was observing the teacher, who was African, attempt to drill the alphabet into children as young as two, (the missionaries personally saw to God's drilling) imagine an infant holding a pointer and attempting to hit the letters on the board. I sat, without thinking about it, like a lady, with my legs crossed. The teacher's skirt reached all the way down to the ground, to all intents and purposes she had no legs. Suddenly she smiled at me and pointed at my legs and signalled for me to turn around. Around me sat fifteen miniature versions of myself – legs crossed, faces beaming – yes, fun and games, nobody noticed the alphabet out of delight at seeing my legs. I remember especially how John's face shone.'

'The screw is tightening, Alwilda,' Alma said and pulled herself into a seated position.

'One day I decided to take the children for a stroll. They all wanted to hold my hand, they pulled and tore at my hands and at one another to get to my hands. Finally we established that they could hold one finger each. I held out my hands behind me, and one child latched onto each of my fingers, what a strangely wild cargo I walked with. The Lilliputians weighed Gulliver down. Fingers like teats, and thus we entered the woods. It was a listless wood, sparsely vegetated. Never before have I seen a forest with such great distance between the trees. What kind of trees were they, I cannot say. I shook my hands free of the children, and they set off and swarmed around a huge stump, they climbed on top of it and jumped down from it. With the exception of Mildred. She wanted to be carried. Fair enough, because there had been no finger for Mildred to hold. I clasped my fingers together to form a kind of chair which I placed under the back of her knees, she wrapped her arms around my neck, and her bum dangled about in the air. She had me all to herself and out of pure satisfaction, she stuck a couple of filthy fingers into her mouth and began to suck. Maybe she also fiddled with my ears. Suddenly the children began to scream – "Snake, snake." And they cleared away from the stump in one movement, like a school of fish, a flock of birds. And what did I do?'

'Yes, what did you do, Alwilda?'

'I tore my hands apart so that Mildred landed on the ground with a heavy thud, and then I ran – fifteen, twenty metres. I noticed two of the children helping Mildred to her feet. It had been a false alarm, or else the snake was gone by now. Because the flock was calm. I walked back and wiped off Mildred's cheeks and picked her up again. The entire way home she cried mechanically and inconsolably. If it had been little John or little Mary, I would never have let go.'

When Alma said nothing, Alwilda continued: 'And now I want to talk about greed.'

(Would you like a pointer, Alma thought.)

'All meals were consumed in a refectory. It was self-service. Next to the stack of plates were bowls and pots. There were a lot of missionaries, a lot of people eating. The first day Edward and I arrived relatively early – I mean, there were not many people in the queue in front of us when we arrived. That day they were serving rice with beans in tomato sauce and a little onion and some avocado slices. Outside, over the fires, the same bean dish was stewing in the pots of the African women. I had seen that on the way to the refectory. I had passed the women earlier that day, when they had been sitting in front of their huts observing everything. Little John had fallen and had sliced open his big toe on a sharp rock. I grabbed him and ran towards the nurse's domain, in the main building. His foot was bleeding and he was screaming. I looked at the women as I ran past. I sought solidarity, that together we could feel sorry for the child (because he must have been in real pain), but all I found was complete indifference, perhaps outright coldness, or else it was listlessness. They did not move. Their faces reflected nothing.

We were terribly hungry. We were far out in the country, and there was very little food to go round. We took one spoonful, and another. We could not stop. We must have thought that the pots would be filled again, that there was more food, behind the curtain where the

137

kitchen must be. When we sat down at one of the long communal tables, hundreds of eyes sought out our plates and crept all the way around the portion like flies, measuring. We had taken at least twice as much as everyone else. My face contorted like it had blood dripping from it. We could not put the food back. We had to work our way through each of our voluminous portions. I did not know whether to eat quickly – so that my crime disappeared. Or slowly, to show how much I enjoyed the food that I had purloined. Edward leaned as far over his plate as he could. At one point he fenced the plate off with his arms. But it seemed so possessive – that I elbowed him in his side. The last person in the queue got next to nothing. Tiny blobs on big plates and ours were full, oh no. And do you know what, at the next meal, there was someone at the counter to dish up – so everyone got the same amount. To guard against our greed.'

'Don't you want to tell me some more?' Alma asked a little later.

'Alright. On the trip, Edward obstructed my access to every person we met. I would ask a passer-by for directions, and immediately he leapt in front of me to be the one to receive the answer. Then he displayed all his charm and cleverness – towards a stranger he was going to be separated from a minute later and in all likelihood would never meet again.'

'More,' Alma said.

'The rest of the trip, I remember only in points, such as – you know, I've dyed my grey hair since I was eighteen – several times I kneeled by the shore of rivers or lakes and washed the hair dye out, risking being taken by a crocodile.'

'Fearful, greedy and now vain as well,'

'Do you want to hear more?'

'Is there more?'

More honey, more words, she is stuck with me, and just like A. A. Milne's tough Rabbit I consider whether there is anything I can use her for now that she is here; something hushed, which demands no movement on her part, no mental activity.

I love the sight of her on the sofa in the morning, but by noon I feel like her slave. I think she must have had servants growing up.

'I'll let you have a couple more points.'

'Then I will connect the dots myself, and they will be connected.'

'When we landed in Cape Town, there was still some of the colossal packed lunch that Edward had made and brought with us from Copenhagen remaining. "First we have to finish with Denmark," Edward said punctiliously, "then we can get started on Africa," and it was his punctiliousness that I was so sick and tired of. We found a park and began to eat, the tropical climbers climbed above us, or else they were brown and tired, withered, listless from the heat – I thought something was hanging down over the bench. A woman stopped in front of us and held out her palm. Edward offered her a piece of rye bread. She stared at it and shook her head. "I guess you're not hungry then," Edward said and shooed her away. A couple of weeks later. Mozambique. Way out in the country. The bus stopped at a station. Street vendors came running up and displayed their wares to the passengers who were hanging out of the windows (if it was possible to open them.) It turned out that everyone sold the same thing: whole roast mouse, fastened to a kind of frame. Edward shook his head, "I guess you're not hungry then," I said – and the stiff little fellows were even the same colour of brown as rye bread. All around the bus people were crunching on the crispy rodents, the tails were tossed onto the floor. I got out to stretch my legs, since there was time. A white coating had fallen over a number of the residents' eyes (the residents of the bus station); and those for whom the world was not entirely switched off led those who were completely blind, but led them where? Just back and forth a ways, along the row of sheet metal shanties that had been erected by the bus station, then to the right into nothingness and then back again, to the smell of roast mice and overheated tyres and diesel, there was nowhere to go, there was nothing to see, other than cracked earth and dried scrub. But I had them to look at. And it makes me shudder – the whitish eyes directed at the heavens and the click-clacking of canes on the earth. And then the women's breasts dangled under their dresses and did not seem to end until they reached the waist, children clinging to their apron strings. A large white eye and below it a long breast.'

'On TV I saw Africans making burgers out of mosquitoes,' Alma said, 'the air was dense with mosquitoes, it was a veritable invasion, they caught them in nets around nightfall and received a much welcomed nutritious meal out of it. Black mosquito burgers. Pest turned to protein. Boy, I fancy some prawns now. I don't think I can stand staying on this princely furniture any more, it makes me feel lordly, should I change to a straight-backed chair?'

'I'll look in the freezer. But first, another point ...'

'Paddle out in your kayak and catch us some prawns.'

'I want to talk more about the poverty in the country, in the African provinces.'

'But you have to go fishing.'

'Sit in your straight chair.'

'Thou who professes knowledge of sport, knows humility – towards godly body. You, Alwilda.'

'Why do you say that?'

[Alma]

Pale grey at six o'clock, bright red at seven o'clock, light blue at eight o'clock, nine o'clock like a red flash, a warning, this is it! Brown at ten o'clock, yellow at eleven o'clock and black at twelve o'clock. White at one o'clock and white at two o'clock like a ticklish childminder, paid for mildness, three o'clock green and with folds: now the afternoon is drawing to a close. Four o'clock: yellowish as a dough packed with butter: perdition. (If I read magazines, I would reach out for one on the shelf under Alwilda's round girlish coffee table.) There is nothing to be done but postpone all activity until tomorrow at seven o'clock. Tomorrow is another day, for my part, to pull my finger out. Does *anyone* want to take charge of me? Where is Camilla? Is she lost?

[Alwilda]

'I'll continue. Now I want to talk about fear.'

'But you've already done that.'

'Fear II. Location: the African provinces. The heat, the poverty, incessantly we felt the need to bond, inside the car, or up against the car, easy prey for wild animals.'

'You're sending me straight into Edward's arms.'

'Take him, he's yours, you won't be able to put up with him for very long.'

'I don't want to hear any more about fear. I want to hear about beauty.'

'At that wretched place such as the bus station was,

141

a rose suddenly shot up – I was back in the bus when the petrol attendant emerged from the hut. He was beautiful. He was healthy. He was seventeen years old, or eighteen. He looked like he had just stepped out of a Benetton advert, with his beauty and his white teeth. There must have been a small green cap resting on his curls, and it must have been sitting to one side? And he was surrounded by blind people. But he did not realize that he was in the forecourt of hell, because he did nothing other than smile and laugh. He was wearing dungarees, with no T-shirt underneath. The straps were fastened over his bare skin. He had strong arms. He was a boy. I could see how soft his skin must have been, and how taut it was, stretched over hard muscles. I wanted to be a girl again and once again have a boy who smelled of fresh salt and had skin like fine upholstery over rock-hard pecs.'

'And something-or-other like dashing waves.'

'Dashing waves! That reminds me of the beach at Dar es Salaam where a Coca-Cola advert had just been filmed...'

'I have to get up early tomorrow, Alwilda.'

'The beach was a quagmire of fish guts and rusting ship's hulls with their noses buried in the sand, big as houses and polluting like blazes, everywhere the beach functioned as a kitchen, with small, crackling orange fires, and as a public toilet, expressed by people squatting & squeezing, one person even folded his hands all the while. And there Coca-Cola had chosen to summon a flock of doughty fishermen, provide them with torn red shirts and toothless mouths, and have them pretend they were dragging a fishing boat out to sea, all the while clinking glasses and drinking.'

'Good night, Alwilda. No prawns tonight then.'

'Good night dear Alma, adorner of my sofa. Good night.'

IF ASHES HAD EYES

[Edward]
It might be a kind of defiance that makes me walk the dog to the grave each day. My mother, even though I am a grown man and have long since made the decisions that had to be made, did not think I should get a dog. Once, in her final year, when I aired the idea to her on the phone, the line went quiet, finally she spoke: 'Don't do it!' she said, and it had come from deep inside her, ominous and emphatic.

'No, of course not,' I said, 'I'm building castles in the air.'

The purchase of the dog, on the safe side of her death, so to speak, was almost an act of liberation. So now we stand by the grave for a little while each day so that if she were able to see me from wherever she is (if ashes had eyes), she could see who makes the decisions; and that I have company, you might add; that I, single and an only child, was not going to wander alone in the cemetery and alone through life for ever, but I have found myself a companion. That must make both of them happy.

'It's hard to be a person, little dog,' I say.

I happen to put my hand in my pocket by chance, where the dog biscuits are, causing the dog to lick his mouth.

Note to *Mourning Diary*: My mother's being. It's so clear to me I feel like I could reach out and touch it. Like a substance. Maybe that's what it means when someone says they sense the existence of the dead, 'a presence'. I have a hard time dealing with my longing. She is so clear to me, and I am never going to speak to her again, never going to embrace her again. Am I going to miss her this much for the rest of my life? My grief has stagnated; no growth; no development. It happened almost two years ago; it feels like it happened last week. I keep tabs on the date. I count the months and regard them as shovelfuls of dirt. But the dirt does not keep the mind at bay. I don't feel like working. I feel like walking and walking and walking. I have purchased an opportunity for myself: the dog. My feet are horned. The dog is thin.

On 1 August 2007 I saw her for the last time. I had bought five plaice and a bunch of yellow roses. I also had some books with me. She let me in, and I put the bags down on the kitchen counter. She had some potatoes on the stove. She walked back to the bed, I wanted to start on the fish and put the roses in water, but she said: 'Come sit with me. And let me look at you. I've really been looking forward to seeing you.'

A little later we went into the kitchen, she sorted out the plaice and I placed them in freezer bags (three of them) wrapped rubber bands around them and put them in the freezer. Then I had to cut up the parsley. In the living room, her on the sofa (Dad was not home, he had an appointment), me with the parsley (complaining about how dull the scissors were), we talked about Granddad's grindstone, about a book called *Gården*, about all the phenomena she knew from the country, for example how raindrops on a dusty road can turn into small balls of dust. We talked about Granddad and Grandma. About the time they had briefly lodged with some Danish Nazis, how the wife shouted to Grandma: 'Our friends are coming, Mrs Poulsen,' when Denmark was being occupied. How they quickly moved out to then live with a farmer named Stampe who was cruel to his animals and refused to acknowledge European

Summer Time, so that the boys and girls working the farm arrived late to their appointments (physical education, for example). Granddad had written a verse about him and the sun in Jutlandic. She recited it. I thought it was fantastic and wanted to write it down. But I never managed to do that. She told of a trip to Copenhagen, her and Grandma were going to visit Granddad who was somewhere on Amager (with the ship). There was a funfair, and they convinced her that it was Tivoli. (She had been promised that she would be taken to Tivoli when she made it to Copenhagen.)

She talked about a barge (gravel hoover?) that Granddad had worked on (maybe it was called Hektor), he was earning more money than at any other point in his life. Later they lived in a house with another family, and the husband had also worked on Hektor. They had agreed that if they saw Hektor out in the sound, they would get hold of the crew and then they would throw a party. One day Granddad wanted to tease Grandma and came home and announced: 'Hektor is coming.' That made Grandma race up the stairs to the wife upstairs and shout: 'Hektor is here.' She was in such a hurry – because it was time for a party after all – that she strained a tendon and was bedridden for several weeks.

About how the calves (at Stampe's) came running up to the fence to be scratched on the forehead – when they saw Granddad coming down the road in the evening, on his way home from a job at the sugar mill. He was so exhausted after having lugged sacks around all day that he lay down on the kitchen floor and remained lying there for a good while before he had the strength to clean himself up and get changed.

After she had eaten, she was tired and went back to bed. I told her about a conversation I had had with Dad earlier that week, he told me that in parts of the animal kingdom, there was a demand to share the prey, 'share-demanding'; and it made her think of the time she had gone out to buy a pack of biscuits for Grandma, and all the children on the street came running over and wanted some, in the end she stood with her back against the wall, the pack was empty, 'And you know who didn't get any, me. All I got was a telling-off.'

When I left, I saluted her (in jest) wearing my bike helmet.

The burial plot has started to resemble her. Before Christmas it had appeared neglected, the heather and the lavender had withered; and I recalled the dull and worn appearance the house sometimes had, the walls yellowed with cigarette smoke, as well as the bed and herself. I decorated it with spruce, catkin branches and red berries and now envisaged a more comfortable her, one with a healthy, bronzed face. The grave, that's her. A stone, a granite stool that I still had not sat on, but which I had placed at the grave because I seem to think better when I'm sitting down – and because there is such a transience in standing up; and then a few various plants or flowers, all framed by a low hedge.

I have had comforting dreams, and destructive dreams. The latter have dealt with what takes place in the grave, the putrification; for my own sake I refer to them (in my mind, as well as here in my *Mourning Diary*) as 'dreams of decomposition', without getting into any details, but nevertheless the details stuck with me over the days that followed. My mum had been cremated, which in itself was no reason to dream about the unmentionable things that happen in the grave, the decomposition. All right, one dream had a natural explanation. Her ashes had been divided into two urns. One urn was lowered into the grave, I scattered the ashes from the other one into the sea, at a place my mum used to enjoy swimming. For that reason it was a rather logical dream, that when the lid fell off the coffin, lying inside was half of her, practically split lengthwise.

In another dream I saw her from a slight distance, beautifully made up, wearing a red hat, but it was clear that she was dead, a made-up cadaver – she had returned for my sake. She had always gone to great lengths for me.

In one dream we spoke together. She told me she was not dead, but had gone to another place. A place where I could not visit her. The following day I was slightly intoxicated with peacefulness.

It struck me, on one of my perpetual walks through Østre Anlæg, that I myself had already set out on my departure from this world, a departure that would hopefully last a very long time. I am heading towards fifty and have long since begun greying.

I have begun 'to thwack' – in the mornings I cross the large lawn in Fælledparken and walk over to the lake with the fountain, then I bang the lead against a particular bench a couple of times and say: 'To a day without bitterness and dispiritedness.' But I seldom manage to keep my spirits up for very long.

The one thing that would give my life a tremendous boost is love, and I have not found any since Alwilda. I wanted it all. But I was weighed and found wanting. Of one thing and another.

It is the small dog that makes the women's voices go all shrill and languishing. That is what they look at. I am invisible at the end of the lead. On the odd occasion we exchange a couple of words about when the dogs are in heat. I have begun to view him as my forward operating base on the love market, just like in *101 Dalmatians*. But he is a little restrained.

'It's down to the breeding,' a man said to me.

'What do you mean?' I asked.

'Danish men wouldn't harm a fly,' he said.

And I think he would have preferred to see us Danish men performing rape in droves.

'But we are in Afghanistan now,' I said, 'and we were in Iraq, as well.'

(The other day when I came home from the shop holding an ice cream, the small dog got an erection; everything is slightly blurring into one for him, but on the other hand: all the various pleasure centres in the brain et cetera.) In San Francisco I saw a gay man come strutting towards me with a poodle that he had sprayed royal blue. If he had done that in order to be seen, I have to say, I was unable to see the man for the poodle. It was majestic in its blueness. I did not turn to look: what kind of person would think of doing that? Still, I can remember that he was wearing shorts. So he *did* reach my retina, my memory.

If I get told off, it can stick with me for an entire day. Those incessant workplace assessments have not made it any easier. And now in my spare time as well. If I am just a little too slow getting the bag out of my pocket when I have to pick up after the small dog, cyclists will sometimes brake suddenly and motorists will roll down their windows and shout. The bags have a tendency to stick together, that can delay me, but I counter with friendliness. 'Good thing you're keeping an eye on things,' I say, or: 'Sorry, I'm such a clumsy clod.' It's the shit war. The other war is a matter of space, too many rats in the same place and so on, obviously down by the lakes is only for champions, and they do not stray from their path, 'If it doesn't move, I'll kick it,' people shout. It's wrong if it is on the loose, and it is wrong if it is on its lead – particularly when it's dark. I have one of these leads that acts like a fishing line; you can cast off (eight metres) and reel it in with a ticking sound. In the darkness the long lead functions as a snare, 'sorry' I say to the runner as he stumbles, 'I didn't get a chance to haul the cod to shore,' (obviously the cod is the small dog).

I was almost more frightened the time my mum took a tumble in the garden than the time I found her and my father dead in the bedroom. The garden is made up of a cultivated section and a wild section that we called (and I still call) the wilderness. This is at the house that I have taken over. My childhood home. Down in the wilderness there is a toppled willow tree that has still not died, and in its crown wild honeysuckles grow. There is also a hollow from an artificial lake that my dad emptied when I was with Alwilda, back when they hoped to have a grandchild; out of fear that the child would fall into the lake and drown. The previous owner had covered the hollow with thick black plastic to retain the water; with great pains my dad managed to tear this plastic off, and now there are ferns growing in the hollow; there is also an area with yellow flowers which I don't know the name of, and there are several areas with tall stinging nettles, and there are piles of garden refuse and a lot of trees. I have no idea why, one day at Easter, my mum decided to enter the wilderness.

The terrace itself resembles a wild ocean. It is due to

the ants digging passages under the flagstones, causing them to shift, they either sink or slope. In some places the terrace is simply dangerous, at least for old people who walk unsteadily and fall heavily. Old people who fall like they have no hands to ease the blow. As though they have lost all volition and so leave their arms hanging feebly; people who have lost faith in their arms. The fact that first they and now I have not had the flagstones relaid in order to have a new and completely level terrace is due to the wild strawberries and the poppies and the thyme that grow between the flagstones, which would then be lost. For that reason we walk around on rolling ground warning one another to be careful.

At any rate we got up from the terrace that Easter and walked down towards the wilderness. A couple years earlier my father had built some round brick flowerbeds and planted wild strawberries and decorative pumpkins in them; but these beds had long since been swallowed up by the wilderness and now lay like traps somewhere beneath the tall grass. When we approached them, I took my mother by the arm, and we made it past them safely. She leaned on me heavily. We walked around a little at the bottom of the garden and looked at the strange shape that the prostrate willow tree had taken on, and we talked about the stinging nettles and about her long, bitter battle with them, and how for a long time she had actually succeeded in keeping them at bay. She did not have much of a head for gardening, and in her great naïvety (that was how she put it) she initially began – because she could not really solve the problem of how to get rid of the garden refuse – to stuff the stinging nettles into black bin bags. But she stopped when she began to realize how much refuse there was, and how many filled bags it would amount to.

While we walked around down there and talked about how tall the trees had grown – the rowan tree, for example, which I had found in the woods and planted. 'As a child, you were mad about rowan trees,' she said, and I nodded – we also recalled an afternoon where we had sat here in the wilderness, which back then was not a wilderness, but a lawn with two imposing weeping willows, in garden chairs, waiting for some sort of builder to arrive. We sat drinking Noilly Prat. She was irritable and restless. It must have been in March or April, there was an air of weariness and neglect, not just to the garden, but to nature as such, it had been brown and decaying for a long time and was in need of some greenery; the black, waterlogged earth, the fallen branches and the yellow tubes that poked up and were left lying on the ground as part of last year's stinging nettles and last year's ground elder – it was a hopeless mess. I told her about an essay I was working on. When I outlined the contents, she looked away in annoyance. She thought it sounded foolish, but refrained from saying so. Nor was that necessary, the impetuous shrug of her shoulders said it all.

Maybe we both remembered that conversation we had in the garden chairs nearly ten years earlier because we were having a drink in the middle of the day, something we almost never did, and because we were sitting somewhere in the garden where we normally never sat. We had sat with a view of the road so that we could see when the builder arrived, 'sorry,' she now said, 'I thought it sounded completely irrelevant and it turned out to be the best thing you have ever written. Don't you think so?' (Obviously that did not make me happy, annoyed before all else, because she preferred that dusty old piece to everything I have written since.)

When we had wandered through the wilderness that Easter day and enjoyed what there was to enjoy, we set out in the direction of the more or less civilized section of the garden – the terraces and the lawn. Suddenly my mum spotted a large preserving jar in the tall grass. I have no idea how it ended up *there*. As she bent down to pick it up, she fell to the ground heavily without using her hands to ease the fall at all. I let out a cry. She remained on the ground for a moment, checking to see if anything was broken, then rolled onto her stomach and got up on her knees. She had tripped on one of the treacherous bricks and had a superficial cut on her temple and had hurt her arm. I must confess that I gave in to tears and was powerless to stop. I cried (though noiselessly) while I helped her onto the sofa and cleaned the wound with chlorhexidine. I cried, even though she had been very lucky and was virtually uninjured. My dad was not there. He never was. And ten minutes later I was still crying. While inwardly berating myself: 'Mummy's boy. In your late forties. You blubbering idiot. Grow up.'

'You really love me,' she said from the sofa. The words came from somewhere deep within her, and were spoken with deep and raspy marvel.

A moment later she said: 'Perhaps you should try to love me a little less so it won't be so hard on you when I ... oh, fiddlesticks, we can't control these things.'

'It's going to be difficult when you're no longer here,' I said, 'but I'll manage.'

And difficult it was. We had talked about death so much – or in any case openly considered the possibility – but when it arrived, it did not do me one bit of good. But I manage. And furthermore, I have not cried since that day. But once in a while, when the small dog attempts to grab an object with its paws and fumbles with it, it pains me that he does not have hands. Now don't misunderstand me – it's not because I want to have my hand held (in any case not by a dog); the fumbling is just so pitiful. So I step in, with my superior set of hands.

At night we spoon, and I wrap my arms around its lean loins; fur is much different than skin. And the body of a dog is hard and angular, you can't sink into it. The species are indeed different. The fur has a strong odour. And when we wake up, the bed is covered in white hair. Perhaps the canine body is more like that of a man than a woman – so hard and streamlined. If it was a man I was longing for, it probably would not have felt so wrong. The small dog is a restless partner. It gets too warm and extricates itself from my embrace. A moment later it wants to return to the warmth – it positions itself by my head and practically knocks on the duvet, with a scratching and a brief bark. And so on, all night long.

The other day the neighbour leaned across the hedge and looked across the wilderness. Then he said: 'Tell me, do you not have any vision.'

I simply replied 'no' and remembered the song we used to sing in the old dinghy when we were bailing or jigging for cod. 'Put on an old sweater oh, and let your beard go,' and I added for my own account: 'and let the hedges grow, and stop staring over my row.'

Finally he withdrew from my wasteland and continued back to his own, you have to believe: visionary plot of land.

I was left overwhelmed by the memory about fishing. I still did not have a beard, granddad's stubble was grey. I think he only shaved on Sundays, so he was in the habit of letting his beard go, not just when we were at sea. The dinghy was named after me, the name Edward danced on the bow. I was sucking on a piece of brown barley sugar while making regular small tugs on the line to make the silver-coloured jig on the seabed move like a herring.

'You're not crunching, are you, Edward? Let me see.' I opened my mouth and showed him the sweet, and if we had not been jigging and were quiet so as not to scare off the cod at that precise moment, he would sing or call me 'Good Edward,' it would be nice to hear those words here in the garden. It makes me remember what one of my psychologists once said to me (I had just decided against buying one of the semi-transparent rock crystals she sold at her desk, and which resembled, and perhaps were, the frozen tears of her clients.)

She said: 'You have to love yourself. There is no guarantee that there will always be other people to do that.'

Back then I shook my head. But now she would be able to boast that she had been right.

'I love you, Edward, I love you so much. Don't leave me behind, baby,' I say.

'My neighbour doesn't love my garden / but he sure likes me,' I say.

I would rather think about what it was like coming out of the harbour, current wind surging against us, and for that reason the outboard motor was put to use, it was difficult to start and made in Sweden, so we called it 'the Surly Swede'; the prow rammed the waves in short, hard skips and with a hard thud – that's how we arrived, in short hard skips. I sat with the wind in my face, it was fresh and salty too, the wind and the salt made my skin soft. If I turned around, the barked fist, as they say, was on the tiller, his large shoulders and a face that, back then, was what I imagined when someone mentioned the

155

Heavenly Father. When we had the harbour behind us, I got the sense that it was not merely the sea that was spread out before us, but the world itself, the wide open world, there you have it good Edward, there you have it, divine granddad, there are already twenty metres of greenish-black water beneath you, filled with cod, and 'if you don't crunch, but eat them in moderation, you can have another one, awright.'

Note: I asked my mum to appear in my dreams and give me some advice – when I speak to her, the gravestone serves as her face, I looked at it earnestly as I quietly lodged my prayer. But she has not appeared. Which is why I no longer feel like going to the cemetery. But maybe she didn't come because I no longer need her; because something is happening – within me. It is getting brighter. A weight is lifted. I feel incredibly alive in the wind. A ways behind me walks an old lady. I feel like, no, I need to address her, I slow down and let her catch me up. Then I say: 'We better be careful we don't take off.'

'Yes,' she replies, 'it's a matter of standing your ground.'

And then we look at each other with unadulterated delight.

NATURE AS A SERIES OF BACKDROPS

[Camilla]

There is a veil of mist above the lake. Five heavy swans go to take off, their wings snapping against the water, and although René, who belongs to my first period of youth – which has sprung a leak, on the chair, next to Charles's bed – even though René did not resemble a swan wearing his white head waiter uniform, on the contrary he was a small meticulous man, his voice would snap out like a gunshot, like wings against water, when late in the afternoon, before the evening's great invasion, he went over the menu with us and subsequently tested us on it. Restaurant Peder Oxe, ten minutes to five. When we (the waiters) stood outside the kitchen and he inspected our uniforms, that they were clean and ironed, he would sometimes grab someone's hand and check their nails. He would sometimes bend over and sweep a lock of hair under the virginal white cap that was part of our uniform, 'don't touch me,' I screamed inwardly. Then he went through the menu in Danish and in English – and then the shelling began. He snapped out the name of a dish, pointed at a girl who then had to describe the dish, accompaniments et cetera. The only word I remember from back then is 'watercress', followed by the inevitable 'sauce', pronounced with a rounded vowel.

'*Brøndkarse. Engelsk*,' René shouted.

'Watercress (sir, yes sir)!' I shouted back, that's the closest I've ever come to being a soldier.

Gråbrødre Torv, where the restaurant still lies, and where René probably still wreaks havoc, was always filled with people sitting talking drinking. One night when I had finished work, I too sat down, on the square, to rest my aching waiter's legs. A car approached, driving down a side street. Suddenly the driver hit the gas and screeched towards us, the people sitting there – we flew back like poultry, he slammed on the brakes and leapt out of the car. He was a small meticulous man, with black hair that stuck to his head like he had combed it with his saliva, wearing black clothes and black driving gloves. He rained down abuse on us that indicated a certain education, 'plebs', he shouted and spat on the ground, 'I despise you, the common herd,' and jumped back into the car and reversed, screeching away. Someone shouted 'psycho' and a little later everything was as before – sitting drinking talking. Perhaps it was white René's dark brother who would have preferred to have smashed his car into the walls of Peder Oxe.

Nature, I have that. I have learnt to.

'Look, look, look,' someone has said to me, conversations were interrupted with pointing and unnatural silence at the sight. And now I see it, I see the red tree, all autumn, as if I have never seen it before. But can I take nature with me into the living room when I come home (to the sick bed), can I retain it inside of me as a comfort and a strength, can I meet with it as though it were a series of backdrops my gaze can lift into my memory? Today I cut across the cemetery – and there was Edward, walking. He did not see me, and frankly I was in such a bad mood that I did not feel like talking. He looked like someone moving from one secret to the next. I mean he looked triumphant, in a sympathetic way. I reckoned he was on his way to the family grave. A little ways off three gardeners were working. Even though they were only a couple of metres from one another, they did not utter a single word. The sound of their tools could be heard, chopping and tearing. Think about how builders always holler to each other all the way through the building, up and down the scaffolding, with the radio playing.

There is a mountain of swept-up yellow leaves, a tree with yellow leaves rises above it, is the mountain the corpse and are the quivering leaves on the tree the soul that is standing firm? I ask dutifully, since I stand at a churchyard. The certainty of soon lying flat and trampled down, in the pile with the rest, is dismal and dreary, as with the leaf, as with me. And Edward has come here every day for several years. Break free from the grave, Prince Edward.

But he is whistling. He *has* cast off the sorrow – and a whistling forces its way out.

The dog is limping. Edward has inflicted a hip injury on it by exercising it too much. For two years he has marched his grief away, for hours at a time. Now the dog is paying the price. He has bought a lamb's wool coat so the dog does not get cold while he speaks to the gravestone; it (the dog) looks like a decadent sheep, with its collar turned up.

Now the dog is wagging its tail, because who is that coming? Wearing red gloves, my heart stops, it's Alma, my Alma. What a place to arrange a rendezvous with a woman, or maybe it's not that crazy, maybe all that boxwood reminds a person that it is a matter of taking life by the scruff of the neck. They embrace. Alma holds Edward's head in her red gloves and observes him closely. I don't know what she is looking for – the final remnants of an illness, a rash. It's gone, he's lucky. I beat a hasty retreat down the tree-lined avenue. Could there be anything better than seeing your best friends falling in love? Then why do I feel so bitter and lifeless inside, as though I were a pile of compost? Because all I have is my youth to reflect on: when something actually happened. And I am not even forty. Nothing happens now. For me.

'I almost hope something extraordinary will happen,' I said to Alma, 'If life is going to be like this for ever, I won't be able to endure it.'

'Don't wish to be in my shoes,' she said, 'it's a right mess.'

'I wasn't thinking about a man.'

'But I'm always thinking about that.'

Don't be bitter now – and with pursed lips. Smile, with bared teeth. Ready to take a bite out of the world. And then remember, for those of you who are interested in yellow, the tulips have arrived. And yellow tulips are the thoroughbred of yellow, the best of the best.

THE FACE OF RUBBISH

[Kristian]

3 May. Two days after the great party, Fælledparken still looks like a rubbish tip. I can see small figures walking around the field with nippers and rakes, I feel a stab of jealousy at how manageable it appears, I would prefer to be nipping rubbish than have to go home and write the article I can no longer put off writing; knowing exactly what I have to do all the time, nip nip rubbish, free the green carpet bit by bit as I drag the waves of paper into the bag. I walk over to a member of the clean-up crew and ask if she is a volunteer. She's a communist, and if she doesn't help clear up the park, the police will fine the party. That's what happened last year. So it is not because she fancies it. But I do, I feel like taking the implement from her hands. Her face is red with burst capillaries, her eyes are watery, her hair is drooping, she's wearing a boiler suit. The communist encourages me to check out the memorial for the battle on the common, 'at the spot where the police trampled the workers, there are sushi boxes lying there, and it is littered with expensive wine bottles.' (She has apparently scrutinized the labels and knows a little about wine.)

I ask her if she knew that back then, B&W paid Louis Pio ten thousand kroner to emigrate to America. She did not know that. But she takes note of it.

At that very moment her nipper seizes a party brochure, and she passes it to me, it's a little stained, but I dutifully stuff it in my pocket, were I to join, one year to this day, I could be standing with a rake in my hand. I walk in the direction of the memorial. For the sake of courage and fighting spirit. To make it through yet another day. That is how my situation appears, I realize I need something greater.

And then I think what I have so often thought. I think: I am choking with despondency over perfectly ordinary existential grief – Alma left me; but in all likelihood, everyone has been abandoned once or twice. On the other hand, society and the course of history and nature are with me for the time being – I am not subjected to catastrophes from these quarters, above, like so many others, a torture regime, drought or flood. It is not because it comforts me. I'm just saying it. Imagine if I also had to endure that. But then my Western grief might be swept away by The Great Big Disaster, 'hey, hey, grief is not a layer cake,' Camilla says inside my head, 'feel free to cry, Kristian, feel free to be dispirited.' But I am not merely dispirited or despondent. I am also disillusioned and disengaged, and for that reason I have no great cause. I note with a 'well' that the North Pole is melting; I cannot even expect to be dead by the time the more serious consequences take effect. I am indifferent. However I have considered taking a flight to Darfur and trying to make a difference, as they say. A dull life concluded with a dramatic death – which in all likelihood would occur immediately after I have left the confines of the airport. What a life I could lead, I thought, and serve my country to boot, even though I don't know if my country is worth it, when I saw an advertisement that the security services were looking for agents. I spent an entire evening revelling in the thought; me in a 'safe house' in Kabul, me crossing a desert or setting out to acquire contacts at a teahouse. But the one time I was in a desert, all I wanted to do was get out of there. It was grey, rocky, undifferentiated. And besides, I don't have a driving licence and only speak Western languages.

I wish someone would arrive and hand me a cause

and say, 'there you go, Kristian, now you have something to pursue,' and with those words, turn me in the right direction and send me off with a gentle nudge. In my mind the cause is practically swaddled in white. Oh, in reality it will be a tiny successor that is placed in my hands, but for that a woman is required, and then I am back to where I started.

Still May, still rubbish. I am developing an unhealthy preoccupation for rubbish, or is it a passion? In the morning – spread out across the large field (still Fælledparken) – there are magpies and crows and gulls; because the grass is so flat it resembles the sea. And the birds get so big. They are feasting on the rubbish from the evening's festivities and it unleashes morbid thoughts. Big city experience, it echoes inside me, and then I picture a dead duck upside down, buried in a slimy sickly gruel of rotten chestnuts and rubbish, down in Sortedams Sø; and a bottle with a wreath of feathers. Incidentally it is not called a nipper, but a snapper or a grabber. Both. The lawn cleaners are becoming my friends; I position myself in front of them and they patiently remove their headphones; each time I begin in more or less the same way: 'What a sty. Isn't it odd that people simply walk away from all of this? It's one of the first things you learn as a child, don't drop your ice cream wrapper...' And one of them says to me: 'With that attitude I'm sure your children won't be leaving their rubbish on the grass, unless they are very drunk.' And I don't know if I should say that they aren't born yet, the little Kristians who always take their disposable grills and empty bottles with them when they leave.

THE HOUSES AND THEIR BRILLIANT
SUICIDE VICTIMS

[Alma]

When the clouds drift across the range of hills, their shadows transform the land below: then the darkness runs through the grass.

We walk around up there for an entire day, at one point the path disappears, and Camilla walks in one direction in search of it, and I walk in the other. A moment later she is out of sight, and I sense how easily the enormous hills and the wind could swallow me up and do away with me; I am superfluous here, in this great landscape, a blot that the wind attempts to rub out.

This range of hills is called the South Downs, and they could be seen by Virginia Woolf from The Lodge, the small summerhouse where she wrote. Now the view is obstructed by trees.

> 'As for the beauty, as I always say when I walk the terrace after breakfast, too much for one pair of eyes. Enough to float a whole population in happiness, if only they would look.'
> — Virginia Woolf

'Why,' I ask the lodger at the house, whose task it is to tend the garden, 'were trees planted at the end of the garden, so that you can no longer see what Virginia Woolf saw?'

(That is why I am here. To see what she saw. Camilla is meant to have come with Charles. But he is ill. So I am here in his place. Camilla does not have a driving licence, and she cannot find her own way around.)

'Because the view is no longer the same,' the lodger

164

says, 'it's not attractive. It's marred by limestone quarries and the work that takes place around the quarries.'

She is immensely overweight. And I think about the discrimination overweight people are meant to be subjected to on the labour market; but is it really wise to have chosen such a heavy lodger? Doesn't she place unnecessary wear and tear on the place, shouldn't someone skinnier have been chosen? She and her husband live on the first floor of Monk's House. Meaning there is no access to it. Leonard Woolf had his bedroom on that floor. Now this giant walks around up there, perhaps the ceiling is cracking under her weight. The entire ground floor is a museum. Volunteers sit on a chair in each room and keep watch. A sign invites people to sign up for this task, knowledge of Woolf's works is not a prerequisite. I speak to the ageing custodian of the sitting room, he thinks that her books are lacking in plot, that nothing happens in them. I feel compelled to enlighten him and say that is how modern novels are, generally nothing much happens. He laughs and says something along the lines of 'well done'. He believes that first and foremost she was of significance to 'feminism'. Again I feel compelled to enlighten him and say that he is mistaken, she is one of the foremost literary innovators of the twentieth century.

'How so?' he asks, suddenly stern.

'By means,' I reply, 'of her...' I hesitate, should I mention how she condenses time so that a day becomes a lifetime? Should I mention the emphasis she places on the life of the consciousness and the exchange between the consciousness and the world, or how easy she makes time move both forward and backward? But it is her ability to compress and saturate that makes me happy. Where is Camilla? She would be able to answer.

'She liked to smoke cigars, at any rate,' he says pointing at a box on the mantelpiece.

The lodger has come down from the first floor to treat the custodians to coffee and cake. She stands holding an empty plate.

And it is true that there are some white surfaces visible, and a crane and maybe a couple of other machines operating in what was once Virginia Woolf's view, but are we not used to that these days, everywhere being so built up (back home in Denmark, at any rate), overlooking a windmill or a concrete pigsty whilst enjoying nature?

At a petrol station, in the newspaper rack, I saw something unforgettable. On the front page of what was probably *The Sun*, a young woman posing in suspenders and high heels. She stood with her backside in the air and was looking out between her legs. On each buttock was a rather large black beauty mark. Did the marks emphasize her buttocks? In that case, do the lime quarries not emphasize the hill? The lodger was still standing there, I could have mentioned it to her. (As time passes, and my trench coat gets increasingly tatty, I feel more and more like Columbo, seemingly naïve, but in reality with the upper hand.) Instead I said that it must be an enormous task to tend the large garden. And 'yes,' the lodger said, you really have to love gardening to take on such an assignment, and in addition both she and her husband had full-time jobs.

She must get incredibly winded when she has to bend down to do the weeding or reach for the pears.

In 1934 the Woolfs visited Shakespeare's house:

'That was where his study windows looked out when he wrote *The Tempest*,' said the man. And perhaps it was true. Anyhow it was a great big house, looking straight at the large windows and the grey stone of the school chapel, and when the clock struck, that was the sound Shakespeare heard. I cannot without more labour than my roadrunning mind can compass describe the queer impression of sunny impersonality. Yes, everything seemed to say, this was Shakespeare's, had he sat and walked; but you won't find me, not exactly in the flesh. He is serenely absent-present; both at once; radiating round one; yes; in the flowers, in the old hall, in the garden; but never to be pinned down. And we went to the church and there was the florid foolish bust, but what I had not reckoned for was the worn simple slab, turned the wrong way. Kind friend for Jesus' sake forbear – again he seemed to be all air and sun smiling serenely; and yet down there one foot from me lay the little bones that had spread over the world this vast illumination. Yes, and then we walked round the church and all is simple and a little worn; the river slipping past the stone wall, with a red breadth from some flowering tree, and the edge of the turf unspoilt, soft and green and muddy and two casual nonchalant swans. The church and the school and the house are all roomy spacious places, resonant, sunny today, and in and out [illegible word] – yes, an impressive place; still living, and then the little bones lying there, which have created: to think of writing *The Tempest* looking out on that garden: what a rage and storm of thought to have gone over any mind.

There is a church here as well, St Peter's Church; it is visible from the garden, old and grey, the fence surrounding it adjoins The Lodge; which would later turn out to be a source of great pleasure. Still I have not considered whether I could sense Virginia Woolf in the house and the garden – just as she senses Shakespeare. To believe that possible one would probably have to suppose that some kind of authorial spirit could be drawn from her works; an essence from her works that can be transferred to the house and retrieved there. At least when it comes to Shakespeare, whose biography is mere guesswork. For Virginia Woolf there are diaries, letters, photographs to construct a person out of – in addition to the spirit of these works.

More than anything, I have felt intrusive, an infringement on someone's privacy. I keep thinking of a spot in one of her diaries where a man stops his car outside the house and gets out and stares, and Leonard Woolf goes outside and says to him... something along the lines of: 'Kindly get in your car and leave. Mrs Woolf has no interest in this sort of attention.' And Virginia Woolf takes the opportunity to air her disdain for people intruding on her life like that man.

I am afraid she won't care for my kind of attention either, and that makes me feel ashamed. I was already beginning to be ashamed when we arrived at Rodmell (her village). We took up lodgings at a bed & breakfast 'a stone's throw from Monk's House'. And as soon as we had parked and dragged the luggage into the house, we set off in search of it. The village consists primarily of stone houses. But this one is made of wood and painted white. It has no front garden to speak of, but is smack up against the road (like a story without an introduction). It offers a feeling of intransigence, of not being welcome. I stood for a moment and pictured her slim figure (I could only conjure up a silhouette) hurrying down the narrow village street where she went for many a walk, and moved at a fast tempo.

168

Since I started to read her diaries, I have dreamt about her on two occasions. Dreams are seldom exciting, myself I always skip them in novels et cetera, whereas a rule they function as some kind of symbolic bonus material, but they don't do that here, they are sheer curios, and I will keep it brief:

Dream 1: Virginia Woolf, ageing, naked, she presses a moist sponge over her body and stands with one foot up on a stool.

Dream 2: Virginia Woolf and I are at a social gathering and we both agree to jump out the window. She does it straight away. I dare not. I run out the door and find her in a puddle. She is near death. I am told not to attempt to save her, because that would cause her limbs to dart about madly in the water, as if she had been subjected to an electric shock.

2 x water plus death. It probably points towards her death in water, in the River Ouse. I'll get to that.

The garden is large and consists of several sections, there is a large flower garden, ponds, a kitchen garden, an orchard, and a large lawn for bowling, something Virginia Woolf was obsessed with and used to play late into the afternoon. She was bad at losing. The large, wonderful garden makes me wistful. I'm only here for today. From her bedroom she stepped outside into that. She walked through it to reach The Lodge. It surrounded her when she wrote. She looked beyond it to the range of hills. Such a profusion of beauty to have access to, 'what a rage and storm of thought to have gone over any mind.'

The view from my desk (at home) is of the rubbish

bins in the courtyard and, thank heavens, a rather attractive yellow wall. That is the backdrop to my thoughts. Camilla urges me to nick a poppy head, 'because it would be funny to have a poppy from her garden back home.' (It would have to be kept in a flowerpot.) I do so, clandestinely, but a little later I realize that I have nicked the wrong part, I mean it was not a seed capsule.

There is no admittance to The Lodge. You can only look in through the window. Her desk is there, facing the range of hills, now hidden behind trees. Lying there are three portfolios in which she used to store loose sheets of paper, and writing implements, and her glasses. Organization and nakedness. I am not really content with merely looking inside, because the literature I hold most dear has come into existence there. For example, *The Waves*. And in there she made an entry in her diary only ten minutes before lunch:

> The idea has come to me that what I want now to do is
> to saturate every atom. I mean to eliminate all waste,
> deadness, superfluity: to give the moment whole; what-
> ever it includes. Say that the moment is a combination of
> thought; sensation; the voice of the sea. Waste, deadness,
> come from the inclusion of things that don't belong to the
> moment; this appalling narrative business of the realist:
> getting on from lunch to dinner: it is false, unreal, merely
> conventional. Why admit anything to literature that is not
> poetry – by which I mean saturated. Is that not my grudge
> against novelists? That they select nothing? The poets
> succeeding by simplifying: practically everything is left
> out. I want to put practically everything in: yet to saturate.
> That is what I want to do in *The Moths*. It must include non-
> sense, fact, sordidity: but made transparent.

Monk's House is only open to the public on Wednesday and Saturday afternoons. We have to continue our journey Saturday morning. But I have to see The Lodge one more time. First I decide to ring the bell at the lodger's and in my capacity as a writer who is contemplating writing about my visit, ask permission to gain access outside of opening hours, just to the garden. Earlier that day I spoke to a taxi driver who told me about a Japanese writer who succeeded (in gaining access outside of opening hours). Writers from around the world, join the queue. It is not that I somehow imagine that the spirit of Virginia Woolf will be more noticeable if there are no other visitors. I just have to see The Lodge again. It is the heart of this place, literature emerged from it. The Lodge moves me, just as the thought of Shakespeare's small bones moved Virginia Woolf. However there is a sign at Monk's House requesting that people respect the personal lives of the lodgers. Meaning I can't open the gate and ring the bell, I can't even see a door anywhere. Instead I would prefer to climb over the wall of the garden when it gets dark. I start to feel my way around the wall, it is, as mentioned, a large garden, a decent walk, which takes me across a field of cows, a cricket pitch and through the courtyard of the village school. All the while I see the range of hills (the view) out of the corner of my eye. My endeavours lead me to the churchyard, and from there I can stare across the stone wall and into the kitchen garden where earlier that day I nicked the wrong part of a poppy. I feel my way along the wall to the corner and walk under a large tree: From here I can look directly into The Lodge. It's night. I've brought Camilla.

She spends most of her time on the phone with Charles, first they argue, then they coo. It is going to be expensive. Camilla has got a terrible cough, at times she is close to choking, maybe it's false croup. When we are dining out, people move away from her, they are worried about swine flu, and Camilla coughs and waves her arms and coughs out: 'It's not the flu, it's not the flu.' I have suggested she get that printed on her T-shirt. She suggests to me that she might be coughing instead of crying (over Charles) however she does cry at times too. She is someone from whom there comes a lot of sound.

Someone (most likely the lodger) has lit a green bag-like lamp in The Lodge. It illuminates the desk and its objects. How should I (prosaic spirit) put it – yes, there is something magical about this green-lit room, seen from the corner of a churchyard at night, with my face pressed against the branches of the large fig tree that stands on the terrace in front of The Lodge, and which also stood there in Virginia Woolf's time. The absence of someone sitting in the chair behind the desk, the near awe-inspiring absence, evokes a kind of presence. (The soul, mine, requires deliverance, I cannot live with this suspense.) Virginia Woolf is not missing from the room. She is there. Finally she is there, an X-ray-like spirit emitting concentrates or saturation. Columbo discovered her even though the chair was empty.

Leonard and Virginia Woolf's urns are buried in the garden, beneath the elm trees that they named Leonard and Virginia, both of which have fallen. There is a plaque on a stone wall where each urn is buried. Leonard Woolf's speaks of justice and tolerance; hers bear the closing words from *The Waves*: 'Death is the enemy. Against you I will fling myself, unvanquished and unyielding, O Death! The waves broke on the shore.'

Death and water, again.

Suicide as a rebellion against death.

Camilla would like to see the place where Virginia Woolf walked into the river, and so we travelled there, to Southease. It was only a couple of kilometres from her house. It was an unassuming location she had chosen as a setting for her death. The River Ouse was narrow at that point, the sloping banks made it look like a dug-up ditch. The banks consisted of bleak brown stones. There was a bridge, exactly at that point; the bridge was supported by wooden structures – to avert collapse. She filled her pockets with rocks before she went out, in March 1941. The water must have been ice-cold. She had made another attempt a few days earlier. She came home soaking wet. Told Leonard that she had fallen in a ditch.

What does it mean to fling yourself at death unvanquished? That its essence has not penetrated you? What then is the essence of death? Abandonment and withering, resignation? Are you unvanquished if you choose it freely, death – not allow yourself to be overtaken by it? Fling yourself towards it. She flung herself towards it, she waded into it. A conclusion. And the waves broke on the shore – again and again and still today.

II.

[Alma]
And then on to Devon, it is a long drive, and it is not always easy having Camilla in the car, gasping whenever she thinks a dangerous situation is about to arise, it distracts me from driving. She is afraid of lorries, and she wants to get out and walk every time we approach a roundabout, and there are a lot of them (Charles told her they are the most difficult thing to navigate when you are not used to driving on the left.) But obviously she does not get out of the car. A constant stream of messages arrive on her mobile, she and Charles are arguing via text message this morning, to save money. 'FATIGUE KILLS / MAKE TIME FOR A BREAK' signs dot the side of the motorway, usually when nearing a service station. Every time Camilla urges me to stop. At one of the places there is a small group of protesters with a couple of dogs lying next to them, dogs that look like miniature horses, covered with blankets. Greyhounds. The people are protesting against dog racing. 'Why?' Camilla asks. She has always wanted to experience that type of race. 'Every year thousands of dogs disappear without a trace,' one of the protesters says. The dog at her side raises its pointed head, then it falls back into a heavy slumber. I wonder if it has been sedated. These two specimens must have been rescued. 'But what happens to the dogs?' While one demonstrator replies by running a finger across the throat, another simultaneously holds out the collection box. Camilla squeezes twenty pounds into the opening. She has a weak spot for animals, all animals.

It is evening by the time we arrive at our bed & breakfast

174

in North Tawton. We drive up to a white Georgian house, out scampers the landlord. He grabs Camilla's suitcase.

'We're here to visit Sylvia Plath's house,' she says dramatically.

The landlord tells us, he's afraid that won't be possible; Ted Hughes' second wife lives there now.

'Then we'll have to climb a tree and see it from there,' Camilla says, they have not even crossed the drive yet, 'you can see it from the churchyard,' he says. She doubles up from coughing and presses her thighs together.

We pass through a hall that ends at the foot of a staircase with red runners. An imperial staircase painted white: it runs along both sides of the hall, it is perfectly symmetrical, very beautiful, like in *Gone With the Wind*, a staircase made for corsets and ruffled petticoats, for great activity; one person can run up, another down. In the hall there is a distinguished-looking wooden rocking horse. Resting on some kind of runner. I touch it in passing, and it does not move up and down, but forward and back, at a smooth, well-oiled gait. Hanging on the wall is a photograph of Prince Charles surrounded by a smiling family, I recognize our landlord. First floor. Our room. What a view, green, green, green and fat grazing sheep. So fat that their cheeks quiver when they lift their head. Camilla sits down on the sofa and starts to make a phone call while the landlord and I drag the rest of the luggage up. We are halfway up the stairs for the second time when a furious scream is heard from the bedroom.

'Is there something we can do for Camilla?' the landlord asks. Now having an unbalanced person with swine flu staying in his home.

'I'll find a doctor tomorrow,' I say, 'it's not the flu.'

'It's not the flu,' Camilla says when we step inside with the luggage, and she raises her hands in the air as though she was about to be arrested. All the same, the landlord is wearing a mask when he serves us the next morning. His wife is not, 'she's the healthy type,' he says and gives her a quick and circumspect English hug. He has small feet and small hands and looks like a restrained version of Mr Bean. His wife is pale (yet composed), that same morning she was going to a meeting to discuss the erection of wind turbines that will obstruct their view. It would deprive them of guests. Wind turbines are loud. They are ugly. The energy cannot be stored as is the case with hydroelectric power (she is now speaking very warmly of Sweden). The battle is almost lost. But she will not surrender. I look at the long strokes of green outside the window, this English prairie with ample space. I imagine her exiting the hall on her steed, riding there with a fixed gaze and her sword drawn, ready to face the turbines in the battle against reflection and rotation.

Camilla is busy demonstrating that she is mentally stable and recuperating physically. She asks if she might enquire as to the occasion on which Prince Charles paid a visit to their home and was photographed with the family.

'It was back during the outbreak of mad cow disease. He visited some of the hardest hit families in the region. And then it was decided that he would have tea with us, and that it was safe here, that we were not the types who would consider blowing him up.'

'Oh.'

'Oh, yes.'

And what about the horse – in the hall?

It is a made-to-order rocking horse, from a factory

in Dorset, you can choose the colour of the body, the mane, the forelock. It was originally a present for their riding-mad daughter, she had long since outgrown the rocking horse. (We never see her, but at one point the son passes through the dining hall, all bent-over and transparent from puberty. The cat exists only as a meow from the kitchen, a ball under the chair.) On behalf of their daughter, they had chosen brown for the body and black for the mane and tail. Very horse-like. And the long mane bears a resemblance to the Dartmoor ponies out on the heath, their long manes. The dining hall also serves as a concert hall. There is an organ, a harp, and a piano. The entire family plays, maybe they also played for Prince Charles that afternoon; in the photograph Prince Charles looks startled, the landlord fawning, the wife happy, the children empty and blank. The family organizes concerts, invites famous musicians, everyone in the region flocks there, people drive all the way from London. They fill the large house with music. We have taken up residence in a cultural hub, in the midst of all that green. Where it rains three hundred days a year – 'that is, out on the heath,' the landlady says.

I am exhausted. Camilla's coughing is keeping me up at night. I give her a sleeping pill every night, in the hope that she will sleep through the coughing (Camilla loves sleeping pills, but her doctor keeps her on a short leash), she washes them down with her opium cough syrup. But nothing helps. I feel like putting a lid on her. I suspect that the sleeping pills are making her unbalanced. One minute she is crying, the next laughing. Soon I'll be needing a holiday – from her. When we get home, I will take a good long break. No pills for her tonight.

'Excuse me, could you please tell us which house is

Sylvia Plath's?' I ask a man outside the church, because the churchyard is surrounded by houses.

'Well, it's not exactly Sylvia Plath's house. It belongs to Ted Hughes' second wife.'

'I mean the house that Sylvia Plath lived in for a time,' I say diplomatically. And then he is happy to help. (I meant her house in – let's call it a 'spiritual sense'. She has been dead for forty-six years. She only lived there for sixteen months, from 1961 to 1962.)

As far as I recall, Ted Hughes' second wife also took her own life, in the same way Sylvia Plath did, using gas. Actually it must be his third wife who lives in the house. But I don't dare ask the man about that. I later find out that number two was merely his cohabiter, they were never married, so she does not count.

The house is white and surrounded by a brand-new lath fence. Perhaps Ted Hughes' widow is sitting inside the house observing us through a pair of binoculars, or through the sight of a handgun, exhausted from the hordes of pilgrims flocking to her house. We can glimpse the house both from the churchyard and from the road. I did not realize I was a voyeur, I think a moment later, when I am again pressed against a tree in a churchyard, squirming to catch a glimpse of a house and a garden. And why do I do that? What am I looking for? Before we departed, the idea of it almost seemed unpleasant to me...

I have to stick with it: the idea of trying to see what she saw. At any rate, standing in the churchyard is the yew tree (it may be) that Ted Hughes challenged Sylvia Plath to write a poem about (they assigned each other such tasks at times). The tree was visible from Sylvia Plath's bedroom, and according to Ted Hughes it is west of the house. But I have no compass, and the sun is not setting.

On the contrary, it is morning. Her poem depressed Ted
Hughes, he found it far too bleak:

THE MOON AND THE YEW TREE

This is the light of the mind, cold and planetary
The trees of the mind are black. The light is blue.
The grasses unload their griefs on my feet as if
    I were God
Prickling my ankles and murmuring of their humility
Fumy, spiritous mists inhabit this place.
Separated from my house by a row of headstones.
I simply cannot see where there is to get to.

The moon is no door. It is a face in its own right,
White as a knuckle and terribly upset.
It drags the sea after it like a dark crime; it is quiet
With the O-gape of complete despair. I live here.
Twice on Sunday, the bells startle the sky –
Eight great tongues affirming the Resurrection
At the end, they soberly bong out their names.

The yew tree points up, it has a Gothic shape.
The eyes lift after it and find the moon.
The moon is my mother. She is not sweet like Mary.
Her blue garments unloose small bats and owls.
How I would like to believe in tenderness –
The face of the effigy, gentled by candles,
Bending, on me in particular, its mild eyes.

I have fallen a long way. Clouds are flowering
Blue and mystical over the face of the stars
Inside the church, the saints will all be blue,
Floating on their delicate feet over the cold pews,

Their hands and faces stiff with holiness.
The moon sees nothing of this. She is bald and wild.
And the message of the yew tree is blackness – blackness
    and silence.

It is Sunday, and the bells are bonging today as well, an infinitely long chiming that is initially beautiful and then nerve-racking as it sounds again and again. The chiming is not solely to blame – music has that effect on me, all music, it quickly gets annoying, as though someone was grabbing my soul with their fingers. I generally prefer to be able to listen to my thoughts undisturbed, no matter how unpleasant they may be. While we stand among the chiming, in the churchyard, by the yew tree, Camilla tells me about a carillonneur at the Church of Our Saviour that created the most wonderful compositions, except when she was too stoned, which was clear from the ringing of the bells. (I imagine she might have been content with only a few notes in that case, however she drew them out into infinity, like chanting monks: Oooom – if that is possible with bells.) But it was not like that, Camilla says, there was talk of particular discordant patterns, for the local residents it was as though a mosaic roof was jingling down on them.

The house is large. The garden is large. Labour-intensive. That much I can see. And just as with Virginia Woolf, a churchyard neighbours the house, death practically a part of the garden. Here Sylvia Plath walked around and attempted to be the perfect housewife and mother in the model of the 1950s woman while writing *The Bell Jar*, and while writing her poems. Here she was abandoned to be a single mum with two children and wrote some of her best poems from four o'clock in the morning until the infant ('the fat jug,' that is what she lovingly calls him in one poem) woke up around six. Everything is possible when you get up early, but perhaps exhaustion leads to death.

'That is the socio-feminist approach,' Camilla says.

'What do you think?' I ask, 'what is the answer to the riddle of her suicide?'

'I think that the loss of the husband reactivated the loss of the father. And I believe what she wrote in a poem, that there has to be a death every tenth year – and according to her personal mythology it was time: her father died when she was eight, her first suicide attempt was at the age of twenty, and the last one, which was successful, when she was thirty. Ten-twenty-thirty.'

If I count correctly, she wrote twenty-four poems in October 1962 alone. She was abandoned the previous month. And took her own life in February 1963.

In her zeal to be a good housewife she even decided that she wanted to make her own honey. (That was before she was on her own.) Everything had to be homemade. But maybe she also wanted to keep bees because they paved the way back in time, to her father. He was an entomologist and published a book about the lives of bees.

We distance ourselves from the house, we can barely see anything.

The bells are still ringing when we step inside the local Spar to buy some cheese. Camilla enforces a strict budget, I don't get enough to eat; she holds the purse strings; she feeds me in exchange for my driving. My financial situation is rather fuzzy at the moment. But maybe it won't hurt to return home a few kilos lighter.

181

Camilla agrees. We eat in our room, something the landlord clearly does not like – he has given us a list of the local eateries – and we smuggle the rubbish out each morning.

At Spar an older man becomes erotically infatuated with Camilla, in the bread section. With my hands behind my back, I politely wait for a brief interlude in their conversation about fibre, then I jump in and ask whether the village has considered honouring Sylvia Plath in some way – perhaps a small location named after her? A bust? Alarmed, he looks in the direction of the home of Ted Hughes' second wife, and says that would display a lack of consideration for her. The second. As recently as the other day there was something on the radio about Sylvia Plath, and it is terribly unpleasant for the second wife to be constantly reminded of the first. Besides, Sylvia Plath did not live there very long, and she was apparently rather reserved: 'She probably wasn't one to go out for a drink with the boys or talk to the local fishermen.'

THE BEE MEETING

Who are these people at the bridge to meet me?
They are the villagers –
The rector, the midwife, the sexton, the agent for
    bees.
In my sleeveless summery dress I have no
    protection,
And they are all gloved and covered, why did
    nobody tell me?
They are smiling and taking out veils tacked to
    ancient hats.

I am nude as a chicken neck, does nobody love me?

Yes, here is the secretary of bees with her white shop smock,

Buttoning the cuffs at my wrists and the slit from my neck to my knees.

Now I am milkweed silk, the bees will not notice.

They will not smell my fear, my fear, my fear.

Which is the rector now, is it that man in black?

Which is the midwife, is that her blue coat?

Everybody is nodding a square black head, they are knights in visors,

Breastplates of cheesecloth knotted under the armpits.

Their smiles and their voices are changing. I am led through a beanfield.

Strips of tinfoil winking like people,

Feather dusters fanning their hands in a sea of bean flowers,

Creamy bean flowers with black eyes and leaves like bored hearts.

Is it blood clots the tendrils are dragging up that string?

No, no, it is scarlet flowers that will one day be edible.

Now they are giving me a fashionable white straw Italian hat

And a black veil that moulds to my face, they are making me one of them.

They are leading me to the shorn grove, the circle of hives.

Is it the hawthorn that smells so sick?

The barren body of hawthorn, etherizing its
    children.

Is it some operation that is taking place?
It is the surgeon my neighbours are waiting for,
This apparition in a green helmet,
Shining gloves and white suit.
Is it the butcher, the grocer, the postman, someone I
    know?

I cannot run, I am rooted, and the gorse hurts me
With its yellow purses, its spiky armoury.
I could not run without having to run forever.
The white hive is snug as a virgin,
Sealing off her brood cells, her honey, and quietly
    humming.

Smoke rolls and scarves in the grove.
The mind of the hive thinks this is the end of
    everything.
Here they come, the outriders, on their hysterical
    elastics.
If I stand very still, they will think I am
    cow-parsley,
A gullible head untouched by their animosity,

Not even nodding, a personage in a hedgerow.
The villagers open the chambers, they are hunting
    the queen.
Is she hiding, is she eating honey? She is very
    clever.
She is old, old, old, she must live another year, and
    she knows it.
While in their fingerjoint cells the new virgins

Dream of a duel they will win inevitably,
A curtain of wax dividing them from the bride
    flight,
The upflight of the murderess into a heaven that
    loves her.
The villagers are moving the virgins, there will be
    no killing.
The old queen does not show herself, is she so
    ungrateful?

I am exhausted, I am exhausted –
Pillar of white in a blackout of knives.
I am the magician's girl who does not flinch.
The villagers are untying their disguises, they are
    shaking hands.
Whose is that long white box in the grove, what have
    they accomplished, why am I cold.

                             3 October 1962

English pub food is sticky as beeswax, these pies, half dissolved bread bowls with their contents heated past the pain threshold, straight from the oven, served in oven-proof dishes, and before that directly from the freezer, and before that straight from the production line, for example eel and ale pie, I can make Alma moan nau-seatingly just by saying it. And for dessert, a flat cake with thousands of raisins, popularly known as 'flies' graveyard'. Not a meal to raise your spirits – but rather to completely rid you of them, the spirit escapes the flac-cid, overfed body during a hiccup. We have stopped in Lyme Regis on our way home. We have just consumed this spirit-sapping meal outdoors, with a view of the pier where the French lieutenant's woman (in the book, in the film of the same name) stood and kept an eye out for her French sailor. Meryl Streep, dressed in black, ostracized because of this romance, every day waiting for a ship, come back come back, but did he really exist? Or had she made him up to give her dreary life a focal point. I don't remember. In any case a child was born – and christened Lalage, which means 'babbling brook' and is well suited to the sounds of the early years. In front of us the fish and chips social class is wading in the bay with rolled-up trousers. One had 'fuck' tattooed across his back. Several have dyed their hair colourless. A couple of tables away an overweight teenager hits his dad because he is not allowed to have two courses. He holds the menu in front of his face in defence. But no more blows come. The teenager knocks over his chair and walks down to the beach, into the sea. The beach is white, the slopes black. The waiter has a jagged scar across the throat. We could also visit John Fowles' house, he made the city famous with his French lieutenant's woman, but we are content with staring at the pier. And the waders there, presumably force-fed on low quality from the moment they opened their eyes, seem to enjoy the water in spite of everything. A social dystopia, does it not sound like constipation? The pier where she stood wishing for something magnificent – where tragedy was better than having a tedious life with no drama.

CHARLES REVISITED

[Camilla]

'How,' Charles asks, 'did you end up in the company of hippies?'

He rarely asks about my biography, we have known each other for a long time; I get all excited in my chair by the bed. (Usually we talk about the pain. Is it dull. Or wild, raw and ferocious. Like walking across a frozen field with sleet on your face, no visibility, the heart dreary, that is what I think when he says: Today it is raw and ferocious.)

First Charles missed out on the spring, then he missed out on the summer. He is lying on a mattress by the window and looking up at the sky. The other day when I went to go for a stroll in Østre Anlæg, he said: 'I'm going for a walk in the heavens.'

Now it is autumn, and he is still lying there. The crowns of the rowan trees are teeming with orange berries. And in the soft light, dust disappears, and wrinkles fade, oh yes, in part. He talks about the future, when he will be able to get out of the bed and walk around again. Then he will miss his windowsill. The windowsill is his actual view, more important than the little he can see of the sky and the rowan tree out on the street. Let me start by describing his view from the left of the windowsill, furthest out is a paradise tree, 'that must be the Christian section,' Charles says, there is also an orchid, so the Garden of Eden is somewhat fleshy. And goodness me if that isn't an apple lying there today. In the middle, India is represented by Ganesh and his rat as well as a vase from Punjab, then comes Africa, the desert, a number of small windswept palms arranged in a group, as though together they could better withstand the storm.

I was led there, to Torremolinos, which still had a rather hippy feel to it, by an Englishman I had met, his name was Tim, Tim King, but since Charles and I no longer talk about previous relationships (we got through that long ago), I say that I would rather tell him about how I made it back from there. We had a falling out, Tim and I, because I did not want to sew a patch on a pair of his jeans that practically consisted only of patches, which he was proud of. The jeans can be compared to one of these big brown adventure suitcases with corner reinforcements that used to appear on the baggage carousel at the airport, and maybe still do, plastered with stickers from various destinations, so you could not help but realize that the owner was a globetrotter, that he or she was constantly trotting across the globe; the jeans too had travelled far and wide, and it was their advanced age, everything they had gone through, in the hot south and in the far north, that he was so proud of, the trousers were an embodiment of his travels, and the frugality he exhibited in order to afford these travels, which was his way of distancing himself from his English lower class background, better to travel than to stand in a factory (though I did not understand that back then, I just thought, increasingly annoyed, that his journeys would later enable him to comment and pass sentence on cities and countries in subordinate clauses, and how painful was it when he lectured me about Christiania) and had I not on one particular occasion, at a cheap Italian restaurant in Torremolinos, infuriated him by asking him what he felt like drinking, 'What do I feel like drinking?' he repeated, with growing agitation, obviously we're both having tap water, how could you think I would be part of such extravagance, he raged, while I sipped from the chalice of shame, a glass of house white. The factory.

The East End. When his money dried up, he returned home to London and for a number of months worked at a factory where he sat at a machine and sewed logos onto sweatshirts in the middle of the night, for example *Genesis in concert* God-knows-what-year on black, blue and red sweatshirts, I had worked there too, but only for a few weeks, where my job was, using a small sharp object, to remove the tacking thread around *Genesis in concert* et cetera. I have never been good with my hands, I could not keep up the pace, the sweatshirts piled up around me (one time I accidentally poked a hole in one, which was diligently deducted from my wages, paid out in the morning, after a completed shift, payment in cash), though I was better rewarded than the Indian workers on the night crew, something I found impossible to accept, but there was nothing to be done about it. The Indians smiled, they were gentle and shrugged their shoulders. They wanted (obviously) to keep their jobs. Probably because I was so slow and practically a guest on the crew, I was often sent to collect food, I left a little before the break, from an Indian restaurant that was open around the clock, around three, at any rate I cut across a deserted construction site, it was January, pitch black, and with my heart in my mouth and a firm grip on my scout knife, relieved to get away from the pile of sweatshirts, and picked up vegetable curries in small foil containers that could not have been sealed properly, because when I returned, they were always greasy and yellow on the outside, and I don't think I have ever tasted better Indian food, not even now when I have an Indian friend and have it homemade, she is the one who contributed to the windowsill with the vase from Punjab. Maybe the odyssey across the construction site added something to the food.

189

In Tim's bedsit, you had to insert coins to get the gas oven to work, ditto the water heater in the bathroom – but I never learnt how to get hot water from the water heater, all I managed to coax out of it was coughing and a loud banging, and on one occasion a proper discharge of soot. The fireplace (in the room) no longer worked, but someone (a poetic soul, perhaps him) had covered it with aluminium foil and placed a bunch of tea lights inside, and when we lit them (when we got home from the factory in the morning) the fireplace was transformed into a deep silver cave. ('When we got home from the factory in the morning,' had such a romantic ring to my middle-class ears – even though time dragged when I was there – and I used that very expression in a letter to Alma.) And on the mattress, in front of the candles, we came to realize, again and again, what we wanted from each other, and that we wanted it to last, preferably for ever. At times we sat up and grabbed hold of one another, our eyes filled with tears of joy, and to recover a little before we were again swept away 'by the river of flesh', you might say. Several times a day he toasted hash over a tea light, and after he had smoked it, he began to pluck at his guitar. Charles is the only man I have met whom I have not had to listen to play the guitar. To appreciate Tim's guitar playing required a lot of love. And even though I did not enjoy smoking – it usually made me ill at ease, a receptacle of self-reproach – I continued until Tim was out of the picture. I thought about it the other day when Edward said: 'Whenever I start something, I keep with it. If I killed someone, I would become a serial killer.' I had just turned nineteen, and Tim was twenty-one. He kept his clothes in a rucksack. He had no fridge and bought only a little food at a time, but there must have been a table where the food was kept. The walls were almond-green. It seems to me now that he lived a valiant life. His notion of the future did not differ from his present, he wanted to travel for all eternity, and I imagined him (with concern) as a fifty-year-old, as a sixty-year-old, a faded man unrolling his sleeping bag on the ground; whereas I was simply taking a break between school and university, a guest in his life, and he was a guest in mine, disparaging all my education, himself a student at the school of life (when he said that, I looked down and nodded) and here, on the chair, in the living room, I truly hope that he has survived; and here, on the chair, in the living room, I think that we grabbed hold of one another so firmly, in front of the silver cave, because we knew that we would soon go our separate ways. His father had a criminal record, a small hairy man with a lot of jangling gold: chains, bracelets, rings and a sports car. His mother had been a model in her younger days and dated Tommy Steele, she was still blonde and still luscious and ran a fish and chip shop in Brighton with her new husband, who was dark and equally luscious; she made shepherd's pie for us and told me that she could not be alone in the house, then Tim could not endure her any longer and we left. When I went with him to visit his dad, who looked like a mafioso, he (his dad) took pleasure in ordering me around and equal pleasure in my refusal to obey. Maybe I made him a cup of tea when he asked. But I did not tidy up. I did not pick up his dirty clothes. I remained stubbornly seated while he practised his cockney, sitting in his leather sofa, the coffee table in smoked glass, and lying in front of him at all times, that's how I remember it, drawings of furniture that he had thought up (it was unlikely that he had drawn them himself), which consisted of large blocks, and since his surname was

King, these furniture building blocks were called King's Cubes, and the idea was, like Lego, that people could re-build their furniture according to taste, I don't know if the blocks ever went into production. One time we, Tim and I, were alone at his dad's place and wanted to watch a film, but there was already one in the player, and instead of taking it out straight away, Tim pressed the start button, and a couple came into view, bleeding to death, all the while using their last ounce of strength (literally) to engage in blood-curdling intercourse, outdoors, in a smoky and desolate landscape. It made my stomach turn; Tim swore and decided he could not endure his father a moment longer, it was time to leave the country, again. Four months later, though he looked like an angel with his long blond hair and his perfect nose, he threw his precious jeans at my head, on a beach in southern Spain, and then the mending kit, and I got up and left, trembling with rage. I went into a café, a little later I saw Tim standing outside, he was obviously looking for me, and I ducked until he was gone. I counted my traveller's cheques, I did not have enough for a train ticket home, so I would have to hitchhike, that was after all that we had done over the previous months, you would have thought I had learnt how to do that, at the school of life. And I wanted to set off now, straight away, the first road sign I saw was for Lisbon, so I headed in that direction. And that very evening I rode into Lisbon as a conqueror, on the back of a lorry, windswept, armed with a supply of tortillas wrapped in aluminium foil from the family in the cab; the children leaned out the window and waved at me, the sun was sinking, and driving through the suburbs, with the stench of exhaust, outside under the blood-red sky, with my foundered love behind me, I believe I felt 'the nerve fibres of life quivering in my hands'

– in other words, that I had situated myself as near as possible to the course of events.

Now Charles is asking if I then went to Copenhagen. I did not, I told myself that I would remain in Spain and Portugal for a time and muster the courage for the long journey home, because I was scared, each morning when I stood on the roadside, I was terrified of being cut into tiny pieces. Men. If there was more than one, I refused their offer of a ride. I remember three happy men in a car, laughing loudly, in a convertible with the top down, they continued driving next to me for some time, I walked along the side of the road, I had turned them down, they laughed more and more and licked their lips like dogs and shouted that I had probably made a wise decision, then drove off, I started to laugh as well, and I waved at them, because clearly we were all in on the brilliant joke that if I had got into their car, they would have maltreated me all the while splitting their sides with laughter. There were the restrained ones, who warned me against the unrestrained ones while placing a hand on my thigh. There were also the genuinely restrained ones, who kept their hands on the steering wheel. There were the pragmatists, who stopped and offered to drive me wherever I wanted in exchange for sex, then drove off as soon as I said no. No women stopped, which I thought displayed a lack of solidarity. Then I met up with a man who looked like Alma's grandfather, an upright man of the old school, wearing a faded green corduroy jacket. He wanted to take me with him to Morocco, as his secretary, but I did not want to travel any further away from Copenhagen. We drove around for twelve hours, at the bottom of Spain and Portugal, we ate a number of meals at nice restaurants where he embarked on lengthy attempts to persuade me – about Morocco, about me and him. Every time we went to a restaurant, he tried to comb my hair with his black comb, like I was Granddad's little girl. Seeing as he was so old, I considered myself to be on firm ground. I could just as well remain in his car. After all I was not headed anywhere in particular. His hair was black, so maybe he was not that old after all. Late that evening he stopped the car at a lay-by and tried to kiss me. I slapped him as hard as I could and jumped out of the car. My rucksack was in the boot. I waited for a long while. He sat with his face in his hands, finally the boot opened, and I grabbed my rucksack and left. The road was dark. I walked on the shoulder. I wished I had had a torch so the cars could see me. It was properly dark, there were cicadas singing, it was a relief to be out in the open. I thought of both the car and the man with the comb as something sticky. I must have walked a couple of kilometres when I saw light. A lot of light, like an amusement park. It was a hotel. I trudged into the reception and asked how much a room cost. Far too much. So I had to return to the dark road. I was afraid of getting run over. When I stood outside, an Englishman came over and told me that he had noticed how disappointed I looked; he wanted to help. I could spend the night in his bungalow. He looked like Marty Feldman (1934-1982), I really liked him when I was a child. Google him, Charles, then you'll see how he died! His death was right out of one of his comedies. I went with him. It was midnight. While I, in the bathroom, was putting on my light-blue tracksuit (cotton) that hung from my body like elephant skin, he was having an overwrought conversation with his wife. I had lost ten kilos, thanks to the school of life. (The next time we went to see Tim's dad in the East End – Tim and I had been reunited – he said: 'The last time I saw you, you were a fat little girl, now you're beautiful,' and he invited his mafia friends round to see me, finally displaying a little pride in his son, but I locked myself in the toilet until they had left.) I even put a cap on. And a pair of woollen socks. I stuck my scout knife in the waistband and hoped it would not slip down one of the trouser legs. Shrouded in that way, I stepped out. A person wrapped up like that, there was no way he would think I wanted something from him, in the double bed. Before I could allow myself to sleep, I had to thoroughly check out the bungalow, both inside and outside, where there was a natural pond with a grotto to match; he was put out by the splendour of the place and wanted me to be too. So I was. I thought he had mentioned something about wanting to order food, but nothing came of it. We climbed into bed. I moved all the way to the edge and crossed my arms over my chest.

'And then what happened?'

'Nothing. We slept. And in the morning we ate breakfast on the bed. He asked whether I would like to wake up in such lovely surroundings every morning – instead of sleeping on the beach. But sleeping on the beach is adventurous, I said, and then repeated all the things Tim used to say when I complained about the cold and the dank sand. He asked whether it would also be adventurous to make love, right now? That would be adventurous, I replied, but I did not fancy it. He put the tray down and cupped his hand around my breast and said: "Just the right size."

I leapt off the bed, my trousers slipped down around my ankles and the knife landed on the floor. "Imagine, I slept in the same bed as someone who carries a knife," he said, exhilarated. At least I got to try the pool before I left. A little later when I stood by the road I realized that I was only twenty kilometres from Torremolinos. And the first person I met when I arrived in town was Tim. I had been gone for exactly one week. He had been beside himself with worry and for that reason he was gentle as a lamb for a long time.'

'So did you ever get out of there?'

'Yes, but then I went back again.'

Charles looks expectant, and a little disappointed. But I am not Scheherazade. I just enjoyed being on my own that week, that something happened, that I managed on my own.

'Here is a slice of autumn,' I said to Charles later that day, and handed him a red leaf. He stuck it in the pot with the paradise tree to support it. Yes, then it could be a fig leaf, in the Christian section. The sky reveals how cold it has become. The sunset looks like a piece of architecture, the purple and red colours appear to have been forged. And Charles's body is in ruins, 'I'm split down the middle,' he says, 'I don't know how I'm ever going to get out of here.'

'Here' meaning the bed. I am used to 'here' meaning the world. I hear the elderly members of my family say: 'I long to get out of here,' meaning they want to escape this world. For that reason a brief clash occurs within me when Charles uses that turn of phrase.

Charles's body is only in ruins internally. On the outside there is nothing to see. Just before, a moment ago, he called me from the bathroom: 'Come and look at me.'

I wanted to look at him. Most of the time he is under the duvet.

'Look, I look like myself,' he said, 'don't I look like myself?'

I went over to him, into the shower, through the water

in my stocking feet. I delicately embraced him then stepped back and looked at him again, and here it ends, in the shower, as my cheeks get wet – all the time that has passed, such a huge part of our lives, without being able to open the folding doors of our bodies and enter one another.

A THEATRE OF SOULS *or* THE ENTIRE PARTY

[Camilla, Alma, Alwilda, Edward, Charles and Kristian]
'Oh, I wish that today the world would present its best side, now that Charles is finally going out into it. The world is a large tray that I hold out to him. The world is my invention. For a long time I have brought objects from it into the living room for him, a red leaf, a black feather. And then there is the tree. And there perches the bird,' Camilla says.

'The eggs are too big,' Edward says, cupping his balls in his hand (his temperature was nearing forty-one degrees, he was delirious), 'they have to be trimmed / with a cheese slicer.'

'I am drowning in the night. I am trying to find good things to get me through the despairing hours between one and five,' Camilla says, 'my soul feels hard and full of bumps, like a runway that is impossible to land on. So I am circling above myself. I can't descent and take hold.'

'Promise me that if I die, Camilla will not get the dog.'

'I walked today. I sucked in my upper abdomen, as I was taught, to engage my inner corset,' Charles says.

'Today Charles and I walked down the street together, for the first time in an entire year, I had thought he would walk hunched over, like an old man. But he was straight as a tin soldier,' Camilla says.

'No, that was no geriatric patrol,' Alma says, 'I saw the two of you arrive.'

'The scar on his back from the operation – doesn't it look like a piece of laced-up pork?' Alma asks.

'Not at all. It looks like a ladder.'

'Death, I don't give it a second thought,' says Charles.

'But you wear your heart on your sleeve.'

198

'Nor do I,' Alwilda says to Charles.

'And I held my head high,' says Charles.

'I'm not walking towards the red trees – they're the ones that move. They move forward and into me like peacekeepers,' Camilla says.

'From the glossary of therapists, the word I am most tired of is "accommodate" – two people standing opposite one another and screaming: accommodate me, accommodate me,' Edward says.

'You're forgetting about society,' Alwilda says, 'you're only thinking of yourselves.'

'I always buy a magazine from the homeless,' Kristian says.

'Nor in all decency can you do otherwise. When you come out of the department store barely able to carry all of your merchandise.'

'Couldn't we juuust squeeze the magazine in between two delicacies.'

'No, there's no bloody room for that today/then the bag will break.'

'Feel free to pick up anything I drop, it's yours.'

'I don't know if I'm dreaming,' says Edward, 'there's a husband and wife and a black Labrador. The woman looks at the Labrador, she says: I love you, and the dog's face bursts into joy, it leaps up and kisses her. Now the exact same thing is repeated, between the Labrador and the man.'

'How symmetrical,' Alwilda says, 'but I want to go to China, I want to eat an eight-metre-long noodle, anyone care to join me?'

'I'd rather go to Iraq,' Kristian says, 'I want to tempt fate. No, I want to travel through Afghanistan on the back of a donkey. Since our time here is so brief.'

'May I suggest a camel,' Alwilda says, 'and then I'll

join you.'

'Cut the heel and chop the toe, then into marriage you can go,' Alma says.

'When I have a child,' Alwilda says, 'I'll chase it up a tall tree every day.'

'You should have been alive back when time was one great mass and not chopped up into tiny little tickets, for example, 3 p.m., 4 September 2007,' Kristian says, 'I'm talking about the Stone Age, I think.'

'Then your time here would have been even shorter.'

'Afghanistan, go to Afghanistan, that's the closest you'll get to the Stone Age.'

'I know what Kristian's final words will be.'

'So do I. *Da capo*, he'll say.'

'*Da capo*, he'll rattle.'

'We stick together like lyme grass.'

'But none of you like me.'

'I like you, Kristian.'

'We're pieces on a board game. In the end we'll all have stood on all the squares.'

'Let's take off our clothes and play Twister.'

'Who's going to disentangle us afterwards?'

'Kristian. He won't want to take part anyway.'

'I'm scared you'll accidentally push me,' says Charles, 'then I'll be split down the middle again.'

'You're wrong about that. Kristian is happy to take off his clothes.'

'O, hast thou a dog then heap ye praise on it,' Edward says.

'When you smile, it's like you're all teeth, Camilla,' Edward says.

'To fall asleep and wake up as easily as an animal.'

'I feel like a broiler hen on a hook, that accidentally ...' Charles stops short.

200

'Good morning, here's today's roll of tickets.'

'What do I do when the last leaf has fallen? When there's no more yellow or red remaining,' Camilla says.

'Five fruit flies flew through three fields, thirsty for free flower meals,' sings Edward.

'Then you just have to chug through all the withered leaves,' Alwilda says, 'it helps to shout Choo-choo.'

'What do we do with nature / it must teach us how to die.'

'Let's split up into two teams. Then we'll sing it in rounds. Wouldn't it sound almost Gregorian? The first line in treble, and the next in bass.'

'You can't sing. You know nothing of notes. To you, there is only high and low,' Kristian says.

'But I have a good sense of rhythm,' Alma says.

'I've been lying in bed for such a long time. The world passes like an express train. And I'm standing completely still,' says Charles.

'Do you want to hear what I'm dreaming about?'

'No.'

'I'm standing on an oil platform, far out at sea. I'm fishing. I've got a turtle on the hook. It's moving at a furious pace. Now I'm getting on a bus in order to catch it.'

'Edward, oh Edward, here's another blanket, you're shaking with fever.'

'Yes, the body is a fantastic factory.'

'Men like us need old-fashioned womanly care.'

'You're not feeding the dog chocolate, are you, Camilla?'

'It's my pleasure, I used to tie my grandfather's shoe-laces all the time. But when I'm lying here, I can see how dusty it is,' Alwilda says.

'I can't manage everything,' Camilla says.

'I went to see a psychologist,' Edward says, 'because

of all the loss I suffered, but it seemed immodest to air my thoughts to a complete stranger.'

'Tighter,' says Charles, and wriggles his foot.

RELOCATIONS

[Camilla]

I have two thoughts in the same breath, so to speak; the first, how often my mum moves house, and the second, about a scene at a bar near Death Valley.

My mum had moved again, she had bought a small yellow house on Orevej in Vordingborg, where she worked, I had travelled there to visit her and stood out in the garden whitewashing a wall in a muted yellow tone, my mum might have been gardening near me, or maybe she came up to me, in any case she said that she considered her stay in this house a temporary one, and that she would probably sell it on soon; I was infuriated and put the brush down, because working on the wall seemed pointless now. Why waste my energy on this place if she was only thinking of getting rid of it, and how many times had I already helped her move? A pylon rested its one heavy leg in the back garden, and her life in the house was accompanied by an unpleasant crackling; in itself reason enough to move, but of course she had seen the pylon when she had made up her mind to buy, so why had she even bought the house? The answer was, to quickly get away from where she lived, a so-called temporary solution, and moreover the garden was long, like her grandmother's garden had been, long – it had stirred up memories of afternoons under fruit trees, with a book, at the end of the garden, alone, free from meddling, free from human companionship, with a purring cat on the blanket with her. A paradise where you only had to raise your hand to pick a sweet-smelling apple, a yellowish pear, where the fruits let go of the branch on their own accord and dropped onto the blanket for you. But towering at the end of this garden was the pylon; and then towering behind the pylon was the sea, practically lapping at the other leg of the pylon where it rested on the shore. At night we went swimming, or perhaps it was only one night, when a childhood friend of my mum's had popped by, unannounced, and I had produced an exceptionally successful dinner of fried plaice, golden-brown and crisp all over, and said something bizarre to him, he was a botanist, that I did not realize that hyacinth grew wild, I thought it was a cultivated plant, a child of the greenhouse so to speak, and it had evoked great surprise in him, it almost looked as though he had smelt something foul when I had the misfortune to say that, god knows how we ended up talking about hyacinths, in the middle of the summer? (For me that flower, still, is associated with Christmas.) In any case the three of us went for a long walk on the beach, after dinner, and my mum and I went swimming while he sat in the sand with his arms crossed. He had flirted with her for years when they were young, now I felt his gaze on me as I sunk into the waves and emerged from them again, wearing my orange swimsuit; my mum must have been fifty, and I was composed of long, taut muscles.

Prior to that (buying the small yellow house) she had lived in a large flat at the hospital where she worked in the old person psychiatry ward, the patients she called her 'geriatrics'. There was a nasty consultant psychiatrist who made life miserable for her, as well as for the geriatrics, and went hunting in Poland where he committed outright massacres, he brought home hundreds of bloody bodies, or maybe simply left them where they fell, in any case I had these monstrous figures passed on to me, boastfully recited over lunch, 119 ducks, 12 hares, and an equally astronomical number of wild geese, put to death by this man alone, in one weekend; it sounded like a distorted unabashed echo of Valdemar IV: '77 chickens and 77 geese is nothing,' he is alleged to have said when he had the Goose Tower constructed in Vordingborg and placed the golden goose at the top of the tower to mock the 77 war declarations he had received from the Hanseatic towns. (At one time Alwilda had a boyfriend who was a hunter and came home and plonked bloody heaps on the kitchen counter, as a gift to her, 'here you go – haven't I been a clever boy,' and suddenly the smitten vegetarian Alwilda found herself in a cloud of feathers that clung to her reddened hands. It was strange to watch her climb out of an oversized four-wheel-drive with two baying hounds at the very back throwing themselves against the grille. I did not much feel like seeing her during that period. But she said it was because he was well-off, and he always closed his eyes when he fired the gun, or whatever it's called. He felt he was obliged to, to go hunting, his income required it, or his social class.)

The flat was situated above some offices. It was newly renovated when she moved in and reeked of varnish, maybe the floors above and below her were also being renovated, because the stench of varnish seemed to linger everywhere. This glistening railing, the large slippery floors, made me think back to the corridors at Stege Hospital, where I lived for a year, before I started school, in a hospital flat, with my mum; she worked at the A&E, and my hypersensitivity to emergency vehicles stems from this time, since the sound of an ambulance usually meant that she had to grab her white coat and run, and I was left in the care of a young girl who preferred giggling with her girlfriend over having anything to do with me. Of the accidents (at the A&E) I only remember a young boy who had worked as a beater, but had been mistaken for game and came in filled with shotgun pellets, which my mum picked out, with tweezers I presume, and I imagined a hail of small metal pieces drumming against the bottom of a metal bowl; I used to slide down the corridors in stockinged feet shouting and at full speed until I was reprimanded by a lady in a blue coat, wherever she came from, probably from somewhere in the kitchen. My mum's coats were starched, and I could not get enough of the breast pocket where a couple of pens were fastened, and a pair of forceps, it was unusual having a pocket with the contents hanging on the outside. One day around lunchtime my immature red cat (separated from its mother too early; and here it could be claimed that if you do not get enough mum time, you apparently remain a child; in any case the cat spent the rest of its days waiting for a sleeping person to have the misfortune to poke a toe out from under the duvet or setting up an ambush behind doors and leaping out at passers-by, until it died tragically – it got too close to a farmer who had been out catching eels and was cleaning them, and the farmer poked a pitchfork into its abdomen, and the cat came home with its intestines dangling behind it) – jumped out the window of our second floor flat, just jumped. It landed in front of the mental patients, who walked in a long chugging row, like they were linked together, carrying or pushing trolleys that resembled milk cans, which I suspect were filled with scalding hot soup, a heavy yellow liquid. The cat falling from the sky made them stop for a moment. They were wearing identical greyish-brown coats and trousers, the mental patients wore uniforms. I saw it all from the window. I waited to fetch the cat until they had disappeared down a basement staircase and were inside the building.

206

On the grounds, a strangely straightforward word, which my mum always uses about the area around a hospital, which for her is connected with a feeling of freedom and rest when she moves across it, on the way from one ward to another (her sense of direction is not well developed, she always chooses the grounds over the shorter route through the hospital's underground system of corridors, if there is such a thing), on the grounds around Oringe you could meet a long-term Greenlandic patient who had eaten his enemy's heart, or maybe only part of it, a titbit I learnt by overhearing a conversation, inadvertently. In one of the wards foundered a number of Faeroese patients, hospitalised twenty-thirty-forty years earlier, at a time when there was no possibility of receiving psychiatric treatment on the Faroe Islands, brutally torn from family and everything familiar, and placed here, for something approaching eternity. There had been a few instances of arson at the hospital, which had frightened my mum and been a contributing factor to her buying the small yellow house. To further underscore the 'fire theme'... after giving notice to terminate the lease, she had been paid a visit by a close friend who emptied the ashtray in the wastepaper basket and caused yet another fire, but this one was able to be extinguished under the tap. She moved out of the fire into the electricity, from crackling to crackling. And there were mice. One night she was awoken by a mouse crawling across her face. Where was the cat? She had taken on a cat from the previous owner of the house; agreeing to take the cat into the bargain (otherwise it would be put down), 'it jumped up on my shoulder and wrapped itself around my neck like a fur collar,' she told me, but its gratitude did not extend to keeping out the mice: and a mouse got stuck behind the cooker and died there, we could not get the cooker to budge (as though riveted to the spot), so my mum poured a couple of bottles of vinegar into the gap between the wall and the cooker in the hope of easing the smell, and perhaps also to accelerate the process of decay, she explains the chemical process to me in the midst of her jostling, but the potent smell of Christmas (red cabbage and pork roast) rose up from the gap and made her want to move even more, she hates odours, and this was desperate. The house of the unfortunate animals, ignoring the cat 'like a fur collar' and so on... one morning there was a crash on the roof, and we raced out of the house, it was during one of my visits, and lying on the ground was a swan and a couple of roof tiles, it had crashed into the roof and had to be collected, hissing and bleeding, by a man from animal rescue wearing enormous leather gloves who placed a firm grip around the neck of the swan, right up by the head, 'so the chap doesn't bite,' and there was, not surprisingly, something erotic about the long white muscle that lived a life of its own between the gloves.

Not until my mum got cancer was I able to tolerate seeing laboratory animals on TV, mice endowed with tumours so large that they could barely walk, yes, I observed them out of pure cool interest. On the other hand I had a proper breakdown, lasting an entire afternoon, when Charles and I were at a bar near Death Valley, sitting at the bar, or rather hanging over the bar, our straw hats duly dangling from strings down our backs, exhausted from the heat, next to a terrarium, on the bar counter, where an inconsequential grey gerbil sat in a landscape that was a miniature copy of the desert landscape outside, nibbling on a piece of straw it held ever so delicately in its mouse hands (I wish I could say that the straw quivered in its hands, because something ought to have quivered, the mouse for example, out of fear; but total calm prevailed; and I seem to remember hearing that when animals are unable to react to impending danger, flight or fight, they often start to eat, or groom their fur, evidently to calm themselves), strange to keep mice, I managed to think, before I spotted the snake. The snake, also grey, was coiled up, staring at the mouse, which did not seem to take notice of it, but it certainly would when the snake got hungry. To be confined with death like that brought to life every ounce of claustrophobia in my body, and I left the bar (after considering whether I should ask the bartender, didn't he think there was enough evil in the world, did he need to throw a scenario like that into the bargain but I knew that I would be categorized as a sensitive, hysterical woman, that at most he would reply with a shrug), and let myself into our car, where I launched into a lengthy fit of sobbing, interrupted only by posing the same questions (to Charles), over and over again, as though he'd have an answer: 'How could someone think of something so cruel?' 'Why not wait until the snake was hungry before putting the mouse inside?' And when my mum got cancer, she had long since sold the small yellow house and said thank you and goodbye to the trigger-happy consultant psychiatrist and had (temporarily) moved in with me, it was a couple of years before Charles and I moved in together. When she had told me about the tumour, I slipped down on the floor and for a long time lay with my face pressed against the carpet and recalled what she had said one evening as we walked round the corner onto the road where the small yellow house was situated (I remember we had just turned, because what she said, in my mind was linked with the expression 'to round a sharp corner'), devastated, exhausted, upset about the consultant

again, out of breath from smoking far too many cigarettes, she said: 'Yes, you slowly begin to realize what
will put an end to you. As for me, it will probably be the
heart or the lungs'; I had nodded in the dark, her voice
was embittered, the words seemed completely abstract
to me, because here she walked, alive and full of vigour,
beside me (so vigorous and embittered that I dared not
offer any objections), not the least bit ill – all the same I
must have believed her since this tumour in her breast,
cancer in a family that had never known cancer, gave me
a feeling of being taken for a ride, cheated through and
through, victim of the complete unpredictability of existence. When I could stand on my own two feet again, I
went out to buy her a nice present, it was the only thing
I could think of (after having repeated the family mantra, 'it's going to be alright,' probably in an imploring
tone, half a dozen times), and brought home, blind to the
symbolic value at the time, a mother duck in turquoise
and silver, with her ducklings standing in a row behind
her, which she still keeps on her windowsill. Because she
survived, but the cancer left her in a panicky state that
gave wings to her desire to move, so to speak, and made
her move house five times, relatively quickly, one after
another. Clearly, she and I living together did not work,
after many years of living independently, even though
she did her best not to interfere in my life, and I in hers,
I remember (with shame) how in anger, I plunged a knife
into an orange, pierced the skin and twisted the knife
around in the wound, which made her raise her arms
in terror. She was ill, and I was strong and angry. She
did not have the strength to move out, but I drove her
to it. I found her a flat and moved and unpacked and arranged everything. Stepping inside the flat was a big
moment. She went inside and walked over to a wall and

slid down slowly until she reached the floor, wearing her coat and clutching her bag, exhausted, incapable of starting over, yet again. A little later we walked, through the rain, towards Kongens Nytorv, through her new neighbourhood, I was disappointed, she ought to have been delighted that I had taken such good care of her, but most of all she wanted to die. I had played doll's house, but the doll did not want to, could not, was incapable, skin yellowed, ill. Since I had practically forced this place upon her, it was not that strange that she gave notice to terminate the lease soon after and moved out. Every time she moved, there was a good reason: first there was a motorcyclist who started his motorcycle in the courtyard every morning at five o'clock; then there was no lift in her block, and stairs would be so difficult to manage – in the future. I recalled how often she had rearranged the furniture when I was a child, and how little I enjoyed coming home to discover that stars and planets, while I had been at school, had formed new constellations, that arch enemies leaned against one another affectionately, that separations had occurred. Everything at floor level. I wound my way through the labyrinth, oh, there it is, but where is that, and how could you think of doing that, in my room, it looks like war; but the rearranging always wore her out to such an extent that I simply had to yield, give her a hand, so the finishing touches could be made, against my wishes. My steadfast mother's hair was dripping from her exertions, and the floors so tremendously clean that you could eat off them, the rearranging always included spring cleaning. My mum was declared healthy just as Charles grew ill, she had reached her goal and passed the baton.

When she was most afraid (the cancer had moved to

her bones, though she did not know that yet) she began to send round her furniture with removal vans, I think of it as the frantic circle dance withered leaves perform when trapped in a corner, in the wind's embrace. Some furniture she sent (to their surprise) to friends, some she sent to me, and other pieces still were driven out to her summerhouse. I remember how surprised I was one October day when Charles and I were going to weekend at the summerhouse, and there was the table we had eaten at the previous day, in her flat, and her bed was there, and other pieces of furniture that belonged in other places suddenly revealed themselves. But that bookcase! But those chairs! Here! The removal men had forgotten to close the door behind them, and nature had trespassed, there were leaves and twigs on the carpet. I was confused, to put it mildly. And I began to sweep the new backdrop. Fear of death, that was what it was, in its pure and simple form. In turn she had, simultaneously, from an acquaintance who collected antique furniture, received seventeen chairs, and a sofa that had reportedly belonged to Admiral Gjedde. It had collapsed, as though the centuries had taken its breath away. And I found my mum in her flat, on the floor, in a sleeping bag, surrounded by all the chairs, and the deflated sofa, quiet observers of the bronze light that suddenly surrounded her, because everything about her was now bronze, her skin, her hair. She was admitted to hospital, and it turned out that the Crab had teamed up with the bones.

One sentence continues to haunt me: 'Therefore no ruins may be seen from a flower passage.' (I stumbled across it in an article about horticulture from 1802.)

Have I conjured up flower passages in my story? Or are they pure ruins?

212

And if I have successfully constructed a flower passage, have I then allowed a ruin to be seen from it, or have I only allowed it to reveal itself at the end of the passage? 'But to suddenly move from pleasant objects to ruins leaves a splendid impression,' D .C. Fester continues – does he experience the splendid impression as a stab of melancholy in the area around the heart, at decay and impermanence, the area around the heart precisely where a lightness was felt, the nostrils still in convulsive contractions, from the scent of flowers on the path?

III. THE PARTY BREAKS UP

'Someday, she mused, one's past must be put in order. Retouched, retaken. Certain "wipes" and "inserts" will have to be made in the picture; certain telltale abrasions in the emulsion will have to be corrected; "dissolves" in the sequence discreetly combined with the trimming out of unwanted, embarrassing "footage", and definite guarantees obtained; yes, someday – before death with its clap-stick closes the scene.'
— Vladimir Nabokov, *Ada*

THE PATIENTS *or* CAMILLA AND ALMA'S EARLY YEARS

[Camilla]

I.

Other people's homes have a dreary and engrossing effect on me when I see them from the outside, like flies and flypaper (I am the fly). The thought of having to spend my life there. I would hate to wait out my years in there as the walls squeezed the life out of me.

My own previous homes have had more or less the same effect on me. On occasion I go to Jægersborg and stand outside and look up at the flat I lived in until I left home. I look at the windows in the room that was first called 'the playroom' and later simply 'your room'.

Up there they allowed black material from their heavy hearts to drip on me whilst they gave me the title, Sol.

At this very moment I am sitting on the train (I've been to Jægersborg again) racing past a series of superbly built but harsh brown façades – and I begin to feel disheartened and threatened by the walls, completely at their mercy, as though I have unwillingly had a series of lives forced upon me. In the short story 'The Destructors' by Graham Greene, a gang systematically destroys a house *from within* so that only the walls remain; fastened to a lorry the walls too collapse in the end – yes like a house of cards, but with a crash and in a cloud of dust. The reason for this destruction is beauty. The house is old and beautiful. In the hall there is a two-hundred-year-old spiral staircase, and there is tall wood panelling on the walls.

(There are other reasons; one of the boys who came up with the idea is the son of a failed architect, perhaps

216

the attack is directed at what would not come to be in the father's world: buildings; perhaps his failure weighed on the family like a heavy cloud and has led to quiet embittered family meals.)

OF, the gentleman who was unfortunate enough to set fire to my mum's wastepaper basket in Vordingborg, was a weekly guest at our dinner table from the time I was fifteen or sixteen, and that continued long after I had left home, in fact maybe until his death. The first time I met him, Alma was also there, we were both wearing her slim, long-legged boyfriend's worn skinny jeans, written down Alma's left thigh were the words 'fuck me, baby' in felt tip, when my mum saw that, she froze, she covered her mouth with her hand. The rest of the afternoon Alma made sure to cover the spot with her hand, it looked a little awkward when she got up, and in fact, OF had probably noticed it straight away, because the black writing stood out against the pale blue, almost white material, but he was not that prudish. Alma and I sat thigh-to-thigh on the sofa, and sitting across from us in separate armchairs were OF and my mum, we all smoked, OF incessantly so. He had a long melancholy face, dyed-black hair with brilliantine (flat, not like a wave in suspense), wore black-rimmed German glasses, his skin was white, made even whiter by the black frame, and soft, I must have brushed it with my lips when he arrived, and again when he was going home and grabbed me and pressed me against his green polar coat so that my stiff back and neck cracked.

The smoke served as a curtain between him and the world, he sat behind it observing, with a friendly smile and a veiled gaze (veiled by erotic thoughts? veiled by melancholy?), then a vigilant gaze, depending on

217

whether he listened to something within himself or to us, and when he spoke, he leaned forward and slowly poked holes in the smoke with his cigarette. He seemed to exist in constant fear of being attacked (which we did not have the least urge to do, he was sweetness itself), and to disarm us he offered us florid praise and a steady stream of compliments, very distracting, very flattering, eventually very tedious as well. Because are we meant to praise him in return, or can we continue the conversation? No, we cannot, we can only extract these flowers from the bunch and hand them to one another. Everything kept coming to a standstill. We have to placate one another, no matter how placid we might be. When he walked through the living room, he ducked his head. He was tall, but in no danger of banging his head against the ceiling.

He was lean and always wore a suit and sat with his legs crossed and his arms over his chest, only his smoking hand poked up, his overworked right hand. But within this cage of limbs, laughter was not infrequently heard. How old was he? He was a journalist, now on early retirement. Being out of the workforce was not easy for him. It was not easy for him when the war had ended, and the action film had reached 'The End', he had liquidated three informers and stashed his wartime weapons, one evening he brought his pistol with him and let us hold it, it felt dangerous in my hand, like having an independent life that could suddenly break out, and I put it down again, after a couple of steps. Naturally it was not loaded. To my mum's great surprise (and delight I think) one evening he brought it loaded to a nine o'clock showing at the Grand in order to be prepared for the walk to Central Station around midnight. The other day I was stopped in the street by an elderly lady who introduced herself as a childhood friend of my mum from their time as supply teachers in Stege, and she said: 'Your mum was wild. We were three supply teachers, always together. She was without a doubt the wildest.'

I asked her how the wildness manifested itself. And she mentioned a summerhouse they had rented on Ulvshale, red wine, midnight dips, visits from young men, supply teachers too, perhaps, all either seventeen or eighteen.

When my mum was a young child, her life revolved around a desire for two things – to one day host a literary salon and to accomplish great feats, to be strong and brave, and she passed that on to me, she had swum across the channel (with the ferry surging towards her), she had swum across Grønsund, she had swum with a pack of seals far off the coast of Anholt and had completely forgotten about the distance back to the island, fascinated at being so close to the seals that she could see their eyelashes. She was expecting me. The story inspired Alma to write a mythologically influenced poem in the spirit of (the late) Bjørnvig or of Lundby's, 'The Seal Woman', where she concocted a story about a conception via seal semen during her swim, but she was very young. When she read it out loud to us, for a moment I was scared that my mum would react in the same way as the time I prepared a recorder concert for the family on Christmas Eve, where she and my grandmother cried with laughter because I breathed through the pipe, drew the air in and blew it out again while I (indefatigable) whistled, which had also made my music teacher decide that I should only pretend to play at the school concert since he could not exclude me. I still have the small brush that looks like a pipe cleaner that was used to clean out the recorder, supposedly of saliva, now

219

I use it to clean the small hole in the fridge that keeps getting blocked by bits of food without understanding the function of this hole, but if it is not kept clean, the entire fridge fills with water, and I think of the music teacher, Mr Florian, a light name for a heavy man of thirty, and his wife, also a music teacher, who once saw me, while walking down the corridor to our classroom, pull a girl's hair (not very hard, really just a friendly little tug on her brown ponytail because it was so thick and enticing) and so she snuck up behind me and grabbed my ponytail (in an iron grip) and pulled my head back so hard that it nearly struck the floor. Music classes took place in the basement, in the same place we collected school milk, and the couple never seemed to leave, but overweight and old before their time, with, respectively, full beards and double chins and pearl necklaces, lived a basement life filled with music. I'm afraid of dark, deep water (what it might contain) and have only managed to conquer that fear whilst intoxicated, I swam across Hald Sø one night, rather tipsy, with a three-man-band (incredibly white against the darkness and Hald's majestic trees as they pulled off their clothes with their backs turned to me, I still remember the one with the squidgy, slightly too fleshy buttocks), so that I did not shudder at the thought of the thirty-one metres of black water beneath me, incidentally a titbit (the depth) that one of the band offered up, swimming, that this lake with its thirty-one metres of water was the second deepest in the country, but articulating the information frightened him so much that he turned back. And across Peblinge Sø, which is not deep, in the same condition. It was after a wedding (that had featured street vendors who sold jewellery from Helligaandskirken on Strøget, or played guitar, or sold hash), that Tim and I had been to, as Tim went with me back to Copenhagen, and we lived with my mum for a couple of months until we found a sub-let with hideous purple and pink walls that I woke up to each morning with a heavy head; I was working as a waiter at Peder Oxe, and when I finished around mid-night, the other waiters and the Irish cleaner – 'Jesus, Mary and the fucking donkey,' he shouted every time one of us slipped on a kitchen floor that grew gradually more and more slippery and covered with scraps of food as the evening wore on, and dropped a stack of plates – used to go out and spend all our tips on drinks. Here it is necessary to mention Jeanette, also a waitress, a former model, I recall a cover of *Vogue*, Jeanette wearing a white bathing suit on a beach; when her career was already over, she was no more than twenty, due to drugs, at this point she had just begun to snort heroin with her idle boyfriend Mikael and his idle friends whom I met once in their messy flat in Nyhavn, where Jeanette showed me all her covers and told me about the terrible things from her childhood. She had grown up in a tower block with large glass windows, one wall in the living room might have been made entirely of glass. Her dad perpetually threatened to take his own life by jumping out the win-dow, and once out of desperation Jeanette had said: 'Just do it, then,' whereupon her dad had got up from the sofa (which I imagine was made of leather) and threw himself out, he could hardly have thrown himself through the glass, so maybe the wall was not made of glass after all. When she threw her head back in laughter, her breasts made up half the laugh, even René, the head waiter, was amenable. Jeanette and I wanted to sell sandwiches at Roskilde Festival, and she arranged to buy everything for the project through Peder Oxe so the large quanti-ties of cheese sausage ham salad cucumber tomato bread would be far cheaper than if we had purchased them ourselves, and we also used the kitchen and produced an astronomical number of sandwiches and René drove us to Roskilde in a Peder Oxe van. The sandwiches sold like, well like hot bread, even when they got soggy, everything could be sold if it was accompanied by Jeanette's chortling breast-shaking laugh; when there were no more cheese sandwiches left, and when a male vegetarian wanted to buy something from us, Jeanette opened the soggy wet sandwiches and picked out the sausage or ham with her not particularly clean hands and pressed the wilted salad into the butter, and the vegetarian was happy, the marks from her nails in the butter perhaps even a bonus. Tim was also at the festival, but we were growing apart, he hung out with a group of foreigners who hung out in front of Helligaandskirken, two Americans and an Israeli, all jewellery pedlars (ceaseless guitar playing, ceaseless hash smoking) and married to Danish girls ten years their junior, girls who were about to become anthropologists or sociologists, and there was also this small group of Peruvians from the Andes playing pan pipes in ponchos. The thin man in a suit with the sheepish expression who sold roses, whom Alma said owned a house in Hellerup, stopped holding out a rose whenever he saw me, but nodded instead, figures who had until now only served as points of reference on Strøget for me, but thankfully Tim had not become friends with any of those people who pretend to be a statue, sprayed either bronze or silver or completely white (or had he, all of a sudden I sense a strange rubbery person sneaking around the outskirts of my recollection), I am hypersensitive to them, I cannot stand them, this posing, the arm extended and the leg stretched back 'look how still I can stand,' this alleged stillness, in an uncomfortable position to boot, they infuriate me, I consider them malicious, and in fact I was once confirmed in my aversion towards them in Madrid when I passed one and the person in question suddenly leaned forward with a hiss and pinched my arm like I needed to be woken from a dream, and I had needed that, because I had just come from a Goya exhibition; maybe, I thought, he is taking vengeance on behalf of all the living statues because I find them so incredibly revolting. Maybe they remind me of depressives (frozen stiff out of sheer misery) or of corpses. Every time I see one, an imitation statue, I hear the following lines in my head: 'Tordenskjold, he was roguish / went around and sold fish.'

And Alma was there too, I think I neglected both her and Tim in favour of Jeanette (having new friends has always made me so happy), until I saw two Red Cross workers with Alma between them walking towards the Red Cross tent, and I ran after them. For want of something better, Alma had eaten an entire jar of caffeine pills and was wriggling like an eel out of anxiety. Not long after I lay down next to Alma after a brief but brilliant spell (speed), and Sunday night we went home together, stooped over our racing hearts, taking slow steps, like two old frightened people. I don't know where Jeanette and Tim were. The last time I ran into Jeanette, some years later, the time at Peder Oxe was long past, it had only been one spring and one summer, she came to see me, her face was covered in inflamed spots and she did not laugh. Someone she owed money to had torched her flat, with her two cats inside, it was impossible to recover from such an atrocity, of course. She was flat broke, and I remember giving her a block of cheese with black rinds when she left, it had been lying in the fridge for a long time and I didn't like it because it was matured. That was the last I saw of her, I hope she isn't dead, I can't remember her surname, maybe I never knew it. But I do remember all her various tops and her eagerness to make money, which led us to try our hand at selling sandwiches. Once, maybe she could not get hold of anyone else, all bridges to that scene burnt, I went with her on a photo-shoot for leather clothing, I was a size 10 but not that tall, but she managed to get me teetering on a pair of incredibly high heels and made me up, she was very pleased with my transformation and searched her memory for the name of a French model she thought I looked like, and she encouraged every bit of affectation on my part, like for example my reluctance to wear white, 'white doesn't suit me,' I said, I had heard Alma say that about me, 'isn't there something mmm a little more soft,' I said and flicked through the clothes racks, the photographs were taken, and we got our money, but not as much as Jeanette had expected, and she flew off in a rage at one of the leather guys, who called her attention to, I remember it clearly, her fall from grace (after appearing on the cover of *Vogue*) and my status as a complete novice, only previously photographed for family albums, which was true enough and not the least bit insulting, but I thought I should show solidarity and support Jeanette and her exasperation. Then we teetered off again, I couldn't cope with her talk about heroin, and I couldn't get her to talk sensibly, she kept interjecting my reprimands and pleas with the story about her dad and the window. Around the same time Alma and I took part in a hair show, a promo for our hairdresser, a stocky pockmarked gentleman who had hired Lotte Heise to organize the show at a hotel; with our hair up in a kind of tight whip high on the top of our heads (like the Chinese men you see in martial

224

arts films) and wearing six-inch heels and extremely tight dresses we had to walk up and down a catwalk
while playing pink violins (replicas), it was difficult to
appear relaxed whilst simultaneously trying to work out
what reality this scenario feigned to have stemmed from,
maybe we were meant to depict some kind of overgrown
geishas. Alma stoops, and the heels made it even worse,
it made her appear furtive, her shoulders hunched up
by her chin and her head protruding and bent over the
violin, I could not reconcile myself with the violin either (even with my previous experience pretending to
play an instrument), 'you're holding it like a nun holds a
sailor's cock,' Heise screamed at me with her usual sen-
sitivity, and during the break she told me to only eat one
sandwich, 'more won't do you any good,' not two, like
the others, a strangely hollow sound escaped me and I
took a second one anyway. Several years later on a TV
show, after she was unable to spell Nietzsche when asked
to, she buried her face in her hands and broke down over
his name as though it were a flogged horse, and I nodded in satisfaction. Nietzsche went up to join violin and
sandwich number two.

Tim (in that period) was a dishwasher at a restaurant
in Kongelunden. My mum was worried that I wor-
shipped and submitted to him, she said that she had
looked out the window one day when we left her flat, and
that I had walked a couple of metres behind him 'like a
squaw', maybe my skirt had been of a Native American
cut, 'so, have you found yourself a new guru,' she said,
but for her part, she delighted in making his favourite
dish, lamb with mint sauce, just for him, and moreover
she was the one who had a guru who had assigned her a
mantra, and she sat meditating in the evening when the
house was quiet, the mantra was secret, but after she had

225

(long since) stopped meditating because it became too intense for her, she revealed the mantra to me, one time she had had an orgasm while meditating, sitting bolt upright staring straight ahead, with her palms facing up in a receptive gesture, and another time a black goat, apparently the Devil, had exploded before her eyes, and I had expected some wonderful word, one that I had never heard before, but then the mantra turned out to be 'Jesus'. I was disappointed in the same way as when you are given an object you already have, a duplicate.

Back to the wedding, to round off the talk about water and swimming. I was nineteen, I stripped down and quickly made it to the opposite side of Peblinge Sø. When I climbed ashore, a water rat poked its head up, depriving me of the pleasure of swimming back. So I had to run across Dronning Louises Bro in my knickers and collect my clothes where I had left them. On the bridge a police car had stopped at a red light. I kept my right arm over my breasts and kept my balance with my left.

Tim. He was not my first love, my first love was a receptionist (Crete), maybe I'll come back to him.

No, now.

For the first time a melted soul in a melted body, in his room, in the basement, beneath the reception where he worked. He called me *glicka* (sweet) and offered me eucalyptus pastilles (from his lips), and we walked together in the darkness outside the hotel. How did this first walk come about? It was the very first evening, my dad and I had arrived at the hotel, we were spending the half-term break in Crete, and we went for a stroll. I was fifteen and did not wear make-up, only lip balm, all the time. He was eighteen or twenty-one, I don't remember, and his eyebrows were joined. Brown pageboy haircut.

His face slightly triangular, like a goat, or maybe I am confusing it with the peculiar sight of a goat in a tree viewed from the bus on a trip somewhere in Crete where ice-cold retsina was served at the restaurant where we ate lunch, long pieces of cucumber and bowls of runny honey that we dipped the cucumber in. I (the child of fifteen) had generally stopped eating. Every night my dad and I walked down to a long narrow restaurant at the harbour. When I moved through the restaurant, the guests turned their heads, they could see I had become someone else. I thought so. What did we talk about, the father and the child who was no longer a child? That I could eat nothing? Beautiful dishes were placed in front of me, souvlaki on a skewer, blackened meat with lemon, tomato salad with feta, moussaka, stuffed peppers, fried potato wedges, yoghurt with honey and a drizzle of sesame seeds, but it was all too heavy for my pollenous body. I considered the food to be elements of the senses, part of the storm that blew through me, not potential nourishment. All it took was his name. Ni-cho-las (three syllables like in *Lolita*, and like in *Lolita* the tip of the tongue makes three small steps – and ends in the bed in the basement). My hands shook. I shook. I went out to the harbour and photographed the waves. My dad told me about Hokusai. And I have an entire series of waves captured directly before they turn. It's windy. There are black cliffs, a yellowish-grey sea and the Second World War rears its ugly head: a concrete fortification.

I have a photograph of myself sitting on a donkey, in shorts, the owner of the donkey, an old man, rests his hand on my bare thigh, he looks sly, I am far too big for the donkey, and it looks like he is holding everything together, the donkey and me, with his hand and proprietorial air. I had been taught to be very polite, almost submissive, with people who clearly had less than I did (money, opportunities, education), that must be why I agreed to climb up on the donkey and why I found myself in this man's hands. My mind had long since been set with the idea that people or entire groups of people who have been victims could not exercise bad behaviour or malice. I thought (still at the age of fifteen) that all Native Americans were good, all Jews, all black Americans and all poor, old, donkey-owning farmers in Crete.

Endlessly tiring pent-up wet hard stiff, we did not sleep together. Nor do I think we removed much clothing. I think we must have touched each other beneath our clothes and kissed for hours. But maybe that's not right. Now I suddenly remember his bare legs. And that he had a shower afterwards and blow-dried his hair whilst I lay on the bed watching. Every moment he did not have to work, we sought out his bed. My dad had to see the labyrinth in Knossos alone. He had to see all of Crete alone. I only wanted to go with Nicholas, down to the basement, down to his bed. Then the bus arrived to drive us to the airport. I dissolved into tears at our departure, the very core of life snatched away, I had pressed my face against infinity and now sat alone, buried in my father's handkerchief. And the grown-ups on the bus, probably well meaning, probably considerate, my loud sniffling heard throughout the silent bus until the guide found his voice, on the microphone. I had to believe that what I was going through at that moment, they had all been through it, that it was a kind of childhood sorrow. I had to believe that love and goodbyes were something they used to get on prescription, in measured doses.

We never saw each other again, but we wrote to each other for seven years, spanning new loves, and for him, marriage and children, and each year around Christmas he went to the photographer and sent me a photograph of himself, always well groomed, with the upturned (using a hairdryer) ends resting on the edge of his top or shoulders, all depending on what fashion (in Crete) dictated that year. (When Charles was going to move in, I threw out all the photographs and love letters I had, his too, but I remember these photographs particularly well, even his pullovers, a new one each year, the pattern on the patch of pullover that was included in the photograph.)

Alma and I met Tim in Amsterdam where he worked at the bar of our hotel, actually it was a youth hostel, he looked like a contented angel, long reddish-blond hair, freckles, scout knife. His black T-shirt was a washed-out whitish-grey, and there was a faint odour when you got right up close to him, not really unpleasant, just a whiff of sweat. Nothing more happened than him asking for our address; his address book, it turned out, was his bible because he was travelling the world and was happy to have some destinations. A few days after Alma and I had returned to Copenhagen, he rang at our door – we lived together. That same night the door to my room opened. He later told me that he had been in doubt as to which door to choose, mine or Alma's. It turned out to be mine, because he said 'Alma is big, big with a capital B,' he was fairly slim and no more than five foot six. Alma is tall. And it's true that Alma was a little overweight at that time, but I was too, I worked as a cleaning assistant at Gentofte Hospital as a part of the emergency response team, we appeared when an operation had finished and quickly readied the operating room, the floor often strewn with pools of blood and unidentifiable organic material, for the next operation. During the operations I killed time by drinking fruit cordial and eating tea biscuits, leant over my mop or my little handy cart (handy if the wheels had worked properly and did not drive to one side so that we had to zigzag across the corridor when the surgeon opened the door to the operating room, taking long strides as he pulled the mask from his stone face and removed his gloves... then it was our turn, me and the mop.) A lot of students at my secondary school (from which I had graduated with terrible results, and now worked as a cleaner) worked as cleaners at the hospital on the weekends, and white hospital vests with blue-striped sleeves (the name of a commercial laundry imprinted on a blue patch on the stomach) were the fashion at school, making us look like escaped patients – and white hospital bathrobes for use at home, this white terrycloth had a touch of Hollywood to it. At parties we drank a strange sweet nectar made with medical alcohol, it sent several people to the hospital, to have their stomachs pumped, whereby it (the medical alcohol) returned from whence it came, home, you might say. I too had smuggled a bathrobe out of the hospital. When my mum discovered that I had appropriated something from an institution, she was beside herself, and I had to hop on my bike straight away and smuggle it back in, to the scrub room, in the laundry basket.

OF also owned a cannon, he kept it in a storage unit on Amager. But we never saw it. He did not arrive with his cannon in tow every Friday night, only his shopping trolley, the Mercedes of pensioners (he loved expressions like that; just as he loved jingles and took part in jingle contests and was happy when he won, his favourite was used by the Traffic Safety Commission, or so he claimed, 'Why save a second, if it's going to be your last'). But the shopping trolley worked against the appearance of youth his black hair was meant to present, it made him into an elderly man who could not manage the weight of his belongings. He had barely stepped inside the door when he began to take presents out of the trolley (in that way disarming us before he had even crossed the threshold), a tube of pea soup from Irma, a dark chocolate Guldbarre, newspaper and magazine clippings covering topics we had touched upon the last time we were together (when my mum got breast cancer he sent her, with the best intentions, an article containing gloomy statistics about survival and recovery rates that completely took the wind out of her sails, on this occasion there were also stickers of Charlie Brown and the Peanuts gang stuck to the envelope since they have a line for every situation in life. When she received the diagnosis, she rented a house where she was far from any neighbours, on the island of Nyord. A house where she could scream.

She rented a house where she could scream.

But she did not use it in the end and terminated the lease after a couple of months. I don't think she ever did any screaming. Maybe she screamed into a pillow. I could not make it to the substance of the sentence when she told me about the house where she could scream; as if the words themselves and the act (the lease) stifled the desperation behind it.)

And he brought sleeping pills if anyone had complained of not being able to sleep – he would also send sleeping pills by post, unsolicited, swathed in cotton wool and placed in yellow Läkerol boxes, with rubber bands around them. The rubber bands always surprised me, because the boxes were closed, the pills were packed in cotton wool, there was no risk of them rolling out of the envelope, the rubber bands became the very picture of the pills' strength, that they had to be stopped from breaking out of the box. They were old school sleeping pills, so to speak, Rohypnol, which his doctor let him accrue in a seemingly endless stream or maybe he bought them at his local, Polar Bodega, where according to him you could buy a little of everything, passports weapons pills, and ten minutes after you had swallowed a Rohypnol, it felt like you had been struck on the forehead, and if you dared to get out of bed and stand on your feet, it was like sailing on the high seas during a storm, the walls came crashing towards you, you raced towards them with outstretched arms. Or you went out like a light, deprived of the inconvenience of slipping off to sleep, and that was probably when my love of sleeping pills was established, but my doctor keeps me on a short leash, I receive a quota of ten sleeping pills per annum, altogether mild pills with the effect lasting only three to four hours. You can walk around unaffected after taking one. If you change your mind and don't want to sleep after all – I often get the feeling that I don't actually want to sleep, but think that I should, as though simultaneously acting as my own reluctant child and my own parent – you can simply stop yourself. Nabokov believed that humanity can be divided into two groups: those who can sleep and those who can't. His father believed that humanity can be grouped depending on whether or not they appear attractive to others – as that which determines how life will take form. But if you stumble around in a haze of sleeplessness, you can scarcely notice your effect on others, or you misjudge it, like you misjudge so many other things.

'He bent down with a grunt, cursing his knee, to fix his skis, in the driving snow, on the brink of the

slope, but the skis had vanished, the bindings were shoelaces, and the slope, a staircase.'
—— Vladimir Nabokov, *Ada*

The character in the novel *Ada* does not suffer from sleeplessness, but is in a highly emotional state because of a romantic betrayal, when he mistakes indoors with outdoors. I often mistake occurrences in the physical world. And I ask myself how differently from other people you can experience things that ought to be a given, that is to say where there is consensus, without being considered completely wide of the mark. What degree of subjectivity in the perception is permissible or excusable, how far can you deviate from consensus if you want to be deemed sane? If you are willing to correct yourself (well no of course that's not the sound of water falling, but the sound of electricity, obviously there's no waterfall here, how could I make such a terrible mistake), the people with normal perception would still allow you to squeeze in with their group, it is only when you insist on the rightness of your perception that the group closes before you like a wall. Now I think of something slightly different. My mum had a fever. I was visiting her. Suddenly she straightened up in bed and waved in delight at a blackbird on a branch outside the window; as if it was essential that the bird saw her greet it, now that it had at long last appeared.

Back to the subject of sleep... nonetheless, in the care of another doctor, or lack thereof, I grew addicted to these seemingly innocent oval pills that are so difficult to divide into two. When I shut up shop and declined to take any more because I got so dizzy during the day that I staggered like a drunk and several times sat next to a

233

chair instead of on it, it cost me five sleepless nights, every sound cut me, and I had no skin, the atmosphere squeaked like cotton wool and scraped at my bones and nerves.

Rohypnol meant obliteration from the surface of the earth for the following ten hours. My mum must not have known that OF supplied me with these pills. Or else she trusted that I would use them sensibly, which I did seeing as their effect was horrifying, more or less like – first a shadow (of heaviness) fell upon me, and the next moment a bird grabbed me with its claws and flew me off to its nest, far from the world, giving me a fore-taste of death. The other day when I was out for a stroll with Edward, he had an errand at the pet shop, and I went in with him. The staff had let four or five small birds out of their cages so they could fly around the shop, and I prayed that none of them would land on my head, or get anywhere near my face. Both of those things happened. I felt an intense loathing, I cannot stand the whirring of wings, and the darting movements. The fact that I am short-sighted and my eyes are different, the left is more short-sighted than the right, ('remember "lousy leftie"': my optician) makes it difficult for me to judge distances, and often I think that a pigeon or a gull is about to land on me when I am down by Sortedams Sø or on Rådhuspladsen so I duck and shield my face, while in reality, apparently, it keeps to a safe distance. In *Orlando* a loving touch is praised as being light as the wings of birds. It is the Russian princess Sasha who touches Orlando in that way, like the stirring of plum-age. When I read that passage, I pictured something I could not bear: a bird brushing its wings against my na-ked body, and stop thinking of birds as genitals like in Catullus's poem about the sparrow: 'My girl's sparrow

234

is dead ... It would not leave her lap, but hopped around now here now there ... He chirped constantly to his mistress alone.'

Here, with me, bird means bird. Once I discussed the frequent occurrence of dogs in one of Alma's books with a teacher. He mentioned symbols. I said that the detailed description of each dog meant that it was not a symbol; that the details made it specific, something in itself, the dog, on each occasion one dog in particular.

'I don't buy that,' he said (that is one of the expressions I care least for, perhaps only surpassed by 'that'll teach him'), 'we're talking about text here, not life.'

'Then what do the dogs symbolize?' I asked, 'Do they symbolize wolves?'

'Precisely,' he replied, 'they symbolize something lurking, something uneasy, something subservient, some kind of lone killer.'

'But they are retrievers,' I said, 'gentle retrievers.'

Again he said that he did not buy it, and asked whether I knew that a dog can tear a leather wallet to pieces in less than a minute.

Incidentally, one time in Greifswald, the only thing I recall of my weekend stay there, a raven at the zoo had caught my attention, and I sat down right by the wire cage, and it came right up to me, and we stared into each other's eyes for a long time (a little too long to be strictly healthy, on my part), the bird with its head cocked, me gradually ascribing this to the fact that its eyes shone with intelligence, and was in quite a state that this creature with such an ability to connect had to remain locked up.

OF had been a patient of my mum, now he was healthy, and things proceeded like they sometimes did between her and her patients, they became friends (but he had wanted more, he had chased her round the desk in her office, and I picture her holding up her arms to ward him off and putting her full authority behind her refusal), which had the advantage that she could continue to keep tabs on her former patients and intervene if their illness recurred.

At times the patients drove me crazy. She almost always came home from work late, nearing seven, in a taxi because she was tired, and at long last when we sat down to dinner the telephone started to ring, and it was one of them. I had no siblings. I had the patients, the persistent, those who had permission because they were ill. Because (maybe) it was a matter of life or death. And since her soothing voice could save the ill, or if the matter was less serious, merely relieve the pain, soothe, (her voice as a hand) then it should be able to do so.

Every month she had to fill out a form to record her overtime, but often she was too tired to do it and missed out on being paid for it. Just as she was too tired to get public transport to and from work. She did not have a driving licence. Several times she purchased a theory guide with the intention of engaging in some kind of self-study, but she never managed to book a lesson. Her weekends she spent in bed, reading, exhausted.

Every time Charles and I try to track down a doctor through the hospital system, usually in vain, to get help for his wretched back, I think of how my mum overworked herself and how I often had to act as a buffer between her and the patients, in her own home. The most annoying one of all was Birthe, a dull woman with a voice like a foghorn; my mum had given her permission to ring every Sunday, and for that reason we called her Sunday Birthe, which she also adopted.

'Hi, it's Sunday Birthe.'

(But it's not Sunday, it is Monday, Tuesday, Wednesday.)

She wanted me to call her Auntie.

She wanted me to say I loved my Auntie Birthe. And I agreed, begrudgingly.

It was difficult for her to make her extremely nasal voice sound inviting, it sounded like she stood above it and pressed down. After an ingratiating introduction (I was Saint Peter, my mum heaven) she asked to speak to my mum. If my mum waved her hands in protest, I had to come up with an excuse. Only if Birthe was in one of her rare good moods was she able to accept no for an answer. Usually she insisted until her voice reached its natural pitch – foghorn – and she became truly angry and told me that I was mean and that I should be ashamed of myself and I would be to blame if she had an attack. She suffered from epilepsy. Then I had to hang up, and if my mum was not on call and it was possible to pull the plug out of the socket, I did so. Otherwise we had to come to terms with her calling as many as eight or ten times, growing increasingly angry and crude. I met her only once, on a Sunday, where she came to visit with her husband, Svend. Her appearance was much like her voice, big and powerful, a bear under the guise of a lady, and she held out her arms and drew me in. Her husband was small and wretched, he had been exploited as a child, forced to work as unpaid labour on a number of farms. He was run down and broken. He laughed nervously at everything Birthe said. Once in a while she stroked him on the shoulder and said 'isn't that right, Svend,' and he sunk under the weight of her hand. Svend wanted to get away from her (her violent temper wore on his nerves), but she would not allow it.

237

In the end some government authority must have taken mercy on him and got him into a nursing home. Without her. To her great despair. On the Sunday they visited us, they had brought a jewel box for each of us, cigar boxes decorated with glazed tiles that weighed down the lid, dark blue, light blue and pink tiles (the glue applied generously, bubbling up between the tiles, first whitish, later almost brown) and overloaded the veneer where the small hinges rested, so they ended up sagging after opening them only a few times.

We had had a drug addict stay with us, on methadone, she suffered from a heart that was too big – literally, she seemed out of breath. Being forced to turn away drug addicts due to lack of beds at the hospital was one of the things that made my mum most unhappy and angry with the system (a word seldom heard today) – so she brought this woman home with her companion, Peter, thrown in for good measure; the two of them, Anne and Peter, who had just met in the admission ward, perhaps he came along to help her with the methadone, my memory is inadequate – he came with her, and they both settled in on mattresses, one in each of our two living rooms. Anne was a Marxist, and she supplied me with a long list of books (political theory) for me to pick up from the library where at the time I worked as a shelver (a monotonous job; even the librarians were properly bored, in any case they drank a good deal, apart from re-shelving books it was my task to supply the lunch room with food for their meals, I purchased delicacies of every kind, some of them were rather stout not to mention fat, and wine in great quantities, they had a pre-dilection for plump bottles in straw baskets) so I knew where everything was, of course the entire set of *Das*

Kapital, she could not do without that, Lenin Mao and bi-
ographies about the anarchists Kropotkin and Goldman
and several works that I do not remember (on the other
hand I do remember my mum saying something along
the lines of it being lucky we did not live in a country
where your lending history was monitored, the books
were borrowed on her card), and when I stacked them by
the head of Anne's mattress, I realized that her stay with
us was going to be a long one if she was going to read all
these books. She moved slowly through the rooms. And
when she was going to read, she placed a pair of glasses
on her long nose. She was only twenty-six. But I did not
think of her as young. How could I, I was seventeen. She
preferred tight velour tops and had a long sloping bosom. She was hollow-backed, and it did something to her
bosom, extended it perhaps, or thrust it out. She wore a
chain with a gold heart round her neck, and she pulled
it, the heart, over the collar, letting it dangle over her
tight velour top. And under her top worked her large
overstrained heart.

She had been a 'streetwalker'. It made me nervous
that she had been through so much, she brought the
streets with her – slowly and breathlessly through the
rooms, her bosom that I could not stop staring at, the
books I kept tabs on as to whether she read them – places I would never have access to, would only get a sense
of from the few words my mum occasionally let slip, ca-
sually and intimately, like this 'streetwalker', 'how else
do you think she made money'. No. I would have tipped
my hat (to her), if I wore one, when she drifted past me
in the entrance.

I only treated her as a normal person on one occasion.
She opened the door to my room while I was dancing
in front of the mirror, without knocking – and I said

harshly, exposed and embarrassed: 'you can't just barge in without knocking.' Then she beat a hasty retreat in her slippers with trampled heels, which also seemed deliberate. A detail (I can remember exactly how she closed the door, the embarrassment at being exposed and me putting her in her place has left contours of the door closure in my memory), she looked down at her hand on the door handle and bent over the hand as if it was the guilty party, and she now had to monitor its actions, as she overcautiously (ironically) closed the door.

Peter was a centre of restlessness. He was in a manic phase, he followed several TV programmes simultaneously, he changed the channel every thirty seconds, confusing for the rest of us, but no problem for him. At the same time he talked incessantly, and soon his goal was to seduce me and my friends, Alma was the only one he was successful with, in the rocking chair, during a maths lesson after he had been chosen as our tutor, not a particularly pedagogical one, the explanations lost in associations. And my mum arrived home from work, perhaps a little curious as to whether her menagerie had made it through the day, whether I had bunked off again, always late, just before the shops closed, holding shopping bags, friendly and tired. Peter was a member of the Mad Movement and introduced us to their magazine, *Amalie*. Alma wrote a colourful poem (sobbing owls, midnight, full moon, delirium) about him, 'Mania', it was called, and it was published in *Amalie*. He was a bitter opponent of the psychiatric establishment; he viewed my mum as an exception or as some kind of 'good cop'. Being a psychiatrist was not popular in those years, the seventies and eighties, when anti-psychiatry raged. The left wing, which she ascribed to, considered psychiatrists to be some kind of lackeys based on the Laingian notion that madness is a healthy reaction to an ill society.

As for the rest of the medical profession, psychiatrists (incidentally) were considered, according to her, to be at the very bottom, the binmen of society; whereas surgeons were at the top. If Charles ever runs into the surgeon who poked around in his back and failed to notice (even though he spent several hours in there) that his bones were brittle, he would push him as hard as his back allowed. And a surgeon from Stege Hospital, where my mum and I lived for a couple of years in a hospital flat, whose name resonated like Glasgow and who had a habit of greeting his patients with the words: 'Yes, so we've sharpened the knives, Mrs Xxxxxxxxxx.' Something similar could possibly be said about opticians – unpleasant memory in the queue for later use, all the same it slipped through: We'll get that sty with a knife 'now you lie down, and I'll get up and you'll be in my power' (direct quote, accompanied by a flourishing scalpel, straddling legs); 'Snip there we go do you want to look at your eye in the mirror on the wall up you go yes that is quite the bloody snip.' Neck hits the deck blackout wake up on the floor with two opticians over me alarm bells fight hard to believe anything other than I have been raped after the talk of power. Ashamed of not sharing the perception of reality with two against one. Slinking home.

Folkets Hus, the communal house on Stengade, was Peter's second home, and he said of his activities there: 'First I made tea, then I seized power.'

He sat on the floor with his legs crossed and brightly coloured crocheted items. He had an overbite and protruding brown eyes and thick glasses (when he took his glasses off in order to clean them or rub his eyes, there was direct access to his mind, it seemed restrained and expectant, the small slightly red-rimmed eyes looked outright cute. I could almost kiss those eyelids. But his hair was so greasy. When the glasses were back in place, the covetous staring returned, and I felt like teasing him. His hair was black; I realize that all the people I am deploying here are dark-haired: OF, my mum, Peter, myself, Anne's Czechoslovakian boyfriend: 'dark and intense,' my mum's expression. But Alma is blonde, my GPS, my light in the darkness) and he wore a Peru hat and red corduroy trousers that stopped a good ways above the winter desert boots, the summer sandals, and crocheted waistcoat. He was quick-witted, fast and hungry for love. He had a hard time keeping away from his maths pupils, which he got more and more of from my secondary school class. Exclusively girls. The teaching took place at ours. He must have kept his lust in check when my mum was present.

Anne and Peter's different tempos obviously did not harmonize very well. Peter annoyed her beyond all reason, and one day she decided to move. I returned the books to the library.

When Peter eventually moved out – it could only have happened in a way reminiscent of how a swirling bee changes course, thrust by a sudden movement in the air. But him we just about kept in touch with. Whereas Anne disappeared forever when she went out the front door with her dissident boyfriend, a member of VS, a Danish Marxist Party and 'terribly brilliant', that was how he was introduced to me; I assumed it was because of him that Anne had wanted to read all those books. We saw him only a couple of times. Once during a visit when he sat holding her hand with our blue painted

242

Mormon clock (sold to us by a Mormon) in the background, while with her toiling and hoarse voice she breathlessly explained something or other, maybe that Emma Goldman had once decided to sell herself too and went out and bought salmon-coloured underwear, but changed her mind and threw them in the river, probably the Spree. And then another time when he came home to pick her up and help carry her belongings.

Peter continued trying to hammer mathematics into us, mania was replaced by depression, and so on. Alma and I visited him once when he was in one of the heavy phases. He had barricaded himself in a bedsit on Fælledvej, in a loft, all the way up on the top floor, and the floor beneath him was almost invisible because of various piles, clutter and rubbish. It smelled like being in a cage, afflicted and ill, with no future.

There were the more peripheral patients whom I never saw, but only heard about or talked on the phone with. Kaj, who always wore black gloves, and whom my mum was afraid to run into when she crossed the grounds between two wards. He had once slapped her so hard that her ears sang. He was a schizophrenic and could not tolerate eye contact. Maybe she had been injured for meeting his gaze. There was an opera singer with a handsomely wavy beard (one day his business card had mistakenly ended up in my school bag and then on the floor of the classroom, I was teased about him, the business card was passed around) and a tremendously deep voice. There was the signwriter Else from Vienna who painted a nameplate for our door, green with gold lettering. And a handsome old Jew with a cracked voice who gave my mum silverware, five short knives and five short forks for eating fruit, strangely short, as if your hands had grown smaller by the time you reached dessert. Charles and I got them later as a wedding present.

Several years earlier that which must not happen happened, something completely inexcusable. My mum had fallen in love with one of her patients and had started a relationship with him. I was eleven. She was forty-two. He was twenty-six. In my mind the relationship is in triple slo-mo; on three separate occasions my body reacted seemingly independent of my will – or of any planning – and it felt as though I found some distance from it (the body) and saw it act (how each of its movements appeared slow, and at once far too clear and dispersed). Each experience is connected with objects (which are all red or reddish). A red bag, a reddish beard, an orange and a burgundy sweater. When my mum told me that she had met him, and that he was moving in with us, I got so furious that my body sent me through the living room with a roar of anger, 'not you too,' I roared and I meant that she now, like my father (the previous year), had found someone else; the anger culminated in me stomping around, jumping up and down on her red bag so that everything inside must have been damaged. Now I have a red leather bag like that. (Nobody has trampled on it yet.) I managed to prevent him from moving in. He came and went with us. I grew fond of him, and one day when he was about to leave, I followed him to the front door, my body shot over to him, and I placed my arm around his neck and pressed my cheek against his. He glided out the door, deprived of all reality. Afterwards I was only aware that it had happened because I could still feel his beard against my chin. He was healthy when he began to stay with us. He got ill. He began to air his thoughts to me; that my mum was out to poison

244

him. I replied that I most definitely did not believe that to be the case. When my mum found out about it, I had asked her one day if it was true, she demanded that he no longer visit us. (So his thoughts would not harm me.) There was a scene. All the while I sat at the dining table spinning an orange in my hands and hating him and supporting my mum. I wanted to throw the orange at him. It developed into him grabbing her by the shoulders. I flew up and elbowed my way between them and shoved his chest (he was wearing his burgundy coloured roll-neck sweater) and rammed my head into it. He left. In the time that followed I imagined that when I was home alone an unseen person wanted to poison me, and so I transported food or drinks with me from room to room. I dared not leave a glass of milk or a cup of tea unguarded in a room. It was a great love. They could meet during his good periods. He had moved to Jutland, and my mum visited him there, on a holiday, on a couple of weekends. He had long since stopped being her patient. When they started the relationship, he must have been taken on by another doctor. She was good for him; and he her. His sisters later told her that; that they were grateful for the happiness that had flowed to him, through her. He had sworn that if he did not get healthy by the time he turned thirty, he would kill himself. And he did not get healthy. When my mum told me about his death (I had just come home from a bike trip on Fyn with Alma), she looked down and banged the edge of her cigarette pack on the table, this tapping and her lowered gaze stated the finality – and how difficult it was to accept.

Around this triple slo-mo there is almost no recollection of him; his coat on the hook and a visit with his friendly sisters, one light and one dark, their toilet seat was sprayed with gold paint. And then the intensity between the two of them, almost tangible, and a pair of wine glasses on the bedside table one morning I went into their bedroom; the two plump glasses leaning against each other was the new love in the house. A love mixed with the thought of poisoning. A love that tore at everything, and that I wanted to conceal. I wanted them to stay inside the flat, not walk arm in arm outside in the world. Not because he had been her patient, I knew nothing about that back then. Because I wanted everything to be the way it normally was. That is what I wanted 'the others' (a word I always used about my classmates) to think. I could not be left on my own with a shattered nuclear family. But I was, and for that reason I stayed home from school for long periods. Until suddenly a liberator entered the picture; Alwilda joined my class and cheerfully dragged a trail of stepmothers and stepfathers behind her. Now there were two of us.

We lived with the secret that my mum herself had taken ill, twice after I was born and several times as a young woman. One morning when I woke up, she was not there; I hit my dad when he told me that she had been taken to the hospital. I was five or six. She later told me that the mania had given her a fever. The first night of her hospitalization, because of a lack of beds, she had been placed in a bathroom. The tap dripped, and she said something to me about the sound, maybe that it mixed with her thoughts, her feverish mind, and that she was thirsty, but did not get a glass of water. Maybe she said that each time it felt like the drop hit her forehead. Then I imagine a stone slowly being hollowed out.

I was too young to have realized that she was getting ill. Later I understood that there was something wrong when she started to reorganize the flat – the start of the belongings' cruise which later in life, when she had been diagnosed with cancer and got ill one time after another like she sat on a see-saw and flew up in the air and fell down again heavily (fear of death made it impossible to keep the illness in check), expressed itself wholeheartedly. She sent furniture and small belongings from one place to the next as if this movement guaranteed life.

How I watched over her.

Maybe once in a moment of weakness she had asked me to do it, to keep watch over her. And if I saw signs of either sadness or heightened activity, I asked her (in a very quiet voice so as not to rouse her anger since I found myself in dangerous territory), 'do you think you might be getting ill?'

It was never chaotic. (And it was always immensely clean, it smelled of Ajax, vinegar and floor wax, and in my mind the smell in the bathroom is dense with moisture and the smell of wet linen, because for a long time she washed everything by hand, in the bath.) Only new forms of order. She took precautions against clutter, the clinging of belongings to one another. She gave things away, including things she thought I had grown out of. It made me beside myself with bitterness. She acquired nothing, made no frivolous purchases, she disposed of things. She talked too much, went way too far in her talking and grew short-tempered – she could not stand being contradicted or interrupted – as though her long chain of thoughts could snap if someone so much as cleared their throat. The usual, patient, gentle and attentive person was replaced by an irritable and headstrong monster.

From that point onward (while I was a child) she managed to keep the mania in check, with the help of medicine and rest.

The second time was depression. Or was it simply complete exhaustion. She was faced with divorce. It was January. She had made it through Christmas (which she had held for the entire family) and had attempted to grin and bear it (my father, the infidelity, his impending move), so that Christmas was not ruined for me. In January she could not take it any longer. The Christmas tree was still standing. A few friends of the family (particularly my dad's), one of whom was a doctor, came by one Saturday afternoon and persuaded her to have herself admitted. They must have come unannounced, in any case she had not managed to put the shopping away, the bulging shopping bags were leaned up against a chair during the entire conversation. She consented to have herself admitted. I experienced it as if she was being taken away. I was given an aquarium in an attempt to console me. I thought that (again) something had happened that at all costs should be kept hidden. I told my friends she was on a holiday. But I came close to revealing it. When I showed one of them the aquarium, I said: 'How annoying that you can't take aquariums with you to the hospi...' I wanted to show my mum the fish immediately. She came home after ten days, and I heard her tell my godmother that she had thrown a slipper at my dad during one of his visits; my godmother pointed me out (pointed in my direction, said my name) to get her to keep quiet, not reveal any more information. My mum might have shrugged, her anger surpassed consideration for me, her anger was volcanic.

After the two hospitalizations she always feared running into a colleague who knew that she had taken ill, one who had treated her or who had simply heard about it. She was afraid it would be held against her if she sought a new position; that it would undermine her authority, that she would be considered incompetent. And she was afraid of getting ill again. She was afraid of coming down in the world after she had become a sole provider.

Maybe the fact that she herself had been ill made her more empathetic, a better doctor.

In my mind, when I look into the house in Jægersborg, I have the impression of destruction, as though I am using a screwdriver against the internal components of existence, against the glass wall that surrounds these secrets. Not that the secrets are subversive now. But they were back then, both for my mother and for me. Well, I am a worm in my own apple.

II.

My mum is the one who has taught me to take notice of nature. But I cannot remember the names of the flowers, in any case not very many at a time. She quizzes me on them – stops and bends down and asks me the name of a flower. And I cannot remember it, or I mistake it for another flower. Not even her favourite flower, periwinkle, do I recognize all the time. It looks far too much like another bluish-purple flower.

It must have been some sort of magic, the time she put a handful of dried hazelnuts in milk and they swelled up and tasted like they had been freshly picked – viewed from my height at the time, that of a five-year-old. And this: by the Neretva in Mostar, long before the bridge over the river was bombed, a small group of children approached us and held out their hands. My mum searched her pockets and her bag for change, to no avail. The children were my age, nursery school children. Then she pulled a perfume bottle out of her bag and indicated to the children that they should hold out their wrists, and then each of them got a puff of *Madame Rochas* on their thin arms. I have a sense that you could feel the water from the river in the air, and that the perfume arrived like a dark heavy gust.

The other day when I saw a painting by Kiefer, a painting of an enormous sunflower at the foot of which, a man is keeled over, (the title of the painting is *Sol Invictus*) I thought, that was how it was to be a child of hers. The sunflower head looked like a shower head. One moment warmth, the next in danger of drowning. I am the one who is keeled over at the foot of the flower. I have died the sun death, I have died the flower death.

My mum is very clear. She wants so much for me, 'I

will fight for you like a lion, to my last drop of blood.'
To help me. She gives me books by the stack. An entire
bookcase. Sound advice. Furniture when I left home. I
was given the sofa on which we followed conversations
through to their countless ramifications, unfortunately
as impossible to relate as music, she'd had it reuphol-
stered. I had chosen the colour. A subdued green, green
with cream. Support me. Understand me, refuse me
(causing a death-like sensation), ('I'm no longer your
grandma,' my grandmother said because I had spent the
money she gave me, on a suede jacket from Flip Machine
with holes in it. She interpreted the holes as an insult. I
could just as well have let the money disappear down a
drain.) They (the women) demand, they command (the
first time Alma met my grandmother she commanded
me to look under the bed for her glasses, I crawled underneath and banged my head on the bottom of the bed.
In the end the bow-wow emerged with the glasses in its
mouth.) They attempt to shape me, and they are so angry at the men because of their negligence that they (the
men) only remain visible as objects for these enormous
waves of anger, weaklings foundering on anger's beach.
Maybe my dad will only become visible in his own right
when my mum dies.

(I am not going to go to that place where I regard her
as almost Christ-like, accompanied by a harlot – though
the harlot went away again – and a handful of lesser
lunatics.) Good thing I have Alma, she preserves the
equilibrium the common sense the grounding. She is
The Voice of Reason, usually, when it doesn't completely abandon her, as with Kristian.

When I was a child, living in the flat below us was a
mother and daughter who to me seemed more or less the

251

same age; they dressed the same, in black clothes, and always looked so unhappy, a kind of eternal mourning. I don't know if the daughter never left home, or if she had moved back home, maybe after a rocky marriage. Never a sound was heard from their flat. It was a grave. On occasion one of them would stick their nose out, holding a bin bag or a net bag. One day one of them died. Shortly after the other one killed herself. Unable to live without each other. The alarming coalescence. Unable to break free of one another. The two of them an example of the worst possible way things can turn out – between mother and daughter.

When my mum was thirteen, at her island's library, she started with A and worked her way through to Z. She ingested everything that could be read. Some things she understood, others she did not. She dreamed of hosting a salon, of becoming a Madame de Staël. And then she ended up with her cabinet of patients. A few close friends. And us: me, Alma and now Charles. I have always wanted her to have the best conversation partners; that her thinking, her knowledge would come into its own. And been unhappy that it does not always do that, that it is stranded within her. She spends her spare time in bed, in her bathrobe and on her heating pad, reading. I often have to stop myself from writing 'book' in a sentence where I should have written 'mum', 'mum' where I should have written 'book'. The two words are more than inextricably bound; they are substitutions for each other.

Sometimes I am unable to take in what she tells me; my thoughts drift somewhere else while she talks, or I just sit staring at her face. Then I strain every nerve, I revise it, like exam material; it could be Golda Meir's biography, European revolutions; I latch onto the material

– so that her efforts have significance, and because I am curious.

Her boyfriend when I was twenty, Mogens, was an (out and out) anti-intellectual. It would have made sense for him and OF to get on well with each other considering they had both been active in the resistance movement and neither of them had ever really got over it, but they did not. They were jealous of each other's exploits, the former resistance fighters approached each other suspiciously. OF had his three murdered informers, Mogens had done something heroic at an improbable young age (and then the enervating period afterwards, to have to spend three or four years in a camp in Sweden just waiting), and they were jealous of each other's relationship with my mum. She had fallen in love with Mogens at school where he was a couple of years above her. They had once shared a kiss, at a school party, where incidentally she had also asked Torry Gredsted, the author of *Paw*, to dance, thereby winning a bet (he was a former student at the boarding school on Bogø and present for that reason). The boarding school is an imposing red building with jagged towers, like a small fortress (historicism), and with large chestnut trees in front of the main building. I have walked past countless times, but have never been inside or so much as crossed the gravel drive. And I have never been able to connect the building with my mum's childhood, only with my own, where at first the building (quite simply) signified that I was halfway up the hill, and later it seemed to me to be a tad ridiculous – borrowing its power and authority from the fortress. On the other hand... now that I am speaking condescendingly of it, I notice that I simultaneously experienced it as a dear old sweater, immensely familiar, and just like the church and the old lighthouse a point that was visible from Grønsund when arriving by boat.

Mogens (surprisingly) went to visit her during a hospitalization when they were at school. But suddenly he disappeared from the boarding school on the island – the resistance movement, the camp in Sweden. Hero was a word associated with him. He looked like Morten Nielsen, with a large mouth, 'still too lowly to die' and 'I am the glow of the cigarette,' she did not forget him. Then one day, after she had turned fifty, he called her and invited her to dinner. She went out and bought a new dressing gown and stood sipping a glass of wine in his kitchen when he suddenly fell to his knees in front of her and wrapped his arms around her hips and buried his head in her bosom. She patted his shaved head, slightly embarrassed, but did not return home until a few days later. He was a telegraph operator on various ships, and she thought that it was ideal having a man who was away the majority of the time. In the beginning she cheerfully gave herself to his way of life, she wore motorcycle gear and sat on the back of his Nimbus, or in the sidecar. (When he insisted on driving her to work, she wriggled out of the leather gear behind a bush, on the grounds, before she set foot in her ward.) She even went to a couple of meetings at the motorcycle club. Mogens believed in the importance of sharing each other's interests and doing everything together. (She quickly began to feel that her long evenings and weekends in bed with books were under threat.) She dutifully ate the rich food he made according to an old fashioned cookbook, until her figure began to bulge, something he (incidentally) had nothing against. He was athletic to behold when after a shower he jumped from bathroom to bedroom in his underpants. I imagined a faun, but a faun stripped of all poetry, not one from *Afternoon of a Faun*. He had a white, well-groomed goatee. Things became different in the flat. A blue haze of cigar smoke hovered below the ceiling, there was always an open bottle of red wine, the one with the bull on it, on the kitchen counter. When he laughed, there was no sound, he leaned forward and fell victim to a silent breakdown, straightened up and continued sucking on his cigar. Like other men with average talents, because it has to be said that was the case with him, he had 'matters' he defended and argued endlessly in relation to. While I rolled my eyes. The traffic, I seem to recall vaguely, was something he had a hard time letting go of. I wonder what he might have thought about that? In all likelihood he made sarcastic comments about cyclists. Himself a motorcyclist. The dinner table where OF, Alma and I were regular Friday guests, became an agitated and tedious place. It normally ended with OF folding in his long arms and legs and smoking within his shell. Mogens read the same two books over and over again. *The Long Ships* volume I and *The Rise and Fall of the Third Reich*. His face was ruddy and worn by weather and wind. His eyes were blue. The stubble on his head was straw or sand coloured. My mum persuaded him to let his hair grow. She associated his practically bald head with violence. So he grew it. But it made him look older and more haggard, like a crofter. He distanced himself from *Information*, the newspaper she had read for the better part of thirty years. He would only watch films with happy endings. He was straight-laced. At the sculpture museum, the sight of *The Water Mother* surrounded by her many children made him spin on his heels and exit Glyptoteket.

A quick detour now that we are on the topic of children,

the other day Clea (who is pregnant) told me the following: '...Stockholm. I was about to go on stage. I was nervous and had a terrible craving for a cigarette, just half a cigarette. Let me hasten to add that until now, during the pregnancy, I have smoked at most ten cigarettes in total. My mum on the contrary smoked up to a hundred a day because she was preparing for her exams while expecting me. I did not grow to be very tall, but that's all right. Naturally smoking is not allowed at the theatre. I went into the ladies' room. There was a queue. I felt the ladies in the queue casting suspicious glances at me. (I always feel as though I am on trial.) It was my turn, and I locked myself in the cubicle. I pulled a perfume bottle out of my bag and kneeled down in front of the toilet and stuck my head halfway down before daring to light the cigarette. It was by no means disgusting, you could have operated inside that toilet, it was antiseptic. While I smoked, I continually sprayed perfume into the air, with the other hand I flushed again and again smoking with no hands and blowing into the cistern. After five or six drags I dared not continue and let the cigarette drop into the water. Now I had obviously flushed so many times that there was no more water. I covered the cigarette with toilet paper and pleasantly dizzy, stepped out into the common area, onto the scaffold. They (the ladies) said nothing, they just looked at me with disappointment and shook their heads. I had not made them angry, I had made them sad. They thought about the little child in my belly. "Sorry," I said. But they could not accept it, they were not the ones who had been harmed. I could beg and plead, I would never be forgiven. Only, perhaps, if I gave birth to a very tall child. I looked at the ladies and said: "The last scan showed that the child is extremely long, it practically has to lie folded over.

It was recommended that I smoke a little to stifle its growth." Now one of the ladies stepped forward: "No, no," she said, "That's not it at all. Do you not want there to be any water left for your child, the way you waste it..." and she grabbed my hand and pulled me into the stall (the obvious smell of smoke) above which there was a sign that I had overlooked.'

My mum had not been with Mogens for very long before she wanted to be rid of him again. She told us that we should guard ourselves against the might of unfinished business, by which she meant that if she had formed a relationship with Mogens when they had been young, this would never have happened. And he wanted to get married. He had already been married six times (though with the same woman twice), but that did not deter him. They shared no social norms; he appropriated small objects from institutions, an ashtray from a hospital cafeteria, shirts from one of the shipping companies he sailed with as a telegraph operator. He liked to pretend he was an officer and wore a uniform at festive occasions; where did these uniforms come from...? It boggled her mind. And once when they were out for dinner, he spat in the food because it had garlic in it, and stormed out of the restaurant. He laughingly told her about a ship's cook who left children at every port, and when my mum objected to such irresponsible behaviour, he said shortly that it was the girls' own fault (*The Water Mother* again). But did he not have a single redeeming feature... yes, in the beginning; wearing a red shirt and with this straw-like hair, the faun bent over the jug of rich sauce; he was interesting to us, first and foremost because he was new. Interesting in the same way as a merry insect. (But how he could sulk.) And because he arrived full of energy and dragged my mum out into the world. I have a holiday photo of them from Madeira where they appear slightly drunk and glistening. One time he drove me home on his motorcycle. I sat on the back and tried to hold onto him almost without touching him. He reached back and made me hold on properly while he laughed at me in his silent manner (shoulders shaking). It made me think of one of his 'matters', that he did not understand how mature men could be interested in little girls (that was how he viewed us) who did not share the same experiences, who had not lived in the same era and did not understand your references; in other words: who were far too young to have experienced the war.

Gradually all of our conversation revolved around how she wanted to be rid of him. They were about to buy a house together. Her need for isolation was seriously under threat. She pictured herself Saturday mornings forced to drink coffee at some random abominable centre. He had told her that if I continued to contradict him, I would not be welcome in their new home. (That did the trick. The lion rose to its feet.) He had already parted with his house on Amager and had moved in with her. His moving boxes were in my old room. In the end she decided that the escape from him would have to take place while he was off sailing. She applied for a job in Vordingborg that included a flat at the hospital and got it. She put up her flat for exchange, it worked out in my favour as I received a colossal flat. I was twenty-five and had long since moved away from home. Still it was difficult to say goodbye to the old place. I had known it my entire life. I lay down on her bed and dissolved into tears. She was doing a final clean-up and did not have time to deal with me. She had all of Mogens' furniture and boxes put into storage. OF came by and disconnected the washing machine. Her own moving van arrived. The flat in Jægersborg became a mirage. In the gap between moving out and moving in she and I went to Portugal.

She sent Alma a postcard of an avalanche and wrote: 'The load we loosen from each other's minds.'

I saw it when I placed the card in the postbox.

OF wrote a rhyme: 'Margrethe the luscious larva has travelled to Algarve.' She sent a telegraph to the telegraph operator. He rang me (when we had returned home), shaken, and said that my mum's conduct both as a normal human being and as a doctor had to be considered irresponsible. I replied that he had not been her patient.

She is old, now. She seldom dresses up. Maybe a pearl necklace at Christmas, a hint of lipstick. To make me happy. Because it shows a certain energy. I look at her mouth, and she says: 'I knew it would make you happy.' I fetch her a pillow, an ashtray, a glass of water, a cup of coffee, the newspaper, and am surprised how strong her shoulders feel. When I embrace her, I see that she has also put her red suede sandals on. They are (by now) the only thing we cannot agree on.

'What do you actually have against them?' she asks, stretching her legs and lifting them up so that she can better see the shoes from the sofa (which has been mine for so long that it needs reupholstering again), at home with Charles and I where she comes to dinner every Friday. And I feel terribly petty, terribly conventional, why can I not just leave her and her red shoes in peace. I ask to be allowed not to like them. I tilt my head and ask whether that is alright. I remind her of some of the worst

259

outfits I have appeared in, which she did not care for.

'The worst one though,' she says to Charles, 'was the time she was going to a party, I ran into her in the stairwell, I was on my way up and she was on the way down – I mention it because if I had been home while she was getting dressed, I would never have let her go out like that – and she was wearing a delightful black velour dress with pink fabric roses sewn on and had bare shoulders, and with that she wore tan tights and brown walking shoes, and then she had rolled a pair of white sports socks down over her shoes. It made me shudder, and I thought: oh no, she'll be teased. But what happened was that one of her friends got drunk and tore off the roses.'

'It was to accentuate the legs,' I tell Charles, 'that's why we rolled our socks over our shoes.'

He contributes by telling us that as a child he could not stay away from his sister's dress-up dolls. He loved them. Then I tell them about a boy I know, who spends all his time cutting bridal dresses out of magazines. Charles says he could have been that boy.

But back to the shoes.

Until my mum got too busy and too tired, she was elegant and always wore powder, rouge, lipstick, had pencilled eyebrows, mascara and eyeshadow. I seem to remember her saying 'the idea of being poor and forced to wear dresses made of cheap synthetic material in ugly patterns is an outrage' on more than one occasion (but at least once when we left the department store Illums Bolighus with a rustle of shopping bags, I had ten new dresses, one for each day of the trip to the Black Sea), 'the idea of being poor and forced to wear dresses of cheap synthetic material from Daells Varehus is an outrage'.

The demand for beauty. The beauty of clothes. The

beauty of the home. Perhaps the beauty of the face and the body too. The absence of beauty – a pit of self-loathing. She herself had impressed the demand for beauty on me. And she herself abided by it until she grew too tired and abandoned it, and why should she continue to be subjugated to the convention of being a 'lady'... personally it makes me think of how bored I get at the hairdresser's, how beauty care and painting my toenails in the summer bore me something fierce, still I take vanity for what vanity is – but it gradually demands less of me. Incidentally the longing to win back her beauty has not entirely released its grip on her, the other day she said to me: 'It's ridiculous, but I still think that if I can just lose some weight, I will be very attractive again.'

I recall an evening many years earlier, in the kitchen at her parents' place, late at night; we had left the loft bedroom we were sharing, and had gone down to the kitchen to grab a snack and take it up to the room. She bent over a piece of bread and spread a quintuple thick layer of butter on top, 'This will give the Heart Foundation something to think about,' she said.

The summer I met Charles, I went to visit my mum at her summerhouse by bike, and when I was going to cycle home, my chain fell off. My mum stood ready to wave, at the garden gate. I did not want my dress to get covered in oil so I pulled it off and fiddled with the chain in my knickers and bra. For me there is nothing worse than objects that are meant to fit together, I can still hear my dad's voice (from my childhood) 'Now try to look after it,' and back then I went all empty inside or was filled with rage, and it's still like that. On my knees on the lawn with the oily chain in my hands, I remembered an issue of *Playboy* that a man from the

United Arab Emirates – who during mine and Alma's trip to Turkey followed us halfway across the country by bus, and along the way a large taciturn character in a yellow sweater joined him, then there were two who disembarked when we disembarked, and checked in at the same hotel or guest house as us and each morning sat waiting for us in the reception without knowing where the day and we would take them, a journey, you might say, in the spirit of Sophie Calle – showed us (sniggering), featuring Le Pen's former wife, Pierrette Le Pen, pictured in a series of cleaning scenarios, undressed, naturally, I remember in particular one image where she was scrubbing the toilet, kneeled down in front of it, with her arm down the toilet bowl and, it seemed to me, her head halfway down as well, in the toilet, from where she sent the beholder a flirtatious-lusty gaze, her breasts pressed against the toilet bowl, embodying the fantasy: the crawling maid, everything, that is the entire photo session, because Le Pen in an interview with *Playboy* had stated that if Pierrette could not manage on her own, then she should live off her lover or take on a cleaning job, and subsequently she and a camera crew from *Playboy* staged these photos.

Then the neighbour came over to gossip. The two women stood looking at my work on the chain, I apologized for my attire to the neighbour, sweating and beside myself, even though it was not my fault that she had barged her way into our garden. And my mum said something along the lines of we were after all women. The neighbour must have left when (glancing at me) she said: 'Now that you've found yourself an older man, you no longer have to be so perfect either.'

She had said something similar once... I had been ill, my skin was spotty, and my hair was flat and lifeless, and maybe it was meant as a comfort when she (laconically) said that it was better to have been beautiful once than to never have been. A despondent remark in a despondent past participle from someone extolling thirsting for demanding beauty. From someone who always found comfort in beauty.

'And that time Alma showed up in a pair of jeans that had *fuck me, baby* written on them. I had a former patient over for coffee for the first time, and I very nearly fell out of my chair.'

Charles nods. He is lying on the floor. She is lying on the sofa. My two fallen warriors. They both have bad backs, they have brittle bones, they are heavy smokers, and her back has collapsed because of bone metastasis whose development has temporarily been halted with the aid of Tamoxifen. In addition she also has degenerative joint disease. And sciatica. But she takes nothing stronger than paracetamol for the pain. She does not want to grow listless and lose clarity and the ability to read. Her greatest horror is that something will happen to her eyes so that she can no longer read. Charles has two unsuccessful back operations behind him. And in addition two failed attempts at regulating his heart rhythm with the help of a couple of proper electric shocks. Next to the two lying here I feel like a kind of floating fairy, very light, pain-free. Quite simply very young, even though I am not. (As if I am their child.) But I am also in the possession of, for the time being, a physical form that is not under attack, and my pulse is regular. Status report complete. Sometimes it is completely exhausting to be around them. One Christmas Eve, we had made it through dinner and presents, the two of them lying down as always, myself sitting, and we were now watching a film, *Delicatessen*. I did not find it interesting, I was quite simply exhausted, so I excused myself and climbed into bed with *The Alexandria Quartet* (to travel somewhere where everything is saturated with meaning, friendships, love affairs, the view of the world, the language. That saturation has contributed to my idea of how everything should be. I think so. I have been reading *The Alexandria Quartet* for the past thirty years, often only a couple of random pages, I know the books so well that I immediately know where I have landed, *Justine*, *Balthazar*, *Mountolive* and *Clea*. And Pursewarden and Darley and Nessim and Narouz. And Melissa – with the flat scissor-shaped thighs.

Justine looks in the mirror and says: 'Tiresome pretentious hysterical Jewess that you are!'

And Pursewarden (author): 'I want style, consort. Not the little mental squirts as if through the ticker-tape of the mind.'

The duck hunt. The masquerade ball. The intelligence officers. The fast rides through the desert. The secret lodge. The alchemist Capodistria who is successful in creating four homunculi, a king, a queen and a red and blue spirit in bottles. The king breaks free and attempts to get in with the queen, his small nails clawing at the bottle. Capodistria gets some ugly scratches that will not heal when he attempts to capture him. I once launched myself into a comprehensive study of the alchemists due to this scene alone.

And here Darley is speaking: 'Like the dead Pursewarden I hoped I might soon be truthfully able to say: I do not write for those who have never asked themselves this question: at what point does real life begin?'

And finally, Darley on his relationship to Justine: 'Possession is on the other hand too strong: we were human beings not Brontë cartoons.'

264

Lawrence Durrell, the author of *The Alexandria Quartet*, did not get in to Cambridge, he applied several times, but was rejected, reportedly because he was terrible at maths. The composition of the tetralogy is based on Einstein, it is an attempt to convert a mathematical theory, the theory of relativity, into language, three of the works are an expression of space, and one of time, 'the soup-mix recipe of continuum'.

The existence of an absolute unique frame of references is rejected; all depending on where the events in the books are seen from, they appear different.

But that is not what makes one's hair curl – that happens when Balthazar drops Narouz's harpoon gun in the water and the harpoon goes off just as Clea has dived down to the wreck, and her hand is riveted to the spot in the depths so Darley has to get a knife from the cabin and dive down and cut off her hand – in order to bring her back alive from the bottom of the sea. And when Amaril tears off Semira's mask and sees that she has no nose, it has been eaten away, and proposes to her on the spot and decides to create a new nose for her, he is a doctor, in fact a gynaecologist, but he launches into a complex plastic surgery, Clea has designed the nose, and the following year it grows on Semira's face, and she is ready to stand before Alexandria after spending most of her life hidden in a dark room because of the darkness of her face, it might be said, and the majority of Alexandria's high society are present when she dances into the hall with her doctor) and left them to each other, I could not manage for a moment longer to be the one they both knew best, with both of them at the same time; it felt as though they each had to be given extra consideration, even more than when I had them on their own.

It can be difficult to manage, both taking care of the

practical matters and sitting down with them and listening and talking – without thinking of what I have to do for them afterwards. At times my mum complains of me being distracted, that I am not really present. It is difficult to concentrate on a conversation – sitting across from a face writhed in pain, a person attempting to find a slightly better body position, at the same time as she and he, because they both do it, insist on conversing, to think of something other than the pain. At the same time – I don't know what word to use – I admire (but that sounds too distanced) them for it while my-heart-bleeds.

Charles seemed to have the idea that I could manage everything. Gradually as my mum lost her grip on things, Charles and I took responsibility for the care of her summerhouse, yes I make it sound like an estate, though it is very small. But the large shady trees and white benches transformed the garden into a park.

Charles had arranged to have a couple of the mighty huge trees felled in order to create more light. As per his request, the gardeners had chipped the trees and left the wood chips behind. There must have been ten to fifteen tonnes. Charles envisaged that the chips would be used to fill the craters left by the trees. The previously wild and soughing location looked like a lunar landscape. I dragged my garden chair up onto a mound of chips and burst into tears. Charles put his hand on my shoulder and told me he envisioned that I would take a shovel and start to level the large property – and fill it up with wood chips. That might take years. I had other things to do.

But he took pity on me. Or I refused to grasp the shovel – or live with the sight of the barren brown parcel of land. The gardeners returned riding a huge machine. And it was levelled. And grass was sown. And then we had a big green plot of lawn, as flat as a pancake. My mum thinks it is boring.

'Men love felling trees,' I say; I am standing with my neighbour on the shiny coin that the garden now is.

'Yes,' she says brightening up, 'I was always disagreeing with my husband about that too. He loved chopping down trees. But I preferred to keep them.'

She looks at me with an expression of superior knowledge, and we allow ourselves a moment of unfathomable oversimplification and share a brief Freudian moment in the garden. A rare moment of agreement. She, the neighbour, often comes running to meet us when we arrive at the summerhouse and follows us into the garden and points at places of decline: 'Such a pity,' she says, 'look, such a pity.'

One day when my mum sat in her flat in the city centre, she had begun to long for the sea. She walked down to Nørreport Station and caught the train to Hillerød, and from there she continued to Hundested. (Several years earlier Mogens had been aboard his icebreaker in Hundested Havn, and she had visited him on this icebreaker.) There is an estate agency next to Hundested Station, a Dan Bolig, and displayed in the window was a small thatched house with a vast garden. It reminded her of the (thatched) home of her childhood. Instead of going to the sea she opened the door to the agency and drove out to the summerhouse with the estate agent. It was close to the fjord. She took me with her a couple of days later so I could see it before she made up her mind.

She had made up her mind. She told the estate agent about the seamen in her family. She said that she thought only sailors were real men.

The estate agent nodded. He concurred. I squirmed

like an eel because she talked too much, made wild associations, like I was ten years old again, and pouted like I was ten years old, and said grumpily that the house was far too small. They did not hear me. They talked about men as they signed. The estate agent's partner was an able seaman.

'This is a paradise,' I have said that to her countless times later (and been happy that I failed as a guardian that day; so that she got her house).

The red shoes make me think that my mum has joined 'the cheap synthetic materials' camp, so to speak, even though the sandals are made of suede. And even though she has not become poor. On the contrary she receives a good pension. But she has been close to dying, and 'when you have been licked by the Crab, a lot of things stop being important. Can't you understand that?'

She had almost given up, she has moved countless times (that is, seven), scattered her furniture to the four winds, given almost everything away, 'so you're not left with all that,' for my sake at that, even though I protested madly at these disposals and wished she had abided by the convention of 'a beautiful home' and not replaced the beautiful heavy furniture with wicker 'because it is easier to manage', but then she placed beautiful little objects, knick-knacks rocks candles flowers within her field of vision and let her gaze be drawn by them.

How many times have I thought that if she hadn't moved out of the flat in Jægersborg she'd lived in for twenty-five years all of this relocating might never have started?

CAN I APPROPRIATE HER MUM?

[Alma]

OF would do anything for us. But it was difficult to get the opportunity to do something for him. He lived entrenched. You could not ring him. He could only make outgoing calls with his phone. At least that's what he claimed. Maybe he just did not pick up the phone when it rang, or he lived with the cord unplugged. And he would never have visitors at his flat. He did not think it was nice enough. It had to be redecorated first. But that never happened. He stalled us, year after year. Camilla's mum was allowed to visit him once. It was a bachelor pad, there were a couple of bikes in the shower cubicle. On one occasion I made it as far as his front door, I rang and rang, there was something I had to tell him, but the door did not open, I left a message. When the flap of the letterbox slammed shut, and my note fluttered onto the floor of his entrance – I didn't know whether he stood there, as still as a grave. But I don't think so.

I had dropped by because I had written a play, a monologue, it was the first time I had written something that long, for six weeks I had worked in a rapture, and now I was finished. I strode from my flat to his, and my head was singing, 'Here comes success, here comes success / Oh hooray success, hooray success.'

He had to hear that I had finished it – that I had created a wonderful piece of work. And he had to help me figure out what to do with it. Where I should send it. I knew he knew a publisher. I envisaged that my monologue would be published in book form. I was not particularly interested in theatre. For a brief time I had thought I would become an actor, and Camilla's mum had arranged for some private lessons with a director. I thought I had seen tears glimmer in her (the director's) eyes when I embodied Portia in her sitting room (wearing a red dress with a wide gloss belt and white boots that went high up my thighs, more *Pretty Woman* than Portia; when we reached the court scene, she pulled a tremendous piece of fabric out of a commode, and draped it over my shoulders as a cape), and even though the tears made me proud, I quickly lost interest. Camilla's mum thought that the main reason I accepted the lessons was in order to boost my self-confidence. (I had a hard time opening my mouth at large gatherings, my group at university was so big that we sat on the floor and in the window-sills; the one time I said something, I got so embarrassed that I raced out of the room immediately after. I had a high and thin voice, Camilla's mum often encouraged me to 'turn up the bass', and when I said something, people turned around to see who the strange voice belonged to. I had recurring ear infections as a child, and once an ear-nose-throat-doctor said at the sound of my voice: 'There is no way anyone can have a voice like that,' my parents were with me, neither of them protested, I had once heard my mum say that I sounded like the kind of toy that peeps when you squeeze it, why would she defend her peeping mouse?)

The monologue was about a man who was so afraid to die that he wanted to be stuffed: 'in order to be *in* the world, without being *of* the world.' He had already killed and stuffed his friend. The monologue was addressed to her and to a stuffed bird that had obviously inspired this human stuffing.

OF made an appointment with the publisher. But before that I had an appointment set up with one of Camilla's mum's former patients who was an author. (Camilla's mum was my second mum, I ate at their place at least once a week, and once I had a falling out with my own mum, I moved in with them and stayed there for six months.) I was allowed to meet him at his home. I was so nervous that I knocked over an entire jug of juice. We sat in his kitchen. When I was finished reading, I hardly dared to look up.

Lengthy silence.

'You must have really suffered,' he then said.

I did not know if that was good or bad. And he said nothing more. I started to feel like a patient.

'It's either brilliant, or else it does not work at all,' I said.

'Maybe it's somewhere in between,' he said kindly (but I did not believe it). I scraped up my papers. The consultation was over.

OF and I met at the corner so we would arrive at the publisher's together. I had a bad feeling straight away. OF appeared drunk, and we had barely got through the door at the publisher's, before he pulled a couple of bottles of wine out of his shopping trolley and placed them on the table in front of us. First they talked about old times, OF's life had ground to a stop, the publisher was an active person, OF was stuck in the past. Then OF began to sing my praises, not mentioning my monologue, but my appearance and my nature, and it became clear that he did not think my monologue would suffice on its own, I had to be part of the transaction. We were here to sell me. The publisher squirmed in his seat and finally said politely: 'We have to watch out that I don't fall head over heels for Alma.' I squirmed. OF persisted. OF drank and with each long gulp his praise grew more fulsome, his final trick was to grab the publisher's hand with one hand and mine with the other and try to hitch our hands. We resisted his efforts, and after leaving my monologue *Satan and All His Pomp* on the table I dragged OF away, two sheets to the wind, got him on a bus and stood watching him and his bag practically slalom down the centre of the bus. And nobody wanted my monologue, neither the publisher nor Radioteatret nor any other theatres. But obviously it was not OF's fault. For a long time, maybe for a couple of years, I read it to anyone I could get to listen.

Telling Camilla's mum about the incident was completely out of the question, even though OF belonged to her, so to speak, since he was originally her friend, and they were much closer in age than OF and I; the incident included alcohol and (an invitation for) sex; elements of mine and Camilla's life that she – Mum – had no access to. Even though we were grown up and had long since moved away from home. Then I happen to think of how we used to sip from the bottles of liqueur and other alcohol she had before we would go out dancing and cavorting, at the age of fourteen or fifteen at Tophat in Bakken in our white trousers that we put on wet to make them more clingy. When Bakken closed at midnight we rode home through Dyrehaven on our bikes, and if we heard bikers approaching on their motorcycles, we hopped off our bikes and hid in a ditch (lights off and hearts, mine at least, pounding).

She would only have one drink when there were guests over, she had no drinks cabinet, the bottles were kept at the bottom of the kitchen cupboard, gathering dust, because they had been there for years. When we arrived, the contents of the bottles quickly disappeared. To conceal our boozing we topped them up with water. Until the time Camilla's mum poured something for a guest that was so diluted, practically water, that we were exposed.

She (Camilla's mum) speaks impeccably. The sentences leave her mouth fully formed, no hesitating, no repetitions. Her speech is like elegant handwriting. I like to imagine that I have spent so much time with her (from the age of four) that she has contributed considerably to my linguistic development. When I say something ambiguous, she forces me to be more precise. They say it takes three generations to create a gentleman. Her father wrote, though was never published. She wrote when she was young. She had poems and short stories appear in *Vild Hvede* in the fifties. She had shown them to me; she had lost her own copies, but OF found them at the library and photocopied them for her, here is one of them, she was nineteen:

ASHES

I rest at your feet like a pile of ashes,
consumed by the fervent flames of love,
whilst the bliss of our embrace slowly fades.

Before this I was a child, now I am a woman,
and the wonder has happened on this night,
sculpted by your strong hand and flaming mouth.

We knelt before our god of love
and quenched our thirst at love's fountain –
the wondrous water, which induces thirst.

I thank you, my beloved, for
you woke me and crowned my brow
with the gold and rubies of love.

Viggo F. Møller invited her to a restaurant in Tivoli to celebrate her debut in *Vild Hvede*, and at the restaurant she had to brush his hand off her thigh. They ate open prawn sandwiches, and out of ignorance she sprinkled salt on her prawns and was informed that only pepper is to be used with prawns, and felt socially inadequate. She went red from head to toe. Had he kept quiet, maybe she would have been able to enjoy everything – her debut, her notion of a future as a poet, the day, the prawn sandwiches, the distinguished company – had he been better able to cope with rejection; had he been more magnanimous that day.

She went so far into her notion of becoming an author that she abandoned her medical studies and sold her textbooks. She sat down and tried to write for fourteen days; but nothing came to her. She thought she had to come up with something. She arrived at the conclusion that she lacked any imagination. She bought back her medical textbooks, poetry turned into terrible limericks like this one by her private tutor: 'On the valvula Bauhini / the final villus stands / waving at the faeces / which near the anus lands.'

At parties the male students hung up huge pairs of knickers and bras on washing lines along with inflated condoms and displayed organs and body parts embalmed in formaldehyde which they cheerfully dropped their cigarettes in with a hideous smell the result, all very cringeworthy.

She has scarcely written since the fifties. If I am considered her daughter, it could be noted that it has taken three generations to create an author. Instead she has this consummate elocution (which my writing has grown out of), which is conveyed by a voice whose tonal range seems enormous, from dark to tremendously bright and all the tones in between.

One afternoon she looked up from Colette's *Sido* and said: 'Maybe you'll write a book like this about me one day.'

She said it shyly, or modestly. The desire by those who do not write for a memento in words. An *illam vixisse*, 'this woman has lived' (as Roland Barthes designates it in *Mourning Diary*. I don't know if his mam (what he calls his mum) had a need to be written about. But he had a need to write about her, an *illam vixisse*.

When Edward called his notes about his mourning over his parents' death *Mourning Diary*, he was not aware of Barthes' diary. He first heard about it a couple of weeks ago. He ran out and bought it straight away. Now we have all read it.)

'One day' pointed towards the time after her death. It sounded like when she talked about her career, her contribution, and with raised eyebrows intended to give the statement an element of self-deprecation she said: 'I ought to be dined at the archeion – that was a way to honour Athenians in antiquity, to invite them to dinner at the town hall, to be dined at the archeion.'

Back to Sido, Colette's mother. A mild woman in a large and lush garden places her hand under the chin of a flower and says something beautiful. She loved her flowers so much that she would not give them away for funerals:

'No. Nobody condemned my roses to die with Mr Enfert.'
—— Colette, *Sido*

At times I think that Camilla's mum still envisages and

hopes that she will become a writer. Like Colette's father hoped throughout his life. After his death, this was discovered in his library:

> 'Two hundred, three hundred, one hundred and fifty pages per volume; beautiful ribbed kraft paper, luscious and soft as cream, or thick exercise paper, meticulously trimmed, hundreds and hundreds of blank pages...'
> — Colette, *Sido*

Occasionally she complains that she has not created something lasting; here she is not thinking of fiction, but of research into depression. Then I remind her of all the gifts she has received from her patients over the years. And she replies that the only thing she has done has been to listen and never judge.

I am just like her in that regard, in that I have chosen a different path from my parents; I pushed off with my arms and dragged the rest of my body over the vaulting horse – she left behind sailors and housewives, me, a crystal decanter on a mahogany sideboard in a sitting room with a desolate gleam and the bourgeoisie precept that if something has not been noticed, it has not existed. They did not anticipate my intelligence, my dad thought that at most I would be able to manage a hotel, but would most probably end up at an ironmonger's; my grandma asked me straight up if getting my foot in the door at Danish State Railways was something that would interest me. She could not drop the idea of me in uniform (back then green-brown) behind the counter in the dining car. They do not know who I am. Can I choose to have Camilla's mum as my own? (And what about her dad... he is gentle and good at protecting himself. He has what must be one of the most beautiful gardens in Copenhagen; every single centimetre is in bloom; a gentle person in a beautiful garden.)

Camilla is, with her voracious appetite for literature, a kind of copy of her mum. Often when I come to visit, they are in the middle of a conversation, sitting at either end of the sofa, under the same plaid blanket. (I have keys and let myself in while I announce myself with a 'cuck-oo.') They look up. They welcome me. They do seem happy to see me. But they are far away – in each other. The living room seems charged. Yes, that's right: I am jealous. Of both of them.

'Your mum said: "When I'm no longer here, you can write anything you like about me."'

'But I don't think she means that,' Camilla answered. 'She also once said to me that even though we are getting along with each other now, you should remember that it has not always been like that.'

'I remember – it was when the three of us were at the summerhouse together, and I had sat writing in the annexe all morning and came in to see you – her studying me and said: "It's not that writing is going to make you outright ugly, I can't say that, but something is happening to your face." I went into the bathroom and looked at myself in the mirror, and it was true. My face appeared dissolved and tired – from the effort of collecting something from deep within and bringing it out; the digging through all the layers of time'.

I happened to visit OF. Not in his home, but at the hospital where he lay with ruined lungs, from all his smoking; it was a couple of weeks before he died. The suit was replaced by a pair of green pyjamas. By the way the nurses treated him, it was apparent that he had worked up a personal relationship to every single one of them. One smoothed his duvet, and another one sat down for a moment on the edge of his bed and held his hand.

For a long time he had not been able to walk more than a couple of steps without having to stop and gasp for air. On these stuttering walks I used to pretend that I was terribly interested in something or other, a shop window or a tree, and stop and look at it in order to give him the opportunity to catch his breath. He saw right through me.

I had published my first book, and he was proud of me. I don't think he ever read it, but he clipped out every single line he could find about me in the newspapers and magazines, and sent them to me.

WEDDING

[Alma]

As soon as the final note had sounded, his cousins and other male relatives grabbed Kristian and lifted him high into the air where he screamed and thrashed about (if he had fallen on the stone floor, and cracked his head open, I think his blood would have looked like fish or poultry blood, thin and bluish, with a cold foul smell), while a couple of others tore his shoes off his flailing feet and cut holes in his socks as per tradition. I could no longer think of him as man. I was happy that Charles immediately turned his back on the situation; that he did not contribute to his degradation. There was something about the way his back billowed in the air that made him insect-like.

I had really gone all out. I had got a French manicure, had my hair and make-up done – I removed the make-up at the last moment, the Polish make-up artist had made my face look like a heavy, dead (and rather Eastern European) mask consisting of a thick layer of shiny powder, light-purple lipstick; it was liberating to watch it run down the drain. For a long time I hoped we could avoid the bridal waltz. I have never been able to memorize sequences of movements as such. But Kristian's mum insisted. She arrived with a CD in her bag and tried to help us, at home in the living room. But she could not get through to me. I decided on lessons with a professional. The woman at the dance school could have been a man. Built like a dockworker, this dance robot. Arms covered in long black hair, she tugged and towed me about. If she had been one of the marathon dancers in *They Shoot Horses, Don't They*, she would have lasted a long time.

The floor – like a fifth element, which let us sway, let us glide, let us breathe. Many lessons later I thought that something near perfection had been achieved, and I wished that she could replace Kristian, just on the big day, during the terrifying minutes it takes the waltz to sentimentalize through time; a melody full of stops and starts, like someone carrying a wardrobe and constantly having to put it down, dragging it for a bit instead. The bridal dance is bittersweet, a frightful word, intimating that peaks follow valleys, but valleys follow peaks again.

On the big day someone had let the dance go on for what felt like an eternity.

'Now we'll forget everything,' he said and started to bounce – easy for him to say, I was the one who had taken lessons. As if from the outset there had been an understanding that I was the hopeless one. While the guests came closer and closer, clapping, I thought of a novel by Alistair MacLean (I loved him when I was very young, oh *Ice Station Zebra*), where the criminals have ended up in a field, in Poland or maybe in the Ukraine, back then the breadbaskets of the world, it was harvest and the harvesters (wearing national dress? All very authentic, quasi-fascistic) close in on the culprits and make a ring around them, with their harvest tools stretched out, scythes and forks, and do away with them, infinitely slowly, in a kind of stomping forward march, chopping, at the ground, the blood, the corn. Our guests had only their hands, and their palms echoed through the air.

In the end, when the guests had closed in around us to hide the sight of us from the world, and there was good reason for that, I placed my arms around Kristian's neck and, still bouncing, buried my head in his shoulder. But what use is *that* on such a day when you are more dress than person. When it was finally over, I fled to the garden. And I was almost unable to bring myself to return to the party, that's how embarrassed I was.

THE WORLD'S GO-GO POLE

[Camilla]

I need to keep my mind active, give it something to work on, just like you use prayer beads or knitting needles to prevent your hands from becoming pendulums that heavily and resignedly pull the body down or on the contrary swing into the air or rub and pick and chewing gum for the mouth, otherwise it (the mind) fiddles with catastrophes the outcome of which always results in coffins or in any case deathbeds or farewell letters, immensely trivial, but for that reason no less troublesome. I can get so consumed by an idea that I do not pay attention to where I am going, but accidentally run a red light and have to get off my bike and walk, but still one of these imaginary catastrophes has not led to a real one. It is normally only some ways into the catastrophe that I realize that I am in the midst of it, then I say 'stop,' but a moment later I am caught up in a new catastrophe. Perhaps catastrophe is too big a word when only one person dies at a time. But the person who dies – it is catastrophic for me. (I once talked to a psychologist about it, and she said that a person should not think that way. But I do. And there we foundered. Death cannot be plucked out with a pair of tweezers.)

It is the people I care for that my thoughts subject to disasters. Those whom I would hate to lose most of all, Charles, my mum, Alma. Or myself, writing goodbye to one of the three, as I find myself on the day of judgement, summing up what we've had together, a long thank you. (How daft. How pathetic.)

I think there was one time where instead I imagined that I saved people from drowning and from terrorists in planes while I sprang from seat to seat; civilization's two possibilities: hero or victim. But the heroic era is presumably past, replaced by departure and the final farewell. What can this mire be traced back to? Have I once, for a rather long time, felt under threat; so that one wall of my cranium is built of fear of loss, and the consciousness, in a kind of pleading gesture, has to play ball (catastrophes) against it with an endless bonk bonk; who knows, but it is exhausting, and at times I would happily exchange my head with someone else's, but of course I could end up with something worse, like for example the voice that periodically tells Charles that he is no good at anything, then I'd rather have deathbeds, thank you, oh generous allocator of unpleasantness.

Late in the summer when I returned to Copenhagen after several months in the country everything seemed rich and beautiful and immense. I saw the world as a platter, the elements arranged / numerous and varied, so many types shapes colours, so many moods, so many possibilities. I felt good, better than I had in a long time. Everything became clear, radiant, practically gleaming. At first it was lovely, then it was as though any object that my eyes happened to fall upon, or which entered my field of vision, made unreasonable demands on my attention. I had to stare. I simply could not stop. And even if it was a familiar object (a lamp at home, a pylon somewhere, with this continuous sound of water across its straddling leg), it was as though I had never seen it before. If I looked down for a moment and then observed it again, it was (again) completely new. It was tiring. I felt like going into hibernation. But it was demanded of me, all manner of things required my attention.

During a bout of staring I realized that in order for

something to be completely new all the time, it (also) had to constantly be destroyed. Death birth death birth, so to speak. The way the death of something then takes form. Visibly, in the blink of an eye. Logical madness.

And thus I ended up where I always end, on the dreary topic of death. Why can I not stop myself. I no longer want to twist everything around the subject of death as though it were the world's go-go pole.

THE HAIR IN THE DRAWER

[Edward]

I asked the undertaker for a lock, but he took a scalp –
judging by the thickness of the envelopes, closer to two
scalps, a Native Indian with his own business. These
envelopes lie in my chest of drawers, sharing the drawer with my socks and underwear, my hands find them
when I rummage around inside; or I see a corner poking up, the escape of a white sail through black reefs (of
socks and underpants). I have never again considered
opening them. I once dared to peek inside, and there was
plenty, overwhelming quantities of white rustling hair
and the memory of the pink scalps (his was also spotted), and what it was like to stroke their hair, those dear
old dogs. I am not in the habit of fetishizing. But am I
not ascribing value and power to the hair in these envelopes... should it be called sentimental value? Should it
be called the *pars pro toto* value? Should it just be called
a dear memory? In any case I cannot bin it. My parents'
hair. It ought to have been burnt, along with them. Now
I am left with it. It is a practical problem that I am con-
fronted with. It is a long time since I clung to life by a
thread, alone and forsaken, and called out to my parents,
but then they had long since flown off to heaven, dogs
have mercy on me.

Why I call them dogs: sitting here at my side, or rather slouched, just like its master (me), as always reflecting
my state of mind, their young substitute, their replacement on the road of life, with a mouldy odour coming
from its mouth, the little dog, the young dog that entered
my life when they died/and left the world desolate, and
in whose company I have walked away my grief for them
while in some or other sense I always experienced it (the

young dog) as their alter ego, reincarnation, ghost, a rutting version.

Of course I could just leave it (the hair) there, then someone in a hundred years will find the chest of drawers in a lumber room and open the drawer, and it might unfold for the person in question like it did in Guy de Maupassant's short story 'A Tress of Hair' where a rich young man, a lover of beautiful things, finds in a piece of Venetian furniture from the seventeenth century, in a secret drawer, placed on a bed of velvet, an enormous and long light-haired plait. This young man already feels like this in advance:

'The past attracts me, the present terrifies me because the future means death.'

So it suits his nature to begin to love the object of the past such as the hair is. He has the plait and conjures up the entire woman. He caresses it, sleeps with it, makes it his companion and takes it with him to the theatre whereby the trap snaps shut:

'But they saw her... they guessed... they arrested me. They put me in prison like a criminal. They took her. Oh, misery!'

Before the young man finds the hair, the Venetian furniture seems irresistibly alluring, he has to own it. Personally I see my own light-blue, slightly heavy chest of drawers first and foremost as a practical arrangement, as a piece of furniture tasked with containing many things, also far too many, whose key often disappears, and whose small hinges hang and dangle and could use

286

a few screws. My chest of drawers, this awkward enveloper of the hair, is of little attraction. I can certainly stay away from it. I am not drawn towards it and its wavy mess. But I can well imagine a man in the future, or a woman for that matter, finding these envelopes and falling in love with the contents, this twinned hair, white and rustling, and let it fall down over her face like a forgiving rain. Afterwards it might be difficult to pick it up again, my dear dogs had short hair, it is not like the long plait in the story, a single beautiful piece, but many small (pieces). Oh, all these locks. If the sensitive person wishes to repeat the action (let it rain down over the face) then he or she must first sweep up the hair and stuff it back in the yellowed brittle envelopes, and would the broom not kill the romance; but without the broom, with the romance the desire the love unchallenged, there can only be talk of a single meeting between face and hair. I imagine the entire thing taking place in an attic.

Camilla's Indian friend is Sikh and keeps her hair covered. She is not allowed to cut it. Whatever she combs off or loses, she carefully burns. I no longer remember her explanation why, according to her religion, she has to do that, but I can ask again. In any case one day I visited Charles and Camilla, their Indian friend had stayed overnight at their place and had (obviously) just been in the shower and washed her hair. She sat in a small room behind the kitchen, Camilla's study. She shouted 'hi' to me. 'Hi,' I shouted back. The door to the room was ajar. All the way along the kitchen counter, in the height between the kitchen cupboards and the kitchen counter, there are mirrors mounted. Camilla has for years talked about replacing them with tiles, because the mirrors constantly get stained with spray of water and grease and have to be polished. I sat in the kitchen with my back to the small room and facing the mirrors. In there I saw (suddenly) this secret hair. It was long and black and shiny, the owner shook her head as she brushed the hair, and the wonderful hair disappeared from the mirror and then reappeared. She knew that I was in the kitchen, that the door was ajar. But maybe she did not think about the mirrors. What more can I say other than: it was a beautiful sight. She is a slightly lean and yellowish and often afflicted person. I think that she showed me her hair. To rise in my esteem.

There are some, for example Alwilda, who think that I am a parent-lover, that I lived and continue to live in a symbiosis with the dear dogs, that I cannot cut the umbilical cord, and whatever else there are of strings and ties (around the neck, like millstones). To that I reply: 'Alwilda and others! If that was the case, do you not think that I would constantly be poking my nose into the envelopes?'

(Yes, yes, it is settled here.)

Then I did it all the same, I opened the envelopes, I defied the ban I had set for myself. And the affection almost knocked me out cold.

('Dog' was a word to keep the longing at bay, cynical from *kyon*, dog, right?)

I could not stand it and tried to tell myself: Paul Celan's mum's hair, for example, was never allowed to turn white, pull yourself together.

(Then I heard my psychologist's voice: Now give yourself permission to be in the feeling, Edward.

The psychologist's utopia: a mind in unison.

According to him (my psychologist), a person ought to start to see a psychologist soon after birth, in order to get a running start; avoid blockages, accumulations; the psychologist as a chimney sweep, equipped with a long pipe or is it a large brush, to knock out the soot. Apropos outfits, the other day I had to call for 'the wasp man' to get him to remove a large wasp's nest, and he arrived, wearing a white silky full-body outfit with collars and an incredible tool wound around the arm, extremely mythological, if only I could say he had met the chimney sweep on the way out.)

NOT DIVIDING, SUBDIVIDING

[Alma]

Standing on the threshold of a new relationship (Edward) I want to try to explain why I ended up having to leave Kristian. I was thirty-five, and my nature had by that point long since forced his nature into a corner. I felt like I was a sack of sand, dry all the way through, ready to be thrown onto a lorry and driven away. We had each entrenched ourselves in our own end of the flat. In the middle was the bedroom with the marital bed which we still shared, and where we met around midnight, each arriving from our own domain. We pulled out our ear plugs from the pillows (small nasty fiddly orange things, Camilla's mum once called them dwarf dicks, 'no, what did I say,' she said straight after with a simultaneously delighted and appalled laugh) and twisted them into place so the other person's sleep or sleeplessness would not disturb. Kristian hopped into bed wearing woollen socks, for the sake of his health, it made his legs look like saplings, rising up from these woollen boats.

When he entered the living room where I lay on the sofa drying up, I had a feeling that he came from the outside, on a visit. He felt like that too, he went awkward and almost hesitant. If I was well disposed, I pulled myself up into a sitting position, so my double chin smoothed out. I was privileged, because as long as I had the sofa, he had to make do with a mattress on the floor, in his room – which was not a living room like mine, but just a room, though with stucco just like mine. Kristian had never unpacked his belongings, they were still in moving boxes in his room, entire towers or pillars or consoles of boxes which clothes and towels were slung over. Wet towels – detour required, the sound of flames, the sound of accidents: our honeymoon was in Paris. During our stay we visited a friend, Maja. We stayed with her for a couple of nights. Morning. Kristian comes out of the shower. He hung his wet towel to dry above a standing lamp in our room. The cover of this lamp was open on the top, like a sieve, so to speak, the bulb was exposed, good lord. We left the flat and wandered around the city all day, among other things we saw von Trier's *The Idiots*, the French did not laugh by and large, not even when the idiots try to sell a Christmas decoration. Twelve hours later when we came home, I turned on the light to our room and continued into the kitchen where Kristian had sat down with Maja. A little later a burning smell. We raced out of the kitchen. A pillar of fire rose from the lamp. The towel had long since dried. One of us, two of us, grabbed a wool blanket to smother the fire as we tried to throw it over and span it like an arched bridge, but the fire greedily ate the wool and received the fuel to jump over to the furniture. Such speed. But not on the part of the fire service. Soon the entire flat was burning, and the three of us stood out in the staircase wringing our hands. (We had taken our rucksacks with us even though we were in doubt as to whether it was the right thing to do now that all of Maja's things were burning.) Suddenly Maja thought: 'Oh God, my letters. My photographs.'

We tried to hold her back, with no luck. She ran into the flat and began to struggle with a large chest of drawers. We followed her and pulled and dragged, but she was practically glued to the chest of drawers. Then the fire service arrived. They got her out. There she came, bent over, between two firemen. 'My hands, my hands,' she wailed and held out something white and flossy as well as black for us. We followed her down to the ambulance and stood watching it drive away. On the way up the stairs we again passed a couple of firemen who were on their way down.

'Is he finished?' I asked them, struggling with my French.

'Is he finished?' one repeated and laughed and nodded. We went up to the completely burnt out flat. The walls were black, the smell was raw. I looked to where we had left our things. I found a small hard orange clump. It was my beloved orange coat (artificial material) with white stitches in the seams from Nørgaard, melted. I stuck the clump in my pocket. The next day we visited Maja at an ultramodern military hospital, but we were not allowed in due to the risk of infection. We had to stand behind a glass pane. Her bandaged hands were placed on a suspended stand and looked like large helpless fins. She lay tossing her head back and forth on the pillow. Her upper body was naked under a sheet, and a long breast was sensed. It ended up occupying a disproportionate amount of my attention, watching it disappear and appear under the sheet. She had just had her bandaging changed, we heard, and it required her getting a large dose of morphine.

She could not work the following year. We had destroyed her life. To top it all off, our insurance company launched a conflict with hers, and it ended up being a long time before she got compensation.

'You were the one who hung the towel over the lamp,' I said to Kristian.

'But you were the one who switched on the light,' he replied.

We had collaborated in the disaster. We had collaborated on the destruction of her life. For a long time, I was angry at her because she had been so stupid as to try

292

to save her chest of drawers. Yes, yes, I realized that the anger was out of self-defence; but we could not pull her out, she was big and strong. The panic made her strong. I thought that we ought to buy her something.

'What do you give someone who has lost everything?' Kristian asked.

And that might have been a fair point. Where do you begin? With a vase? An armchair? I pictured various objects positioned, one at a time, in the sooty living room, and immediately it became an artefact. And very alone. I happen to think of Charles who at the moment is taking photos of the things from his life which have had significance for him, each item is isolated against a background of white cardboard. The project is extensive, and it is growing. He has begun, no, he has always done that, picking things up from the street, things which have a direct appeal for him, it could be a woman's red hat or a screw or a dirty dummy. One thing draws the next with it – because Charles also thinks of what suits what, or what requires what, he would never use an expression like 'the objects speak together'. Thus the other day a miniature ballerina made of yarn required the company of a cod. Camilla went to the fishmonger's and returned with a seven-kilo beast. When they had taken a photo of it, it had to be cut into suitable pieces and placed in the freezer, for future consumption. I could hear on the phone that she was gradually growing tired of the project. In the beginning it had made her sad, 'Charles is giving up,' she said, 'as if he is about to close up shop.' I replied that you don't die of a bad back. 'With all that morphine,' she sighed, 'all those cigarettes.' Then she complained for a long time about the chaos their home had become because of the sickbed. Charles cannot lie in the practically brand new bed that they couldn't resist buying because of its shapely steel legs, because the mattress is too soft. So he lies on a harder mattress on the floor, by the window. Since he cannot have a bedside table, he lives with stacks of books and papers on the floor around him. Leaning against the walls are rolls of white cardboard to be photographed. I don't know what this special type of paper is called. And a long piece is placed on the dining table, supported by a couple of chairs it reaches all the way down to the floor; not a wave, but a ski slope, here the immortalization takes place, here the items become new and alone, icons against the deathly white, items without landscape. Camilla drags boxes up from the basement with things to be photographed. The photographer comes and goes, in addition to a whole bunch of other visitors, often two or three different ones every afternoon, they are kind, they are loving, and go into the kitchen to make coffee themselves, they are also her friends, Kristian coming over to watch a football match with Charles, Alwilda, Edward, and more, including the painter who in my mind is named Clea because she is blonde (and paints) like Clea from *The Alexandria Quartet*. Camilla isolates herself in her study and is close to screaming every time she hears a sound in the kitchen which her room adjoins. She feels like she is living in a public space together with all these coffee sisters and coffee brothers. She is embarrassed about the mess on behalf of the visitors in Charles's room, the bedding scattered with ashes. She needs a façade. She compares him to her granddad who was also a hoarder. 'I am a tape recorder,' he said when he picked up a piece of tape from the road with his walking stick. Charles uses one of his staffs to grab hold of things on the street. He has become a Nordic walker, for the sake of his back. She thinks that he cannot acknowledge the extra

294

workload on her, victim of a hoarder. She has taken on an afflicted expression. And Charles is bitter, he does something or other with his mouth which I connect with Uffe Ellemann-Jensen – yes, he presses his lips together.

Camilla thinks of her grandmother who went on screaming raids against her grandfather's accumulations when he was down at the harbour, how she had to hide what she threw out underneath 'innocent' rubbish, rubbish beyond the grandfather's interest, which there was not very much of, for example he would rinse out all the milk cartons and stack them in his woodshed for later use, he would cut them in half and use them to put paintbrushes in. Back then she always sided with the grandfather and thought that the grandmother was being hysterical in saying that the objects were forcing her into the sea. They lived on a hill, the sea was half a kilometre from there.

Charles's project has made me speculate as to which things I would choose as 'my life objects'; of course there is the plant I have had since I was a child, a hardy growth that has only got new soil two or three times over the past thirty years. If it gets a lot of light, the leaves grow big, and backwards. Then there is my amber tree that the light falls on so golden. It is cleaned under the shower. And my flowered porcelain pig that Camilla's mum gave me when my first book was published. And a yellow vase Camilla gave me last year. The orange clump from the fire I have kept to remind myself that if at some point someone happened to injure me by accident, for example by burning my home down, I should show magnanimity. I will probably come up with more – things.

They have asked if I want the double bed with the chubby legs, then they will buy a new harder one so they can get Charles up from the mattress on the floor and again get to sleep next to each other. And yes, I want that. Not that long ago they were going to stay in Aarhus, at a hotel. They had been to the premiere of my new play. They had brought Charles's mattress with them so as not to risk having a potentially soft hotel bed 'break his back in half', as he says. 'It was,' Camilla said, 'years since I had heard myself laugh so unrestrainedly. (It felt almost as if a physical love was waiting around the corner. Lightness – soon someone will take over from me. Soon I will be someone I do not recognize. Exactly like the sound that had just escaped me, for once my head thrown back in laughter. Foreign. A touch irresponsible.) I laughed at the mattress, that we arrived with our own mattress in tow, into the hotel. That would correspond to taking your own casserole to the restaurant. Almost. In addition there is nothing more impossible to drag than a mattress, sliding and bending, it is alive and does what it wants – and it did that, through the reception and into the elevator. A moment later, in the hotel room, lying on the mattress, Charles began to talk about Jews, in the thirties. I thought that I could smell the dust of the coats. I was locked in with Charles and his Jews. They are mine too. Every time I occupy myself with that, I relive the shock from when I heard about it the first time, every foundation disappears. I asked him to talk about something else that evening at the hotel. So he talked about the Gulag. You cannot think that you have the right to laugh once in a while.'

Now Charles wants to, by the way, have a torture implement tattooed on his back. In the place where the pain stems from, on top of the scar from the operation. His friend the painter is going to make a picture that will then be transferred to the back. Camilla considers it macabre and does not know how she will touch his back.

She has no desire to run her hand across that image, involve it in the caress. You probably cannot say that he has gone over to the side of the suffering, anyway it can mean several things. He suffers, and his obsession with suffering and pain is great. That much can be said. The long flat back no longer belongs to her, only to the pain.

In the end we bought nothing, only a fancy confectioner's cake and a bunch of flowers for Maja's parents who took charge of us on the night of the accident, and whose guests we were for a day or two. But a long time afterwards I considered, apropos cod, to have an enormous Norwegian smoked (flame-coloured, I realized) salmon sent to the family in France, (I must have seen an advert somewhere) but that too remained an idea.

The room smelled of old cardboard. Our wedding certificate and a pile of unusable wedding gifts (fountain pen, silver napkin rings et cetera) also lay on the floor somewhere. Kristian lay there when he was ill, with a sore throat or something, and looked at the stucco with a harried look, or he sat there using a couple of cardboard boxes as a desk. It was hard to avoid the thought that he had not wanted to move in; that in a way he was ready to move out at any moment, the boxes already packed.

It was very dusty, and once I insisted on vacuuming in there even though he was lying ill on the floor, because I was left with all the cleaning, whereas he had arrogated every form of contact with food, he jumped up from his sickbed and grabbed me by the throat. I vacuumed as best I could with his hands around my neck. (The world would run smoothly if everyone carried out their work with a similar enthusiasm. He kept squeezing until I dragged the vacuum cleaner out of the room.) That is the thing with Kristian, he hates rubbish but has nothing against dust, for example he had the notion that it would be a waste of time to clean before we had guests, it made perfect sense to wait until afterwards. Now I do not want to make him sound generally violent, he isn't; I was no better; the only time I gave him a slap, I hit his glasses so that one lens was crushed, and he bled from his eyebrow. It looked worse than it was. I remember that shortly after this incident we coincidentally happened to see an episode about violent wives, all from the English-speaking world. There was a woman who had tried to run down her husband in the driveway several times; it was a drama documentary, a genre (according to me) that seldom succeeds, because the illustrative scenes that accompany the narrative, as a rule, attempt to cover it in a 1 to 1 relation, they are simply cut short and involuntarily comical, fragments of fiction poke their head up from dramatic music, and you see a man throw himself out of the way of the car with the raging wife and land in the hedge, and then once more for Prince Knud, in slow motion (first I have to say something about Prince Knud. Several years ago I went to a university in Gdansk to talk about my authorship with the Danish students there, I launched into a discussion with them about 'warm' and 'cold' texts, and at one point I must have (excitedly or insistently) said 'once more for Prince Knud', because several months later I received in the post a dissertation about my authorship from one of the students who had been present and made notes during the talk, I could read: 'As Prince Knud once said, it can really burn intensely beneath the cool surface of a text.' Her dissertation supervisor was a Danish lecturer, she must have ridden through the dissertation at a gallop) a woman who was always lurking to push her husband down the stairs, and then there was

the very worst woman, the one who one night had melted countless candles on a frying pan, pulled the duvet
off her husband and poured the boiling wax over his
groin. We were introduced to the poor husband after he
had many operations (new skin, maybe even brand-new
genitals). I was happy that I did not belong to this violent
category, that I had only hit Kristian a single time, that it
was an accident that the glasses were broken. But every
day, almost, we said horrible and irreparable things to
each other. He had got rather fat, and if I got a glimpse of
him coming out of the shower, I told him that he looked
like Michael Moore. 'Michael Moore, Michael Moore,
Michael Moore,' I would say, standing and pointing at
him. Over time I felt such a nausea and began to tremble
whenever I heard his key in the lock.

On the kitchen table was a list with two columns with our
names above where we wrote the amount we had spent
on shared food. I ate certain things that did not interest
Kristian, Danish pastries or a tin of bean paste, and so I
did not mark those foods on the list. At the end of every
month we then settled accounts so we paid approximately the same amount of the shared food. This calculation
had a festive feel where we both, while Kristian added
up – he was best with numbers, he thought – tensely
sat waiting for the outcome, wondering which way the
money would travel the following moment. Once I had
been really ill with a chest infection and when I finally
worked up a bit of an appetite, I asked Kristian to go to
the bakery for a bread roll. He did, but only served it to
me after meticulously charging the four or five kroner
to my name on the list.

What did Kristian do in his room... he sat (with an
un-unpacked cardboard box as a desk) writing his PhD

and despaired and rewrote and saved the various versions and did not know which one was best, and crossed back and forth between them like a dinghy on the sea of endless possibilities. When he was not working, he ate. He kept plastic bags containing nuts and raisins and bread slices in one of the boxes. I was not supposed to know about it. He ate all day long while using both hands (like one of our ancestors with a long tail), though not sitting curled up beneath the ceiling on a box the tail whipping against the cardboard, to despairingly stick his foot in his mouth. The right hand up to the hole pop chew left hand up to the hole pop chew right hand already ready with a new load.

'Why do you always have to work?' I complained back when I still missed his company.

'If I don't work, I eat,' he replied.

To eat meant to break down. And I pictured his ego itself, his soul, his consciousness, whatever you prefer, as a ramshackle shed that was braced with a couple of slanted boards – and then someone came and kicked at the braces.

We had not been married very long, the eating cannot be classified by what Herta Müller writes about one of the minor characters in *The Hunger Angel*, who eats his wife's food at the labour camp in Ukraine, but here it comes anyway: 'An old marriage makes you hungry, infidelity makes you full.'

And what did I do on my sofa? If it was morning, I wrote. If it was afternoon or evening, I waited for it to be morning so I could start writing again, with a head not muddled by the day. I lay and was occupied, my mind was occupied with hating, despairing, defending my own loathing, deciding to pull myself together and make it work. I was occupied by the idea of leaving, I played out my break-up endlessly, on my heating pad, my heart growing heavier.

Money sex services, by that I mean housework, in my opinion ought to flow freely between us. But it did not, everything became part of a rigid system, everything had to be agreed, subdivided, planned so that his shed of an ego would not come crashing down. (Near the end we went to bed together every Thursday at six o'clock sharp. Like during the Christmas armistice in 1914 where Germans, Brits and the French celebrated Christmas Eve together, we each dragged ourselves out of our trenches and met in bed, I, the mean one, possibly the German. Quite a few people write about sex as though straight out of a manual, or like grocery bills where numbers are replaced by limbs, rather tedious, you can imagine a meal described with the same circumstantiality, knife and fork, mouth and food actants, or an interior during a storm, but that already sounds like more fun. I will be content to say that these Thursday afternoons were delightful for a long time, and that I could have wanted it also to take place Monday Saturday Wednesday Sunday Friday.) I have often fallen for men whom I thought had a big soul. Whatever I mean by that. I should have gone for something easier to measure or weigh (the pocketbook? But I have never considered that I would not take care of myself).

I don't know how often over time I have confused soul with peculiarity or eccentricity or idiosyncrasies or neuroses or compulsory behaviour or low low self-esteem. The other day I had coffee with a childhood sweetheart (Peter), who after having completed his training at the conservatory left music to become a postman. For two full tedious hours (four cups of coffee) he inveighed against all the music he could think of, it could burn in hell as far as he was concerned. For a moment I was sent fifteen years back in time and I remembered how I once had taken a cauliflower and thrown it out his window, an absurd gesture of powerlessness at the crushing of everything I listened to. Just as long as Edward does not... just as long as Edward is as stable and normal as he seems. After Kristian I want a man without frills, like rye bread, like a blue sky. But I always want something intense, something toppling that makes the soul turn and turn.

Edwards sends an apologetic smile to the gravestone if he does not stop by the grave when we cross the cemetery. But he is now able to not stop. (Maybe I fell in love with Kristian simply because he is a doctor like Camilla's mum.)

A TEA PARTY (AROUND CHARLES'S BED)

[All of the companions]

'Would anyone care to hear a brief anecdote about the small dog and a crow?' Edward asks, 'yesterday morning near the entrance to Fælledparken a crow was pecking at a plastic tray that had contained minced beef. The small dog raced towards the crow and chased it away. It investigated the packaging. It was clearly empty. It raised its hind leg and urinated on it and then ran off. The crow hopped back, took the packaging in its beak and shook off the urine and began to peck at it again.'

'Hmm.'

'It urinates on everything it doesn't want for itself, even bread, in order to prevent others from getting it.'

'The scorched earth policy.'

'Nah, the irrigated.'

'I have been out mating. Again,' Alwilda says, 'and this time I believe it, that there is growth in my uterus. May I please have an extra chair, so I can keep my legs up.'

'Yo, ho, ho and a bottle of organic juice.'

'I had considered Kristian. But the idea of him recognising his son and entering the picture. Better to choose someone outside of my territory, foreign lions, from the other side of town, I thought, and took four different men in a row, stretch and bend. I want three (in time), two sons and a daughter who will come bing bang bong, the diaper stage over in a hurry. Their first words will be "toi-let". They will go to a strict school in the north, and I will cycle them there in a carrier bike, in all sorts of weather, all the way along Østerbrogade, along the railway by Ryvangs Allé, they will be waving from the carrier, and the passengers on the train will wave back. Mum spurts ahead and overtakes the train. Fit as a postman – in advance. They will learn Chinese at school, and I am a Chinese mother. I no longer have time to work, pant pant, but there is no father, so I will have to. Maybe I will hitch the four possible fathers to the Chinese cart, better to have four possible fathers than one impossible, in the year of the dragon, then we can spend the rest of our life guessing, four possible fathers for each little Chinese person, my twelve men, three children and I all sit around guessing, "you," Chang says and climbs on the lap of the Native American from Nordvest,' Alwilda says.

'You're mad as a March hare.'

'Why did that make you shudder, Edward?'

'In my scheme of things, "Native American" is another term for "undertaker",' Edward answers.

'Very personal, very hermetic.'

'My self-loathing is like a ram, it can break the door down. Yesterday I woke up with the following image: me skiing in shit, swooshing down a hill, with shit spraying around the poles. So the tone for the day is set,' Kristian says.

'Apropos self-image, apropos shit,' Edward says, 'then you might consider the effect it has on a dog watching its master bend over its excrements and pick them up in a bag.'

'Such lavatorial company,' Alma says.

'Then let's take a round: What is consuming you at the moment, how are you keeping yourselves busy?'

'Then the sentence is pronounced. There is nothing to be done about my back. Everything has been tried. Now it's time to give up,' says Charles.

'It really pains me to hear that,' Camilla's mum says.

'Then there is only one way – the way of the pilgrim, to the holy baths, the holy baths,' Camilla says.

'Yes. I will let my body sink into Lourdes,' Charles says, 'and hope for a miracle.'

'I'll go with you as a helper and photographer,' Camilla says.

(Charles says nothing.)

'Oh, can't we all go with you?'

(Charles says nothing.)

'I want to be part of the Arab Spring. I long for something greater than myself. I will pitch my tent on a square, starve and strive, die so that it matters,' Kristian says.

'And give you not all, then know you nothing given,' Camilla's mum says, 'that's how I was raised.'

'Raised to sink,' Camilla says.

'Tell me,' Camilla's mum says to Charles, 'have you ever tasted Peking duck in sweet-and-sour sauce? I can really recommend that.'

'Morning in the garden,' Camilla says, 'everything wakes up, everything glitters, shines, crows and is wet and beaming.'

'Yes, here at the house there are so many insects. There are clothes moths, spiders, and of course flies. And moths, the carrions of the micro world, light hunters, with their spotted wings like the one that drowned in the kitchen sink just before, a goshawk in miniature.'

'The other day I met someone unforgettable in Østre Anlæg,' Kristian says, 'she sat on the bottom step of a staircase, with her face hidden in her hands and under a large head of hair. She was young and slender and tall. She wore a pair of cheap white strap sandals that sooner belonged to a grandmother, out in the country, or that you would be able to find among a child's costume – and

305

it made me think that she was Eastern European – and a long skirt and a short white top. I asked if I could help her, but she did not react. In front of her on the ground was a filled plastic bag, not a purse, but a firmly stuffed bag.

"Won't you look up," I asked, "so I can see if you need help?"

But she did not react. And because she did not raise her head so I could see her face, I started to imagine this face, that the eyes were ruined, that I would have screamed if she had removed her hands and thrown her hair back, that she would have had empty eye sockets or a dead gaze, while what I would have seen, probably, was complete surrender, a knowledge of being beyond help.

"It's all right," an old lady at the top of the stairs suddenly said, "I've called the police."

"Why the police?"

But she turned away and said "hello hello" into her mobile, and I thought that she was old, and the communication caused her difficulty. Then I pictured what had taken place before. Had the young girl run around on the road screaming, created chaos with her youth and despair and her big hair, and now she would be sent back to where she came from, in the hands of those who have destroyed everything for her and would continue to do so.'

'Imagine, you almost sound caring, Kristian, fill your flat with trafficked women, now you have a mission in Denmark and don't need/Spring in Arabia.'

'Thanks, I prefer Nescafé,' Charles says and holds out his mug, 'it's not literature, but a con.'

'The difference between delivering material from your mind directly from the sentences (like shooting from the hip) and to use scenes chapters narrator characters to slowly meticulously explain your content. Crudely put,' Alma says.

'Today I longed to rock you in my arms,' Camilla says to Charles, 'he seemed small as a doll's house doll,' (she says to the others,) 'my doll's house dolls had elastic-bandage/plaster bodies that could be bent and folded, everything Charles cannot; just stroking him or holding his knee, and it hurts even more.'

'At first I read to be like you. Then I wrote to do what you did, and become your author. Then all that was liberated from me,' Alma says.

'I would really like to have had a whole heap of children,' Camilla's mum says, rocking her red sandals, 'now I have to get on my feet, whoo-whoo-whoo, give me a hand, would you.'

FROM THE HORSE'S MOUTH

[Camilla]

Married life with Charles is linked to the Osama bin Laden era, we were so in love in September 2001 that it was not until late morning on the twelfth that we realized what had happened on the eleventh, and the dissolution of our relationship took place in the days around bin Laden's death. Two images frame it:

1. Bodies in free fall
2. A face shot to pieces

The end of him. And us. The timely coincidence is the only thing they have in common, obviously. But I can air some slightly more symbolic material. The mark from the wedding ring will not disappear. (The old hide, the far-too-tight ring.) I wish that my thoughts were more organic today, that one grew out of the other, but it's not like that. The idea of the break has a fragmented character, like the sorrow comes in ripples, and the relief too. I am a beach all these feelings crash against.

I look at the fronts of the houses (for For Sale signs) and try to imagine a new existence. I would prefer not to live in one of these massive, red, continuous blocks that surrounds Classens Have, which Charles and I used to call the Apple Orchard, because the ground was covered with bitter wild apples throughout the autumn, Edward's dog never gets bored of you throwing them so it can race after them or catch them in its mouth. Charles shoved the apples away with one of his walking sticks (for Nordic walking). Dogs are strictly forbidden in the garden. It is a park designated for dogaphobes, a man in a boiler suit explains to me one day, again again I am looking after Edward's dog, so that he and Alma can get away for a short break. Alma is completely wrapped up in Edward. She no longer has any time for me, self-pity is unbecoming, up with everything, get back up on the horse, if only one had one, and it was in that moment the thought about the horse was implanted in me.

'I train dogaphobes,' the man says, and I wonder what the boiler suit contributes to, in the training, 'they know that they can come here without being afraid.'

I promise never to return, with the dog.

I get a sense of not being able to breathe, that's how heavy the red buildings that frame the park are, like a four-sided courtyard. My sleepless brain does not recollect the colour of the house I now live in, which I am going to move out of. Charles moved out long ago. The flat is up for sale. I was visited by three estate agents before I decided, the one suitor worse than the other. The worst one wore tight clothing, like a sailor, or a pimp. His eyes glistened, and his golden curls and wide rings also glistened. He suggested that I pack all my books up in boxes and drag them down to the basement and take down the bookcases because they block far too much light, and the space would seem larger without them. The idea made me cry with exhaustion.

The second was too fat, and he had holes in his socks I noticed, when he politely took off his shoes in the entrance. And I happened to think about one of my colleagues the other day, at a meeting at the institute, who had pulled his feet halfway out of his shoes, and sat rocking his feet, the heels worn on the socks, and for the sake of nature, for environmental reasons, he wouldn't replace them, but walked his socks off, to the last thread, and combined with early greying and an unkempt beard this made him look a little like a gnome, I thought about his presentation of himself, in one piece of work after the other, like a giant Cupid, a hard fucker, to put it bluntly, and I thought that he ought to be careful that this elf-ish nature did not damage his self-presentation, because now I pictured him, fucking with his heels poking out of his socks.

'Sorry,' I said, 'I'm a little nervous.'

'Is that the effect I have on you?' the estate agent asked.

'No, it's my entire situation,' I replied.

And he nodded, disappointed maybe. The sight of my bulging bookcases made him, not unexpectedly, start telling me that he was writing a book.

'You too,' I said because soon there will be more authors than readers in the world. He talked warmly and at length about his book that involved a good deal of research and dealt with a military unit under the command of NATO, infused with a dose of fiction. Finally I said: 'If you can get me one of those cheap co-op flats over there (I pointed out the window), I will get you a meeting with a publisher. Then you can talk about your book and not risk simply having your manuscripts returned unread with a standard refusal attached.' (I thought that Alma could easily act as the publisher, that is if she had the time.) He went quiet, and I thought that he probably had not got as far with the book as he was trying to imply. The atmosphere became tense.

The fact that I chose number three was not due to the low price, but because he reminds me of a boy I know and care for, he still (at the age of fifteen) cuts pictures of bridal dresses out of catalogues. He was gentle and girlish. And rather attractive, with icy-blue eyes. Unfortunately my lawyer (because suddenly I have an estate agent lawyer financial advisor and accountant, all I need is someone to help me sleep, a sleep coach who comes every night around bedtime and sits down with me and tells me how heavy my body is, how empty my head is), thinks that I should not have chosen a discount agent, but I have done it now – because of a gentle nature. When he was leaving, and our eyes met, in my mind I bent him over his sales listings and his suppressed homosexuality (if suppressions still exist, in our wide-open age) and placed myself opposite him bent over a book and had us look up and carefully smile at each other one late evening in our life together in this flat which I will after all not need to sell.

No. Because the mere thought of again having to live right up close to another's mood makes me want to run far away. The worse the mood I am subjected to, the more I flutter around the person, it is my moth side, I cannot stay away from the flame. When Charles locked down, or – when he bolted up the door to his soul, I threw myself towards it, open sesame, but not the slightest crack.

The might of his depression. A black black cloud hung over the bed where he lay. Towards evening it became unbearable. It was a prison. Now I've escaped.

I am back from my walk. My house turns out to be red. But at least there are yellow bricks mixed in with the red to create patterns, and the neighbouring houses have different colours. My house is narrow and interspersed with yellow. I do not feel like moving from it. But I can't afford to keep living alone. It feels as if a ditch has been dug from the top of my head down to my belly button, and running through it is undiluted pain. I have said goodbye to Charles. A month ago he told me that he would be ill without me. That he would not ask me for anything else. That I should move on with my life. That the air had gone out of our relationship – and how was the air going to do any different, I have sat on a chair by his bed for three years. That the happiness and desire have disappeared. We have not been able to talk about anything other than illness for a long time; when we tried, it felt unnatural. So here I am, alone. When he gave me the message, my arms became like appendages, and at the end hung my hands like empty shovels. I am no longer going to carry anything. I have it straight from the horse's mouth. Charles will carry himself. Only himself, not my grief at him being ill (over the years my tears have become a deluge), my difficulty in sitting still for very long at a time, my inability to put up with him often not answering me – because it is too far to the words inside his heavy mind. The terrible way he is held prisoner by unhappiness. His own prisoner in a fortress, which he cannot be called out of. Stiffness and silence, not a face, but a mask (of a face). I truly began to fear this becoming stone.

I don't want to lie to myself. I had long thought the same thing during my walks in the parks where I walked and soaked up all the colours. While Charles just lay and lay. The future felt like a tied-up bag. Now it is open... without Charles I feel at times that I am in free fall – through time.

I have probably said earlier that I have devoted more than enough time to death – to last a lifetime – but still I can't stop seeing the origin of the break-up with Charles and I as – no, view the following as a picture of the distance that had come between us... We realized that we wanted (one day) to each be buried in own end of the country and not, as I had imagined, side by side, that is the smooth back of one urn against the stomach of the other, for example at Holmens Kirkegård which is so endlessly French, with a long avenue dividing it into two, and oh the waves of anemones and crocuses across the graves in the spring, and outside the churchyard is the city, teeming. The churchyard that is framed by the capital, surrounded by houses with balconies that people come out on, people who send gazes down towards the graves; but Charles had decided on the district where he came from, at the other end of the country. I thought I dared not be buried in such an empty place, so deserted, so windswept, colder in the winter than any other place, in this final bed.

Our downhill race of beds, through the years. How many beds have I piled up in the basement now and around with friends? We pursued the perfect mattress, the one that could best suit Charles's back; one where my weight on the mattress would bother him as little as possible, a very hard mattress, like sleeping on wood, I thought, a mattress like a door. And then we would usually end up in separate rooms anyway because the morphine and the pains chased him round in the bed and out of bed so that he could smoke. And then I could not sleep. And if I did not sleep, almost everything made me cry, I confused one thing with another – the paper boy jumping on the steps I thought was thunder. I had a hard time recognizing my neighbours, they sprung forth from the same fogs.

The other day I went walking with Edward's dog on a lead, too long, I am ashamed to say that it walked onto the road, but it was not a very busy road. Suddenly a car stopped, and the face of a strange woman appeared in the window: 'Is that any way to walk your dog?' she said.

'Sorry,' I said and looked down and turned around. The car did not drive off, but remained idling in front of me, now I was really going to get a telling-off I thought, then the lady said: 'Camilla, it's me,' and the strange face transformed into Alma's.

What is wrong with me?

Why did I not recognize my best friend straight away?

The first bed I shared with Charles was Swedish, back then we barely took any notice of the quality of the mattress. I was overwhelmed by how tall and wide he seemed, maybe because the man I had been with for a long time was a runt. We were attending a course, each our own, same place. I noticed him, he stood smoking on the terrace coughing and shoulders hunched up. Last year we were in Tenerife together; the hotel room had a balcony. Charles had pneumonia, on top of all the other troubles. The cough made the pain in his back worse, but he did not smoke any less, and when I saw him completely hunched over from coughing lean over one of the cheap white plastic chairs, I remembered the first time I saw him, wearing a leather jacket, in Sweden, and how empty it quickly came to feel if he was not in the vicinity. This feeling of longing was love. From the hotel a donkey could be seen. It stood tied to a tree all day. It was meant to make you stop and notice the greengrocer that lay behind. The donkey had a money box attached to the head strap, where it was written 'Donkey-food'. The money box supplied the sorrowful donkey with even more sorrowfulness. It could not earn a living just by being an advert – for the shop, for all things Spanish as such, and stand under the tree all day getting stiff legs. When you put a coin in the slot, it felt like you put it into the donkey's brain, but then a reassuring metallic clink was heard when the coin hit the other coins in the money box. The shop sold Tenerife bananas. They are short and sweeter than other bananas, they are like

314

confectionery. The banana is a herb, isn't that surprising? Queen Victoria (the stout monarch who cast a shadow over almost an entire century, if for a moment I might be permitted to sound like the narrator in a programme about British history) suffered from indigestion and believed that the Tenerife banana helped, therefore she ordered increased cultivations of bananas on her colony of Tenerife. It was all written in a guidebook to Tenerife. The shop also sold almonds. They tasted very good with bananas. Charles talked about needing a long stay at a convalescent home. He never did, but now he has moved in to a guest house where he is served good and nutritious food three times a day. He has reduced the elements of existence to a minimum. He eats an orange. He lies on his back and looks up at the sky. He keeps in contact with very few people. Not with Alma, not with Edward, not with Alwilda, not with Kristian, and practically not with me either.

Every afternoon, all week, on Tenerife, I went to the zoo and attended an eagle show. Even though I saw it so many times, it is nearly impossible for me to recount what I saw. But it gave me a feeling of Hell, yes yes a dreadful whirring of the fallen angel's wings, the sluices of heaven unleashed a shower of birds, and every time I did not understand how once again I had voluntarily seated myself on the bench in the arena, beneath the sky and the burning sun, as the heavy American eagles as well as vultures and falcons plummeted towards the earth with wings raised and claws outstretched, when their trainer, standing in the middle of the arena, clapped the leather glove and called them down. They flew right above the heads of the audience, and we kept being (through the megaphone) ordered to sit still because the birds could react to movement by attacking

315

(all the same a rather shabby-looking couple with a large group of children let their son run into the arena and were called to order, but they must have given up holding onto him, because a little later he ran in there again, it was really very nerve-racking), and then landed on the trainer's glove and were rewarded with a clump of raw meat. After the large predators had been sent off and had circled high above the arena and were called back (while the furious beating of a drum reached a climax as they were landing), a jumble of various birds were sent into the arena, music made them appear like they were dancing; there were cranes that came and pecked corn out of the spectator's hands (not mine), and there were blue storks and our own storks with the red legs, and there were many other birds I did not know, the air was full of wings. It was a fanfare when they were called in, a fanfare when they were sent off again, and they were free during that time, they could all have flown off, the eagles could have never come back. Next to the arena the vultures again sat on their separate stumps, chained, it was the forecourt to Hell, that's what Satan's soldiers looked like and with bowls filled with raw stinking flesh in front of them, they stared at you when you walked past, so you felt reduced to something that soon could end up in the bowl ...

Sweden, far out in the country. When I had passed Charles who stood in his leather jacket, freezing and smoking on the terrace, I noticed his gaze follow me, and I tried to make my stride light and beautiful. At last, on the final evening, there was a party. Finally we were the only ones left in the banquet hall. We thought. In the middle of a long kiss, when I opened my eyes, at one point I sat on the table surrounded by toppled bottles, with my clothes in disarray and Charles's hands on my back and my shoulders under my shirt, the course leader stood there watching us. I don't know how long he had been standing there. I closed my eyes and kept kissing – as if he would disappear if I could not see him. But a little later when I opened my eyes, he was still there. He must have been a voyeur. Now Charles had also turned his head towards him, the man put his hands to his side, like an embodied superego, and asked us to find somewhere else.

We walked slung together into the morning while we talked about how could he think of standing there leering at us. The air was white, there was a creaking and hollow droning from the lake. The ice was breaking.

It would be a harmonic place to end, at the first meeting, the circle is completed, pure joy. But the mind does not work like that, it pushes on, to stop here would be to park a bus on a flowery meadow.

When Charles moved out, he did not move that far away at first. Not far from where we lived, and I still live – in a forest of For Sale signs, since the housing market is stagnant as they say (incidentally the estate agent's where the agent who wanted to write a book worked went to rack and ruin. So now he has time to write, one would think) – there is a hotel with the strange name of 9 Small Homes, (which always made me think of the seven dwarves) the hotel is founded on long-term lets, and as you can read on their website, one guest was so enthusiastic that he stayed for six months. The guest could be Charles.

Therefore it was unavoidable that we ran into each other on occasion. When I took a shortcut through the Apple Orchard, I sometimes saw him lying on the lawn staring up at the sky, in all likelihood in an attempt to heal a soul that had been torn asunder, maybe he saw me too, but as if according to an unspoken agreement we left each other in peace, yes we pretended we had not seen each other. It was not difficult. He had long struck me as belonging to another world (quite probably the world of the pain and the morphine and thoughts of escape), the past year I had not had the slightest idea of what happened inside him, I thought about it again the other day when I saw on TV a veterinarian knock on a horse's skull; as he lay there on the lawn, or when I saw him come out of Spar carrying an orange, I experienced him almost as a mirage, or an after-image like when you have looked at something for a long time and the image of it remains hanging in the air for some time after the thing itself has disappeared.

'For the time being, I don't want to stick my neck out for another person.'

When I said that to Alwilda, she looked at me thoughtfully, and the following day she came with a present, wrapped in pink tissue paper. It was a self-help book. For divorced women. I duly thanked her, and when she was gone, I hid it in an underwear drawer, it could not be out with the other books, maybe in the kitchen on the shelf with cookbooks where I have also placed another self-help book, about stain removal. The book had a glossy finish, exuding energy, on the cover there was a woman in a life jacket which at first I interpreted symbolically, but it turned out to be wrong. The characters were all blonde, being dark-haired myself I sometimes get the idea that all blondes look alike. Each chapter consisted of a blonde divorced woman's account of how she had attained a new life for herself. Leant against the chest of drawers so I could quickly let the book slip into the

318

drawer if there was someone at the door, I skimmed the first four or five chapters, I have always wanted to read as quickly as the critic Malcolm Bradbury who says (he is dead now) that he can read *Don Quixote* in a couple of hours with the aid of a diagonal reading technique where he lets the eyes race from upper left to lower right corner while it devours everything along its path, the hand long since readying to turn the page. I watch all films on the computer, and every time my Mac identifies damaged areas that it skips over, even on brand new films, whereby it automatically reduces the length of standard ninety-minute feature films to a length of twenty or thirty minutes; simultaneously as I save time, à la Bradbury, my ability to form connections is trained.

All women in the book had apparently approached their new lives in the same way – they had started to row. Since they all lived north of Copenhagen, they rowed, not surprisingly, in Øresund, although in varying vessels, dinghy, kayak, canoe. Many had met a new man at sea. Maybe there was a masculine version of the self-help book. In that way both genders were sent to sea and rowed into one another's hearts, then Peterpiperpickedapeckofpickledpeppers met Shesellsseashellsbytheseashore. The women's accounts were separated by photos of types of boats and sailing equipment with prices discreetly indicated, and at the very back of the book there was a page you could tear out, a form to sign up to Hellerup Rowing Club.

Well. But that was when I had the idea of buying myself a horse and starting to ride in Dyrehaven just like I did when I was a child and teenager. Instead of looking forward, as everyone encouraged me to do, I could look back, or turn back, to a largely happy period in my life, from when I was thirteen to eighteen years old.

Incidentally I was not interested in meeting any men, I had no more interest in that than before I started to read the book from Alwilda. Before, just before, out on the street, the person delivering adverts for pizza delivery shyly asked if I had a boyfriend, and I replied: 'No, and I would prefer not to.' He then slinked away, like someone who would have stolen my debit card if I had let him inside. There is no shortage of offers. The painter who had just painted my entire flat in order to tempt buyers also presented an offer. Which I rejected. I worked from home during the days that he painted, and we could not avoid occasionally passing each other in the hall, or other places, 'I want to kiss you,' he wrote to me, and when I refused, he wrote something less kind that made me angry. Now I get annoyed every time I look at my freshly painted walls that they were painted by such an unpleasant human being.

If I had to describe myself I would say: I require time to function. And I would prefer to be experienced in my own surroundings. I am the opposite of someone who looks good from a distance. I function over time. Though not too long, ten years is too long, ten years, and Charles made a run for it so there was lightning flashing from his walking sticks.

Luckily I had three wedding rings lying around I could now sell to get money for a horse. They are all engraved with 'Charles' and the wedding date. Two rather small ones and one large one. The small ones are for the little finger. When I got married, I got a wedding ring for my little finger because it annoyed me the least there. I suffer from restless fingers. (And also from restless mouth but chewing gum can manage that.) Unfortunately I lost the ring shortly afterwards because I had the habit of sliding it up and down my finger. Then I had to have a new one, I again ordered one for the little finger. Then one time when we had to insulate the flat and sprayed filler under the panels, the builder found it under a panel it had rolled under, and handed it to me triumphantly from a kneeling position. Then I had two. However I had started to think that it was too dangerous having a ring on my little finger; when sweating, the ring would slip off easily, and I had developed the habit of taking it off and squeezing it between my upper and lower teeth. It was a wonder I had not swallowed it. For that reason I decided to get a ring for the ring finger since it obviously was the safest finger of all, I got that, yet it was so tight that I had to stop playing with it, and it had as mentioned left an unfortunate mark. So now I had three rings I could sell. The price of gold is good at the moment. Gold is actually the only thing that can be sold at the moment, I realized. After my divorce I have built up an odd attachment to my internet banking, the first thing I do in the morning is check how much I have, what I spent the previous day. So I knew just like that that I could not afford a horse. Numbers are not my friend. The other day I made a terrible blunder. I visited Clea at her sunlit studio and saw a wonderful yellow and brown portrait, painted from a photograph, of Simone de Beauvoir. My walls have become bare after Charles moved out. That was also how they looked before he moved in; and the first time he visited he told me that he felt bad for me because of the bareness. He wanted to fill my walls. Back then I had nothing against naked walls, I thought that the soul rested perfectly on a background of white. But during Charles's illness I became addicted to colours, and I still am, and the colourless winter looms, it is almost October. So I asked the price of this painting whose colours were like scorched sunflowers.

'Fifteen hundred kroner,' she said and I replied 'thank you, I'm buying that.' We shook hands and parted with a smile, and in my mind I placed it above my sofa with myself beneath it, like being under a shower whose jets were healing colours. It had become rather empty after Charles had moved his things, there were fewer book-cases, lighter, less heavy. It took an entire day to divide the books. We made three piles, one for him, one for me and one to sell at the second-hand bookstore. Seven hours into the process I broke down in tears.

'I got sad before as well,' Charles said, 'we are sad that we have read so much trash.'

'Oh, is that what we're sad about?' I said and for a moment I recognized him from Once upon a time and started longing to belong together again.

Back to Clea. Shortly after my visit to the studio she wrote to me that the picture was now packed up, I could pick it up whenever, and I could pay for it over three months.

'That's not necessary,' I wrote, 'I'll transfer fifteen hundred kr. to you.'

'You must have misheard,' she wrote, 'it costs fifteen thousand.'

'Oh,' I wrote, 'oh oh oh, how could I be so stupid to think that something so beautiful was so cheap oh for-give me, I can't afford to buy it' (I pictured the horse going up in smoke).

Back to the internet banking. In the cool world of the figures I come and go. I calculate and calculate. No soon-er have I set a budget than I have to start from scratch, endlessly counting, I assume that I am building dams against feelings for figures.

Well, but I have to sell my gold, I have to buy a horse.

So I start to look at horses. It is very invigorating after having looked at flats for such a long time. Maybe I haven't said that. When I can no longer dwell on online banking, I normally browse through the flats at www.boliga.dk and www.andelsbutikken.dk.

'Don't start looking at flats until you have sold yours,' Alma said, 'you're just wasting time, you have no idea how much you'll get for the flat, how much you have to spend.'

'It's a good thing,' Alwilda said, 'to familiarize yourself with the housing market, then you're ready to get to it when you've sold your flat.'

(She had come round with a couple of sleeping pills for me – from Alma who didn't have time to come by herself. My insomnia has little by little taken on oceanic proportions. My eyes hurt so much from all the wakefulness that I wish I could take them out and put them down.

'There you are,' Alwilda said, 'at least now you'll get a couple of nights' sleep.'

I was tempted to press a tablet out of the foil at once but I waited steadfastly until the evening, otherwise I would just wake up at midnight. I had been given four pills. Luckily I am the child of a doctor and did not just blindly pop the pill in my mouth, but first checked the name on the product. Ritalin. Alwilda suffers from ADHD. I was so disappointed I could have cried. She had given me the wrong medicine, her own.

'I want to sleep, and you give me speed,' I wrote to her.

She had pulled the wrong foil square out of her bag. She apologised profusely. She offered to come by straight away with the right one. I rejected. Politely. And thought that it was a tiny little bit funny. And I relaxed. And slept for a couple of hours.)

323

In any case I had visited the accommodation portals so often that I knew how many square metres the homes for sale in my own neighbourhood were, how much they cost, and approximately how long they had been up for sale. I could have become an accommodation guide. I don't know if I care for the word 'laytime', I associate it with hens, with nests. All that looking at accommodation made me ready to change nests. But nobody fell into the trap – into my nest. Some thought it was too dark, others that the room divisions were wrong, and yet others were dissatisfied that they could not have a balcony – I approached the committee and asked if an exception could be made on the ground floor, 'the balcony would collide with the rubbish chute, you would have to crawl under the balcony to be able to push your rubbish in the chute,' was the reply, 'such eccentrics,' I said to the estate agent, 'would they sit half a metre above the ground, on their balconies, why can they not sit in the courtyard like everyone else' (apart from me, I never use the courtyard).

You can, it turned out, buy racing horses at bargain prices, unsuitable specimens, so-called lane snails, I see the most incredible horses, young beautiful racing thoroughbreds, for fifteen to twenty thousand kroner. Maybe I won't have to sell my gold just yet, I should maybe wait until everything is sorted out; I had placed a gold bracelet from my grandmother down in the bag with the rings, for sale; and I kept imagining her face back when many years ago, now long since dead, she clasped the heirloom around my wrist. She looked as if something was fulfilled when the click from the jewellery's lock sounded. She looked content and expectant. As though she closed something behind her, opened something in front of her. Gave me a shove ahead, even though I was left standing.

I could just put the bracelet back in my jewellery box and only sell the rings, my tired eyes also belonged in there, those are pearls that were her eyes, oh, it got far too difficult. I needed someone to talk things through with.

I made a new budget and added it up seven or eight times.

I reserved a stall at a riding school near Dyrehaven. I made an appointment with a horse owner and went to see the horse.

'It was called Chicken Heart,' the lady says and leads it through the gate out of the fold which it only leaves reluctantly, 'because it usually loses courage towards the end of the race and comes to a complete stop and just allows itself to be overtaken.'

'But I will call it Brave Heart,' I said, without hesitation, suddenly inspired.

The lady nodded and asked if I wanted to try it. In the advert it stated that it could be ridden by anyone.

'No, I want it to get used to me,' I said.

(It had been twenty-five years since I had last sat on a horse.)

I handed her a cheque. She handed me its papers, I got a glimpse of its forefathers' long majestic names, then I grabbed the end of the rope.

I place my hand on the horse's bent neck, and we begin to walk through Dyrehaven, the forest of my childhood, towards its new home. (The whole thing looked like the bike trip Molloy or Malone goes on with a son somewhere in the trilogy, bumpy and somehow endless.)

It's raining. It is apparently a very tired horse I have bought, maybe it is deficient in vitamin B, or has worms. We fit together because I am also tired. It drags its legs, and its snout hangs by the ground. Why did I do it? I ask the horse.

In a sudden burst of energy the horse curls its upper lip back, tosses its head backwards, the mouth wide-open, so all its discoloured teeth can be seen, in a veritable laugh, a grimace at the imbecility of the world, that you have to be forced ahead when you could just let your head hang and continue sleeping, in the rain, in your green fold.

Wait. There is a moment until the curtain falls.

It was getting dark. It was also foggy. And windy. Yellow leaves scattered through the white air. All very enchanting. I had forgotten how close you can get to the deer when you are on a horse. (I had in the meantime got up on it.) They did not run away, but remained standing, and I stared into several sika bucks' red-rimmed, actually rather malicious small eyes. I could have touched the surreal trees on their foreheads.

I rode out through the red gate, a stone's throw from the stable – and Øresund where I also would have been rowing with Peterpiper and all the rest of them now, had I not bought this horse.

There were some sounds I did not recognize, a monotone electric humming and a hard regular tramping.

I turned into the courtyard of the stable where all the woodwork was red-and-white-striped, and the riding hall was a grey vision, designed by Arne Jacobsen, I had read. It was close to where the sound came from. From an outdoor horse exerciser. And on the horse exerciser

326

walked a horse. Walked and walked a horse on its tread-mill, tramp tramp tramp. Above it on the wall of the riding hall its large shadow walked and tramped in its own blackness.

How should I put it, the red and white woodwork, the sound of the sea and the forest, the tramping of the upper class horse, I thought I had arrived at a condensed place that could come to mean something to me for some time.

THE MARCH HARE

[Alwilda]

We arrived at the wine bar at around the same time, Alma, my ever dissatisfied bespectacled friend Kristian, lively Edward, and myself, from each our edge of the city, like ants where we were each the sugar, in our heavy coats (it was March and the winter eternal). When Kristian and Edward bent down to lock their bikes, it was as though they (the men) were fastened to objects that were far too big, like ants dragging building material many times their weight. I have to say I was satisfied with my outward appearance that evening, and the wine would polish my inward self, or perhaps sharpen is more accurate, so the words could drop like a machete: 'zak,' Edward said, with a karate chop in the air. That's how they prefer me. Maybe I do too. Alma looks like the Statue of Liberty, I don't know how many Russian men or Japanese men have come running to be photographed leaning against her over the years. A little later Edward took a picture of all of us, and I thought about all that bother I had had with the hairdresser. His name is Ulis. And when he had finished, my hair looked like a flattened sticky hat. He stood jabbing his fingers in and out in an attempt to make it rise. In the mirror the difference between our hair was striking, his stood up, mine lay down. He is from Guatemala and not very tall, but has an elongated haircut, his hair is brushed upward, he is small and sparkling, during the summer he wears a straw hat, something I cannot do myself because it does not suit me, but then I lack a pair of long grey ears. When it was Easter, he invited his friends to lunch, both hot and cold, his girlfriend was in charge of the hot dishes, it was quite the coordination, in and out of the oven,

'I was so proud of her,' he has told me several times. He is Catholic and likes to decorate with Virgin Marys, he thinks she is cute. His mum wanted to become a hairdresser, but never did. She forced him to cut her hair when he was a child.

'There,' he finally said – my hair looked like a black sticky hat.

'No, Ulis,' I said.

'I know you are the one who understands hair,' I said appeasingly.

'No, no,' he said defensively, and I was inclined to agree with him. Afterwards I explained to him that he should dry it while I had my head down, and crumple it a lot while drying it. He sighed and moved me over to the sink, 'yes, that's it,' I said, 'over and over again.'

Then it was good. Nearly as high and airy as his own.

There is a lot I cannot remember... Yes. As usual Kristian inveighed against everything, to hell and back. Very drunk, very quick. Billiards table. Young beautiful black man in grey clothes, American, surrounded by insignificant friends, from Sønderjylland, with caps, almost identical, I called them Huey and Louie. Intensely pursuing him. Howling after every good shot, I howled, I danced. He was going to be a lawyer. To establish contact I told him that Alma was a judge. That caught his interest. She denied it. I said she was shy. After I had swarmed around him for a long time, I went to the bar to buy a water. He came over to me. 'What do you want from me?' he asked. 'I want you to kiss me,' I said. Maybe he just had to discuss it with his friends, in any case he disappeared. Then he stood there again. 'Do you still want me to kiss you?' he asked. 'Yes,' I said excitedly, 'in here?' (I meant the bar.) He shook his head. He took

my hand. We went outside. He looked around. I felt like
a pony, whinnying with overconfidence, tripping with
expectation, and my mane was airy. Then he grabbed
the door to a block of flats, it was open, and we went in
and immediately started to kiss. I was very dizzy, really needed a glass of water. He stuck his hand down his
pants, presumably to adjust his genitals, and I caught a
glimpse of black crackling hair. Then a family with children and prams and grandparents showed up. We left
the block of flats. We had probably been there around
a minute. I was twice as old as him. It made me shy. He
said that age meant nothing as long as you had a good
heart (we spoke English). I wondered whether you could
say that I had a good heart. He gave me his number. I
said that he must have a lot of women, since he was so
beautiful. 'No,' he said, 'I have no women at all, you can
ask my friends for yourself.' He looked around for them,
he was obviously so young that he was dependent on
them. 'You call,' he said, 'I don't want to intrude, now be
careful with it.' Reunion with Alma, Edward, Kristian,
Huey and Louie. Finding bikes, changing bar. All of that
was unimportant. I felt really bad, a skin without stuffing, to spread out in front of the fireplace. He wanted
to walk me home. We kissed on the street corner, and I
moved my hand up to stroke him or touch (very carefully) his short trimmed black hair. He grabbed my hand in
the air. His eyes were sad. He did not want me to touch
his hair. It was goodbye. We went our separate ways. I
noticed that he went in the direction of my place, and
I walked away from mine. We had to swap directions.
It could not seem as though I was following him. I took
a side street which according to my calculations should
lead me home, in a semi-circle. Suddenly he came towards me, flanked by Huey and Louie, all on bikes, I

was growing to hate bikes. Without stopping he reached out a long arm and grabbed my head and kissed me, impressively well coordinated. He is far too young, I won't call him, and I would get Huey and Louie with him.

I did not call him. I gave Camilla his number to cheer her up, to give her a nudge. She accepted it with a laugh that came from the bottom of the heart (down in the actual mechanics where it rattles and is heavy).

IV. MAROONED

'I've been waiting for you like a sun that would light up everything for me.'
— F. M. Dostoevsky, *The Adolescent*

ALONE IN PARADISE, WITH THE GARDENERS AND THE HEDGEHOG'S HEART

[Camilla]
'When you're alone, you risk nothing.'

'But is that entirely true?'

(I was talking to myself.)

Marooned – the o's like a spray of water over the railing of a ship that now can just be glimpsed on the horizon.

'That is just terrible, they have all failed you,' the neighbour said, right outside my large garden where we had met, where I stood crying.

'Of course my mum can't help that because she's dead,' I said, 'and Charles – it is as it should be, we couldn't put up with one another.'

'Well, then it's just as well.'

'I've got used to being alone in the house. But the garden, I haven't got used to taking care of the garden on my own yet.'

(Until now I had sat in the house looking out onto the garden; I had not placed myself in it; I had taken it in small bites – through the window.)

I had just let three gardeners in there, now they raged and wreaked havoc with chainsaws and brush-cutters, I was afraid that they brought about destruction rather than tidying up and creating a path – for example to my berry bushes, over to my fruit trees, which had not been trimmed and now bore fruit nobody could reach.

'I don't know if I'm making the right decisions about the garden,' I said; the neighbour promised to come by later and look at it. Whatever good that might do, then it was done, the damage irreparable, 'no, it will grow back again, you can be certain of that.' I slinked into the garden again, panic-stricken, despondent: beneath all the wildness that was removed, it was withered, singed. It looked sad and bare along the edges of the garden, 'just leave the ground elder,' I said to the leader of The Green Fingers, 'or it will be too bare.'

'Is coming fine,' he says reassuringly, he is Polish, and the other two, his employees, are Romanian, two slave workers with flat stomachs and well-developed chest and arm musculature, efficient gloomy young men, probably underpaid, probably illegal, he is fat, he is patronising, I feel like a seventeen-year-old virgin, a confused worried bungling virgin. Later, when he wants his 9,500 kroner for the work, I had also got the garden fenced in so Edward's dog would not run out and get hit by a car while chasing the neighbour's cat, and removed a tree that had toppled into the neighbour's garden, I could not count the money while he looked at me; I tried three times, and each time it went to pot. I had to hand him the bundle and let him count the notes. As if I was dyslexic or dyscalculic, I think it's called. That's what he did to me. That's how he made me feel. Looking me up and down, or intensely staring at my face, it turned me into a fool.

'So do you make a good coffee?' He wanted to come at eight o'clock that same evening for his money; he did not arrive in work clothes, but tidy and shaved, smelling of aftershave, for a moment it made me soft that a man had made an effort for me, but since I could not even count a stack of notes, I did not offer him a chair, I just told him that as far as felling my diseased birches he should wait until he heard from me, I felt like the owner of a plantation, and then he had to go. I was certain that he had ripped me off, that I had paid far too much. But the people really being cheated were the Romanian slave workers that the Pole paid twenty kroner an hour, it later turned out.

I have painted the garden gate – it seems wrong to call it a garden gate, it is a tall and wide gate; I connect garden gates with something short that I have to bend my back a little to open and close, that's what my granddad's garden gate was like, it was his, because he was the one who painted it, or them, because there were two, you could enter the front garden via two different gates and then walk through the much smaller garden along two different tiled paths, where one led to the front door and another to the kitchen door. He had decorated the white gates with tins he had painted blue, it looked completely natural, as if the tins were a carving on the gates, you could only tell that they were tins, if you knew; either he had cut, for example, cat food tins down the middle, so that each tin came to constitute two types of decoration, even though it sounds terribly rigid in relation to the simplicity and ingenuity expressed by it, or else the tins were small, the size of tuna tins. Maybe the tins did not sit on the gates at all, but on the fence posts of the likewise painted white fence. Naturally they did. He used a strong clear blue colour whenever he could get his hands on it; a maritime blue, he had been a sailor, and this blue resembled a dream of the sea in strong concentrate.

It was at least ten years since I had last painted the gate; back then the summerhouse belonged to my mum; she was hospitalised with depression, and I went and wood-treated her house and also the gate, because there was nothing else I could do for her; I could not make her better; but I hoped that it would make her happy – when she was healthy and again able to experience joy. I remember that back then, while I painted, I clung to the idea that I did something for her. (It was an obsession for me, always.) And that I looked forward to her coming to see the Swedish-red gate.

She died: late one morning, quietly in her bed, where she lay fully clothed and with her eyes closed behind her glasses. I took off her glasses and placed them on her bedside table that was filled with layers of unclipped features and articles. Then I sat down on a chair and sent a stream of heartfelt thank yous from an entire life towards her. The glasses left a mark on her nose; and this mark, which had the shape of a furrow, made me recall the time she one day in a straightforward merry way had busied herself with how she was going to get 'away from there', very concrete, wondering in what way the dead her would be transported out of the flat and down the stairs. When she saw the kind of effect the conversation had on me, she brushed the thought away with a 'but I don't have to worry about that' – most likely she then quoted Epicurus: 'When we exist, death is not; and when death exists, we are not.'

There it happened that she was lifted from the bed onto a stretcher, and this stretcher was already – or became – fastened to a kind of lifting mechanism (a back-sparing arrangement, not that she was particularly heavy, for the benefit of the emergency services, or whoever it was that had come), and when this machine was going to lift my mum, now fastened to the stretcher, up into a horizontal position, it was recommended that I leave; and so I did, I have always been particularly obedient towards professionals.

My mum had been happy when she discovered that she

fell under the remit of Marmorkirken; then immediately embarrassed at her happiness, because she was not a person who liked to be associated with pomp and splendour. And then one day we stood in a small group around her coffin, in this church that was far too big.

When the hearse was about to drive off, I reached into the car and placed my hand on the coffin for a moment. Kristian said afterwards that it had made him dizzy, that it had been uncanny, as if I was not going to let go, as if I was going to go with her. Which wasn't the case at all. It was simply meant as a final touch. As close as I could get. Give the traveller's shoulder a squeeze. But it did not feel much different from placing a hand on a wall. I was not able to connect with her, even though she lay inside the coffin. (I have previously said that I would no longer busy myself with death, but this is real death, not the death that the mind winds around itself and uses as its prayer beads – and that is the one I want nothing to do with.)

I inherited the summerhouse. Now I painted the gate for my own sake. It felt empty and strange that there was nobody but me to appreciate it. It only struck me much later that I could have stopped thinking of happiness in relation to the freshly painted gate; but had grasped it pragmatically and thought that the wood treatment had secured the gate against rot. And that's that. But I was clearly locked in the memory about the desire to please from ten years previously. Now I was the one who (with force and power, you could almost say) had to be happy – and I had to do it alone, I had to learn to be alone with happiness. I had to learn to see for myself, not be dependent on other people's gazes, my mum's, Charles's – for example see the garden and the storm of shearing and destruction that blew through it, and the freshly painted gate.

I felt like a jigsaw puzzle whose pieces had been thrown high into the air, that I was rummaging around to pick them up, and some of the pieces had yet to land and might hit me on the head at any moment. I had, but again it sounds so active – the circumstances had caused me to un-know myself to what seemed to me a considerable degree. Just a moment ago I sat flicking through *Louisiana Revy* and looked at photos from an exhibition of self-portraits; how time and the (more or less) personal style still flow in over the self in the portrait, I thought, what actually remains, you could ask, where does a small flake of unique self hide itself, if that even exists – the answer is probably: in the style itself (more or less characteristic of the period). I want to have my portrait done in a shower of puzzle pieces.

It made me think of a conversation Charles and I had had about the obligation for happiness, it was in France, where we drove round and looked at cave paintings, and sitting in the car we discussed how not only you could feel like crap (at times), but when you simultaneously felt an obligation to be happy about everything that there was obviously reason to be happy about but were unable to, that made you even more miserable; a sense of misery and misfortune, of lacking a potency in relation to life, set in. I am certain that Charles quoted Kierkegaard and on the whole exhibited a Christian understanding of the compulsion for happiness, or the duty of happiness. But I am ignorant as far as theology is concerned. The conversation, I remember, ended up isolating us. We sat in the car next to each other, and drove through the magnificent French countryside, but the conversation had kicked us inside ourselves and away from each other. Maybe that was the day we had been in Rocamadour and seen the Black Madonna, a small, if I recall, modest wooden figure (modest in the same way as the statue of the Little Mermaid, unostentatious), and while I sat on the bench in the church looking at her, I thought of my mum: the Virgin Mary was the only one of the church's figures that meant anything to her. I was thinking that my mum's life neared a conclusion, that it had been a hard life with a lot of pain, spiritually and bodily, and I had never been able to bear that it was often so hard for her to exist. Only during the final year of her life was I capable of, when I left her flat after a visit, not thinking about how she was doing until I talked to her the next time, and that was normally that same night, over the phone. I was able to put it aside, as they say. The day she died, I forgot her telephone number. She had had the same number for at least a decade. I was in an incredible rush to empty her flat, I shovelled her clothes and shoes into black bin bags while now and again I could not help checking if she was lying on the sofa. I was afraid. Of the emptiness left by her. I had to do it quickly. Perhaps a little like Muslims who have to bury their dead immediately; if the burial is delayed it is said that neither they nor the dead will be able to have peace later on. I had to get everything out of the way – not to cut off her retreat, but to cut off the idea that she was still there, from letting it conquer my head.

My mum said on a number of occasions (when I had sought help from her to talk something through) that I had to learn to talk to myself (because she was not always going to be there). Now I do nothing but that. I talk out loud to myself. I have started to, without really thinking about it. And if anyone hears, I say: 'Yes, I was just walking around talking to myself about...'

'Yes, I heard,' the person in question sometimes answers.

I need to be both myself and another.

Dream, from the notebook saved from my forgetfulness: A man (anonymous, unfamiliar) approached me and asked me to follow him. He wanted to show me the strange light that just now had descended on the attic and walls of the church. The church had belonged to Mum. I understood that the light *was* Mum, and was happy that she revealed herself to me.

Later, perhaps while the man and I stood in the church (now mine), it was recommended I get the ceiling renovated. It was falling down.

Late one evening Edward's dog began to bark out in the garden, it barked as if it was going to explode, and I hurried out of the house. It stood at the end of the garden, near the new fence. On the lawn in front of it was a hedgehog, rolled up into a bristling cone; in front of the small animal stood the frothing wild beast that did not dare attack and was close to flying off the handle. The hedgehog's heart was beating insanely loud. So much fear under cover of quills. I took the dog under my arm and carried it into the house and closed the door. Then I returned to the hedgehog. It had not moved an inch. And its heart was pounding just as loud. I withdrew from the hedgehog in the hope that it would calm down and be able to continue its journey through the garden. All the way back to the house I could hear the sound of its heart, it was incredible that such a small animal had such a loud heartbeat, that there was resonance space for it – in the chest of the hedgehog. Then it made me think that by fencing off the garden I might have cut the hedgehog off from ever meeting other hedgehogs; now it was for all eternity doomed to be locked up with the dog and me.

This hedgehog is not me. I am alone, but my heart beats gently. The hedgehog alone is proprietor of the fear.

The longing for love has for some time been visualised in this way: A hand passes me a cup of tea or places a blanket over my shoulders, I, sitting somewhere that most of all resembles a sanatorium, I, a centenarian. (The sanatorium perhaps this garden.) I possibly do not have the same need for, or strength for, intimacy that I previously had in my life. How the cost of intimacy often was to be transformed into a whimpering fool, with the tears pouring down the cheeks.

Thomas Bernhard said in an interview that intimacy would kill him.

A small list to note my pleasure at being the only one of my kind in the garden:

> Nobody to complain to, you avoid this pathetic approach to another person to do something for you, cheer you up, et cetera. I now carry, more or less cheerfully, my life on my own shoulders.

I have dragged the garden furniture out of the shed and settled in out here, with a notebook and with the first part of Thomas Bernhard's autobiography, *The Origin*. Around me an undifferentiated mass of trees rustles. They are my trees, and I cannot tell them apart, rustling, crown weaved into crown. Though I do recognize the apple tree in front of me. It bears pitmaston pineapples, small and rugged, they won't be ready till July. An apple falls (suddenly) off the branch with a crack, shot towards the grass by the worm inside it, I believe. Apples and the thought of the family, that could not be more suitable.

I intended to cough all the misery there has been down in this pail, the notebook, which I hereby dub *Document Black*. Behind the verb 'cough' and the entire idea of pails or tubs a literary origin lies hidden: Ron Weasley, Harry Potter's friend, whose magic wand is in pieces, accidentally invokes a kind of curse upon himself consisting of him coughing up slugs; he is literally running over with snails, they pour out of him, and so Hagrid gives him a tub to lean over, where the snails can be collected. Well, I am bending over my notebook and start where my thoughts often founder:

My mum had been depressed for some time when one of her friends rang me and told me that she thought my mum was having suicidal thoughts. I rejected that most definitely, as I believed and trusted what my mum had told me, over the years, on several occasions, that when you have had a child, the thought of taking your own life has to be wiped out, I think she said: 'Then that possibility no longer exists.' (I knew that she had attempted to take her own life when she was quite young because she had fallen in love with a married man, an impossible love; she used to say that she was probably one of the last in the wave following the young Werther. In the hospital room an old lady in the neighbouring bed gave her a turquoise scarab, the resurrection beetle, for the new beginning she had woken up to; she later passed it on to me, and I have it in an envelope, because it is so small that it could easily disappear in my jewellery box.) I did not think that this child, me, had by now been an adult for more than twenty years. I shrugged off her friend's concerns. I think that I forgot all about the phone call.

One afternoon I visited my mum, a suitcase was packed; she who always preferred to ride out her depression at home had personally arranged an admission and was on her way to the hospital. The ward, dull sad futile, the lounge full of smoke and smokers (if as in other parts of society a smoking ban had been introduced at the psychiatric wards, the wards would have been devoid of people, the chain-smoking patients camped outside, but what about the closed wards, the few non-smokers perhaps moving around in a kind of mobile aquarium-like oxygen box steamed up with breath, 'come as your madness': Anaïs Nin placed a birdcage on her head at a party under that theme), it was either later that same day, or the following day, that my mum asked me for her grey bag, in itself gloomy, like a small collapsed donkey, but she changed her mind, as I reached for it, and jumped up from the bed and grabbed it... one of the first nights she attempted to take her life with some pills she had brought with her in the donkey bag, in her hospital room, but ended up vomiting them.

I know that she did it at the hospital out of concern for me (had herself admitted in order to take her own life there), so that I would not come and find her, and I also understand how terrible she was doing, and how difficult it was to make such a decision. She talked about it on another occasion, how difficult it was for her to reach that point, to make the effort to leave life behind, that it demanded a huge effort (maybe she was referring to her suicide attempt when she was very young, now she was at the other end of life, probably around seventy).

344

Thomas Bernhard writes about himself (in the third person):

> 'But he, yes, he had never managed to muster the power, determination and strength of character that was necessary to commit suicide.'
> —— *The Origin*

It is not only the degree of despair that determines the outcome: if the suicide attempt ends up taking place.

The attempt failed, and I was deeply grateful for that, but I felt conned cheated deceived – and guilty, because I had not been attentive to 'the preparation phase of suicide,' in Bernhard's words, unlike the friend who had warned me. A little later she, the friend, committed suicide. (In my mind it is connected to the fact that her husband shortly before choked to death, a chunk of meat got stuck in his throat one day when he was at home alone. After that I, the vegetarian, stopped putting avocado pits in my mouth in order to suck off the remaining avocado – I imagine the pit flying into the abyss.)

Five years later when my mum was near death she had a couple of days of vomiting that she told me were due to a kind of mechanical irritation, caused by taking all her evening medicine at once, instead of in several doses as she normally did, it left me with a doubt as to whether it was in fact another suicide attempt. And if her death was the result of suicide. But she lay, as mentioned, so peaceful when I found her. It looked natural.

'I can't take much more,' she had said, weak after her vomiting. 'Nor should you,' I had replied.

When we then sat together, the day before what would become the day of her death, I said to her: 'When you say that you can't take much more, I feel that I should give you permission to die.'

'I simply can't understand how you can come to that conclusion,' she replied, 'five years ago, back when I tried to take my own life, you said afterwards that you still needed me. And so I decided that I would be here for you as long as I could.' She reached out for my hand: 'We need each other.'

She only did it – tried to take her own life back then – I said to myself sitting in the garden that now mercilessly was mine alone – because she thought I was in good hands with Charles and no longer needed her, and for a time I truly was, in good hands, but then I could no longer endure the marriage, I developed a kind of hypersensitivity towards it.

And after the enormous exertion of deciding to take her own life – and managing to carry out the act, the act of suicide, which then failed – then she was right back where she started, in bed.

Dream: my mum lived in an attic, I walked up the attic stairs, the door was not locked, she had been asleep and was frightened that she had lain there completely defenceless, with the door unlocked.

I feel bad writing about her. I am certain that she would not care for it. And she is defenceless, not sleeping, dead. But I can't stop. I can meet her when I dream about her. And when I write about her. It is a somewhat selfish project, possibly outright improper.

'I have always wanted to gun someone down from behind,' Charles had said and laughed (depraved), so you could see the void where the tooth was missing, or else he said 'shoot someone in the back' and basked in the not very heroic nature of the statement and his own toothless charm, he could get away with standing in the position of the coward because of his charm. Could he also have gotten away with it by saying that he wanted to be a rat, even wanted to rat on someone? The other teeth in his mouth were heavily discoloured, all things considered there was something brown about him. He mentioned it on more than one occasion. Two or three times over the ten years that our marriage ended up lasting, he said that he had always dreamt of shooting someone in the back. Each time I pictured a small town in the Wild West, it could be OK Corral, dust rising up, and the bad guy's straddling legs, the cowardly shot in the hero's back. And while I pictured the western scene (the guy with the brown glow as the baddie), I saw myself sitting in the brown corduroy armchair watching a western on TV, with my legs dangling over the edge of the armrest, while from a bowl, with a spoon, eating something that might be dough, an afternoon during my teenage years, quite possibly a Saturday or Sunday, because only on the weekend would you expect to see a western. In all likelihood I had felt like baking a cake, but had not had the patience to wait until it was baked, or else I had not managed it because the film started, and for that reason I ate it raw (raw food, decades before it became modern), though in all likelihood with baking powder in it. Which makes me remember my grandmother's flat cakes; for some reason she never used baking powder, and her cakes were always flat, and they crumbled easily. When I asked her why she did not use baking powder, she brushed it aside. It seemed as though she simultaneously wanted to bake and not bake, or as though she wanted to bake a little – bake, but bake flatly. There was something immensely unassuming about her cakes, just as there was something immensely unassuming about her, who almost always stood up drinking her coffee with the accompanying flat cake, or if she sat, she sat on the very edge of the chair. All because she belonged to a time and a milieu, she came from the country, where the women waited upon the men while they sat eating, and she had a hard time staying still during an entire meal, even when she reached an advanced age; she preferred to walk back and forth between the kitchen and the dining table, even though everything already, before the meal began, was placed on the table, and the people eating could easily manage to pour and serve themselves.

As far as my family history is concerned, at the age of fourteen I was introduced to a point in it that turned everything on its head. As far as my family history is concerned, I quite simply have to settle my inheritance, no matter how heavy it seems, but with an eye to what, you might ask? A kind of liberation, I presume. To let a heavy burden fall. By talking about it? Would that be enough? Incidentally it seems to me that in my family there has always been a certain eagerness in relation to, prevailed a certain need for, talking about weighty topics. In order to thereby lighten the load? And here I picture the family placed in a row, with a boulder passing from one set of arms to another, the recipient sinking to their knees each time under the weight. Their suffering could be perceived as an attack (even though there is a certain unreasonableness in saying that), like the open end of a cannon pointing at me.

I can't put it off any longer: I was on a trip in the countryside with my cousins, in Ermelunden, we sat on a blanket and ate our lunch when the youngest of them (incidentally it is unbelievable the extent to which she and I share gestures and diction, suddenly in the midst of a stream of words she lets out a high sound, an uh or an uhm, so high-pitched that I am initially taken aback, but then I recognize the voice from myself, and the hesitations, all these small tosses of the head, the wrist's sideways movement through the air, which I find immensely affected when I have seen video recordings of myself, but with her just see as life and consideration) took it for granted that I knew something I (nevertheless) did not know; that my grandma, when her children were little, had slit the artery of first her daughter (my cousin's mum) and afterwards herself. Shock always leads to, in any case on my part, a change in the surroundings, in this case the lake a little ways from us became more radiant, more like a mirror, and my own movements, the movement of everything seemed jerky, as though time had stopped flowing.

My cousin suddenly clapped her hand over her mouth and said: 'No, I'm sorry. I thought you knew,' and they both tried to protect me because I was the youngest, their little cousin, they called me.

From that moment everything had to be approached differently than before: when someone I loved so much, my grandma, had tried to kill her own child. But how differently: with greater suspicion? With a new weight? With a constant feeling of a catastrophe lurking right around the corner? I don't know.

Here sat my cousins, their mum had survived and became a mum herself, and my grandma still walked around baking her flat cakes. Their mum could remember how someone had pressed firmly around her wrist in the ambulance on the way to the hospital.

My dad was in the living room where it happened, but

he was quite small, he has no recollection of it.

'But the atmosphere in the living room that evening may have taken hold of me,' he once said and put his hand on his heart, or somewhere close to it, 'the incident,' he continued, 'has not, by the way, been significant for my life, but it rests within me, encapsulated.' (Then I thought about a bullet from a firearm, that cannot be surgically removed, but which the body over time encapsulates.)

To this story belongs a previous story, or several, which can serve as an explanation, as an interpretation – childhood: my grandma's mum died when she was relatively young, her dad remarried.

My mum: 'And what do you think the stepmother named her own daughter?'

I did not know, but the hairs on the back of my neck began to stand up, because of my mum's voice, her expression

My mum: 'Meta.'

My grandma was called Meta.

My mum: 'As though the first Meta did not exist.'

Or else she said: 'So the first Meta no longer existed.'

Or: 'Then the first Meta ceased to exist.'

Marriage as an explanation: My paternal grandmother's husband got drunk on pay day, and when he came home drunk, he wanted to sleep with her. My aunt remembers how her mum held her up in front of her like a shield – against the man.

When I heard that, I realised that my grandmother could not leave her daughter with him, but had to take her with her into death.

Schizophrenia as an explanation: My paternal

grandmother's head was full of voices. The loneliness. Alone, with the voices; she alone heard them. But I could hear when she answered them, so I (as a child) made her aware that she was talking to herself, and it made her self-conscious, but also present again, and loving, so that her mouth formed into a shy small loveable smile. She was very loveable. (Just like my granddad she was very fond of blue, intense blue, all her clothes were blue, dear blue ancestors.)

I have begun to sit out in the garden early, with my coffee, while everything is still damp with dew. Then I sit and watch the garden wake up. I place cushions on the garden furniture, and the dog lays down next to me. At the top of a tree near me there is a pair of doves sitting and tenderly polishing each other's feathers, or they bicker and coo, they can keep at it for hours. Then I pull out *Document Black* again, even though the morning is almost too beautiful for the monster, I have started to think that I never want to leave this place.

My granddad has come to a halt on the tiled path in front of the kitchen door of his house, it is December, he has been standing there for so long that his hands have turned a whitish-blue. He broods over all the installations that can break, the oil burner the cesspool the oven the water heater. When we, that is my mum and I, realize that he is standing out in the cold, my mum grabs his hands and helps him inside. Christmas Eve, he won't allow Christmas dinner to be made, because the oven could break, and he could end up going broke from electricity consumption. We have proposed eating cold food like every other night so as not to worry him, it is his house, he is the one who is depressed, we approach it like scouts, no Christmas Eve this year is fine. When the neighbour's house begins to smell of Christmas food, nevertheless it becomes difficult to accept. We decide to defy him and at least make rice pudding, it would be nice to have something hot, the house is cold so as not to challenge the oil burner to give out. Meanwhile he moves around us complaining, raising and lowering his hands and telling us that we have completely lost it. I don't know if it's right, that he practically attempts to tear the wooden spoon from my mum while she stirs. My mum has looked after him for a couple of months, he really does not want to be admitted, and is getting tired. I am the only one in the family who is never ill. My mum constantly feared that I would get ill, but I never did. Around me they fall like dominoes, soon my granddad will knock over my mum, when my grandma was alive, she was the one who got knocked over, and the other way around. They constantly found themselves on a see-saw, when one rose, the other sunk. My granddad does not want any of the pudding, he waves the plate away with his heavy hands, we eat it in darkness so as not to bother him further, because of the danger of fire there can be no talk of candles. I have come to celebrate Christmas with them and in order to push for my granddad to be admitted before he topples my mum. The following takes place in the living room, by the door to the corridor, where the stairs to the attic are, my mum and I are sleeping in the attic, maybe he discovered that we have filled a couple of hot water bottles, he accuses my mum of something or other, I can see how fragile she is, that it is only a matter of days or maybe weeks before she topples, and so I say to him: 'You old fool,' everything comes to a stop, I have admired and loved him my entire life, there was never a bad word between us before, and I regretted it on the spot and said that I didn't mean it, but he took it (fool) personally and sat down. And I could see how he sat with the word, and that I would never be able to get it back from him.

But he gave it back himself. Later, when he had been admitted, and I visited him – at a medical ward, because there were physical difficulties too, the depression now gone, and he sat in a white bathrobe reduced to at least half his former size – he said that he knew I had not meant it, and we ended up somewhere in the vicinity of where we had always been, before the arguing by the stairs to the attic – not the same place, because he had become so small and was soon going to die.

It was not always like a see-saw, sometimes all three of them, my mum my grandma my granddad, were ill at the same time, so one lay in the bedroom the other on the sofa the third in the attic (and one time I even prepared a document, probably inspired by all the old documents uncovered by The Famous Five, with grandma's name written in full, 'I XXXX promise never again to go to bed during the day,' which she signed, but no sooner had she put her signature on the document than she had gone back to bed), I sat in the living room, the entire time there was the sound of the clock on the sideboard that I hated, the sound of summer or winter ticking away, no the season didn't matter, it was always afternoon in the room, stale afternoon, hence my dislike for afternoons, as soon as afternoon arrives, nothing can turn out differently that day – 'but it does not have to be a crutch,' I can hear Kristian saying.

It seems to me very wrong to deal with only a single aspect of a person, like here the ill, the ill was the

353

exception, the Christmas Eve definitely an exceptional situation (preceded by twenty-nine perfectly normal ones in my memory blurring, because they are probably indistinguishable Christmas Eves.) There has to be something else. There is an infinite row of bright days, it's just a matter of digging in.

An excursion, by boat, a summer's day, to Tærø and Lilleø, which is really only a patch of sand, and which you can almost reach in one long jump from Tærø. Now there are horses on Tærø, there is an airfield, and you have to ask the owner for permission to come ashore. It wasn't like that back then, you could just show up, and I certainly don't think there were horses, only cows, suddenly I remember how careful you had to be so as not to accidentally step in one of the large greenish-black cowpats with flies suspended above.

When we had eaten lunch, my granddad placed his cap over his eyes (and a pillow he had brought with him under his head) and lay down to nap, while I inhabited Tærø alone and walked across the island and looked down a high slope at the beach below, which was full of rocks and lay in shade, and where it was windy, and the waves pounded the coast with a hard sound, until I suddenly had enough of the way the wind tore at the trees, and hurried back to the sunny beach where my granddad in the meanwhile might have woken and started to fill the sacks we had brought with us with sand.

One time I had stayed on the other side of the island so long, maybe daydreaming, leaning against a tree, that my granddad had long since managed to gather the sand he wanted, and already sat in the dinghy ready to sail.

'There you are, I was just about to weigh anchor,' he said and even though I knew he would never have left me on the island, I still felt the isolation of the place inside me and hurried to hike up my trousers and wade out to him.

To set off had demanded, it always did, a certain amount of preparation, with things that had to be transported down to the harbour, stacked up in the clog hall, in the courtyard, maybe all the way out to the lawn, where sails, rather patched, for example a faded green sail with brown patches, were unfolded in order to be inspected. The food was packed in a bike basket, big sandwiches, a thermos, light beer lemon water raspberry fizz green soda, salt pepper sugar, packs of home-baked pastries, mug, cream in a fizzy drink bottle with a cheerful cork made of kitchen roll. And there was also a dog back then, there were always dogs and cats, one replaced the previous. Then we packed (I am tired of first person singular, like a top that is too tight, and of first person plural) the load, my grandma always kind when she sent us off (because imagine if we never returned, but that wasn't nicely put, she probably was truly happy on our behalf) with the goodies in the basket, as long as we promised to come home on time, so she would not worry and go out on the hill with binoculars to look out across the sea, to see whether a white dinghy with a blue railing did not sail into her line of sight soon and behind it a small orange dot: the Optimist I was given when I turned twelve, I wonder what she might get up to while we were gone, maybe late in the afternoon she would sit down with the paper, already back then (when?) I experienced it as if she took on a role, that of the newspaper reader, when she leaned forward for the paper on the coffee table and unfolded it, and holding it at a proper distance, she began to read, with her head tilted a little.

355

She always wore lipstick when she read, as if she were a guest at someone's house. The rest of the family read all the time, and she was outside, because she did not read books, because they did not convey anything to her, because she was unable to form connections, grasp the storyline and the characters. 'So who is that?' she might ask an hour into a film at the sight of the main character. I think of her when I watch a ball game where I don't know the rules; how the match dissolves into moments without connection.

What was her proper element? The embroidery? Because she thought it was better to create beautiful things than to read. The kitchen? No, but acting as the hostess: when the food was ready and was on the table, and she said, bon appétit, smiling and powdered, her hair in place beneath the pearl-studded hair net, Blue Grass on the wrist and behind the ears, everything homemade and wonderful, and she was met with praise; then she beamed, then she flourished – until her husband began to act like an ill-bred child and show a lack of table manners, perhaps to seize the attention of the guests, perhaps to make cracks in her happiness, as revenge for something that happened earlier that day or earlier that year.

My granddad was always happy when he was heading off, and for me, that was what the holiday was all about, these excursions. For my granddad it meant freedom and then to gather sand for cement (for concreting tiles?), so we placed as many pails as possible on the bikes, and also sacks, he balanced a mast and maybe a freshly painted boat hook, resting on the seat and handlebars, we had to walk the bikes, the load was so heavy, and hold them back down the hill to the harbour.

Sometimes I was seized by panic at the thought of

someone coming out of the sea and grabbing hold of the Optimist (I was so close to the water, it was like sitting in a walnut shell), or else it was just because the water was so deep and black, in any case I began to yell practically scream for my granddad who was hard of hearing and could hear nothing, but just waved cheerfully at me from his jolly boat, in his proper element: with his arm on the tiller, a cheroot (Grøn Havana) in his mouth. But when it came time to sail through the passage in the dam, I joined him in the jolly boat. If I could not get right up close to him on my own, because I never became a very good sailor, never entirely familiar with the direction of the wind (once I had to get out of the Optimist and pull it, shamefaced, wading through the low water, home to the harbour, like Gulliver pulling the Lilliputians' navy behind him), he would pull me over with the boat hook, then the two dinghies would grate and crunch against each other. We had to lower the masts. We had to row through the passage, with the Optimist in tow. The walls (of the passage) were made of raw cement, and you could see how strong the current was from the ripples along the walls. There was an echo. You felt locked in, it was a relief to get out into the light again. And there lay the islands – waiting.

Today Alwilda came for lunch, the sun and the wine made us drowsy; Alwilda placed the pillows from the garden furniture on the grass, and we lay down next to each other and fell asleep. It felt both reassuring and a little too intimate to lie there side by side under the whispering trees. I don't think we had done that since we were children.

She is a liberating element in our concerned part of the world that shakes with fear of death and tries to stretch out life like a rubber band by safeguarding the personal safety and health. She drinks too much wine and smokes too many cigarettes. (My dad refers to her as the wild lady.) She does not use sun screen, but flips and turns under the burning sun twelve hours in a row to get dark-brown for her lover, and she drives fast in her car, she circumvents the chicanes by steering straight ahead, so that she does not have to slow down. She is master of the moment. Alwilda, you are an ode to freedom, occasionally a little impatient.

Much of the time I do nothing. I sit looking at all the things that ought to be sorted, the garden, the house. 'I did not take into account that the trees would grow,' my mum once said. Nor did I. There is the ladder, there is the saw, or if nothing else: There is the note with the telephone number for my gardeners. There is nobody to prompt me to make an effort, nobody I can nominate to be my superego. The neighbour used to take on that role, automatically. But she has become conspicuously mild – towards me. There is often a bunch of marigolds or a couple of cucumbers lying on my garden table from her. On the other hand, she fights with her boyfriend out in the open so the garden shakes, I don't know why I think it is worse to hear a seventy-year-old woman like my neighbour shout 'fuck it (the birthday)' than when a younger person does it. I go down to the fjord and walk and look up at the wild slopes and at the many nuances of green, the dark green treetops, the light green tall wild grass, and another green and an almost blue: marram grass. My house is a house of cards, so let it come crashing down. Well, I simply blot out the gardener's gaze the builder's gaze the housewife's gaze and observe the hollyhocks' silky grace, swaying in many colours, on the terrace. The next moment I think: not a chance, I will appropriate every single centimetre of this house and this garden, I will make it into my everything. And I get up and tear off the lid of the tin of wood treatment. (I also like staring at my laundry while it dries in the wind, it can almost make me fall into a trance, I wonder if it is a kind of fetishism, self-fetishism, before I know it I'll be stealing from my own drying line – some might claim that I have already done that, intellectually speaking, with *Document Black*. Ack, women and their washing – Alwilda told me that when she was on a trip with Edward, she felt connection love a strong affiliation to her knickers and tights when they hung flapping in the wind, far out in the nothingness of Mozambique. Representation of Home, I assume, in all the foreign. I have been allowed to use the washing machine at the camping site just around the corner. The person who runs it is also bad-tempered, one of the campers has encircled their tent with potted plants, and when I arrive with my laundry in tow, I hear him shout to her that if she does not have them removed, he will personally kick them away, and afterwards he would give her a proper kick in the arse. I could wash one of the horse's heavy hairy filthy horse cloths in his machine, that would keep him busy for a while, picking out the bristly horse hair. This is not the most peaceful place on the earth. A podgy man walks around hoovering up twigs and leaves from the area around his camper, how many other machines does he have inside the camper? And how much does he look forward to every time he can turn one of them on?)

I don't really know if this belongs in *Document Black*, but it could serve as a horror story, a warning to my future self: this evening down by the fjord I met an older woman with a Danish-Swedish farm dog, a spitting image of mine (I don't think Edward will ever want it back), greying ageing and clearly with arthritis in the hindquarters, it practically has to drag itself along. A little ways away there was a pushchair which the woman told me that she drove the dog in when it could no longer walk. I thought I had seen the dog before and I had, it turned out, that is on a TV programme about dementia research, for which dogs were used, and this dog was in the early stages of dementia.

The woman was very close to it and talked about its loyalty over fifteen years, about all the painkillers it took, she talked about a ninety-year-old neighbour, also with dementia, how the neighbour and the dog both forget what they were doing and in confusion come to a halt in the middle of the room. She talked about how she would never be able to have it put down, 'we don't do that with people, do we?' she said defiantly, she was a doctor. I happened to think about the dog in *The Stranger* that runs away from its owner after being mistreated by him for years. The dog here might have to run away from its owner just to get the opportunity to die in peace. I told her that I had read that some people make a diamond out of their beloved pets' ashes.

'Then you could have it in your bag or attach it to your keys,' I said to her, 'a truly beautiful and shiny one, yes, a memorial shining in the light.'

She picked the dog up and put it into the pushchair and rolled off with it, as if she had to protect it from me. Then I sat alone on the beach and felt like Death.

Another day I walk down by the glittering fjord, in a better mood, I didn't think that it was so bad to imagine myself walking along here in fifteen years, still alone, besides an old dog (or two, though it would make it easier to have lost one of them); once in a while one of my friends would probably drive out to visit me, like Alwilda the other day, especially if I consistently dish up fish, because people always have an expectation about fresh fish when they come for a visit by the sea.

BERNHARD'S SHOES, A NOTE

[Camilla]

In Thomas Bernhard's house in Obernathal the shoes have their own room. In a photograph, which is all I have to go by, there are around twenty pairs of shoes and a pair of wellies. There are possibly more shoes on the shelves, out at the sides, which have not made it into the photograph. Edward has visited the house, and he says that the staff constantly dust these (stationary) shoes. Clean, clean shoes. I am interested in these shoes, this shoe room, for the following reason: during his unhappy time at upper secondary school during the war, Bernhard had been allocated the shoe room (at school) to practise his violin. Each day he camped out in this room with his violin, the shelves around him filled with secondary school students' shoes. He played in a completely different way than his violin teacher had directed. The entire time he was absorbed by the thought of suicide, of hanging himself, from a hook in the ceiling, in the shoe room. Peculiar artistic expression, the thought of taking one's life and the shoes found a place to merge. It is not strange that shoes from then on had enormous significance for him, and that he later in life had to establish a similar room, a separate shoe room, a burning room, a survival room.

A place of refuge. To isolate yourself in order to be able to devote yourself, unfold that which has conquered you, like here the thought of suicide, no matter how terrible or subversive it is, at full sail. The intensity of the sound, the intense movements across the strings, the (playing) style that is the release of one's nature – I expand so that the room has to give way. I play it to bits, I play it pieces, myself included. Then I survive. Presumably. Only the shoes are witness to it. The shoes witness everything. (They absorb it, like sweat.) And from now on there can almost not be enough of these elongated shining cases, in place in the witness box.

THE BOSS

[Camilla]

(Is my skull collapsing, my brain matter seething? Everyone tips over and is combined into one mass; a centaur is conjured up by a person like me who could not decide, but let one be the other, my horseman my manhorse, who is the horse, is the horse even a horse?)

When there is an empty place, something else (presumably) will attempt to be placed there – by me. (There was an empty place, and in stepped the horse.) Now I have the animals with their iron wills instead of the two ill ones, my mum, Charles; I could have told myself that the horse would get ill when I replaced ill Charles with it. I take its heavy head in my arms and kiss its eyelid. Then I pull myself together, the veterinarian has said that it is not that strange that it hangs its head when it hears me sigh so deeply. The veterinarian is a scrawny sardonic creature in an open rider's coat which almost reaches the ground. She moves so quickly that I still do not have a reliable impression of her face. When she arrives, she often has her brother with her; they look like two skinny broomsticks climbing out of the car. There was almost no end to their enjoyment when the veterinarian, after having felt the horse's legs, could tell me that there was talk of an old injury that had flared up; that I had been cheated; that I had bought a horse with a previously injured front leg. She impatiently grabbed my hands and let them feel press touch, 'you have to learn to touch your own horse;' I felt nothing, not the hard or gelatinous gooey areas she led my hands across furiously, but I kept that to myself.

A couple of cats live in the stables, and one day I had Edward's dog with me, it barked and eagerly moved towards them. Then the veterinarian took me to task.

'It has to have its attention on you.'

'You're the boss,' the brother added.

'It's the cats that live here, it has to reconcile itself with that. It is only visiting.'

'You look very tired,' the brother said, 'but if you can't train your dog, then you can't train your horse, and then you probably can't train your children either,' he said and nodded in the direction of a child that impetuously rang its cycle bell a little way from there.

I fuss over the animals and feel sorry for them – the dog (borrowed dog replacement dog, which Edward no longer needs, because he has Alma) that has to stay home alone, its dark gaze when I leave. The horse that is injured and has to be dragged along every day. I am keeping it in a livery stable, close to the summerhouse; it is a curious place, with farmhouse and stables that look like they were taken out of the old TV series *Dallas*, the theme song sounds in my ears every time I cycle towards the house; in addition, stone lions are generously strewn over the area, at every corner the lion guards. The large folds are surrounded by white-painted fences, in front of the house there are several golf carts and other small motorized vehicles whose function I am clueless about, and also a bunch of four-by-fours. The house is inhabited by bodybuilders. These bulging *nouveaux riches* are not the least bit interested in horses, but they have bought a house with accompanying stables and large folds, perhaps because they thought it would look good with some rocking horsebacks in the midst of all that green. One day I walk around with the horse on the track, because there is also one of those, it gets a long thick nail stuck in its hoof. I pull and struggle, but I cannot get it out. Luckily one of the bodybuilders is walking around in the vicinity polishing the vehicles. I shout at him. He approaches me and the horse hesitantly. I show him the nail. He shrugs and says that old building material has been used as a drain for the track, and now it has obviously worked its way up to the surface. I decide against telling him how bad an idea that was, and what the veterinarian and her brother would have to say about that. I point at his bulging biceps and ask him to pull the nail out. He shakes his head. He is afraid of horses. But he'll happily lend me a pair of pliers. He fetches them for me and then lets himself into the house so as not to be met by further demands, the pliers don't help. But then a new bodybuilder emerges from the house.

'Your friend is afraid of horses,' I say to him, 'but do you think you are brave enough to help me?'

He is, as long as I position myself so the horse can neither bite nor kick him. The horse is completely calm, it spreads its hind legs and urinates, intensely and amply, and while he pulls at the nail and gets it out rather easily I come to think of the time I was in a public toilet, it was in the Algarve one afternoon, my mum and I had shared a pitcher of sangria at a café with a view of the Atlantic and afterwards had nearly floated along the beach and over the rocks; when I emerged from the toilet, out to the common area, she said: 'You have such a powerful stream,' and I thought, she means I sound like a horse.

That day or on another day of that trip, in any case with the same powerful sun (it destroyed the skin on my mum's lower arms that stuck out of the short-sleeved dresses, and made it horse-like, that is thickened stiff, and in the years that followed she referred to it several times, as she took a pinch of ruined skin between her thumb and index finger and said: 'That was the sun in the Algarve') in front of the endless Atlantic and beneath the endless heavens, the astounding and unpleasant happened when we passed a group of Portuguese men who threw change at us because, we surmised by the action, we were women without men, although wearing a considerable amount of clothing, with only our lower arms showing, between beached fishing boats, below the horse-skin sun.

'You now have to ride sixty minutes a day,' the veterinarian said late in the summer, 'ten minutes pacing, forty-five minutes trotting for periods of five minutes, with a round of pacing in between, and then cool down for ten minutes.'

    'But I can't manage that in...'

    'Yes.'

    'But, it makes...'

    'No,' and as she hopped into the car: 'Other people can do it. Then so can you.'

THE VETERINARIAN'S BROTHER

[Camilla]

How did I end up in bed with the veterinarian's brother,
I suppose only the veterinarian knows, in any case I am
now embracing his lean body on my blue sofa bed and
wishing I had curtains that could be drawn (I imagine
that the veterinarian is not far away). It had to be either
the leader of The Green Fingers or the veterinarian's
brother, the one fat the other skinny, from one extreme
to the other, nothing in between, out here in the country.

'What is that?' he asks and winces and sticks his hand
under the sheet.

'I'm afraid it's a chew toy.'

And then the dog that has until now stayed in the garden arrives. It wants to join us.

'No, I won't have that,' he says.

'It normally lies under the duvet, otherwise it starts
howling' (it's tilting its head back).

'Well, then it will get angry.'

'It is hot,' I say, 'we can let it have the duvet. Otherwise
we probably won't get any peace.'

I pull the duvet off him and pat the bed, it jumps up
and disappears under the duvet. And so it did not see
how we got our bodies up and running. Everything
that there had been, rested in the body, it was difficult
to become light and free. Like being thawed after a long
winter.

'Do you feel your unassailability shaken?' he asks.

But it is not love, it is kindness. So no, I don't.

A little later a honk is heard from the road, I sit up and
grab the duvet, 'that's my sister,' he says and jumps out
of the bed, in a cloud of feathers (there is a hole in the

duvet), along with the dog which the car makes furious. I must be happy, because I start to sing (a couple of verses of 'Lucy in the Sky with Diamonds', if anyone wants to know).

COLUMBIA, THREE LITTLE CHINAMEN (AND A WILD HAPPINESS)

[Alma]

It was difficult to tear Camilla away from her animals, she has long talked about how she ought to be English, she has become so fond of dogs and horses, I am dog-horse-lady, she says of herself, but I waved the tickets in front of her nose, and along she came. And look how lucky she is, because now an incredibly handsome man is sitting on the chair next to her. I am here because I have had a short story included in an American anthology, I am on a panel with the publisher and another author, soon I have to read. I am only allowed three minutes, the publisher does not care for readings, he thinks you get to know more about the author by hearing the person in question speak. We have met twice, and both times he has asked me if I like cooking. I could see that there was a right and a wrong answer. I guessed 'like,' 'but I do not swear by any particular cuisine,' I said, 'I take a little from everyone.' They, it was him and his assistant, thought that Camilla and I ought to try a proper deli now that we were in New York, so I sat with a bagel with cream cheese and smoked salmon and pickles, it was no great experience, first and foremost chewy, difficult to deal with when talking, and add to that a peculiar drink recommended by the assistant, a so-called Egg Cream Soda (even though there is no egg, only milk, chocolate syrup and seltzer, mixed, it's foaming). While we ate, we talked about food, I told them about the Icelandic dish called the Black Death (maybe I am confusing it with a schnapps) which consists of flesh that has been buried in the ground for a long time thereby making it tender. It induced a certain response. So I continued with the

Icelandic and also told them about shark with fried onion and gravy – again, reaction. Then I thought I could rest a little, and sawed off a couple of bites. I thought that if we ran out of material, I would tell them about *grindadráp* on the Faroe Islands, it took place when I was there once. Then the publisher told me that he never cooked just for himself, and looked sad. And I said that I wouldn't do that either, and looked down and made my face heavy. Camilla said nothing, she was in constant phone contact with the veterinarian, it was to do with scans of the horse's legs. Actually, she said one thing. She said: 'I have started to make budgets again, all the time, it is because I am nervous, and just before when I sat calculating, I saw a black wall in front of me, and it felt like I hit my head against it. Everything stopped there.' 'I have brought Camilla with me because she needs to relax,' I said to the publisher and his assistant, there was also a Croatian translator present, 'she has bought a horse, it is very expensive, in fact it is close to giving her a nervous breakdown. She is afraid to check the post because the vet bills are pouring in.' 'That's not true, she emails them,' Camilla said. Then they started to talk about the horse meat scandal, and Camilla got up, 'easy now,' I said, 'you have said so yourself, it has been given so much medication that it cannot be used for consumption,' but she had to go outside to smoke. I am sitting now wondering whether Jews eat horses (galloping koshers, sorry.)

Then Camilla returned and said: 'I recently saw a profile about an American war correspondent, she was a contemporary of Hemingway, but was much older before she finally took her own life, I can't remember what her name was. But when her mum who she was really close to died, she wrote in a letter to a friend that she felt like a compass that had lost North. She felt aimless, and that's what it's like for me. The thought of having to live another twenty-five to thirty years,' she sat down.

'Camilla,' I said.

'It has to be Martha Gellhorn, right?' the publisher said to the assistant.

'There were two things she was sorry not to have experienced, to write a bestseller and have had a lasting romance.'

'I would only be sad about the latter,' I said.

'I don't believe that.'

Alas. I have read from the translation, it went well, the beautiful man next to Camilla laughed. It's not a big audience, probably thirty people. We are in a library at Columbia. But now comes the baptism of fire, the conversation. The publisher turns to me to talk to me about my short story: 'Is it normal for women in Denmark to try to sell their husbands to prostitutes at strip bars?' he asks. 'No,' I say, 'it also takes place in Berlin.'

'There are three Chinese characters in the story,' he says, 'why does it say *three little Chinamen*?'

(I think: If there are Chinese people in the audience, I will die. I hardly dare look up. But luckily there is only one mixed-race person. It was a good thing I didn't read about the mixed-race stripper.)

'I'm not a racist,' I say. If there had been a bible, I would have placed my hand on it. Now I've finally made it to Columbia with my literature, and I have to sit and say I'm not a racist.

'Of course we know that the Chinese are little (he says *Chinese*, not *Chinamen*), there's no reason to write that,' the publisher says.

'No,' I say, 'but actually it is a quote from an old

Danish song.'

'Then there ought to have been a footnote,' the publisher says, 'so how does it go?'

'It's a nonsensical song,' I say and look at Camilla.

Now help arrives, *deus ex machina* gets up from the chair next to Camilla and says: 'I lived in Denmark until I was seven. It sounds like this,' and then he makes like he is playing a mouth harp: 'Tri smi kinsiri pi Hibri Plids stid i spillidid pi kintribis, si kim in bitjint spirt hvi dir vir hindt tri smi kinisiri pi Hibri Plids,' he sat down again.

'Fantastic,' Camilla said.

'Thank you,' the beautiful man said, 'the system is,' he said to the gathering, 'that you can vary the song with different vowel sounds and pretend you are playing different musical instruments.'

'Mhm,' a researcher said, 'we are familiar with that in Mali.'

'Don't you feel like trying it with o?' Camilla asked.

'Mhm,' the publisher said, 'but what does it mean?'

'You have to remember,' I said, 'that Denmark is not a multicultural society like yours, Chinese people were once, for a long time actually, rare in Denmark.'

'Yes,' the beautiful man said, 'you did not see a Chinese person every day.'

'How old are you?' Camilla asked.

'51,' he said, 'how old are you?'

'46,' she said.

'5 years' difference,' he said.

'Yes,' Camilla said.

'What does the song mean?' the publisher asked, patiently, with his hand on the axe.

Camilla got up and said:

Three little Chinamen at Astor Place
stood there playing on a double bass.
Along came an officer.
What the hell is this?
Three little Chinamen at Astor Place.

'Thank you,' the publisher said and turned to the next author, he was finished with me, I had lost.

'Sorry,' I said, 'but since there are also tall Chinese people, there was good reason to mention that they are little.'

(Afterwards I thought that I could also have talked about the possible power in the image of small men buying sex from tall people or in any case taller women.)

'We can ascribe that to translation issues,' the publisher repeated, 'there ought to have been a footnote.'

'A footnote for the translation,' I mimed to Camilla, but she was whispering with her neighbour.

Afterwards there was a reception with red wine and cheese and biscuits, each time a new person from the audience came up to me, I thought I had to repeat that I was not a racist, but they didn't believe that I was, they understood the spirit of what I had said. I walked over to Camilla who did not retreat from the beautiful man's side, 'isn't he beautiful,' she whispered to me, 'I'm in love,' 'that's nice and quick,' I said. Then we can get those *beep* animals sent to *beep*.

Well. Then there was no more wine and we had to leave. We were going out for dinner, but before we could leave, the assistant had to help the organizers pack up the biscuits and cheese, even though almost everything had been eaten. It was incredible how long it took, but it was the kind of biscuit from a box where each type belongs to a hole shaped like its shape. 'Shouldn't we just go back to our hotel and drink,' I asked, 'I'm completely wiped.' Camilla turned to the beautiful man, now it was about getting him to come along. He wasn't sure, he was telling the publisher about his relationship to Denmark. 'Let's grab a taxi,' I said. He wasn't sure, 'we have loads of duty-free alcohol,' I said, 'let's drink it in our hotel room,' 'we're going to have to take them all with us,' I said to Camilla, 'otherwise he won't go,' 'yes,' Camilla said, 'I can't be a dog-horse-lady for the rest of my life, can I?', 'no,' I said, 'time for a change.'

When we finally made it out of Columbia and stood on the street together, he still wasn't sure, the publisher stopped a taxi and crawled in and then the assistant, but he remained standing, 'then I guess you don't love Denmark that much,' I said and crawled in, and he sat down in the front seat. Camilla sat on my lap.

[Camilla]
He sat down on the chair next to mine, and after only a moment it was almost impossible not to reach out and touch his hands. When he got up and recited the stupid song, I thought, I would like to spend the rest of my life with him, that's how quickly it happened. And I know I know.

When the others had left, and we were alone, I reached out my hand towards him and said 'come,' he said 'yes' and got up, then we finally touched, and he began to pull me towards him and push me away from him again with his arms around me, and all the while he kissed me, with short quite fast movements, it was at most a few centimetres, away from him, towards him, and with that rhythm

375

he drew me out of myself, I stopped thinking I should do something, be someone, I'll just follow, I thought and allowed myself to be pulled back and forth, and the entire time his face was so close to mine, once in a while I had to see his eyes and pull back a little, they were half enclosed in darkness, two or three times he said 'oh God' very quietly, but I heard it and it made me happy. He spoke to me in Danish, but I asked him to speak American, because I wanted him to speak his own language, so I could be sure that he knew what he was saying. Then he did, he said in American, 'should I speak American? It feels strange to speak American to you,' then he spoke Danish, and I didn't try to force him back into his own language. He sounded young when he spoke Danish. The voice became too young for the rest. Otherwise he said almost nothing. I asked him to say his name, because although I was completely captivated by him, I had for a moment forgotten his name. How can I store the strength and rhythm his body possessed, which drew me along? I can't. I was close to accidentally saying that I loved him, because I knew no other words for the rapture and for no longer being left to myself and my own head.

It was morning, 'we've been making love for hours,' I said, 'we've been making love for five minutes,' he said. We sat up to drink some water.

'Are you married?' I asked.

'Yes,' he said simply.

'So that's why you haven't said anything to me,' I said. (I thought about a line by Peter Walsh, a character in a novel, something along the lines of that when you are over fifty, you can no longer be bothered to tell women they are beautiful. The veterinarian's brother had at least said my skin was soft, and asked if I used herbs.)

'No,' he said, 'I never say very much.'

'Maybe you should wear a ring.'

'Do you think that would have helped?'

'Then why did you do it?'

'I was unsure about that too. But then the taxi arrived, and she said to me, then I don't love Denmark enough,' the notion seemed to make him despair.

'How can you speak to me in such a horrible way,' I said and hid my face in my hands, but a little later I looked up, 'what are you looking at?', 'your eyes,' he said.

We lay down again, but it could not be like before, 'sorry,' I said, 'No, I'm sorry,' he said.

'It felt harsh after such an attachment. Do you know what *attachment* means?'

He did.

We thought we had better get some sleep, but I'm not very good at that, and when he had fallen asleep, I got up and started to empty the ashtrays and throw out the bottles. A little later he also got up.

'I'm happy. I think it was a lovely night.'

'You're sweet,' he said, 'yes, I won't forget it.'

It was raining, I wanted to walk with him to Grand Central Station, he put his arm around me, and there we walked, 'you look very American,' I said a little later and took his hand, he did not understand that, he was used to being attributed to various northern European nationalities, and he was also heart-rendingly blond or at least he had been, now he was probably rather grey, but actually it was his coat I was looking at, I had seen a man the previous day on the Upper West Side with an identical one. I thought that now I only needed to hide my despair for a moment longer, because there was the station. We embraced, and I turned and left. While I walked back to the hotel, I remembered how for a short time in my garden a couple of months earlier I had thought that I was just like Thomas Bernhard, that intimacy would kill me, now I was already close to dying without it. And a week later the great wild happiness still rested in my body.

My consciousness is a burning room. I have conversations with him, in there; and show him things. My thoughts are directed at him, you might say. We walk together, we two homunculi, through my brain, he has placed his arm around me and turned up the collar of his coat, we walk away from the station.

He is a straw my thoughts cling to, I know it.

If it were real, he would gradually know a good deal about me, what I love, what I don't love. But I never tell him the sad things that have passed, because I have had enough of them myself. This is an opportunity to rediscover myself, like every time you meet a new person. I can be the one I am, as a result of this-and-this-and-this instead of that-and-that, it is clearly pure guesswork what has formed someone. Nonetheless there are people who for decades travel in set stories around themselves.

I talk the most. He only offers a few clarifying questions once in a while. I am the one with the wheels. He is like a box that has to be pushed across the floor. And he is a gaze – on me. My idea that he observes me when I walk across the street, is so alive that I nearly dance. There is a ring at the door, and I imagine that it's him. I talk out loud. I am exhausted. I drink wine in the middle of the day.

It is insufferable, this fever this passion, my longing is great, it has to stop. But what did my mind fiddle with before I met him... it made budgets endlessly and wound its way around death. It had become such that certain thoughts settled across so that nothing else could get past.

The scenario with him is better. One day there will be no more fuel, and the fire will die out.

FRAGMENTS OF THE COMPANIONS'
CONVERSATION IN THE GARDEN

[All of the companions]
'Nearly four weeks later, I still listened to *Wicked Game* on YouTube, which we had heard that night, and watched Helena Christensen and Chris Isaak's stupid narcissistic display on a beach,' Camilla says, 'like I was a teenager.'

'You can't have an empty consciousness, it won't allow that to happen, it will always be the opposite of a room painted white,' Edward says.

'I'm sorry to say this,' Alma says, 'but your American reminded me of a camel or maybe a giraffe or an ostrich, yes, one of those animals that carries its rocking head high and deals you one hard unexpected blow.'

'The fact that he put his arm around me when we came out of the hotel and walked to the station, that meant something too. After doing so much walking alone, it was lovely to walk with his arm around my shoulder.'

'Yes, that sort of thing is dangerous,' Alma says, 'the night I met Kristian, I remember it all started with me saying to him, at a party where we sat next to each other on a sofa: "Try putting your arm around me." And it felt good and solid. It saddled me with a marriage. It cost me seven years.'

(...)

'And after all those years of stubborn insistence on acquiring knowledge, then the enormous exertion of deciding to commit suicide – and managing to carry out the act, the act of killing yourself. Which then failed, and then she was back where she started, back in bed with all the books, and leaned up against the bed: the future:

black bin bags full of library books, such courage and such bravery, continuing to spend so many hours of the day reading, for so many years,' Camilla says.

'I want to go to Syria and fight,' Kristian says.

'You're always interrupting, Kristian,' Alma says.

(As though not constantly expressing your opinion about one thing or the other would be synonymous with your complete disappearance. He completes people's sentences. He has an opinion about everything. He puts up fences with his chatter. When we were together, I quickly stopped having any opinions at all, and became rather quiet, Alma thinks.)

'That's suicide,' Edward says.

'Syria is our Spain.'

'Fuck all to do with you. Or me.'

'Wasn't she meant to get the book delivery this morning?'

'Maybe she couldn't manage another stack of books,' Kristian says.

'There is a need to reconcile oneself with, to be able to endure (where is the right verb), history (because what else can you do, have you ever heard of anyone setting fire to themselves because of a calamity far in the past, a thousand-year-old bloodletting?), whether it comes to world history or family history, even though for example it might seem impossible to endure the fact that the mathematician Hypatia was skinned alive by a Christian mob in Alexandria, around two thousand years ago, or that excavators shovelled bodies of gassed Jews into mass graves, humanity's absolute zero reached, where steel grapples human flesh like it was stone, only seventy years ago, only a few hundred kilometres from this garden. As far as my family history is concerned, at the age of fourteen I was introduced to a point that turned everything on its head, just as facts about the Holocaust had done – I assume that I concern myself with all of this, because I have to believe that in some sense I am the result of what I have heard and seen, that trawling through the Holocaust in history books and in one documentary programme after the other has done and continues to do something to me, apart from (over and over again) filling me with pure and utter horror, but precisely what that is I don't know, perhaps it makes me more distrustful of people as such, and makes me guard against the herd mentality within me at every opportunity, I hope that's the case.'

'Yes, well I think so.'

'I have only once had the opportunity to prove it, and that was not my actual intention. Alwilda, it was back when you took me along as your guest to an AA meeting. It was in a large hall, there were several hundred people, at first we sat listening to a talk by an American pilot who talked about how drunk he would get when he was flying – passenger planes. He also told us that a week went by from the time his wife left house and home until he discovered it ...'

'How did he find out?' Kristian asks.

'He found a message from her, dated. Anyway, afterwards someone said something along the lines of, can all the alcoholics please stand up and hold hands. Soon everyone was standing by the walls, hand in hand. Apart from me. I was left alone, with all the empty chairs. Since I'm not an alcoholic, I figured that I should stay seated. Until you, Alwilda hissed "come, come" at me.'

'Then you got up dutifully and joined us.'

'C'mon, Camilla, there are a lot of things to say to what you've just said. The way you're muddling things together, what does the Holocaust have to do with your family?' Kristian asks.

'Nothing. Only that I heard about my grandmother's attempt to take the life of her own child around the same time I saw the pictures from the concentration camps for the first time.'

'Another thing, your eloquence is offensive, you're turning incomprehensible hell into linguistic artwork,' Kristian says.

'Yes, you've got to stutter and stammer / the syntax goes to pieces / before you know the thesis,' Alma says.

'Your rhymes are hopeless.'

'A language that mimes inability, makes the spoken authentic, it comes all the way from the gut directly from the screaming soul.'

'And one more thing, Camilla, there are stories about people who took their own lives long after putting the calamity far in the past, think of all the suicide victims among survivors of the concentration camps,' Kristian says.

(...)

'The Second World War has taken up so much space that there are limits to how many other wars I have been able to absorb, yes, I'm reasonably familiar with the Vietnam War as well, and the war in Iraq, but even though I have read about the Balkans wars in the nineties several times, they remain blurred, I have almost given up on letting the war in Syria in...'

'Kristian will see to Syria.'

'... instead I'm starting a fresh round, on TV, with World War Two, lately about the French resistance movement, and about the blitz over London and about the American soldiers' relationship to their dogs during the War in the Pacific and and and *World War Two Lost Films*.'

'I dream of flying in a Spitfire,' Alwilda says, 'I love watching clips of dogfights between Spitfires and Messerschmitts. Such elegance! Such spirit.'

'Every time I turn on the television, there is a pro- gramme about the Second World War. I lie on my sofa and gorge on all that war.'

'I suppose you stuff yourself while you watch.'

'I occasionally grab something from the kitchen. But I finish chewing before I continue watching.'

(...)

'Last night, in a dream, I heard the words "Camilla and I" spoken inside of me, and then "I" turned out to be a long foot with the heel sunk into the sand, pointing straight into the air. "I" landed (with a hollow thud) in the sand and then began to leave prints around "Camilla", and it was clear that she was going to be sacrificed,' Alma says.

'Trampled alive.'

'Now I have to tell you something,' Camilla says, 'what started out as emptiness after my mum and Charles has slowly turned into peace and quiet.'

'I could have had the incident removed,' Camilla's dad says and taps himself on the chest, somewhere near the heart, 'I could have had it suppressed. But I never managed to do that.'

'In the beginning I had felt like showing Charles ev- erything – how big the rhododendron has become, and I think he would have been happy about the horse.'

'But now we've seen it.'

'It certainly is shiny,' Alma says.

'Tell me, do you ever hear from Charles?'

'He wrote that he had replaced his hard-soled shoes with soft soles, and it couldn't be helped if it ruined his image, since it was good for his gait, I mean his skeleton.'

'So no more of those hard clack-clack-clacks.'

'At night I keep the lights on and the doors open, then the insects come in and slam against the lights.'

'Clack-clack-clack.'

'Why do you leave the doors open?'

'When I am closed in with only myself, there's too much of me.'

'So you're airing yourself out.'

'The last time my mum was here, she looked around the garden before we left and said: "I don't think I'll be coming back."'

'You'll never know whether she slammed the door behind her (her own expression) – or if the door was shut on her.'

'This cod is delicious.'

'Yes, it's difficult being human, Camilla, for me too,' Kristian says.

QUEEN OF THE JAMS WITH THE STICKY LEGS

[Alma]

Write like I'm stretching (I want to), or like when the dog stretches, when it makes itself long and swims or crawls across the lawn, one long free movement, (the skin wrinkles sensually near the base of the tail) such a delight, then it rolls onto its back, then it continues swimming, the long white dog on the large lawn. Edward has given it to Camilla, I was so tired of it wanting to crawl into our bed. Camilla sleeps alone for the most part.

It stings, what Alwilda told Edward when she left him. He told me about it. She expressed it so hideously: that he was not much fun.

Alwilda has no sense of boundaries, we all know that. There was even a time when she flirted with Charles, with large flower arrangements and jams (she makes jam to calm her nerves, keep the anxiety in check, preserve, preserve, all year long, she has a freezer full of berries), she sat on the edge of his bed (low-cut top, her breasts right under his big nose), 'I love you,' she wrote to him, why didn't Camilla send her packing?

'Alwilda is like an insect that gets carried around by the wind,' she simply said, 'she'll be off somewhere else soon.'

'She wants to see how much power she has,' I answered, 'the queen is bored.' (Queen of the Jams with the Sticky Legs.)

(I don't know why I picture her making jam with her entire body, her feet down in the preserving jar stomping up and down like with grapes.)

Camilla has always been slow on the uptake, 'sometimes I wonder which world you actually exist in,'

Charles once said to her, 'the same one as you – as all of you,' she said to us, wounded and on guard. But I think that business with Alwilda destroyed Camilla's love for Charles. She stopped wanting to be with him, to be by his bedside. She hid in her office behind the kitchen. She hid behind busyness and obligations. Behind her tears and angry roars.

Alwilda dragged Edward along to places where people copulate in public while watching porn; clubs. And he did not care for it. Room after room, left in darkness, only these glaring colours and sounds from the screens on the walls. He told me about the time he was in one of those rooms, banging away on top of Alwilda. Then a young man came in and sat down in an armchair next to them and started to wank while watching them.

'The idea of having to get up and put my trousers on while he was looking at me,' Edward said, 'was unbearable. I stopped moving. "Are you dead?" Alwilda said and wriggled out from under me and got up and smiled at the man on the chair, who incidentally looked practically in awe of his erection which he grasped with both hands. He looked like someone holding a divine statue. Fortunately he was not looking at me."'

I prefer what I call primal sex (primal as in screams, not numbers), and apparently Edward does too, with only the darkness and the humming of flesh; like a swing where you are flung back and forth between the other person and yourself, and you never want it to end.

THE LIST OF ITEMS AND MATTERS
ALREADY WRITTEN

[Edward]

Camilla is now where I once was: at the mercy of mourning. Mourning (mine) is now something that occasionally rears its head, and which I can shove aside if I don't have the strength or time to handle it. I am happy that I wrote *Mourning Diary* (even though I felt like some kind of accountant while doing so), so I can go back and see what it was like, what and how I thought and felt.

Alma writes everything down. I am being recorded. Camilla's mum once said that when she was young and wrote poems, she got a sense that she only looked at things in order to be able to write about them; and she did not like that. She was not at it for very long anyway, writing, probably only a few years. Alma mentions, if I can express it a little rigidly, being in the world and her transforming the world and existence into writing have long gone hand in hand. It is equivalent to reading, she says, experiencing and interpreting simultaneously. To exist and to write absolutely belong together, they can no longer be understood separately, she says. All of that I understand very well. I have never believed that analyzing destroys anything. On the contrary. But I felt offended when one day I pointed something out to her at the sea, and she replied that after she had written about the sea, she had stopped looking at it. As though it was emptied once and for all. I almost felt offended on behalf of the sea. It had been crossed off the list of items and matters already written.

'I wonder if I'll end up there one day?' I asked cautiously, and I pictured her sitting in a wasteland, an emptied world, holding a thick book (with a pencil stub fastened to the book with twine, just like my granddad's ledger.)

Then she got angry and replied that she wanted her literature in peace. And I replied that I wanted to be able to say something without later having to see it in print.

It developed into an argument, our first. And now I have an irrepressible urge to flip through her notebook to see what she has written about me. But I keep away from the rows of cutting alphabet marching; enclosing annihilating not-summoning; Alma, you ought to be ashamed.

EEYORE WITH A STICK OF DYNAMITE IN HIS MOUTH

[Kristian]

The others (my so-called friends, the pack of comfort companions, where, if we are talking about Pooh and company, Alwilda is Tigger, I'm Eeyore, with a stick of dynamite in my mouth, argh, the rest of them I can't place, oh yes, the always-kind Edward must be Pooh, but still no little Roo in our midst) don't know, and they are not going to know either, no, of course they are not – I have accepted the consequence of wanting to make a difference in our raving world, but am rooted to the spot, more about that later maybe. It would take a very loud bang before the others (airy-fairies arseholes sods maggots) would so much as raise an eyebrow, let alone raise their head above their teacups, has it always been like that, that they were completely indifferent to the world that surrounds us, apart from Alwilda of course, but the closest thing to compare her to is a blind force, she plunges headfirst into anything, for her it is simply a matter of using her many strengths, her restless energy.

Once upon a time we planned a series of meetings to talk about what was happening to our society, and what we could do, it was back in 2001 2002 2003 when we had Anders Fogh Rasmussen and the Danish People's Party and the war in Iraq, as big a shock as bin Laden, almost, and much of what we had assumed was solid began to collapse; Alma tried writing essays, about Danishness for example, something that was discussed to the point of vomiting, but thinking has never been one of her strengths (what actually is? And she could also have taken better care of her bikini line), it became a kind of third-rate column; we ended up sitting around talking about Iraq and genetically modified crops and Afghanistan and milk-no-milk and opium fields and the corruption of the financial markets, all kinds of crap was swept onto the same dustpan – or the other way round, like the other day in Camilla's stable, the shovel under a pile of horse apples, a cluster of shit that divides into countless turds upon contact, and what I was thinking is that I would blow myself up, not to compare it with anything other than a giant fart, hello I would like to direct your attention to the fact that we have a problem, several problems; a lot of people blowing stuff up, let off without providing a reason, the surroundings are forced to conjecture, that is how I leave it (to others to find the reason, for example to the soft toys).

But before that I ought to have hung up a sign in the gateway, for my neighbours, a proclamation, about sorting their rubbish better: I hope you burn in hell if you keep putting things in the wrong place!

Now we have containers for hard plastic and metal and one more I can't remember at this raging moment, as well as the classics, paper and cardboard and glass respectively, but what does that matter if someone is not sorting properly. I understood it as such, that if just one object ends up in the wrong container, the entire contents of the container are burnt as normal rubbish. It is insanely frustrating, when I take the time to sort mine properly, that someone goes and ruins everything. The idiocy the indifference knows no bounds: some people even throw normal rubbish bags in with the hard plastic. Maybe I should set my banger off in a container, in the courtyard, then it would not be difficult to find the cause, no guesswork necessary. On the other hand it would scatter the entire mess. Everything that had been laboriously collected & sorted. But wasn't that the very

point? Yes, it was, just hop up in the cardboard and light
the fuse, teeth-gritting hand-wringing. First I get undressed, so I can meet the jury of houris in puris, they
might as well see what they are getting straight away. (I
see myself climbing out of the cardboard like a wet dog
if it is a dud.)

ONCE THEY START TO LOOK

[Camilla]

Yesterday I went to the hospital with a bite that had got infected on my back. I went to my own doctor first, and he sent me to be admitted, he thought we were dealing with a boil. (He took a photo with his mobile, so I could see it, after promising to delete it afterwards. And it looked rather ugly, with a number of small festering growths. I have no idea who would have enjoyed looking at it if he had not deleted it, but sent it out into the world.) It was appallingly busy, and I waited for ten hours, in a bed behind a curtain, first to have blood tests taken and then to meet a doctor, behind another curtain in the room there was a very old person with pneumonia who simply wanted to die. When the doctor finally arrived, she stood by the end of my bed and said: 'You might think it strange of me to ask, but when was the last time you had your period?' When I did not reply, she continued: 'Is it possible that you're pregnant?', she straightened up and said that the elevated levels of hCG hormones in the blood were an indication that I was.

'Once they start to look,' Alma later said, 'they always find something.' (Later still she told me that when I told her the news, she had heard a loud bang in her ears, like the sound of a drawer being slammed shut. 'Something has come to an end,' she said dramatically, 'Camilla, it's going to be a long time before we go travelling again, just the two of us.' And then she launched into an almost shameless wallowing in the highlights of our various journeys.

'Do you remember the time in Venice you slapped me because you were starving, and I couldn't decide on a restaurant? Do you remember the time on Kos you couldn't find our guest house and were gone an entire night, and I was frightened to death? Do you remember dragging your typewriter around all those years and not typing a single word? And what it was like taking the hundred-metre-long escalator down to the underground in St Petersburg, racing along, with the lights flashing by? And when the pack of wild dogs approached us early one morning in Belgrade, and you chased them off with your umbrella?'

Then she burst into tears, and I said: 'Alma, Alma, only yesterday you told me that you love the ordinary; the everyday. You had just passed Søerne around lunchtime and were enjoying watching people on the benches unpacking all manner of fast food. And I prefer to be at home, you know how miserable I get when I travel; floating about; without any fixed point whatsoever; something the wind simply takes hold of. But when I see Paris on TV, nonetheless I get a little wistful and feel life passing me by, as if it is there right there on the Left Bank that life is being lived.'

'Besides, you've got Edward. And I have decided,' I said, contrary to my intentions, but in order to get some peace, 'to let you have a look at *Document Black* before I throw it out.'

Then at long last she sniffled a little congratulations.

'Anyway,' she said, 'we can go to New York together if the father is American.')

And they certainly did (find something), the issue with my back was very minor, the doctor drained what turned out to be a blister filled with fluid, while I lay on my stomach on a gynaecology bed, the only free bed at the overcrowded institution, considering the advantages and disadvantages of the two possible fathers, the one overseas, Mr Camel (with the unexpectedly harsh kicks), married and absent, and the veterinarian's brother who along with his sister would probably enforce harsh discipline, raise the child like they would raise a dog or a horse. Maybe they, that is he, whichever one it was, did not need to know. And suddenly I saw us in the distant future, the child and me, sitting across from each other at a table, the child demanding an answer from me. Then I saw the two of us walking, along the fjord with all the glittering water, and I shifted in the uncomfortable bed and looked at the doctor who stood holding a cotton swab, bent over me, and asked when it might be due. Because it was. Then we started to calculate, and it was very reassuring (only for a moment) to sink down into the world of numbers.

MY TWO MAIN CHARACTERS

[Alwilda]
These are the two traits (I am/about me/mine) that I
know best:

1. Spitting out plum stones is something one ordinarily connects with a certain cheerfulness, and I am doing
that, my pockets are full of mirabelles. I have just pulled
the branch down in order to get hold of the best the rip-
est the reddest. But I am not the least bit cheerful, despite
all the spitting, the flying stones.

Who knows whether anyone thinks it is natural to
live, to feel like a fish in water, here in life.

I who love the city yesterday sat in Christianshavns
Torv and felt completely isolated from all the walking
cycling driving laughing coughing hawking old young
those with dogs or children and those without. Alone.
Isolated. I have always had to haul others in after labour-
ing to catch them in my net. Nobody ever hauls me in.
That is the price of suffering from an abundance of energy, all initiative is left to me. So it was a matter of getting
into my car and driving out to the country, where people
are few and far between. She had just returned from the
stables, and dusted, booted and spurred, she told me that
she is pregnant.

'... and she appeared for a second like some insolent
and powerful captain, returning booted and spurred
from a field of triumph, the dust of battle yet upon
him, confronting the sovereign powers whom he was
now ready if need be to bend to his will.'
— Iris Murdoch, *A Severed Head*

But I did not try to talk her into having an abortion, even though she is getting on in years and does not know who the father is. I just thought I should have been the one expecting.

2. I have met a frail woman, a touching individual with a few ailments. I am so on top of the world that I can't keep still. She is a colleague, a new employee. When we walk down the corridor together, to the staff room, during lunch break – I could pick her up, high in the air, and run off shouting. Then I picture myself as a rapist with a porcelain figurine. She has small, delicate hands and is disproportionately aged in relation to her years, wrinkles around her mouth and eyes, furrowed cheeks, an old neck. She is from Russia and her name is Swaka. And so delightful. And she has a sense of humour and has nothing against it all being over one day. For that reason she merrily grows older and older. In a mood like that I feel like giving women I pass a smack on the bottom. Men cannot deal with me – that's why I have no boyfriend. This mood, this me... yesterday I saw a red evening bag in a shop that sold nothing but black items, and I thought: That's how it feels when this mood comes over me, like a crimson flash of lightning in my brain, bang then I am nothing but energy bang spanking new, every kind of reservation swept aside, I shine and sparkle, I charge ahead on a backdrop of black.

In *A Severed Head* (which Camilla lent me) the characters live with their front doors unlocked, or they all have keys to one another's houses, and for that reason they constantly run in and out of one another's houses, and they run into one another, in one another's houses. And this wide-openness shapes the very atmosphere in the novel. Then one of them has settled in, drunk and despondent, in the basement, and the sister of the owner of the house (who looks like a cliché of a lesbian from the beginning of the twentieth century, close-cropped hair wearing thick-soled walking shoes and a tailor-made suit in heavy tweed, imagine Gertrude Stein) accidentally bumps into him down there. The novel is cut like the episodes of Sherlock Holmes I love watching on TV (gas lamps, carriages, opium, falls from great heights, London in fog and rain, not to mention the capes), one person says something crucial about another and then cut: we find ourselves in a scene with him, where all of his dirty work is plain to see.

The characters are well-off and either they do not work or work very little, and therefore they have time to ensure love is the most important thing in their lives. The actual drama. They have affairs with one another, left, right, and centre, they run in and out of one another's hearts. (For that reason it is also very difficult for the novel to end – because who is going to finally and conclusively remain in whose heart?) When the characters are not loving or (briefly) mourning for their lost love, they are talking about love. A conversation might sound like this:

'– What anyway does a love do which has no course?
– It is changed into something else. Something heavy or sharp, that you carry within and bind around with your substance until it ceases to hurt. But that is your affair.'
—— Iris Murdoch, *A Severed Head*

I come to think about it, because I have stood on the

398

sidelines and observed how Camilla has recovered from her darling over the ocean, oh, this small addition: 'But that is your affair.'

Camilla talked at great length about her romance; I underlined the following in *The Unicorn* by Murdoch, which Camilla has also lent me (so when she rereads it, she can find herself there): 'With that pride which accompanies falling in love at what passes as an advanced age he was but too eager to display it to everyone.'

In fact she wrote to him and told him how much she had fallen for him that night, at the hotel in New York.

'If only you knew,' he replied, 'how many people are falling for me.'

Afterwards he listed and described a number of these women, one of whom was his wife, still madly in love after twenty-five years of marriage. He could not have done her a bigger favour; who wants to be one among many, one person in a chorus of sighs. The love (Camilla's) subsided in one afternoon; nearly. As it does with the characters in *A Severed Head*, where the next one is generally better than the first. And here I place a pensive (but with the beginning of a smile?) round yellow micro-face. I am the only admirer of smileys among the companions.

BY THE BANKS OF THE BOOKCASE

[Camilla]

I stand by the banks of the bookcase and observe that a good deal of flotsam has drifted in since I last made my rounds, but I also discover that a good deal of what I require is missing. My Gogols are missing, *Dead Souls*, *The Overcoat* as well as Vladimir Nabokov's *Nikolai Gogol*. *They Shoot Horses, Don't They* is missing, and *The Lover* is missing, *The Illusionist* is missing, and Murdoch, beloved Murdoch is missing.

When Charles and I were getting divorced, we took the books down from the shelves (mouldy dust covered those most seldom read) to then build three towers in the living room, one for him and one for me and one for the second-hand bookseller with the white hair and beard. A few made desperate attempts to abscond by leaping from the towers, each attempt always resulted in broken spines snapped necks – and several times the suicidal ones at the very top dragged the books beneath them along in the fall. I swept up the dead and dying into a pile of their own. During the process of division the towers sometimes collapsed and some landed in the wrong place – which is why I am now missing some. And so once again I have to take the heavy route to the second-hand bookstore (from where I always depart with more than I set out for) to see if I can buy some of my old books back. Those that ended up with Charles by mistake are obviously lost for ever.

John Bayley and Iris Murdoch spent their entire marriage living in a sinful mess because Iris Murdoch was a hoarder, just like Charles, and just like him she loved rocks and gathered them in great quantities; dust beget rocks, which draw their life from water and light, a death-like quality; as soon as something had entered their home, she could not let go of it again, they lived among piles, accumulations of junk that they had to take with them when they moved; when Iris Murdoch got Alzheimer's she even picked up cigarette butts, dead worms, bits of paper from the street and brought them home. This did not particularly bother John Bayley, *Elegy for Iris* is the account, it could be said, of a happy marriage, about each side's joy at living together. This joy, it is understood, had to do with them not being ridden by some idea of development; they did not envisage their marriage or their love life changing or leading anywhere. When Iris Murdoch got Alzheimer's, the illness forced change upon their marriage, their roles were drastically changed – this change or development tragically and ironically became the chief concern.

Back to the joy of being together (before Iris Murdoch grew ill):

'We were together because we were comforted and reassured by the solitariness each saw and was aware of in the other.'
—— John Bayley, *Elegy For Iris*

(I often look up words even when I know what they mean, because I enjoy reading the explanatory examples accompanying the references. Like now, 'solitariness': 'It was the overwhelming solitariness of his existence that caused the marooned sailor to go mad.' What a gift – driven to distraction considering how the madness of the marooned sailor manifested itself, did he run screaming up and down the deserted beach? (When men scream, things have truly gone wrong.) Had he collected piles of sticks but long since forgotten the meaning of fire? Or were the piles of sticks intended as a sign to God? And who was there to attest to his madness? Could the sailor, until he definitively sailed into his own darkness, see it for himself and account for it?)

I don't know if I have ever felt like that about another person – in any case I have never considered someone's solitariness in that way: as a mirror of my own. Charles's solitariness – I felt trapped with it (in the same house as it), and I felt locked out from it / with no access to him, because his solitariness was so great. If I had accepted it as a condition, not as something I had to confront, change, it might have been easier. And the same goes for my solitariness. If I had not wanted it to be redressed: by the marriage. Well.

If I were to ask Alma if a person can take the liberty to write anything at all about another person, what would she say?

'I would say yes,' Alma said, 'it is only a matter of tactfulness. You have to be tactful – and put yourself on the line too, place yourself in exposed positions, pass judgement on yourself (Ibsen believed a person did that automatically when writing).'

I ask, because I am not certain that I have enjoyed reading about how John Bayley had to fight to take Iris Murdoch's trousers off before they went to bed every night – when she grew ill, she wanted to sleep fully dressed. Nor do I like to read about how disgusting he finds her odour. Had that been necessary to write... and what things has he not written about; where has he drawn the line. In any case he passes judgement on himself by writing about his fits of anger, which arise when

402

he can no longer endure hearing his wife repeat 'When are we going,' or when he gets far too upset about her watering their potted plants to death.

'The part you do not like to read,' Alma said, 'is that these things happen to a person; that a woman who has written twenty-six novels, whose headstrong mystical alluring worlds you have loved residing in, ends up only being able to find peace by watching Teletubbies on TV, emitting a musty odour, the same as that of the house. And you do not like reading about how angry a person can get from living with someone who is ill, worn to the bone. And anyway can I be spared this didactic conversation, it's unworthy. Let's talk about your foetus, or let's talk about Gogol,' and she pulled Nabokov's *Nikolai Gogol* out of her bag and slammed it down on the table.

'So you had it! Would you be so good as to find me a good word.'

'Alright, how about: Nose. There you go.'

Acknowledgements

I would like to thank Jacques Testard with all my heart for publishing *Companions* in English, and Paul Russell Garrett for his fine translation.

I am also very grateful that my agent Laurence Laluyaux has succeeded in bringing *Companions* outside the borders of Denmark and into the world.

I want to thank my Danish publisher of many years, Jakob Malling Lambert, for all his enthusiasm and support.

And finally I want to thank the translator Roger Greenwald, who previously translated some pieces from *Companions* which appeared in various literary magazines and in the *Best European Fiction 2013* anthology; and allowing us to reproduce his translation of 'Three Little Chinamen' in this edition.

Fitzcarraldo Editions
243 Knightsbridge
London, SW7 1DN
United Kingdom

ISBN 978-1-910695-33-3

Design by Ray O'Meara
Typeset in Fitzcarraldo
Printed and bound by TJ International

DANISH ARTS FOUNDATION

This book is supported by a translation grant from
the Danish Arts Foundation

Fitzcarraldo Editions